Introducing "The Last of the Line"
A new Series by Jez & Julia Cæsar

THE LAST PASSENGER

BY
JEZ & JULIA CÆSAR

Published 2014 by arima publishing

www.arimapublishing.com

ISBN 978-1-84549-639-5

© Jez & Julia Cæsar 2014
Book Jacket artwork and design Chris Howard of Blondesign.
Blondesign@gmail.com

Printed and bound in the United Kingdom

Typeset in Garamond 11 pt

In this work of fiction, the characters, places and events are either
the product of the author's imagination or they are used entirely
fictitiously. The moral rights of the author have been asserted.
Any resemblance to actual persons, living or dead, is purely
coincidental.

arima publishing
ASK House, Northgate Avenue
Bury St Edmunds, Suffolk IP32 6BB
t: (+44) 01284 700321

www.arimapublishing.com

DEDICATION

For Charlie Anderson and the proud generations of Railwaymen who served the Railways when Britain was Great.

For the lost generations of both World Wars who gave their lives in the service of this country, particularly those whose cap badges adorn the Downs above Fovent.
"They came, gave their all, and that sacrifice should forever be imprinted on the hills of home."

Lastly to the men, women and children who strive to keep the love of Steam and the pride of British Engineering alive.
Thank you for letting us into your world, sharing your joy in the precision of your craft along with your memories of our great heritage.

CONTENTS

CONTENTS (contd:)

Slow Train

Lyrics by Michael Flanders & Donald Swan

No more will I go to Blandford Forum and Moretehoe
On the slow train from Midsomer Norton and Mumby Road
No churns, no porter, no cat on a seat
At Chorlton-cum-Hardy or Chester-le-Street
We won't be meeting again
On the slow train.
I'll travel no more from Littleton Badsey to Openshaw
At Long Stanton I'll stand well clear of the doors no more
No whitewashed pebbles, no Up and no Down
From Formby Four Crosses to Dunstable Town.
I won't be going again
On the slow train.
On the Main Line and the Goods Siding
The grass grows high
At Dog Dyke, Tumby Woodside
And Trouble House Halt.
The Sleepers sleep at Audlem and Ambergate.
No passenger waits on Chittening platform or Cheslyn Hay.
No one departs, no one arrives
From Selby to Goole, from St Erth to St Ives.
They've all passed out of our lives
On the slow train
On the slow train.
Cockermouth for Buttermere
On the slow train
Armley Moor Arram … Pye Hill and Somercotes
On the slow train
Windmill End.

Written in 1963 by Michael Flanders and Donald Swann, these popular satyrists succeeded in capturing the poignancy felt by passengers forced to watch helplessly as the Government inflicted savage cuts to our railway system. Lines and stations were closed ruthlessly, however Dr. Beeching's plan not only failed to save money, his short-sighted strategy caused needless hardship to whole communities and may contribute to creating a situation in which incalculably higher costs are incurred by the need to re-open lines as people are encouraged to "Let the train take the strain".

Author's Notes & References

Nearly all our reference material comes from living during the 1960's not too far away from the villages on which we modelled "Padways" and its surroundings. Both of us had the pleasure of travelling through the New Forest to school and college, and of using the train along Castleman's Corkscrew when that line was working. We had the joy of living in a village environment, attending village schools, chasing New Forest ponies (and deer) from our parents' vegetable plot and of growing up in a time when children could roam at will. Those times may be gone, but we hope that our readers will remember and take pleasure in sharing those memories with us and for those who want to read further, here is a list of other relevant material or sources. You perhaps won't be surprised to find no reference to Padways; it exists only in our imagination, but Silver Street Station is certainly based on the histories of a number of Victorian railway stations along Castleman's Corkscrew Line, it is for you to decide which is the most likely candidate and applaud the devotion and tenacity of those who worked that line, and those who travelled outward bound along it, many of whom were destined never to return.

Below is a small sample of sources we have used. Set out with the details of Title: Author: Publisher year & ISBN where possible. Note X stands for OUT OF PRINT.

55 yrs. On The Footplate: Stan Symes; The Oakwood Press; 1995
ISBN: 085361 484 9

Castleman's Corkscrew: B. L. Jackson; The Oakwood Press; 2008
ISBN 978 0 85361 686 3

LSWR: Peter Cooper; Kingfisher Railway Productions; 1986
ISBN: 0 946184 20 8

LSWR Locomotives: D. L. Bradley; Wild Swan Publications td; 1985
ISBN: 0 906867 38 X

Memories of Holmsley Station & the Brockenhurst to Ringwood Railway:
Phil Grant; P .S. Grant; 2007;

Rail Routes in Hampshire & East Dorset: David Fereday Glen; Ian Allan
Ltd; 1983; ISBN: 0 7110 1213 X

Map: Inspired by reference to Phil Grant's "Memories of Holmsley Station" & redrawn by Chris Howard of Blondesign.com for this book.

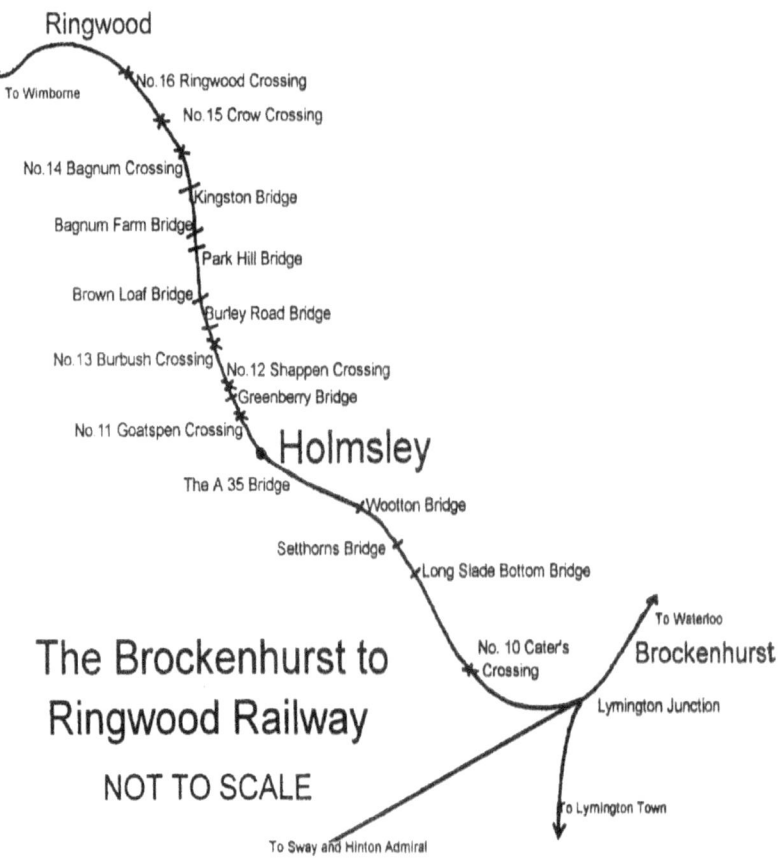

PART 1 - AT THE FALL OF AN AXE

Prologue

"Mid-September and the sun's still hot. I wonder how long that'll last."

With this thought running through his mind, Sam Smart pushed his cap to the back of his head, watching a squirrel scamper into the sheltering arms of an oak tree which overhung the wicket gate of Silver Street Station. Grinning, he started to sweep methodically, ignoring a stray acorn as it bounced from the gently tinted corona above him, until he spotted his tormentor waiting to hurl another.

"Tree rat!" remarked the porter amiably, and moved off in the opposite direction, listening to the squirrel's frustrated chatter, while keeping one eye on the downline signals.

"Soon be home time." he observed cheerfully, as the station cat carried her kitten into the parcel office, intent on settling down before passenger services stopped for the night.

Carefully locking up his broom and yard pan in a cupboard, Sam heard the "clack" as the signals changed, and turned to see a small black dot in the distance, growing rapidly larger as it approached, topped by a plume of steam. The 6.15 drew in with its usual symphony. Squeals, clanks, and shudders were drowned beneath the staccato slap of descending windows as "the City suits" prepared to detrain. Bowler-hatted gentlemen rustling newspapers and flourishing briefcases, made their purposeful way towards the exit, tickets at the ready, as the Station Master appeared resplendent in his best uniform jacket.

Crossing the footbridge at a measured pace John Oswald was frowning as he prepared to board, reaching for his silver pocket watch (with elaborate care). Glancing up and down the platform with marked irritation, he beckoned Sam forward to attend to a large bale of newspapers, which lay uncollected beside the guard's van. Hoisting them onto a trolley, Sam's Dorset burr became deferential.

"Sorry Mr Oswald. I'll take these on to Padways with me. Mrs Fleet's having a might of trouble with that old van of hers, I did say I might fetch them if needed."

The friendly face with the steady grey eyes, didn't betray by so much as a flicker the exaggeration, but John Oswald, (naturally full of his own importance) remarked pompously, "Railway employees work for the railways Samuel Smart. Not for shopkeepers, gamekeepers, parsons or publicans, to name but a few of the folk you run errands for." He swung up into the guard's van as a whistle blew and to the accompaniment of the guard's stentorian bellow, "Mind the doors now! Mind the doors!"

Sam swung them shut with a satisfying "thunk". Leaning through an open window as the train moved off, the Station Master chanted a familiar litany of instructions.

"Barrows away, doors double bolted gates chained…" his voice drowned as the train rounded the bend and chattered away to the west.

"Chuh chutch, chuh churh. Chuh chutch, chuh churh. Chuh chutch, chuh churh."

As sound faded to a remote chuckling, then finally died into the pulsing thrum of the vibrating line, Sam, still standing with the fine miasma of coal driven steam in his nostrils, sighed with pleasure, turning back to pick up the papers. Then his world fell apart.

Headlines hidden by a protective page baled about them, were revealed as an errant breeze blew the sound back down the track to mock him.

"Forest lines close as the Beeching Axe falls."

In stunned silence, he sank on to the trolley, remembering an odd conversation from earlier that year. He'd been shopping in Lymington (following the worst winter in decades) when he was waylaid by a colleague.

"Well Sam, won't be long before we're all out to grass. Last week it was trains that drive themselves! Now we'll see whose jobs pay for that!"

Reg, Lymington's morose ticket collector pointed out a hoarding which announced "Railway Rationalisation". Sam, who hadn't read the headlines, stared in astonishment.

"Trains that drive themselves? How come I didn't see that?" he demanded. "Honestly Reg, you see conspiracy round every corner! What's in this one then?"

Leaving the paper unread on the bench where it was discarded, he listened as the Lymington man expounded his latest theory. Deep set eyes gleaming triumphantly, his face assumed a "knowing" look, as he slid a forefinger (stained with nicotine from an endless chain of roll-ups) to the side of his nose and tapped it.

"Some of us Mr Smart stay ever watchful." he announced conspiratorially. "Some of us collect the London papers when our gentlemen come home to roost!"

Reaching into an inside pocket, Reg produced his wallet, and extracted a newspaper cutting, unfolding it to display the headline.

"Train drives itself". He handed it over silently and Sam read the article before commenting.

"Well, I'm glad neither my Dad nor Uncle Norman lived to see that!" he'd declared, handing back the cutting. "However, just thinking about automatic trains gives me the heebie-jeebies, and I'm not a driver. Surely you don't think the two things are connected? The risks are huge. The costs of those Underground trains are enormous. Overground couldn't afford then."

Reg's mouth turned down grimly.

"Exactly my point lad!" he exclaimed (ignoring the fact that he couldn't have been more than ten years Sam's senior). "Someone's getting bloody rich to the cost of the railways! If these cuts go ahead whose pockets are being lined with our wages, that's what I want to know."

The memory of the man's thin bitter voice was disturbing as Sam hunched in misery recalled what now seemed to be prophetic words.

"Just think of all the wage packets they won't have to pay, rail maintenance, drivers, and station staff all to go without a backward glance if this man Beeching has his way, and this looks like the start of it! Once we have automatic trains, who's next for the chop? Ticket clerks, station staff, and all they'll need are platelayers, signalmen, and freight loaders. Passengers can carry their own property, they don't need porters. They'll get in cleaners; take out waiting rooms so passengers freeze under open canopies. They'll get rid of cafes, paper kiosks, and everything that makes a railway station comfortable. They've invested in road transport, all they have to do is make journeys by train tough and expensive, and then Mr Everyman will take to the road. Now do you see where I'm going lad?"

Sam recalled saying scathingly, "It'll never happen Reg.", but it was happening right now! That vision of the unimaginable had begun, and there was nothing he could do about it.

He was still struggling to absorb the news, when Fred Cummins (the up-line porter) called across.

"Better get that trolley away Sam. Bus coming up t'hill!"

He followed the instruction mechanically. Feeling old, and as cold as last winter, he trundled the trolley across to the other side and into the entrance hall. Sliding the ticket clerk's window down, he absently slipped the padlock in place and locked it, before slinging his jacket over his shoulder (in flagrant breach of regulations).He locked the entrance doors, checked the waiting room, and chained the up-line gate swiftly, before trotting across the bridge to where the newspapers waited; then, dangling the bale from the twine, he went to meet the bus with a heavy heart.

Chapter 1 – An End, or a Beginning?

Oddly isolated from the rest of the queue, Sam waited miserably until it was his turn to board the bus, hardly daring to acknowledge the conductor's greeting. Loading the papers into the consignment cubby hole, he allowed habit to take him to the long sideways bench seats he usually chose, fighting the hysterical urge to chant, as if in time with a departing train.

"Forest lines closing, we're for the axe. You'll need a car, we'll never come back!"

He forced his mind from the crisis, oblivious to the hum of companionable chatter, or the shrills of children on the top deck as the bus groaned and swayed back onto the narrow Forest road down to Padways.

By concentrating on the cold sick lurch of his stomach, he reminded himself that nobody knew (except Samuel Smart), not until Mrs Fleet marked up the papers for Tommy and Tony Long to deliver that evening. It was his job now to protect them from that knowledge until they were home, safe amongst the friends and families that would help them face a devastating change in their lives.

The bus drew up with a protesting squeak at the gates of the boarding school as Sam agonised. Two women got on and slid into the front seat, carrying on an intensely expressive conversation in French. Sam (who was a man of the world) knew it was French because he overheard the one expression he had learned.

"Merci mon ami." said the small lady elegantly attired in grey, taking a book from her companion and turning towards him. Sliding past the conductor (who was busying himself taking fares), she came briskly to join Sam who completely failed to recognise Miss Ellen Armitage, the English teacher, all dressed up in "Town" finery, until she frowned at him in sudden concern.

"She didn't travel down on the last train. I'd have seen her.", he found himself thinking stupidly, as his inner focus shifted, back to the endless refrain.

"The lines been axed, the lines been axed, it's going, we're going, the lines been axed."

Perhaps his frozen immobility, his air of bewilderment, must have touched that chord that tells a teacher or a mother, there is something seriously amiss. Ellen looked at her normally cheerful companion, saw the deep misery in his eyes and made swift decisions.

"Right then Sam. We'll discharge your errands in the village, I'll post a card to my sister in America, and then we'll get that cup of tea." She watched a sliver of relaxation appear, cursed herself when it vanished as she suggested "Shall we go to the Bay Tree?", then she said comfortably, "No, that won't do at all. I was about to ask if you would move my piano Sam, so perhaps tea at my house would suffice?"

The strange rigidity of his muscles eased then, allowing him to respond to her naturally as the bus swung round the corner and down an incline, gliding into the bus stop as around them, eager travellers prepared to leave. Three chattering women carrying new babies in slings passed them, followed by young Mr Carter who owned the local shoe-shop. Children clutching lollipops, satchels and shoe bags came next, then folk from the upper deck flooded down the stairs, as Ellen stepped out to wait for Sam, who carefully hoisted the papers by the string securing them and joined her. She put her head on one side as he shifted the bale to a more comfortable position, then said quietly, "Now Sam, there's something dreadfully wrong, I know it, but I shan't ask questions until we get back to my house. Why don't you take Mrs Fleet's papers straight over to her, I'll just drop my post in the letter-box, then we can get some crumpets and go home for tea. If you want to tell me what's wrong then we can talk, and if you can't then I'll understand, but you must talk to someone soon."

It was so easy Sam thought dully. One minute everything was chugging along famously, then the trolley came off the tracks and you didn't know who you were, why you were there, or what was going on. He reached for the lifeline gratefully and as she took his free arm, Ellen was appalled to find him trembling. She soothed him, like one soothes a frightened animal, turning him towards the newspaper shop, and under the guise of steadying the bale, assisted him to cross the road and take them into the dim little place.

Mrs Fleet was fulsome in her gratitude swiftly getting her son to swing the package up onto her bench. She hardly noticed Sam's glance of apprehension as she deftly sliced the twine, allowing the wrapping paper to tear, revealing the dreadful contents to all and sundry. In appalled comprehension, Ellen swiftly took Sam's arm, taking him out into the evening sunshine and silently round her allotted tasks, before heading down the path that led to her cottage.

Sam remembered nothing of that, or very much of his tea and crumpets. He did remember sitting on Ellen Armitage's sofa, hearing her low sweet voice telling him that he was suffering from shock, then no more as he fell fast asleep. He remembered only the embarrassment of waking, lightly covered with a travelling rug, and Ellen's low voice saying gently, "Sam, I think it's time we got you home."

She wouldn't listen to his protestations, but calmly put on a cardigan, and walked back along the village as lights began to spring up in sitting-room windows. They exchanged greetings with one or two villagers and then, just as Sam would have taken leave of Ellen by the church gate, the Reverend Martin Short appeared over the rectory wall waving the Evening Standard.

"Dreadful news Sam. Poor fellow! This must have been a terrible shock. Mrs Fleet came straight over to tell me you looked like you'd seen a ghost when she opened up the papers. Are you alright my boy?" at which Sam tried to get his churning thoughts under control. However, Ellen Armitage said sharply, "No Vicar, Sam is far from alright! More than one of your parishioners will need your advice once the long-term ramifications become clear. It is even possible that Padways itself will cease to exist as we know it, after the railway closes. Patients seldom survive a main artery being cut when there is no plan to replace it!"

Whether her unaccustomed acidity sparked the Vicar into action or not, Sam was grateful for the ex-rugger blue's care that night. He went quietly up the steep narrow path to his home, let the Vicar find his key and let him in, then grateful for the gentle prompting, washed, got into pyjamas and went to sleep, too tired to battle the thoughts and feelings that beset him.

Martin Short (who was anything but), let himself out of the house muttering, "Poor fellow. Wonder what he'll do now?", as he went back down the strip of sweetly scented night stocks, to pray for all those touched by this modern tragedy.

Chapter 2 – Undercurrents

By the time Sam was aware of anything outside his own state of misery, quite an undercurrent of rebellion had arisen amongst the inhabitants of Padways and surrounding district. Finishing that week's shift was torture. Nobody spoke about the situation; even the Station Master was conspicuous by his absence, distancing himself from the staff by hiding in his office. By Friday evening however, Sam began to hear the comments as he ran his usual errands around the village in preparation for his weekend off. When on Saturday he ventured into Lymington market, his attention was sharply focussed by the Lymington ticket collector's comments as he checked Sam's rail pass.

"Better make the most of it Sam.", he remarked kindly. "We thought that fat blighter would be the death of the Forest line from the moment he took charge."

Startled out of his train of thought, Sam (thoroughly bewildered) asked cautiously, "Which fat blighter Reg? Do you mean Beeching?" at which his colleague chuckled derisively.

"Lord, love a duck! Ain't you the innocent?" he leant closer, saying with rough sympathy:

"There's more than one stoker fuelling this loco's firebox boy. Old man Flaxman knew that line like the back of his hand, but the moment he got sick he's out on a miserly pension, and the fat boy's in. He knows nothing about the area, nothing about the station, except how to cook the books! I bet you he won't lose his job when the line goes. Mr. Ruddy Oswald has presided over other station closures before; in fact he's an expert on the subject, though I'm not at liberty to reveal my source of information!"

Sam, fascinated and repelled at the same time, finally turned his feet towards the steeply ascending High Street, thronged with market traders; his mind continuing to hear the vindictive inflection as he trudged the steep ascent.

"Mr. Ruddy Oswald", the Lymington ticket collector had called Silver Street's temporary Station Master and Sam, who had never had cause to doubt anyone, found his mind reluctantly turning to what he knew of the line and the station he loved. True to say, passengers from the surrounding district were not huge in number, and since the war freight had been dwindling away due to the new roads and better vehicles. He paused by a stall, eyeing sturdy khaki trousers, ex-military jumpers (with leather patched elbows) and workmanlike boots. Momentarily distracted from his cogitations while he selected some socks, he continued to evaluate his colleague's comments as he sorted through a handful of change.

"Seven and six with that jumper." he reckoned ruefully, "I hope I shan't need anything else this winter!"

He shivered remembering the Arctic conditions that had laid England low only recently, and studiously ignoring the balaclava that would keep his ears warm on the allotment, walked up the left hand side of the pavement, glancing in at the windows of shops he couldn't afford to frequent. Making his way past the cavernous bus yard, he continued along the High Street, heading for Scats (the seed merchants).

Pausing to run an amused eye along a rare serpentine wall to the left of a car park entrance, he eventually turned to contemplate the best shop in town, whilst consulting his list hopefully. His order for Spring, (provided that it arrived at the right time next year) might see him comfortably harvesting potatoes, spinach, peas, runner beans, leeks, onions and the usual variety of salad vegetables. He needed to be thrifty for the pay on the railways was constantly under review, and now he was going to be unemployed in the near future, he would need his allotment even more. For a moment, he wondered if his allotment could support him, realising that he had been lucky to have any crops to talk of this year. During the Big Freeze (in which the entire country was caught by surprise), land, roads, and all forms of transport were locked in an icy grip from Christmas almost to Easter. Even the sea had frozen for a mile into the Channel, fuel had been in short supply, and food just as scarce and twice as expensive. Now six months later he was hopeful that it wouldn't happen again as he pushed the door open into the dim, dusty shop. Redolent with the mixed aromas of animal feed and linseed oil, it enfolded him (before he could be dissuaded) by the horrid thought.

"Maybe next year I won't be able to afford the allotment either!"

A thin, elderly voice greeted him warmly.

"Now then young Sam!", and looking about, Sam spotted one of his late father's gardening cronies seated behind an enormous seed catalogue.

Despite age and infirmity removing him from his beloved garden, Percy Adams still haunted the seed merchant's shop daily, and could be relied on to offer all sorts of advice, so Sam joined him in speechless admiration for all the products advertised.

Perched on a high wooden stool like a proverbial garden gnome, Percy pointed to some bright red pea-like plants, commenting slyly, "Remember those growing up the path? Charlie thought the world of them asparagus peas. Took me a hell of a time to persuade him to try them though!" and they settled to reminisce. Sam remembered the strange little pods, no more than an inch long, almost square in section with odd little wings. He could almost hear his father saying scathingly, "Well, that's daft Percy for you! What size of peas we'll get out of those I can't imagine!", but they had persisted, until Percy visiting one day, admired their crop and showed them how to harvest and cook the delicious vegetables (pods and all).

Since then, Sam had listened and learned a great deal from Percy, adding asparagus peas to his order, figuring that anything that grew in flower borders and provided a little extra food was worth the effort.

They passed a few moments more in comfortable reminiscence, Sam refusing to let his situation creep into their conversation out of regard for Percy's own courage. He couldn't bring himself to contemplate a time when his own gardening would have to stop, and admired the old man's determination to pass on his pearls of wisdom while he enthused others to seek the active life that he had once enjoyed. Eventually however, he dug out his list, consulted a salesman, placed his order, and had just turned away to leave when from the sloping old desk where the catalogues lay, Percy called after him.

"Sam! When one door closes, another's always there for you to open. Your Dad taught you a great deal and you're a grand gardener. What you need is something to take your mind off those wretched trains. Charlie was a driver for more years than I care to recall, yet he walked away from the line when the time came, and so can you. Why not get a piece of ground and create a smallholding?"

Sam stared back in amazement, seeing the wizened little face with its neat corona of silver hair as if he'd never seen it before, without realising that (in that moment) Percy had planted a seed deep within his mind. He smiled, raised a hand in acknowledgement, and went out into the September sunshine, crossing the road and turning down the High Street towards New Street, where he planned to take his lunch at the small cafe called the Spinnaker.

He loved the simple décor, the bright sails on the menus and the clean simplicity of the food. Here, there was nothing to make him feel uncomfortable or out of place. The Spinnaker had a reputation for attracting young mums, busy shoppers and even the occasional library bound visitor to its well-cooked, pleasantly presented, but utterly uncomplicated meals. None of that fancy sauce drowned stuff with foreign names to trip the tongue. No elaborate napkins or tablecloths. Simple seating and good wholesome food beckoned, and Sam was suddenly aware of how hungry he was.

He hadn't been sat more than a minute however, when a familiar voice said cheerfully, "Well Sam Smart, now I know where you go on your off-days!", and Ellen Armitage was grinning at him from the next table. She continued conversationally.

"I've not even ordered yet, if you're on your own why don't we at least share a table?"

He liked that idea, but hesitated long enough for her to lean forward and say confidentially, "We'll go Dutch Sam. I wouldn't dream of anything else!"

Suddenly emboldened he smiled into her pretty brown eyes and said happily, "We'll have none of that nonsense. You were there for me at a very bad time and I've been struggling to think how I could thank you. This is my treat!"

They slid into the same table space, ordered the same meal, and chattered happily about everything other than railways, before walking round to the library, arm in arm. She seemed to like poetry, picked up a historical romance, then stood waiting for Sam to choose from the small selection of books on market gardening, before she whispered self-consciously, "I need a book about growing vegetables Sam. Perhaps you'd advise me? I hear there's an allotment going, and I want to apply for it."

He stared at her seriously, trying to imagine what a schoolteacher would do with an allotment, when she had marking, writing lesson plans and other activities to occupy her evenings. She ploughed on bravely, keeping her voice to the merest murmur.

"On Monday, I found out that Pine Trees High School is relocating. I think Miss Silversmith had advance warning of the proposed rail closures and has decided to relocate to Boscombe. A suitable property has been selected…Oh damn!" said Miss Ellen Armitage as her voice (remarkable for its unemotional clarity) trembled treacherously and failed.

Sam swept up his books, grabbed one that had earlier attracted his attention, then catching hold of Ellen's arm, he steered her unresisting form to the checkout desk, solicitously watching Ellen's shaking hands as the librarian slipped the book "cards", into their tickets and meticulously stamped the date onto the lending record, before sliding the tickets and book cards into long wooden trays.

"See you in a fortnight then.", the librarian said easily and Sam thanked him as they left, realising as he cupped Ellen's elbow, guiding her deftly back into New Street, that they were the last to leave, even the market was beginning to pack up. He instinctively turned to the left at the end of

New Street, then paused, shifting his now heavy shopping bag as Ellen came to an uncertain stop, as if she would go the other way up the High Street.

"I suppose you came in by train?" she asked in a subdued voice, adding almost before she could stop herself.

"I came in my little car. It's parked behind Scats. I don't suppose you'd care to come back with me would you? I could do with someone to talk to."

It wasn't a very elegant invitation, but Sam saw her hands clasp convulsively on her shoulder bag, and felt a sudden kindred spirit with her. She was obviously distressed, had tried to hide it and now, she was offering him the chance to really repay her earlier kindness.

"Cor!" said Sam Smart appreciatively, "What turn down the chance of a ride through the Forest in autumn with the prettiest girl in the village! Strikes me that wouldn't be precisely sensible!"

"Fool!" said the lady in question (blushing helplessly) but she didn't look displeased.

Chapter 3 - An Exchange of Confidence.

By unspoken consensus, neither of them talked as Ellen carefully reversed her Morris Minor out of the narrow parking space, slotting it neatly into the traffic turning out of Lymington High Street, onto the main road.

At first, Sam didn't realise that they weren't headed directly back to Padways via Brockenhurst, but was content to look around him as they passed through the satellite villages of Pennington and Everton. However, when they reached the outskirts of Milford-on Sea he broke the silence.

"We're going to the seaside then Miss Ellen?" at which she grinned.

"Well, I fancy an ice-cream. There's a place we can sit and look at the sea on Hordle cliffs, then, we can either cut up through Hordle and Sway on our way home, or cross the Forest via the Cat and Fiddle. I know a lot of shortcuts, I used to teach in Brockenhurst remember? Game to try?"

Sam, (who always saw the bright side quickly), thought about it before responding with a chuckle.

"Well now." he said thoughtfully, "Having been kidnapped good and proper, I suppose the prisoner can demand a Mivvi?", and Ellen gurgled as she manoeuvred her little car through Milford neatly.

"I never had you down as a Strawberry Mivvi man; I thought you'd like a cornet!"

He considered this for a bare moment before agreeing.

"You'd be right about that as well. I can do almost anything ice-cream. I like lollies, ice-cream, cornets, cones, wafers, choc-ices ..." he mused on until they began to crest a hill which opened up into a right hand bend as the Solent opened up on their left.

"Lovely.", sighed Ellen Armitage, observing the sweep of the bay nestling below tan coloured cliffs. Sam craned his neck for a glimpse of the sparkling sea that separated them from the dark hills of the Isle of Wight which stretched out along the horizon to their left, and then Ellen clicked something on the driving wheel. He almost "felt" the flick of the amber trafficator arm as it lazily emerged from its nest between the doors and idly blinked in the sun, pointing towards their intended direction, as Ellen steered them neatly into a cleared parking area on the cliff-top.

Coasting into a parking bay facing the Solent, she came to a halt, then wound down her window letting salt-laden air bring their environment in to tease them.

Eventually, she asked seriously, "Am I being silly Sam? It seems that Miss Silversmith knew about the line closures for months. She seems to have decided to re-locate the school simply to save what is after all, a business. She has taken no-one into her confidence, just assumed that we'd all be grateful, and move with her. She sat there in our Staff-room and talked about the need to keep everything about the move private and confidential. We're not even supposed to mention it amongst ourselves at work in case the girls overhear. It's totally unreasonable. Their parents are sure to tell them, they read the newspapers when they go into Lymington to change their library books and not all of them are boarders. The nett result is that no-one's talking to anyone and you could cut the atmosphere with a knife."

She pulled a face as she spoke, adding distastefully, "I don't suppose I've added anything to the atmosphere, but I consulted a solicitor on the subject. That's where I'd been when the story broke! I had a morning off, so I took advantage, but he wasn't able to find any solution to the problem. Pine Trees is a private school, and as proprietor, Miss Silversmith calls the shots!"

She sighed and Sam turned in his seat, finally feeling that he'd found a friend that understood.

"Yes. I know how horrid it feels.", Sam thought for a moment, continuing slowly, "It's like everyone knows, in fact everyone knows that everyone else knows, but because there's nothing official like, you daresn't talk about it, in case it really happens."

Ellen stared at him, her face sober. "That's exactly what I was thinking Sam. You put that "am I being watched?" feeling into words very well, but it's "dare not", rather than daresn't."

As she added the habitual correction absently, Sam grinned.

"Go on." he said admiringly, "I never knew that Miss.", and Ellen Armitage looked up for a disconcerting moment, honey brown eyes smiling into his (very closely).

"Oh get along with you." she said with mock severity. "There's not much that escapes you Samuel Smart."

She opened her door. "Let's go and find that ice-cream man.", so that's exactly what they did.

Solemnly locking her car, they turned along the short grassed track and wandered to the next parking bay, watching the shingle beach over the edge of the great clay cliffs. These, streaked by greeny grey rivulets of water and iron brown mineral deposits, were still tufted with grey-green sea pinks. Here and there a late flowering Campion waved bravely in the breeze but along the hedgerows in the distance leaves were turning, despite the late arrival of spring.

"Oh the world's gone mad.", Ellen caught the direction of Sam's gaze.

"Pinks, Campion, suntans and autumn colours all together. Coal too expensive to buy and eggs! Don't talk to me about eggs! This time last year two and six a dozen, now look at them. Four and six a dozen and not worth saving for. I wonder that the price of ice-cream doesn't rocket!"

She marched off indignantly, a grinning Sam in tow, then, after collecting their ice-creams, they retired to the formal brick shelter nearby.

Just like a little house (complete with tiled roof), the four alcoves provided a wonderful coastal view on the Solent side. They sat on the wooden bench overlooking the sea, thankful for the fine weather, diligently devouring their treats until Sam (ever curious), got to his feet and explored the other three sides. Facing south was the whole west channel of the Solent, facing west (in an identical alcove) he could see the wide expanse of cliff-top, the continuance of the main road by which Ellen had brought them, which separated them from large residential properties on the northern side. He moved round the corner until he was facing north, gazing across the road at the salt battered gardens, the weathered fences, a marine environment in which he couldn't imagine gardening successfully. However, he could see bright planters, neat borders, and window-boxes so it must be possible.

The Solent Court hotel sported bright terrace planters behind an enormous car park. Bravely striped awnings shaded windows from the sun, and glad that the summer had succeeded the impossible winter with apparent disdain, he waited for Ellen to notice his absence. She greeted a passing dog cheerfully as he moved round to the eastern face of the shelter, staring back down the road towards the bend that hid Milford. He reckoned the houses here were bigger than normal, and was idly wondering how many people lived in each one, when Ellen peeped round the corner at him.

"I thought you'd escaped!" she laughed at him, gathering up his lolly stick and wrapper, and turning back to dispose of them in a waste bin as he followed her.

Returning to the side facing the sea, they stared into the eye-aching dazzle as the Solent shone in the late afternoon sun and watched bathers struggling up the steep wooden steps set into the cliffs, from the shingle beach below.

Finally Ellen (without turning her head) said apologetically, "I don't have any right to burden you with my problems Sam, but I would value your advice if you don't mind. I'm sure you will respect my confidence won't you?"

Sam said easily, "Look Miss Ellen, I knowed you since your poor mother came home after the War. She were that sick it was pitiful and I well remember old Reverend Ambrose getting me to chop kindling and light her fires that first Winter before you joined her. I reckon even if our paths only cross on the bus, you know better than to think I'd gab your business around. That's not what friends are for."

Mortified, Ellen said hastily, "No Sam, I'm sorry, I didn't mean that, it's just that I'm seriously thinking that I don't want to move with the school. Somehow, I feel wrong about this secrecy angle. It's as if Miss Silversmith doesn't trust us with our own futures. I know that I don't feel willing to continue until she gives us leave to speak. Furthermore, she has positively banned any of us from actively seeking alternative employment until she decides to make a formal announcement!"

Sam turned, shock written all over his face.

"That's unfair!" he stated flatly. "How are you supposed to keep body and soul together if you can't look for other work? Haven't you got a Union to represent you?"

Ellen laughed ironically. "Yes, of course we have a Union, but it's not very militant. Teachers are supposed to put the welfare of the children they teach first, loyalty to the school second and think about themselves last. No Sam, I'll have to wait till the end of term like everybody else. We won't be moving until the Easter term, so I have time in hand, but it's so frustrating, not being able to plan anything ahead. Miss Julian, the French teacher has family in France, and she plans to look for work there during the Christmas holiday. She says, Miss Silversmith can't dictate to her once she leaves the country, and she's right, but I'm dreading it. I have been there for ten years and I hadn't made any plans for change. Of course the cottage is mine, but I can't keep it up without a job."

Sam, looking into her wan face said nothing, but felt very much as if he wanted to put his arm round Miss Ellen Armitage and protect her from a world suddenly turned crazy, only, he needed protection himself. He stretched out a booted foot and dug his heels into the worn path that fronted the shelter, and thought blankly.

"She's got a home but no work or money, I've got a house but the line is to go. So many other people will lose their jobs and way of life, there has to be an answer for it.", then he told her what the ticket collector had insinuated.

"At least one of the Lymington crew said they suspect our temporary Station Master of helping to dismantle the line. Seems the government has been considering cut-backs for a long time, but Beeching apparently has based everything on data collected over just one week!" he seemed unaware that his face was screwed up in a scowl of ferocious concentration as he said seriously, "It's insane, decimating an institution that directly affects half the country's ability to move goods and passengers. MacMillan needs long-term strategies to save money, not the quick fix they're planning now. The railway is a service, not a product that isn't selling." He was thinking almost as he spoke, and Ellen leaned closer to hear his low voice better.

"I suppose we all knew things would change after the war, but this has snuck up on us, almost as though we thought it wouldn't happen if we didn't look at it. However, it isn't just railwaymen and railways that this affects Ellen. It's people like you, teachers, students, office workers, executives. We've got to raise public awareness, somehow we've got to get people to talk to the Government, otherwise what did we fight that war for? A country heroes can't go to work in?"

He had become more animated as he spoke and Ellen gazed at him in admiration. His keen grey eyes were flashing, (oddly she hadn't noticed how luxuriant his eyelashes were), his face was flushed with righteous anger and his chin had lifted with pride.

"I know what I'll do!" he said abruptly. "I know loads about the railways, their history, how they came to be built and what part they played in the Wars. I've got my old man's medals to display, tons of photos he and my Uncle Norman took when they drove the trains, I've even got the original plans of Silver Street from the mid nineteenth century. I could give talks about the railways, and then ask those present what they'll do when the lines close? That's not drumming up trouble, after all, it's current news, and so without doing anything other than reminding people of what they're likely to lose before it goes, I might get someone else to start a protest!"

Ellen gazed at him speechlessly. Whatever she had expected from her friendly railway porter it was certainly not this vivid firebrand, who was plainly determined to do something to protect his way of life. She felt his warm hand close about hers as he pulled her to her feet and tingled expectantly.

"Come on then trouble!" he chaffed her laughing, "Just remember that I'll get the sack quicker than you if old Oswald finds I've told anyone anything. I'm just a lowly railway porter and it's not my place to comment!"

Ellen poked her tongue out at him, and chanted, "Porter, odd job man, carpenter, messenger, friend and local railway historian as well.", as she skipped alongside him on the way back to her car.

They made themselves comfortable, and then sat gazing out over the Solent as the shadows shifted along the bay. Here and there a sail disturbed the sparkling expanse of water, and by turning his head to the right Sam could just see the feathery foam as the relentless waves curled against the shore. Families were trudging homeward with rolled wind-breaks (riotously striped in primary colours), lilos rolled and deflated, semi deflated and in some cases none of these conditions applied. He grinned at the struggles of one small boy who stumbled along carrying one end of a bright red lilo (the front end of which was carried by a girl very obviously his sister).

"Wouldn't pair those two in a pantomime horse!", he commented dryly, smiling as Ellen catching a glimpse of the boy's enraged face burst into helpless giggles.

"No, I wouldn't either, and there's no prize for guessing whose going to catch it when Mummy and Daddy aren't looking! She's setting a cracking pace, no wonder he can't keep up."

They politely turned their faces away as an indignant wail went up from the boy.

"Bella slow down. Daddy, she's nearly pulling me over!", but they both had quivering lips as they tried to contain their laughter. A man's voice rang out.

"Bella you heard your brother! Why you had to carry that thing between you beats me. Giles, your plimsolls are undone again. How you didn't fall down those steps I don't know."

A wealth of memories carried Sam back to a visit with his cousins at Keyhaven. The taste of salt-laden air, the smell of brine sodden sea-weed, the feel of scrunching shingle and the sound of constant reminders.

"Sam don't you sit on those stones, they're coated in tar!", then Ellen spoke regretfully.

"What a lovely end to the day, but I have to get back to Padways. Shall we go by old Milton? I can cut across from Naish Farm to the Cat & Fiddle; we'll be home before lighting up time."

She didn't wait for a response, just gave him a grin, inserted her key into the ignition and with a deft tug on the starter switch, the little Morris sprang into life. Sam swept a parting glance down the darkening bulk of the Isle of Wight, the familiar humped rocks that formed the Needles with their vigilant lighthouse, then the car was swinging round and they were facing inland. He could see large houses sheltering behind windswept pines as Ellen turned out onto the main road towards New

Milton. Sighing with unaccustomed pleasure, Sam settled down to enjoy the cross-Forest trip back to Padways, the road unfolding ahead of them as evening began to fall.

Chapter 4 - The Seeds of Rebellion

Sam watched as the open cliff and the seascape to his left began to change. They were leaving the built up area opposite, and on the right open fields appeared with a huddle of roofs showing beyond. On the seaward side, the grass grew longer, tufts of bracken appearing as woodland took over. Almost hidden amongst the trees, he noticed large buildings close to the cliff edge and sat forward as they entered the left hand sweep of a double bend. There was an entrance to the left as they swept round the right hand curve, which they'd almost passed, when Sam caught sight of a sign.

"Hordle Cliff House School", he mused although he hadn't meant to say it out loud. Ellen said quickly.

"It's another private school. Unfortunately well within twenty-five miles of Boscombe, which puts me out of the running if there was an opening, and I was prepared to live so close to that particular cliff edge. It's been crumbling for centuries."

The road had straightened up in front of them as she spoke, and Sam, glancing to his left was shocked to get a glimpse of what looked like gravestones as they passed a gap before a farm. Ellen was forced to stop so that a queue of traffic ahead could turn right down a narrow lane, and she said absently, "That's all that remains of Hordle's original churchyard. The cliff is thought to have collapsed during the twelfth century, forcing the villagers to move inland. It's a bit of a mystery; we must go and have a look one day when we have more time."

All along the seaward side, stunted hawthorns criss-crossed the cliff-top fields (bowed by the constant breeze into permanently leaning shapes like so many ancient men. At their feet, rough shaggy grasses leant, bleached by salt and sun, interspersed by brilliant yellow gorse bushes. The occasional cow browsed on the fields to the right, but the unfenced cliff fields seemed empty, populated only by seagulls. The road wswung inland as they passed the junction to Barton, then they paused before the next town. Looking carefully about her, Ellen slipped smoothly into the home-going traffic taking the road through Old Milton, sliding away from the new conurbations of retirement bungalows and onto the road to Highcliffe with a rueful grin.

"I'm glad that Padways doesn't have so many drivers or attract so many seasonal visitors."

She deftly negotiated a deep bend, swooping the little car over a hump-back bridge as if it could fly Then, at Sam's gasp of shock, she was spinning the wheel to take them to the right, into the road that would bring them out opposite an ancient smugglers inn. Her visible relief at leaving the continuous two way traffic was laughable, she was a brilliant driver, but as they waited to cross a main arterial road (thereby avoiding the Saturday shoppers and the coastal developments) Sam was curious.

"You should like driving Ellen." he commented, "You seem good at it. I can't co-ordinate. One try was enough for my Uncle Norman to leave his van to my cousin, and my Dad said I'd never make a train driver. Too easily distracted me!" he chuckled at the memory of his father's disgust, but Ellen frowned.

"You shouldn't give up Sam.", she coaxed the little car over the crossing and into the narrow roads leading through the Forest.

"Learning a skill sometimes takes several attempts. It's been fairly obvious through my years of teaching that not everyone can play a piano, but occasionally I've noticed that one year a pupil will try and fail, the next year they've "settled into their skins", and take off as if they've been playing all their lives. There's no accounting for it, adults and children alike are affected the same way. You'll learn when the time is right."

He responded gruffly, "Well, the time will have to be right pretty soon if I'm to get another job. Bert Credding (you know our signalman) is packing up altogether. His family's in London and he's going to look for work in the Smoke. He often gives me a lift if I have to cart a lot of tools on a private job, but once he's gone there's nothing I can do about it. Once the last passengers come through, it's all up for us, there's little other work available, and too many folk will be looking for too few jobs."

They were passing through a stretch of woodland as he spoke, the trees hung sullenly over the road, and the bright gloss of the day was gone. He pondered the problem silently not wanting to depress Ellen, but she was irrepressible.

"I know." she suggested brightly, "Let's visit the white witch at Burley. I'll pay her to get you co-ordinating then you'll be able to get a van of your own."

She giggled as Sam rolled his eyes.

"Seems to me that we wouldn't have to bother if we sent that man Beeching or his lords and masters to see her.", he said bitterly. "Iffen she turned that lot into slugs I'd happily pay for the beer to drown them in!", then they were coasting down into Padways, the day was over, and Sam felt unbearably sad. For half a day he'd had someone to talk to, someone with a sense of humour, and now he had to face his lonely cottage by himself.

Ellen had drawn up by the church wall, and he scrambled out of the car, gathering his shopping bag, rescuing his library books in a rush. She leant forward and put a hand on his.

"Thank you for a lovely day Sam. I've really enjoyed it.", she coloured faintly then said diffidently, "I really need to talk to you about that allotment. Do you think I could borrow that book you mentioned?" she gulped, and then threw caution to the winds.

"In fact, if you'd like to come to Sunday lunch we could discuss it then."

This was too good to be true. Gathering his belongings Sam stepped out, shutting the door firmly, before leaning in through the open window.

"I'll look out the book, get a list of things you'll need and meet you after church." he offered, then found himself blurting out.

"However, I'll thank you to remember that I'm on the allotment Committee, and bribery is against the rules!"

She covered her mouth with a hand to choke the shout of laughter he'd provoked, and sat watching him stride up the narrow path to his door, rucksack over his shoulder. She would see him again tomorrow, at which thought Miss Ellen Armitage smiled, her warm brown eyes glowing.

The Vicar didn't pull any punches either. The theme of his sermon that Sunday morning had many of his parishioners nodding and nudging each other surreptitiously when he spoke at length on the subject of "putting money before the welfare of ones fellow man". After the service, (as was his common practice) the Vicar lingered in the porch of the church, and Sam, waiting for Ellen to collect her music began to notice that several of the locals who used the trains to get to work were talking to the Vicar at length. He had just moved forward to take Ellen's bag when he heard his name being mentioned.

Ellen said briskly, "I hope you were serious about talking to interested parties about the history of our Station? Martin asked me to recommend a speaker for the Parish Meeting next month. I think he's about to ask you when we leave. I've noticed him talking to the Parish Councillors already. Are you still prepared for it?"

Sam nodded. "Meeting's not till the end of October; I started sorting out all my Dad's diaries and odds and ends that Uncle Norman left me. Reckon I could get something interesting together in time. Trouble is, none of us know precisely what is happening so they won't be able to ask me why, what or when!"

Ellen took his arm and said in tones of deep satisfaction, "Thereby raising the indignation of all who should have been informed of those details. Sam, don't you see that this involves a much wider swathe of people than those who travel on the trains? It involves the wider community, from shopkeepers who ship papers, to urgent parcels delivered to the local station by Red Star. It touches holidaymakers, troop transport, children travelling to school, rail investors, and businesses all over Great Britain. It will affect who develops their business in towns that lose their rail links, those who are moving from one town to another to start new lives. There isn't a man, woman or child that it won't affect in many rural areas, and all in the name of saving money!"

She sounded so indignant that Sam stared at her in surprise, and then the Vicar was taking his hand and saying warmly.

"How much better you're looking Sam. Quite a nasty turn you had the other week. I hope you're feeling more the thing now?", and Sam forced to admit that he was feeling much better, added ingenuously, "Did I hear you taking my name in vain Vicar, or is there something you wanted to ask me?"

Martin Short (who towered head and shoulders over most of his parishioners) glanced at Ellen's innocent features, and said quickly:

"I understand that you know a fair deal about the station Sam. I knew your father was a driver of course, but Miss Armitage tells me that there is a great deal more to Silver Street than anyone might realise. Unfortunately we've been unable to secure a speaker for the Harvest festival get together, so I wondered if you could cobble together something on the history of the place. I don't like putting you on the spot, but Miss Armitage made it sound rather intriguing. Could you manage the 28th October? There's a free supper of course, I can lend you a slide projector if you need one, and I'd be delighted to help you set up anything you need."

Sam considered quickly. His late father's room was lined with bookshelves holding records and files going back over most of this century. His Uncle Norman's photographs had pride of place on every wall of the cottage, and from Ellen's approving nod he knew he could also depend on her to help him.

"I'd be delighted to help out Vicar." he heard his own voice from a distance, and then he was out through the door into the late September sun, and heading down the path with Ellen on his arm. Somehow the closure of the Forest line seemed a remote proposition, although at the back of his mind he knew how devastating it would be. For the time being he had the prettiest woman in the village on his arm, people actually wanted to listen to his extensive knowledge of the railways and in the back of his mind he heard Percy saying prophetically.

"When one door closes, there's always another ready to open. Just you look around and recognise it and you'll be alright young man."

He smiled down at Ellen as they turned in at her gate, and prepared to set about sowing the seeds of rebellion in the fertile ground of the New Forest.

Chapter 5 - Dreams and Aspirations

Ellen set a small table in the garden at the back of her house. She used a cheerful red and white gingham checked tablecloth, and set out a handsome ploughman's lunch, complete with a pint of shandy for Sam. He worked his way steadily through a chunk of mature cheddar, (appreciating that it was no shop bought pickle that went so well with the cheese), finishing off the crisp salad with a hefty slice of crusty bread, before he spoke.

"Well Miss Armitage.", he said with deep satisfaction, "I reckon that you keep a very comfortable establishment here. That was superb and that cheese wasn't local was it?"

"You're right of course Mr Smart.", she responded happily. "My father had shares in a hamper company. There's no point in my cooking a roast just to serve myself, so unless it's very cold I like to eat what I grew and use the hamper I get every year to top up for special guests. That cheese was from a priory farm. Mrs Castle made the pickle; I bought it at the fete last month. I grew the cucumber, the tomatoes and the lettuce, they're over now, but they've lasted better than anyone might have expected after the Freeze. I hope the rumours of poor winters for years to come are wrong, which brings me back to discussing allotments. What do you think of what they're saying?"

"Well...", Sam leant back with his shandy, and after taking a long pull on his glass, turned a knowing eye on the brightly lit garden. Carefully fenced, it held a tiny lawn, a bird-bath, a potting shed with a cold frame huddled to its side, and about eight foot square of vegetable patch. Ellen watched his appraising eye anxiously, and then Sam answered her question.

"I wouldn't depend on anyone predicting the whole course of a winter?" he said thoughtfully, "Look how many times they get a single event wrong! Take for example all the folk lore you've heard bandied about. Why (if hindsight showed them so many indicators of an unnaturally long winter) didn't they see it afore it happened? Don't you worry about it yet, I don't think it's imminent. Everything's been late, but we've had good harvests. I've laid by everything I can and Mrs Thomas (the Vicars cook) has jammed, jellied or pickled half what I grew already. The other half is bedded down in straw, drying on racks, or has been salted down in my Gran's Kilner jars! All the allotment members have shared or swapped their produce so there's little chance of anyone in this Parish starving!"

Ellen nodded seriously, and then started stacking their dishes ready to return to the house. "I know about the pickling parties." she smiled and invited, "You should see my pantry, it's scandalous for a single person, but I bet there's stuff there you've never seen. The W. I. really got stuck in to foraging and we are going out again in October. We've dried and pickled mushrooms all through this month, the berries are jammed, jellied or converted to syrup, and next month we start on the nuts!"

Sam finished his drink, and then turned serious.

"So what do you want an allotment for?" he queried, shocked to see Ellen's lips trembling as she replied.

"Because I'm being forced out of teaching for at least a year! I won't be bullied into a move that won't suit me at all. I love Padways; I've lived here since the war. My parents are buried here, and I won't be forced to give up my way of life by anyone, or anything, beginning and ending with your Dr Beeching and his mad ideas."

She stood abruptly, sweeping crumbs from the tablecloth, and depositing them on her bird-table.

"I may need to depend on what I can grow for food." she announced quietly. "I haven't the room here for main crops and I can grow more variety on an allotment."

She waved a hand round her neat little garden. "If I could grow runner beans, cauliflower or cabbage, I'd be able to eat better for less. I can go without meat if I have cheese, nuts and fungi. Thankfully my mother was an expert on those. She taught me how to make cheese; I have foraged all my life and know what grows locally. I can earn enough by teaching piano, but I won't be brow beaten into moving, even if Miss Silversmith offers me the chance to live in."

Sam looked at her mutinous little face and said slowly, "Why do you have to give up teaching rather than move to Boscombe?" to which Ellen answered unhappily.

"As they move before my contracted period of employment ends, I will not (according to the terms of that contract) be able to teach English Language or Literature within a twenty-five mile radius of the school for one calendar year. Miss Silversmith has let it be known that she considers us under an obligation to support the move, and will view those who don't as being in breach of contract."

Sam, shocked, stared at her blankly as she burst out indignantly.

"I can't think how I didn't realise how that clause would affect me if I left. I've taught there for ten years damn it, she has no need to enforce such a stupid rule, but she's going to. I wonder how I didn't see how like a cat that woman is. Nice and fluffy, soft and purring while you are doing what she wants. Calculating and cruel if she doesn't get her own way."

She stood abruptly, clearing away their dishes and standing them in the sink of her modest kitchen. Sam took the coal scuttle and filled it with an aggression that surprised him.

"How dare anyone upset Ellen, who only wanted to remain in her family home and earn a living!" He returned from the coal bunker, banging the scuttle down beside her Aga somewhat harder than he'd intended. Ellen had washed up already, but Sam, conscious that she still had lesson plans to prepare grabbed a brightly coloured tea-towel extolling the benefits of visiting Norfolk, and began drying up. Ellen bore it for three minutes, then rescued her crockery saying gently, "Why so indignant Sam? I signed the contract after all.", and he grinned sheepishly.

"Doesn't seem fair to me that's why. She's got her business to protect, but she's moving away from you, not the other way round. You didn't ask for any of this, she's just making life tiresome for no good reason."

He leant back against the draining board and wondered why Ellen had never married. Most attractive girls did these days, and then she asked the question herself.

"How is it that a nice man like you never married Sam?", and he stared at her open mouthed.

"Don't really know." he muttered, "Never met the right girl I suppose. Then again I had my old man to look after till a few years back and the job doesn't pay that much. I worked as a chippy with a local builder when I left school, but he went to war, and never returned. I went on the railway mainly to please my Dad. Portering might not seem much, but it pays more'n four shillings an hour, and when Flaxman was around I got to do a lot of maintenance jobs too. It gives me plenty of time to think, time to research railway history, and I get free travel too. Course that'll all go soon, so I won't appeal to many women. No looks, no money, no job, no chance of marrying!"

He turned away to the Aga, opening the firebox and riddling down the clinker before opening the lid and refuelling the fire. He heard her say in a muffled sort of voice.

"I shouldn't have asked you Sam, I'm sorry.", then she was stood beside him, touching his hand solemnly.

"We should be looking at that gardening book shouldn't we? We can't solve any problems without a plan, and I'd like to start with being more self-sufficient."

Sam lifting the massive gardening book onto the little table thought suddenly, "I'd like you not to be so self-sufficient my girl. In fact I'd like to take care of you myself!", but he said nothing, keeping that particular revelation to himself as they discussed everything but the loss of their jobs, as though that subject had never been raised.

They moved into Ellen's sitting-room, spreading out the seed catalogues on the pale blue carpet, each taking note of things that especially appealed to Ellen's eye. Eventually, laughing, Sam held up a hand as she waxed lyrical over some distinctly foreign sounding produce.

"Hold on there missus!" he protested, "you won't grow stuff like that without a greenhouse, and they'd need a heated one at that. Allotments aren't like having your own garden you know. You can have a small shed for tools, but we can't provide anything more than basic services. There's a main tap for getting water, some plots can even reach that with a hose, but you have to understand that you can't always guarantee that half a dozen other gardeners won't need access at the same time. There's rules to follow about use of watering cans, buckets etc., as well as rules about weeding, destroying of weeds, compost making, burning etc., and if you don't follow them, you'll become highly unpopular."

Ellen, sprawled on the carpet on her stomach, cupped her chin in her hands and resting on her elbows not ten inches from his own face, regarded him steadily.

"Sounds complicated." she commented, and then said irritably, "Oh how I wish I could win the football pools! I'd buy a plot of land and turn it into a small holding. I'd have all the vegetables I need, a goat for milk and cheese, some chickens for eggs and a goose for Christmas!"

Caught up in this vision of delight, Sam said promptly, "A cow for milk, different cheese and butter, a few ducks on a pond and enough ground to grow all them fancy goods to sell for Christmas. In fact, iffen we had that much land we could buy a big old van and turn it into a mobile shop. I saw one of those down in Lymington one time. It went out to all the little estates, all the properties along the coast, right down to Everton I think.", then they sat up simultaneously, as a single idea formed in two minds.

"That's it.", said Sam exultantly, as Ellen exclaimed in triumph.

"Sam! I used to drive an ambulance. If we could find one that would convert, we could take Mrs Fleet's deliveries and our own produce once we're set up!"

Shaking with excitement, Ellen rose to her feet, anxious not to let her enthusiasm run away with her, and turning swiftly suggested.

"Tea Sam?" in a high brittle voice that didn't deceive him for a moment. He stood, frowning down at the catalogues a little, and wondered how to break the news that they first had to find the money to buy and convert an ambulance before they could dream of starting a business. Even if he had the skills to refit a vehicle, and he knew a gifted mechanic, they needed land and money to give it a go. He heard Ellen fill the kettle, sliding it onto the hotplate of the Aga, and bent to collect the catalogues thoughtfully. He wasn't sure yet, but somewhere, he thought he'd caught the sound of Percy Adams door opening, so he went along the passage to the kitchen with renewed hope, and the merest idea that he quite liked the sound of domesticity, of Sunday tea with Ellen, and a project or two to provide for their future.

The evening was quite advanced when Sam gathered up his seed catalogues and took his leave of Ellen. Deep in lesson plans, she'd excused herself from walking home with him regretfully, but he'd shouldered his rucksack, slipping quietly into the lane, and made his way home in a daze. He felt at once enthused and full of trepidation for Ellen had taxed him with a task.

"Sam.", she'd pleaded, "Can you find out from Mrs Fleet if she would entertain us doing her deliveries if we go ahead and look for the right vehicle. That van of hers is on its last legs, all her money is tied up in the shop, and we'd need her on our side if we were to succeed. I for one don't want to invest Lady Jane unwisely!"

He'd stared at her bemused, before asking faintly, "Whose Lady Jane?", then more truculently, "What's she got to do with it?", until Ellen gurgling with laughter had admitted ruefully, "Oh Sam, sorry you don't know half my faults! I name just about every machine I touch. It makes them work better I think, they seem like part of the family, and Lady Jane is my car. If I sell her, I might just have enough to buy that ambulance, but I'm not in the habit of making quick decisions. I'm far too fond of her to contemplate letting her go if Mrs Fleet thinks we're setting up as rivals. However, that van of hers is about as disastrous as Bert, and she won't recognise that by herself. She had some idea that young Rory would drive it when he finished his National Service in 1962, but of course he was a tradesman and promptly joined the regulars. She says all her men are a disappointment to her, poor lady."

She leant close to Sam and said confidentially, "Please take care who you talk to Sam. I don't want anyone learning our plans before we evaluate their chances of success. Most folk are decent, but the odd one or two with money to back them now would steal the idea before we can put it into operation, and I'd hate that."

He remembered her perfume on the way home, the smile in her deep brown eyes, and the hope in her face as he took his leave. He promised himself that he would take very great care of this lady, for hadn't she entrusted him with her dreams, her hopes, and awoken aspirations that he had buried for far too long.

Chapter 6 - Monday Morning Blues

It was dark when Sam, (huddled in his donkey jacket over his uniform), clambered aboard the Hants and Dorset bus, and shuffled to the back of the downstairs compartment. Upstairs the raucous laughter of some of the Wellworthy contingent only served to underline the fact that for the next week, Sam would travel to his early shift without the compensation of Ellen's company. Outside the weather had turned against him too, and he slumped down into his jacket and tried to ignore the dismal sheen of rain that had blustered into the bus shelter behind him.

He steeled himself to resist the Monday morning blues, but somehow he couldn't stir up the remotest interest in his surroundings. Tom Collier (a bluff hearty man from Burley) leant forward and said conversationally, "There's retraining on offer apparently Sam. One of my pals who works further downline is going to look into the Royal Blue coach service. If you've got a driver's licence, they're looking for drivers to pick up passengers once the line closes. Want me to find out a bit more for you?"

Sam stared at the man silently for a moment, and then his innate sense of courtesy came to the rescue.

"That's good of you Tom." he responded as easily as he could, despite his momentary irritation over others discussing his business in public.

"If there's an advert I'll pin it up on the Parish notice board if you like, it might help someone else although I'm afraid I don't drive. I've already sorted something out for myself, but it was good of you to think of me."

Tom's face crinkled in a broad grin. "I'll do that then mate. What are you going to do? It'd better be something that leaves you free for cricket next summer!"

Sam, conscious of listening ears all around him, forced a grin. "Still ironing out the details," he said with dignity, "but you'd better believe that thrashing Burley isn't something I'd miss if I was painting the Whispering Gallery at Saint Paul's."

There was a muffled giggle from a group of girls going into Lymington on the early train, and Tom (wicket keeper of the rival team) glowered and remarked tartly, "No need to get nasty Sam, I only asked!", before retiring behind his paper.

Resisting the temptation to apologise, Sam made his way forward to the conductor's platform as the bus climbed the slope towards the station, keeping his own counsel as he thought.

"That's my problem! It's like Ellen said, everyone involved knows everybody else's business. The moment I start looking into our plans

41

seriously, there'll be no disguising what's afoot.", but thankfully his distracted scowl prevented further conversation until it was too late and Sam dropped from the bus as it slowed to a stop.

He slipped rapidly away from the cluster of men travelling into Lymington via Brockenhurst, despite acknowledging a couple he knew that worked the Isle of Wight ferry. Time was tight first thing in the morning, and the co-ordination of bus, coach and railway timetables gave Sam and his fellow railwaymen little time to prepare for the working day, which in rural areas started very early. He went through the wicket gate on the down-line platform, as the up-line passengers patiently tramped across the modest passenger bridge that linked the two sides. He unlocked the downline parcels office, hung his donkey jacket (still bedewed with early morning rain), and set his cap to rights before crossing the line by taking the shortcut via the trolley-crossing at the end of his platform. He went down as the platform sloped away, over a solid path of sleepers and then, by dint of using a cunningly inset "hop-up", onto the opposite platform. He patted his waistcoat pocket, extracted the key to the up-line ticket office, and opened the ticket clerk's hatch, solemnly retrieving the padlock and tucking it safely away. He was only just in time to open the outer doors to let in the season ticket holders, then, as they spread out onto the platform, he retrieved a barrow, and wheeled it out, complete with the Royal Mail sacks to load onto the guard's van.

Not five minutes later, he unlocked the up-line gate, let in the stragglers (and Fred Cummins the up-line porter wheeling his bike), then the lines were humming, the signals dropped and the locomotive drew in past him with a roar and hiss of steam. Sam checked along the carriages as passengers prepared to embark. Only one door opened as the train glided to a stop, and sure enough John Oswald stepped out, magnificent in his Station Master's uniform.

Sam, (normally even-tempered) physically restrained the urge to shake the truth out of the self-important man as the Station Master strutted toward his office. Grey eyes brightened (then chilled), as the porter saw the thick "Staff" file under Oswald's arm, then he turned to assist with loading the mailbags, glad that his hands were only grasping those, rather than his senior's throat!

John Oswald paused until the guard blew his whistle and the train drew out towards Brockenhurst, then with a swift glance around let himself into his office and settled down to work.

Sam placed a pot of flowering shrubs on the platform, dusted off the glass on the station clock, and unlocked the main waiting room off the ticket office, and began the daily chores. About ten minutes later a small car drew up at the unloading bay outside and Mr Richards (the ticket clerk) scuttled inside, ducking behind the counter of his meticulously tidy cubby-hole and settling himself into the tall stool where he worked. Sam waited for him to unlock the safe and take out the trays of tickets, then touched his cap, and made his way across the passenger footbridge to his allotted duties on the down-line side.

Harry Armstrong (the parcels clerk) had arrived by then, and they chatted as they loaded parcels for Dorchester on the mail barrow, ready for the 8.30 service. When it arrived, it brought plenty to occupy them. Sam was kept busy swiftly unloading parcels and bags of mail to be weighed, and then entered into Harry's way book, to be signed for as the cumbersome Mail van picked them up. Afterwards, Sam and Harry shared the sweeping of the down-line platform, occasionally watching as goods trains shunted into the sidings on the up-line side. Sam thought (with deep melancholy) that he would miss the familiar sounds of the station, and mentally began to list them in his mind.

"The squeak of the up-line gate; the rattle and clunk of the goods trains; the odd purring of the telephone as the signal box conferred with the Station Master; the puff and chuff of departing trains; the hiss and clank of arrivals.", he was so engrossed that he jumped out of his wits when Harry lifting down a fire bucket full of sand, let out a shout of laughter.

"Well, damn that squirrel of yours Sam. He's gone and hidden his acorns and a whole load of hazel nuts in my fire-bucket! Crazy critter scattered sand all along under that bench and the "old man" will have our guts for garters iffen we don't sweep up sharpish!"

It was a light-hearted moment, but Sam only embraced it with a shrug.

"It's not my squirrel Harry." he protested, "He belongs to Silver Street, and will probably have the run of it in the not too distant future!"

"That's a fact my friend," said Harry the parcel, "but I'm going home to Wales, even if my wife says she won't come with me. My old man has a post office and shop, so he can do with my help. I reckon on working for someone a damn sight more grateful than Dr Beeching and his cohorts. In fact, I've got next week booked as holiday, we're going home to see the lie of the land and if it's favourable I'll beat a hasty retreat and let Mr Oswald weigh his own parcels from now on."

Sam, busy sweeping up discarded sand said nothing, but his spirits plunged even lower, and so it went on all week. Mundane tasks, few if any distractions and every train repeating the chant in the rattle and whirr of the line.

"You're going to close, you're going to close, there's no more work, and you're going to close."

On Friday John Oswald called Sam into his office. He had open in front of him the Padways Parish magazine, and was frowning at it suspiciously. He pointed a stubby finger at an item ringed in red pen, and barked crossly. "What's this then Mr Smart? Taken to rabble-rousing have we?"

Utterly unprepared, Sam squinted innocently at the list headed "Forthcoming Events", as his heart plummeted. There in black and white was the announcement.

"After the Harvest Home Supper, Mr Samuel Smart will give a talk on the history of Castleman's Corkscrew and the various uses this famous old railway line has been put to. An extensive collection of old photographs and diaries will be on display to illustrate this talk, and visitors are invited to bring any documentary evidence they own to show our well-known local historian and to contribute to a truly local event."

John Oswald glared up at Sam from beneath beetling brows. "How come I've never heard of your interest in the line? Why are you giving this talk now eh, and why Mr Smart were you seen deep in conversation with one of railways most troublesome employees at Lymington last Saturday? Just what are you plotting Mister? I'll have none of your union troubles here. No go-slows, no working to rule, and absolutely no incitement to public protest see!"

Sam was so astonished that he snatched up the Parish Magazine and ran his eyes over the Forthcoming Events right up to and including Christmas. It gave him the opportunity to think for a moment, and then he decided that the only defence was attack. He schooled his face to total urbanity then returned the magazine, even giving it a little pat of satisfaction as he did so.

"Mr Oswald. I have been a loyal employee of the railways for seventeen years." he stated with dignity. "My grandfather worked to build this line and his father before him worked on the line as it came down from London. My late father and his older brother were drivers on this line through the end of the First World War in my Uncle's case, and through the second in my father's. They drove munitions between the coast and the airfields at great risk to themselves, they also drove troop trains taking better men than you or I to their deaths in our service, for which both my father and uncle received recognition. The Harvest Home

Supper with guest speaker (on a local topic of interest) is a long tradition in Padways. I expect the Vicar can supply the evidence in my support going back over a number of years. I don't think the Reverend Short subscribes to any union, or political activity, nor I suspect would he allow what you call rabble-rousing in his congregation. I have been an avid collector of railway memorabilia since I could sit on my father's shoulders and wave to my Uncle's train. I have spoken to the local Women's Institute, to Lymington Sea-Scouts, to steam railway enthusiasts on the Isle of Wight, and if the railways are to deny me a living by closing this line, then I intend to use my knowledge to replace that living. Only by getting practice with small groups interested in local history am I likely to become fluent enough to go on radio, or write the book that I'm thinking about, and I don't think there's anything remotely controversial about planning my future if I haven't got one here. I don't think our current masters would find fault with a talk that embraces the great entrepreneurs of the Victorian era who financed this line, nor of the recent war history associated with Silver Street."

He'd braced himself against the Station Master's desk, hands splayed to either side, totally unconscious of how remote and chilling his dignity made him. John Oswald shivered as though the temperature in the room had suddenly dropped by ten degrees, and looked into Sam Smart's flinty face, and smiled weakly.

"Oh, I see." he essayed a look that Sam later described as a conciliatory simper. "Just a local group? Mostly congregation at Padways eh? Well, I don't know that I won't come along myself. It sounds interesting."

At that point, Sam lost all respect for the man. "Interesting! Too right it's bloody interesting. Men died to lay that line, fortunes were invested and lost, bombs that killed thousands were transported from here to God knows where on those tracks, and all he can say is it sounds interesting! I tell you something Ellen, it's blooming diabolical. The line is going to close, they've made their decision, but don't they know what they are throwing away? Lives, livelihoods, the millions invested nationally and it's so short sighted. We'll suffer the effects on and on into the future. You can take the Great out of Britain if they go ahead, but when the petrol runs out, and they can't get coal from the mines to the power-stations, because they closed the lines, don't ask me to apologise to generations yet unborn. Let Beeching ruin ICI, but leave the railways to railwaymen!"

Miss Armitage, (sat on her living room floor listening as Sam enraged strode about fists clenched and eyes aflame) gazed up adoringly.

"Oh Sam!" she said very softly.

"You were so brave to face him down, but it'll be a hoot if he turns up at your talk! They'll cut him dead, he's so unpopular. Of course you'll talk on radio, and write that book! I think you're wonderful!", and the object of her affection glowed happily in front of his one woman audience.

The month wore on, getting progressively chillier, reflecting the atmosphere at Ellen's school. Sam (now on the opposite shift) found himself worrying as her pinched little face came into view each evening, her normal vivacity subdued. He made her giggle by offering gallantly, "Carry your books Miss?", but more often than not she seemed on the far side of a high wall, wan, withdrawn and scarcely engaging in conversation.

At the end of September John Oswald called each man into his office and told them solemnly that the line would close to passengers the following May. He gave few specific details, and was plainly not in the mood to answer questions, reminding them tersely that if they wanted to register a protest, Silver Street was not the place to do it, and that anything which brought the railways into disrepute would result in instant dismissal without references. It was a dismal little group who returned to their duties, the rest of that Monday washed out in the dismal contemplation of unemployment.

The following day dawned no brighter and even Sam had to remind himself that he loved coming to work as he lifted a heavy suitcase from the hand of a young man who descended from the last train to Dorchester. There was a large car to greet the visitor, a chauffeur relieved Sam of the suitcase, then, the tall bronzed young man (looking a little overwhelmed himself), slid into the passenger seat as the car door was opened for him. He flicked the ghost of a grin at Sam, spoke to the chauffeur, and the Bentley pulled away smoothly, turning towards Burley as it glided into the Forest.

"Blimey! Royalty do you think?" said Harry looking down at a first Class ticket, and Sam laughed at his awed expression.

"More likely one of these film stars." he said thoughtfully. "He's staying at Burley Manor and he's an Aussie. I heard him speak to the chauffeur. Mind you, that isn't the Manor car, nor is it the Garden Hotel's car. I reckon he's hired it privately, so he's got money!"

Harry grinned maliciously.

"Yep, and looks, as well as everything we ain't got, and he's young enough to enjoy all of it. Still, at least my time in Wales wasn't wasted."

Still staring after the stranger's car, Sam muttered absently.

"That's good then." as Harry explained.

"Well, the old man really took a shine to my Deirdre. She's always worked in a little village store, but there's no chance of advancement there and she wants to manage a shop. I'm leaving to do a Post Master's training, and then I'll run the post office while Deirdre runs the shop, and Dad can retire. I've made my application already, young Trevor Steadman is happy to come down-line for a few months so everything will sort itself out nicely."

Sam stared downhill, watching the old bus creep off the road and thought bleakly.

"Everything except me. Whatever I do now, I must try and cheer Ellen up, but with everyone moving away, I soon won't have any friends left!" Then, feeling sorry for himself he got on the evening bus and went home in total silence.

Chapter 7 - The Box of Delights

That week wound on slowly, even the weather seemed against all Sam's plans, and by Friday the temperature had dropped, rain threatened and he was thoroughly depressed. To make matters worse, Ellen appeared at the bus-stop on the Saturday dressed in a warm Navy blue raincoat and carrying a rolled umbrella, dressed for an excursion from which he was excluded. She smiled at Sam, (who was working that weekend and was as cross as a crab about it), then continued conversing with the Vicar's wife.

Sam fumed silently. He'd been looking forward to telling her about the Australian visitor and now she was tied up with Jane Short and he couldn't get a word in edgeways!

The Vicar (with unusual interest in Sam's irritation) remarked comfortingly.

"There's no hope for us Sam! Now they've put a woman into space, there'll be no holding them back. You'll soon learn that once women start chatting, we might as well cease to exist. How's that talk coming along?" They exchanged some ideas on laying out the Committee room (set aside for Sam's display), then the bus jolted to a halt by the stop as Saturday-go-to Lymington shoppers crowded on board.

Reluctantly, Sam remained on the footplate with the conductor. There were no seats to spare and four standing already, so he travelled in sight of Ellen Armitage, and dropped off at Silver Street with a sketchy wave as the bus drew away loaded to capacity.

Fred Cummins worked Sam every bit as hard as John Oswald would have done, listing and labelling railway property to go to other stations. Every day seemed to bring another reminder of their fate, and by the time the day drew to a sullen close under miserably dripping skies, Sam was grateful for the lift home laid on by their crossing keeper. He went into the paper-shop, chose a quarter of lemon sherbets, and went home with one tucked into his cheek, wondering what Ellen had been up to in Lymington.

He hadn't long to wait to find out. She arrived in a gust of rain, cheerfully pulling off the scarf she'd wound round her hair and folding her umbrella.

"Sam!" she exclaimed as he took the damp "gamp", shoving it into a large jar his grandmother had used for walking canes. "It was horridly crowded in Lymington. I really regretted not going in the car, but Jane Short is so busy that we never seem to go shopping together these days. Martin had an appointment, so I've been to market and just look what

I've got."

Belatedly he realised that she was struggling to drag in an old tin box. It was only when he saw the unusual "hasp bar and lock" system, that his interest was really piqued, but as he lifted it onto the large deal table that filled the centre of his kitchen, his eyebrows lifted in surprise at its weight. Hastily drinking his last mouthful of tea, he turned the box until the catch faced the edge, and then crouched, eyes level with the lock as he examined it closely.

"It was too heavy for the trader who had it on his stall to carry around with him." Ellen shook her scarf out, laid it on the rail of the range to dry, and commandeered a chair explaining excitedly.

"He says he bought it in Padways "when he was on the knock". He described a large house on the outskirts, which I think might even be Pine Trees, but he's never opened it, having lost the key. He was really fed up when I asked a few questions, so I don't know a lot about it, but Martin helped me get it home. He'll be round in a minute, but Sam, the description he gave me fits Pine Trees in the forties. A large house standing derelict until builders cleared it out. I was so intrigued I couldn't resist it."

Her eyes glowed, and she clasped her hands around her knees demanding.

"Can you open it Sam? I can't wait to find out what's inside. Treasure me hearties, pieces of eight!" declared this very upright pillar of Padways society enthusiastically. "Avast there landlubber!"

By now, Sam (not used to female visitors), had drawn breath and was rapidly clearing his supper table. He grinned at Ellen's rueful appraisal of his kitchen, then (having shut the back door, and stacked the sink), he filled a kettle and came back to run knowledgeable hands over the tin box. Ellen had discarded her raincoat, shoved up her sleeves, and while Sam took down bright blue and white striped mugs from the Welsh dresser and prepared to make tea, Ellen had run the hot tap, found the washing up bowl and was happily disposing of Sam's usual evening chore.

"You don't have to do that!" he protested without embarrassment, but she just grinned, and continued in a comfortably domestic role, as Sam caught up a workbelt, and extracted a few tools.

"Don't damage it Sam.", she pleaded, seeing what he was about, then she added doubtfully, "Perhaps it should be returned to the original owners, if we can trace them or their descendants. The trader said the builders were working for the Fullingford Trust. They administer loads of properties round here, although Martin Short seemed to think that it would be difficult for anyone to be certain whose property it is now. Perhaps the Trust left the builders to dispose of any contents? Legal title might have passed to them quite properly. On the other hand, the trader might have got mixed up; it might not be anything to do with Pine Trees."

She sounded so doubtful that Sam poured her a mug of tea, and said cheerfully.

"If you bought the chest quite openly then legal ownership of the chest is likely to be yours. If the contents turn out to be gold bullion, we can ask the Treasury later. Seems to me that you've probably ended up with some chap's collection of fossils."

She was giggling now, perched on the corner of his father's old chair, hands clasped around her mug, rosy tints in her cheeks.

"Well, if I have, I shall auction them to pay for my allotment tools. I haven't half the things I need, although I didn't have to pay for the box!"

Sam, bent over the subject of conversation raised his eyebrows enquiringly, "How come missus?" he asked, reaching for his mug and straightening up. "Iffen you knocked the poor man down and nicked his box I shan't protect you from the long arm of the law! What have you gotten me into?"

She was still gurgling when there was a rap on the back door, and then a gentle voice intruded.

"Ellen? Sam? Any luck with our trophy?", and the Vicar peered in hopefully.

"Our trophy Vicar?" Sam enquired as he bent over the box once more, eyes level with the old fashioned lock.

"That's what I've been trying to tell you Sam.", Ellen chortled as Martin came in from the chilly evening, closing the door behind him with a shudder. "It's nasty, wet and cold out there." he remarked unnecessarily, and crouched by the table, peering at the box from the other side.

"Strikes me that this box is uncommon. Probably from before the Great War.", the Vicar said slowly. "I don't suppose anyone would have a key quite like that, though I'm sure I've seen plenty of box keys in my time. I've brought the church keys over to see if any of them are remotely like this one. When I was curate here, we had several boxes at least as old. One (which was larger) held the Church plate. Nowadays that has to live in a safe, or we wouldn't get insurance, but the petty cash box was of a similar size, although we don't use it now."

He produced a huge bunch of keys, many of them obviously old and far too ornate. He patiently separated two or three smaller ones, hesitated, then offered them to Sam.

"Try not to be too forceful old chap.", he requested then Sam took the bunch and it was only a matter of moments before they realised that the lock on the box was anything but the simple lock it appeared to be.

"Oh dear.", Ellen sighed in disappointment, "After getting the box for nothing that's a bit of a let-down isn't it?", but Martin added.

"We'll have to get a locksmith interested. It's a shame he didn't have the key, but we can't spoil the box without establishing that there's no other way."

"How come you got it for nothing anyway?" Sam refilled the kettle and prepared to refresh the teapot.

"Well, the market stall was suffering pretty badly, and I think the man running it had about given up trying to sell anything when the rain came down good and proper. He was struggling to load up his van toward the bottom of the High Street when the canopy collapsed and he nearly drowned under the flow. He was carrying the box at the time, and couldn't raise his hands to save himself or his stock."

Sam stared transfixed as Ellen chuckled. Her eyes flashed hazel sparks as she continued gurgling.

"Oh Sam! He was soaked and so cross, and I don't think it was for the first time either, but he was so funny!" her mouth curved deliciously as she recalled the incident.

"He was swearing dreadfully. Martin started to come to my rescue when the trader dropped the box and kicked it.", her eyes creased, as she gave a peal of laughter, only recovering as Martin picked up the story.

"He was extremely angry, his language was appalling, but the Good Lord still has a sense of humour, because as he turned on Miss Armitage, the box skidded into the pole of the next stall, and the water from that canopy ran off straight down the back of his neck..."

Martin was chuckling himself by now, and commented dryly. "We were instructed that if we were that "blankety-blank-blank" interested in the "profane blankety-blank" box we could take it away, and chuck it in Fiddlers Race for all he cared!"

Ellen was roaring with laughter, tears streaming down her face as she confided. "It was hysterical Sam. Martin had a scarf round his neck that completely hid his collar, and when the trader started swearing he was making terrible comments about women who wasted his time. He uttered a string of profanities just as Martin (hurrying up to help rescue him) took his scarf off.

Martin grinned happily. "He said 'Sorry Vicar. Didn't see you there.

Sorry Miss, that there box has been a trial for years, if you want it my dear it's yours', then he rushed off after his partner and the van, leaving Ellen and me with the box!"

"Well I never!" said Sam (leaning against his range), "However, if it came from Padways, it's in the right place to trace its origins. Shall I take it down to your cottage for you Ellen? On the other hand, does the Vicar want to take charge of it? Seems you two ought to sort out what to do with it.", but they were staring at him hopefully.

"I can't even lift it Sam.", Ellen protested. "I don't have the room for it; besides, I've such a lot to do before Harvest Home. Can't I leave it here?"

The Vicar agreed rapidly. "Jane nearly had a fit when we told her how we got it. She's convinced it holds some dreadful secret and won't have it at the Vicarage. I similarly can't take risks with Church property. It's probably alright, but if the Church Commissioners thought I was using the Church for stashing my ill-gotten gains, I'd never hear the end of it.", his eyes strayed to the box as he added wistfully, "You know I'd really like to be there when that's opened."

Then they were gathering macs and umbrellas and a few minutes later, Sam found himself alone staring at the mystery box and wondering how it fitted into his topsy-turvy life.

Chapter 8 - Special Licence

There was no time to investigate the mystery box as the month crawled by. Sam finally decided that the best way of finding out more, was to display it at their traditional Harvest celebrations and see if anyone remembered anything about it in Padways. Both the Vicar and Ellen greeted this suggestion with enthusiasm, so (wrapped in clean sacking), he wheeled it on his barrow, down to the Community Hall. Locking it away in the committee room in preparation for the Harvest get together, he pushed it to the back of his mind as he went about a changeable existence at work, where once he had enjoyed peace and security.

Miserably aware that every day at Silver Street took him nearer to its closure, he watched the squirrel energetically preparing for winter with a jaundiced eye, realising that he wouldn't be sweeping the platform next year, when his little friend might take a mate and raise a family. Molly (the station cat) was re-homed with Harry Armstrong and his Deirdre, who triumphantly bore her off when he left for his father's Post Office in Wales,, and Sam missing both, took refuge in the parcel's office less and less.

Under his gaze Silver Street was changing, some of the heart of it left with every train, until Sam began to loathe the thought of going to work. He walked the station-yard during his lunchtime, poring over odd notes that his father had given him, trying to work out where great baulks of wood had been hauled from the Forest. Destined to make pit-props amongst other things, such loads had been sourced and produced locally, hauled to the station and then sent out across the country from the saw-mills manned by the women whose men had gone to war.

He speculated about the troops who had passed through Silver Street, spending evening after evening talking to the villagers who remembered them, noting the local names on the War Memorial, then cross-referencing them with his father's diaries.

Ellen (looking pale and miserable) sat silently by his side as they journeyed to and from work, until a week into October she touched his sleeve as he rose to let her off.

"Sam, I meant to tell you that the allotment Committee have decided to give me a plot. Could you come with me and take a look at it this weekend?"

She sounded anxious but Sam (who had picked the plot himself), smiled reassuringly and agreed with enthusiasm.

"Saturday or Sunday?" he asked slyly confiding, "It's my weekend off.

I'm hoping to go into Lymington. There's a book I reserved at the Library and I can go to Scats for you if you like."

She tipped her head on one side and said thoughtfully, "Saturday morning early then. You might tell me what I'm going to need immediately, then we could go in Lady Jane!"

He smiled as he remembered her habit of naming machinery, and then said gravely, "If you're sure you won't get a bad reputation through kidnapping young men?"

He'd intended it as a joke, but to his horror Ellen's eyes filled with tears. She gulped and slid past him, almost running as she left the bus, and Sam greatly puzzled stopped with his hand raised and her name on his lips. From the front seat Annette Julian said swiftly.

"Monsieur Smart? Today Madame Silversmith sank to new depths. She openly accused her of "indulging in unwise associations"; even going so far as to question Ellen's moral standards, and her commitment to the school. Ellen is deeply distressed." the low voice continued, "If you care for her…" the melodic inflections died away uncertainly, but Sam was already bounding down onto the pavement as they left the bus. He paused only to throw a quick "Thanks.", over his shoulder, and then he was running.

Ellen had already reached the path leading down to her cottage when he caught her up. She was walking determinedly, head held high, but the tears streaked her face nevertheless. He caught her elbow, swinging her round, then at her whispered "Sam!" he suddenly knew that this was right, this was the woman he had been waiting for all his life.

The shadows enclosed them as he bent his head to hers, gently touching her damp cheeks with his lips. She sighed like a weary child as Sam slid his arms round her and drew her close, feeling the throbbing of his heart as she nestled under his chin.

"Come on trouble, don't cry. Let's get you in and warmed up. You're shivering." he said comfortingly, as Ellen raised a tear-stained face to his doubtfully.

"I've really blown it Sam.", she tried to confide, but he tucked her arm under his and firmly guided her flagging feet down the path to her front door. She let them in, shutting the door before turning on the hall light, and at that moment Sam drew her into his arms again. He kissed her gently, stroking her hair, until Ellen said breathlessly, "Sam, she gave me notice. Not because of the quality of my teaching, but because I'm a woman of loose morals, who has unfortunate liaisons with local men!"

Her outrage was beginning to surface, as Sam took her hand and led her to the kitchen, solemnly turning off the hall light as he entered the next room. It was warm, the Aga was ready to boil a kettle and something smelt good in the oven.

Ellen grabbed an oven cloth and opened the oven door to reveal a casserole bubbling merrily. Selecting two large potatoes from a basket, she scrubbed and pricked both, then slid them onto the floor of the top oven, shutting it firmly. Sam watched her push a kettle on to the hob, slide two large plates into the bottom oven, then come back to him, leaning against him wearily. For a moment, she had seemed quite ferocious in her whirl of domestic activity, but he felt her defences melt as his arms closed about her once more.

"What's it about sweetheart?" he asked her, resting his head against clean scented hair. "What's she accusing you of?" she turned her head, smiling shyly at him.

"It seems I've been too particular in my attentions to you." she murmured. "It seems that travelling to work together, meeting up to shop or go to the Library together is viewed as "an unfortunate liaison". Your visiting my home alone makes me a woman of loose morals, and when I flagrantly visited yours with my overnight case, that was a matter that could not be ignored..." her voice dropped uncertainly as Sam's head came up in challenge.

"Overnight case?" he questioned abruptly, and then as the light dawned he gave a muffled groan.

"That ruddy box!" he said ruefully, "I helped you in out of the rain with it too! Stands to reason some narrow minded body got the wrong end of the stick, but they obviously didn't see you and Martin leaving did they?"

Ellen agreed, but returned to the subject of Miss Silversmith's interpretation of events, and Sam was forced to hold down righteous indignation as Ellen started to lay the small table for two.

"She has no right to question my actions, unless I bring the school into disrepute, and that seems to be what she's accusing me of.", she whispered painfully, her distress so obvious that Sam went over to her, sliding his arms around her, offering silent sympathy until she drew away as the kettle began to whistle.

Sam stared at the floor thinking furiously. If Ellen got the sack for such a reason, she'd never teach again. In fact, he thought it unlikely that she'd get a job with any prospects if the school principal stuck to her guns. He cleared his throat as Ellen checked the progress of the potatoes and said quietly.

"It won't come to anything Ellen. I'll get Martin to confirm that he was with us at my house, but I'd like to know why she's acting like this. Is someone stirring things for you, or is she normally so vindictive? There's more to this than meets the eye."

Ellen grinned ruefully, "Actually Sam, I'm at fault I suppose. The Education Authority sent a Miss Symington Smythe to lecture the seniors about Moral Welfare. I sat in on the lecture, and quite honestly I've never come across such drivel. From not wearing clothes likely to "give men the wrong idea", to how many times to dance with a boy, all wrapped up in Victorian moralistic twaddle. It totally confused several girls who had to be swiftly disabused of the idea that dancing with one particular boy more than four times in an evening could leave them pregnant! She was utter rubbish and I told her so, but that's backfired badly. She's the Moral Welfare Officer for Ringwood, with eyes on the ground in Padways, and she doesn't like me at all. Whatever am I going to do? I've really mucked it up this time!"

Secretly impressed, Sam didn't hesitate for a minute. He seized Ellen's hands in his, looked into her worried face and said calmly.

"Iffen one of those spuds was for me, I reckon you're going to dish up supper, which we'll eat, then you're coming with me down the village to see the Vicar. He'll know how to get a special licence!"

Ellen stared at him in bewilderment. "What licence?" she demanded, "What crazy ideas have you got now Sam Smart?", but Sam was taking hot plates out of the oven and didn't answer immediately. He stood grinning at her as he slid them onto a wooden serving block, and returned to the top oven, retrieving baked potatoes and hastily dropping them onto plates as Ellen placed the casserole dish on a mat.

"That's the way my lass!" Sam Smart declared as she ladled rabbit stew onto his plate, adding with an engaging sigh of satisfaction, "Proposing takes all a man's energy, so feed me now, then we'll visit the vicar! I'll show Miss Symington Smythe that she can't cast "nasturtiums" on my girl!"

"Oh Sam!" exclaimed Miss Ellen Armitage, clasping her ladle impulsively. "Oh Sam, I love you, and yes I'll marry you, but darling it's "aspersions", not nasturtiums."

"Yes Miss!" said Sam Smart meekly, and kissed her lovingly before turning his attentions to eating supper.

Chapter 9 - Checks and Balances

Meals consumed, washing up done and they still held hands across the table, looking at each other and grinning like Cheshire cats. Sam studied Ellen carefully, noting the faint blush on her cheeks as he did so. She had honey coloured skin, dark golden eyelashes, and smelt faintly of peaches he decided. His eyes lingered on the lobes of her ears, snuggling under her hairline, and drifted back up to her mouth as she bit her lower lip. Now she blushed properly and put her hands to her face, taking away the warm contact they'd been sharing.

"Stop it Sam.", she said gruffly, "That comes later, after we're married!", then she chuckled. "If you could see your face, talk about a naughty schoolboy!" his lips quirked, then she grew serious.

"Martin is going to ask us some very searching questions my dear. Don't you think we ought to cover the ground before we get there?" then in a tight, brittle tone, as if she didn't relish what she was about to say, she demanded, "Bagsy I go first!"

She knitted her fingers together, face lowered as she spoke quietly, and Sam was suddenly aware of a feeling of oppression in the room. He waited patiently for her to begin, aware that she was about to tell him something very difficult, and his current happiness might depend on his reaction.

"Sam. I don't want anything I tell you now to hurt you, but I can't and won't attempt to hide from you things a man should know before he marries." Her head came up defiantly, and she looked at him directly as she spoke. Her eyes were sad he thought, and for a moment he didn't want to hear what she was about to say, but then she held out her hand and pleaded, "Hold my hand darling, help me to be brave.", and instinctively he reached out and took it firmly. She sighed then began in a low sweet voice.

"When my parents came home from India we lived in London for a while, but my father's health was failing and war was imminent. They came down to the Forest because an old friend of my father's owned Burley Manor, and while they were here, they found the cottage and bought it, thinking that they'd use it for weekends. I was at University then, only took my finals a month before my father died suddenly, not long after which we discovered that on his death, we were penniless."

She grinned, admitting reluctantly, "He may have been brilliant militarily, but he never had an idea about business, and unfortunately neither did his investment advisor! The annuity he'd relied on to provide the necessities once he retired simply didn't materialise. As for his so-called 'man of business', he apparently dematerialised shortly after Father found out. Of course he didn't tell Mother or me anything, just went round worrying himself to death, advising anyone who invested to put in place as many checks and balances as they could before parting with a sou. So in a way that's what I'm doing now Sam, so please bear with me."

He remained still, face grave as she moistened dry lips and continued.

"We can spend a lifetime getting to know one another, but some things have to be sorted before we start, so that you don't feel that you've made a mistake. You see Sam, you are not the first man to propose to me."

She reached into her neckline with her left hand and withdrew a fine gold chain on which was suspended two rings, a small sapphire engagement ring, and a narrow band of gold. Sam stared at them, forcing himself to put his feet squarely on the ground, pressing down slightly to balance himself, ready for the next blow as she delivered it.

"I met Douglas before my father died. He was an officer, very acceptable to my parents, and we were engaged. I was still trying to settle Father's estate when Douglas was posted overseas. Mother was in a nursing home recovering from one of her frequent attacks of malaria, when I was called up.", she paused rubbing her tired face with a bewildered air as she picked up the story.

"He got back once, long enough for us to marry, then he was gone with his unit and I never saw him again." her voice had grown husky, and despite the heat given off by the Aga, she drew her cardigan around her shoulders shivery with pent up emotion. She returned her hand to Sam's warm clasp, saying simply, "We only had the one night together, but it was enough. I hadn't heard from him (not that it was always possible during that phase of the war), so I wrote telling him we were to be parents, that I was safe and about to escort Mother down to the Forest, where we'd wait out the war for him, then the telegram came."

Sam caught her up in his arms as she finally let go and wept bitter scalding tears. He nestled her on to his knee and let her weep, certain that she had never wept for her poor dear lad before. It was like snow melting he thought. He'd seen glimpses of Ellen, odd flashes of a personality and humour others never saw, but until now he had never suspected what lay behind the high wall of her inner resolve. He gentled her quivering shoulders, soothing her back to control, then she raised her brimming eyes and said simply, "That's not quite the worst of it Sam. I lost the baby. I was determined to carry on, ignored my own pain to deal with Mother's, and paid the price. I'm afraid you're getting the worst of a poor bargain if you still want to marry me Sam, there may not be any children."

He drew a clean tea-towel down off the rack warming in front of the Aga, and tenderly mopped her face, before he answered her. His feet were firmly on the ground as he spoke, his words solemn and sincere.

"That doesn't matter Ellen, I want to marry you. If babies come we'll welcome them, but if not it's still you I want to be with, whatever happens. I have some checks of my own for you to consider." he went on slowly. "Things you don't know about me, things you might not like to hear. I couldn't go to war Ellen, so it's chaps like yours who kept me and mine safe. My mother died just after I was born, that was when the family were living up North. They didn't know it then, but what seemed like 'flu or bronchitis was TB. She must have had it right through her pregnancy, with the result that I was small, very unhealthy, and probably typical of many TB babies. My Gran took me on, freeing my Dad up to work, but I wasn't thriving. The mills where he maintained the engines that drove the looms, closed and my Dad was laid off. Just after that, my Uncle Norman came south on the railways, and settled in Ringwood. I was so sickly, that Dad took me to a doctor, who told him I'd be lucky if I lived to go to school!"

For a moment, Sam's face clouded, and then he grinned at Ellen.

"He didn't know my Gran! Every day she'd listen to the radio, borrow papers from those who took them, and then she heard of an Open School scheme. This lady was giving a talk, and though she walked nine miles to get there, she went, and got advised to get me plenty of fresh air, milk and exercise. They were not to worry about school but to do everything in their power to build me up. They had to get away from the mills and my Dad took a tied cottage where he could work for the local parson. My Gran was a great one for the church, and so we moved a bit further south. However, it wasn't enough. I had pneumonia that year and the doctors said I wouldn't make old bones unless I could be taken further south, to the seaside if possible. The Reverend Heyworth knew Martin's predecessor, and apparently decided to write and see what he could do for us, and remarkably, he too was looking for a skilled maintenance man for his church, the school and community centre. He offered Gran and Dad the cottage beside the Church, and an introduction to a doctor who could advise on my care. In the same post with that letter my Uncle Norman wrote to say that he and my Aunt Mary had just settled in a railwayman's cottage at Ringwood, and were expecting their first child. So we came here, shortly followed by my Uncle Bert who came with the coastguard to Hurst Point. I've cousins in Keyhaven, cousins in

Brockenhurst, and don't remember living anywhere else myself."

Ellen's face lifted momentarily from his chest and she peered up at him, saying softly.

"The move was good for you Sam. Fresh air, fresh produce, woods to wander in. Did you have a lot of bad health after you came?"

Sam thought about it for a moment, then said doubtfully, "Not that I remember. I did have a spate of ordinary childhood illnesses, mumps, measles etc. However, I also remember being in a sort of hospital, where all the windows were left open come rain come shine, but although I know I never had active TB, from my current doctor, it does seem as though I had some sort of treatment or investigation shortly after I arrived here."

He held up his hand laughing as Ellen prodded his chest, remarking that it seemed perfectly sound to her, and then he grew quiet again, his eyes reflective as he recalled his shame at being turned down for the military.

"I went to sign up as soon as I could, but the medicos took one look at my history and turned me down flat." he said wistfully. By then Uncle Norman had got my Dad onto the railways himself, and they drove ammunition trains right through the war, while I apprenticed to a Burley builder. I was to be a chippy, but then he went into the Special Boat Service (due to his knowledge of the coast hereabouts, only he never came back. His widow couldn't keep us on, so I ended up doing Dad's maintenance work, kept the cottage on, and just drifted into my job at Silver Street because by then Dad needed me about."

Ellen shifted restlessly as he said, "I'm not very ambitious Ellen. I like my life at a slow and steady pace, can't do all these alarms and excitements without feeling quite unable to think. I'm no catch for an educated lady my dear. I like to read, listen to the radio, can't bear tub-thumpers, cruelty to animals and get mighty confused if I have to juggle too many thoughts at the same time. Perhaps you'd better apply some of those checks and balances you spoke about, before investing in a redundant railway porter who can't even drive!"

She sat up, and took the thin gold chain from her neck, kissing the rings and refastening the catch before she laid them on the table beside Sam's hand.

"When my Douglas left that day, he said (and I quote), 'If anything happens to me, just wear my rings until you meet a man you can love on a hot day, hold on a cold morning, and respect every day of your life. I've done as he told me to, I went back to my old life, went back to my old name, and now if you please Mr Smart, I'd like you to propose properly."

Sam suddenly feeling as though a third party had quietly entered the room said helplessly, "Ellen, I love you. I want to spend the rest of my life with you, but I don't even know your real name."

"I'm Mrs Douglas Anderson.", she said proudly, and Sam felt almost light-headed as he gently drew her to her feet, and stood looking down at her.

"Well Mrs Douglas Anderson, would you honour me by consenting to be my wife?" he asked steadily, and took her into his arms.

They walked arm in arm up the path and into the village, careless of who saw them. There were cheerful lights showing at curtained windows, a gale of laughter spilled out from the Hay Rack as they passed the pub's doors, then Sam opened the gate to the Vicarage and they went to tell Martin their news. He was suitably underwhelmed, claiming that he "had known it all along", but was outraged at the idea of a special licence or a marriage not performed in their own little church.

"We never see la Silversmith anyway my dears." he said, toasting their health with Jane's famous elderflower wine. "I won't hear of you marrying to stop idle and vindictive tongues chattering. Miss Symington-Smythe is a deeply unpopular woman around the village anyway, so don't take any notice of such matters. You two have done nothing wrong, and besides Ellen, you both deserve better. No, I shall approach this matter differently. I'll ask the Area Education Office to supply a part-time English teacher for the upper year. It's been mentioned before, and it wouldn't be out of place to try again. Simultaneously I will ask Miss Silversmith to supply a volunteer to cover those duties in the period leading up to the Nativity Play at Christmas. She's very keen on getting her girls involved in that as you know. This year the local Education Committee are sending a representative "to observe" and report, so she won't want to miss out on that."

His friendly face crinkled as he delivered the punch-line.

"Ellen, if you volunteer, she'll not be able to prevent you working at the local school when she pulls out. By then, you and Sam will be married, and she'd look a fool if she stuck to her current intentions. It may not be very Christian of me to hope that she comes badly unstuck in that endeavour, but it strikes me that the sooner those girls and the school re-locate, the better. Miss Symington-Smythe is a poor example of what a Moral Welfare Officer should be, and the sooner her attentions are diverted back to her job, the better. She seems to be, sucking up to the principal of the local private school in preference to doing her best for those who really need moral guidance."

Aware that this pronouncement was as severe an admonishment of Miss Symington-Smythe's lack of professionalism as she would ever hear from their mild mannered Vicar, Ellen relaxed. Sam found himself positively glowing in the congratulations of their friends, and after the practical matters of calling the banns were settled, they wandered back to Ellen's flushed with joy.

"I definitely want a goat Sam.", Ellen said as he opened her gate and stood aside to let her pass him. She lifted the plant-pot by the door and retrieved her key, calling over her shoulder. "I saw a pretty white one over at Sway a week or two ago. Shall we go and find out what they cost?"

He came up the path saying slowly, "You can't keep a goat on an allotment Ellen. If it broke loose it would eat everything in sight and probably die as a result." he unlocked her front door as she absorbed that fact, then she dimpled irrepressibly.

"Oh, I wasn't planning for the allotment." she said. "I had it in mind for our small-holding!"

Completely dumbfounded by his astonishing love, Sam decorously kissed her proffered cheek, and turned back along the path. Heading for his cottage, head spinning, and heart turning cartwheels, he saw (in his mind's eye), a little white goat grazing on a long strip of grass. Oddly, this seemed to be growing on the platform of Silver Street Station, and the thought was so ridiculous, that he chuckled out loud, drawing glances from several of his neighbours.

He sobered abruptly, and then reminding himself to treat Elderflower wine with the respect it deserved, he went to bed, and dreamt of hens roosting in the parcels office.

Chapter 10 - What the Porter saw

"Sam, do you realise it's nearly six weeks since we heard the Station is closing?"

Ellen, peering over Sam's shoulder at the photographs he'd amassed on his kitchen table, marvelled. Sam's plan to display them (just as they were), had been forestalled with difficulty. However, Ellen's intervention had seen every frame checked, dusted, and neatly labelled, loose photo's arranged (by date where possible) in albums, and this was the third (and hopefully last) batch.

She reached down a bag as he carefully wrapped the last frame in tissue and stacked it in a box, and then she lifted the bag onto the top with a smile.

"There love, that's my contribution!" she said, patting the soft outlines with deep satisfaction. "This week they'll cover the trestles so your photos will really stand out, and in a month's time they'll make splendid cloaks for the three wise men!"

Sam grinned at her. "You're nifty with a needle!" he complimented her, "but your Mother wouldn't appreciate her Indian silk curtains being used like that would she?"

"My mother was pretty well indulged in anything she wanted during a long spoilt life!", she said firmly, "and the dreamer who spoilt her wouldn't have appreciated the use to which their entirely practical daughter put many of their things, but that was then, and this is now, so shove over streaky-back and let me tie that down safely."

"Oi!" said her swain, "Shove over yourself missus. I been a porter seventeen years come Christmas, haven't I been lashing down loads and securing passengers' bits and bobs long enough to suit you? Besides, I tie knots I can untie. I don't want you making a muck of my good cord, no I don't. What's more I don't want to have to cut it neither." he indignantly took possession of the box, and Ellen busied herself washing up mugs and filling the kettle.

She looked around Sam's large kitchen cheerfully, she'd spent quite some time tidying, clearing dusty old window-sills, and making herself useful. She liked the cottage, but it was definitely a man's home, with none of the softening touches that a woman would have employed. No cushions for chairs, back windows uncurtained, she sighed inwardly, considering that it would be easier to train a dog to jump hoops, than a man left untended for so long. Through the back door of the kitchen was a useful rear porch off which was the door to a downstairs bathroom and privy. At first she'd wondered what she'd encounter in there, but apart from the usual trappings of a bathroom, nothing seemed out of place. It was neat and tidy, clean and well decorated, and she'd relaxed in the hope that the rest of the house met a similar standard. Sam hadn't shown her around yet, he was too busy getting everything together for the Harvest Home talk. Tonight they were moving the photographs, tomorrow the books, and on Monday evening the Parish would gather at the Community Centre and Sam would give his talk. She stole a glance at him, but he was absorbed, loading his Dad's old tool trolley with everything he needed. She had seen his precious box of books, handwritten accounts from his father's old diaries, maps of the track and ancient notices retrieved from the loft. She helped pin out crumpled wartime exhortations like "Dig for Victory", "Be like Father - Keep Mum!", and together they had spent the last week, mounting and framing, stretching and flattening photos, reports, and now it was done. As her eyes rested on him for a moment, Sam finished fastening his cords then turned, and grinned at her disarmingly.

"Right then trouble, let's be having you!" he greeted her, holding out his hand which she took eagerly as he turned towards the door.

"Last load until tomorrow." he said with deep satisfaction, "Shall we go and see how everyone's getting on?"

As they approached the Community Hall, they could see half the villagers coming and going as the Harvest Market took shape. Today they would display the produce from gardens and allotments. The judges would preside over the competition, and this evening winners would be announced. Tomorrow after Harvest Festival, the serious business of auctioning the produce for charity would take place by sealed bid. After all pledges had been placed, the vegetables, fruit, jams, pickles and wines would be stored away, ready to be collected by their triumphant new owners (after Monday's prise-giving ceremony). The Hall would be dressed for the following evening, then after work on Monday came the Harvest Home Evening.

A local butcher always supplied a Hog Roast and during the day, those who were normally around the village would bustle about, tending the fire-pit, boxing up produce, setting out the splendid collection of trophies for presentation, or generally socialising.

The allotment Committee would have their AGM. The Mother's Union and the W I would prepare a feast, and everyone would return to the Hall to redeem their pledges, and having paid up, collect a warm supper and listen to the local folk group. Around seven thirty Sam would give his talk, followed by questions from the audience who would have viewed his display, then it would all be over for another year. Sam was deep in thought as they paused on the edge of the car-park, waiting for a particularly large trestle table to be carried inside, and Ellen raised a smiling face to Sam's.

"That'll be the wine table." she giggled dropping her voice into more masculine tones. "The 1963 Harvest Home Cup for a truly splendid elderflower wine is duly presented to Mrs Jane Short..." she murmured in fond repetition of earlier years, and Sam wagged a finger at her.

"Now then lass, the Vicar's wife deserves it." Then in mock-horror he said, "Oh no! The bottle's empty, we must have drunk it all!"

They were still chuckling as they made their way through the busy throng putting the final touches to their tables, before the judges arrived.

Sam steered his trolley into the Committee Room, and together they unpacked his precious display. They had the whole side of a long room to fill, long trestles set up against blank white washed walls. Ellen, used to demonstration tables moved them fractionally away from the walls then draped them in the ruby silk curtains. She directed Sam to pull the material this way and that, to tuck it in firmly and pleat the ends in the familiar envelope corners beloved of nurses (and boarding school Matrons.) He groaned inwardly in silent frustration, but had to admit the effect was spectacular as the last photograph was laid in place, and the cunning backboard she'd covered to match was laid against the wall.

"When we bring down the books, they will lie on those props you made Sam.", Ellen explained as she counted the spaces she'd left. "I'll hand write a notice so people won't put sticky fingers on the pages." she offered, and Sam frowned.

"How will you prevent that?" he demanded, and Ellen gurgled.

"Simple.", she stated. "Archives collected by the Smart family displayed on unusual Indian silk. Visitors are advised not to handle the rare silk which contains natural substances used as dyes. No children, food or drink beyond this point."

Sam stared at her contemplatively. "You Madam are a baggage!" he pronounced severely, "Rare Indian silk, natural substances indeed. Your Mum's old bedroom curtains, well washed and free of anything except residue of Omo!"

She rolled her eyes at him, laughing and exclaiming, "Needs must when the devil drives my dear man!", then they left, taking Sam's trolley to the Vicarage to assist Jane and the ladies of the W I to their stall. There was coffee and cake in the tea-room, and carefully balancing a plate on his cup, Sam negotiated his way out to Ellen who was engaged in animated conversation with her friend Miss Julian. The French teacher beamed at Sam as he approached and said something to Ellen that turned her scarlet. Sam grinned and raised his cup to the other woman, who said in rapid but perfect English.

"I congratulate you both. Ellen tells me your news, but I am desolated not to be there. I return to France in mid-December, and I cannot change my arrangements, or I won't get home at all."

Interested Sam asked "Do you fly?", but she laughed and shook her head.

"Me? Oh no, flying is for Beatles and millionaires. I go by ferry. I have a good stomach, the sea won't upset me, but I have no head for heights."

She peered past him, assessing the busy rooms, now quieting down as folk drifted out for lunch.

"Do you think we can go and see?" Ellen's friend enquired, so as both women went in arms linked, Sam stepped out into the car park as a Bentley swept in.

At first he'd assumed this must be the judges, but no it was the tall Australian, and for a strange minute he met Sam's eyes, as if he knew him. The moment passed however, as the young man stepped clear of the car, and Sam inwardly chuckled at the incongruous sight of a chauffeur saluting an Australian backwoodsman complete to the inch including his bush hat.

Sam, who had seen many a thing over the last seventeen years of watching visitors come and go, schooled his features to impassivity as the young man dismissed his chauffeur, then with only a mild glance at the Community Hall, stepped out along the road heading for the Hay Rack Inn. Sam's weren't the only eyes that followed the visitor. A number of teenage girls stood rapt in wonder as he passed them, and after a minute or two, the chuckling porter returned to the Vicarage and assisted Jane Short to deliver her wine, and the W I entry for the Preserves table. Bottles and jars chinking gently he wheeled his trolley back down to the Hall, where he found Ellen waiting patiently. The crowds had diminished substantially by now, and Ellen leant against the entranceway looking pensive as he arrived.

"Hullo trouble.", he greeted her, but she seemed a bit withdrawn, so he helped the Shorts to the wine table, stood Jane's entry up gently, then left both women setting the country wines in place, as he trundled the preserves over to the W I table, and retreated. The French teacher had already left and Ellen kept him waiting as she polished and placed the last of Jane's bottles, but eventually, even the remaining die-hards made for the entrance, casting long critical glances over the Harvest Show, as the judges arrived.

Impulsively Ellen whispered, "Oh Sam, I'm glad Miss Silversmith decided to give me notice.", and he glanced down into her wobbly smile as he collected her on his arm.

"Annette Julian says she's not coming back after Christmas either. The atmosphere at the school has changed completely, and I don't see it improving when they move. I'm sad to lose such a good friend, but France isn't a million miles away I suppose, at least she could come back and holiday with us one day".

Sam's thoughts had been running on other lines, but he had to take notice as she continued thoughtfully, "It's not as if Le Havre is in Australia".

They'd reached the gate to the Vicarage by now, and he stopped in his tracks and asked in a bemused voice.

"What's Australia got to do with it?", as Ellen said blankly, "Absolutely nothing silly! Have you heard or understood a single word I've said Sam Smart? You've been utterly distracted ever since I got caught up with Annette. Why on earth are you staring at the Hay Rack Sam? We're not going there for lunch; Martin wants to see us about the banns, so Jane invited us to take pot-luck with them this lunchtime."

Her voice had barely registered on Sam, whose grey eyes had sharpened at the sight of a man leaving the inn by the half-door that led to the public bar. Ellen stepping forward to grasp his wrist paused, and following his gaze saw the Australian striding purposefully up the street, bush hat firmly clamped to his head.

"Oh joy!" exclaimed the teacher crossly, "Now every woman in Padways will be gawking over the garden gate. I wonder what the fancy dress is in aid of!", then Sam regaining his concentration levels, turned to her and explained what he had seen only a day or two before.

"Cor", said Miss Ellen Armitage ungrammatically. "Do you really think he's some sort of film Star then? Could they possibly be filming hereabouts? I sincerely hope not. The weather's getting colder and wetter, and knowing teenage girls they'll all be off looking for the location, dreaming of becoming extras on set, and not applying themselves to schoolwork or the Nativity play I've worked so hard on. Oh Bother!" she groaned, and Sam chuckled as he guided her up the Vicarage path, little knowing just how the Australian was going to influence the lives of everyone in Padways.

PART 2 - AN UNUSUAL FORD

Chapter 11 - His or Hers

The whole weekend passed in a blur. Saturday afternoon, replete with Jane's homemade soup and bread, Ellen and Sam had discussed their wedding plans with Martin. He carefully examined the folded marriage certificate that Ellen handed him, read the telegram from the War Office announcing her husband's death, and examined his death certificate with a delicacy that quite undid Ellen, who wept silently as he put the fragile remnants of that forgotten future away reverently.

"Oh my dear girl." he said gravely, "Why on earth didn't you confide in us? Jane said there was something different about you after the War, and I feel that we have let you down. You know we could have helped you so much better if only we'd known about your loss."

Ellen miserably dabbed her eyes, then sighing said with honest regret, "I'm sorry Martin. I should have trusted you and Jane, but I couldn't bear to be reminded." her hands clasping her handkerchief tightened briefly as she confessed, "There was another death you see, just a tiny one that never drew breath, but I couldn't...no, still can't bring myself to think about that. This was my bolt-hole. Somewhere that Douglas never came to in life. Somewhere that no-one would sympathise with me, watch me, or even notice when I had a bad day!" She drew a shaky breath as Sam caught her hand in his and dropped a kiss onto the back of it. With a watery smile she said quietly, "I can't abide sympathy, never could. It turns me into a watering pot, as you can see, and so many others lost a great deal more. At least I had my life, most of my health and my qualifications. I could earn enough to pay our way. Mother had a small pension and absolutely masses of Indian memorabilia. My father would be spinning in his grave had he known I disposed of his treasures, but even Mother realised that it was better to keep warm rather than own dozens of saris she couldn't wear in this climate."

Sam was glad to see the light back in Ellen's eyes as she gurgled mischievously.

"At the end she even volunteered the tiger Daddy shot in Bengal. It was his prized possession. They made it into a rug, but we tripped over it so many times that when we needed a new carpet Mother gave it up happily."

Sam gazed at this surprising woman and could hardly believe his luck as they filled in Martin's forms, settled on a quiet Wedding a few days before Christmas, and then the Vicar asked innocently, "His or hers, my friends?"

They stared at him blankly, until he exclaimed quite kindly.

"My goodness. You can't be thinking of separate houses surely? Sam owns the cottage now. It was part of the Parish dwellings, but times change and when Charlie's mother died, the Church Commissioners gave him very favourable terms on which he acquired the property. It gave him security, something to leave to Sam, and I'd imagine that it is larger than your little cottage my dear."

He turned a beaming gaze on Ellen, who said gently, "You're probably right Martin, only we haven't discussed where we were going to live yet, though you've given me some ideas."

She turned to Sam, noting the worried frown on his face and suggested gently, "We could let my cottage. It only has two bedrooms but it's well set up for a young couple to start in, or for an older couple's retirement project. Shall we go back there and talk it over?"

That topic dominated their conversation right up until they returned to the Community Hall for the results of the competition. Sam, who never competed, nodded approvingly as a neighbour bore off the ticket awarding him best allotment. He screwed up his face in disgust, when a gardener (with very few scruples over using questionable methods), won the best kept vegetable plot category. Then, looking away from the triumphant winner, he saw 'his' Australian visitor, standing just inside the door, back to the wall, cheerfully watching the villagers as they clapped politely.

Sam nudged Ellen, who glanced in the direction of Sam's nod. To say her jaw dropped was an understatement, but recovering, she hissed a comment in Sam's direction.

"What's he doing here?" was the gist of her question, but Sam (shrugging) had turned to see Jane Short and Mary McGuire win the wine competition again. When he turned back, the stranger had gone. He frowned a little, but there was no time to talk about it for people were rising, clapping the judges and the evening was drawing to a close.

So they parted, Sam to organise trestles for the following day's activities, Ellen, Jane and the Vicar escorting some of the teenagers home to anxious parents.

When Sam finally went home, he was too tired to consider what he'd seen. He was almost too tired to sleep, troubled by images of an Australian wandering the paths and silent copses of a forest far from home fading as he drifted into confusing dreams in which John Oswald herded sheep up the Forest line, using a red flag to chivvy them along. Why he subconsciously connected the Station Master with danger he couldn't tell, but it was to stand him in good stead in the puzzling weeks to come.

Chapter 12 - Harvest Home

The following morning Sam stared into the long mirror on his landing in dismay. The charcoal grey jacket and trousers he wore were clean, in good condition and very serviceable for most high days and holidays, but they hardly constituted the correct clothes for a bridegroom! He moodily contemplated his reflection as he realised that "Sunday Best" wasn't going to set the tone at his talk either, groaning softly as he realised how time had caught up with him. However, with no time to shop, or money to spare, what he wore would just have to do.

He knotted his tie defiantly, and had just slipped his feet into his best shoes when a knock sounded at his door.

Flushing in pleased anticipation, he swiftly tightened his shoe-laces, ran down the stairs and threw open the door with a broad grin that faded into bewilderment, as a smartly dressed man raised a hand towards the knocker once more. Stepping back hastily, they eyed each other, and then spoke simultaneously.

"Jeepers mate! Did I startle you?" said the tall Australian, as Sam's voice tangled with his in hurried apology.

"Oh, I'm sorry, I was expecting someone else. Can I help you?"

They broke off as Ellen clicked the gate, (Sam brightening visibly), as she climbed the steep path to join them). The stranger smiled apologetically and suggested he return later, but Ellen intrigued, was looking directly at Sam with a glance that needed no interpretation.

Sam (with an enquiring look of his own) said firmly.

"We're off to church right now. We can't miss hearing our banns being called for the first time, but you can call back, or catch up with us at the Harvest Auction later if you like."

He held out a hand, offering introductions somewhat self-consciously.

"This is Ellen Armitage, my fiancée, I'm Sam Smart, and you are?"

His visitor responded promptly.

"Alex Ford, over from Australia researching my family." he shot out a hand, grasping Sam's in a powerful grip. "I was pointed in your direction by several folk. If you don't mind, I'll tag along to Church with you. I'd planned calling on the Vicar tomorrow, so I may as well make my number with him today."

It seemed like a good idea, so they joined the congregation gathering at the Church door, where their new friend instantly became the centre of attention until the Harvest Festival began.

After the service, still marvelling at the ripple of expectation that had run through the congregation on the announcement of their forthcoming marriage, Sam and Ellen were greeted at the door by the Vicar. Shaking the Australian's hand warmly, Martin promptly invited all three to take lunch at the Vicarage, refusing to take no for an answer.

"It's only what my wife calls "pot-luck" he announced cheerfully, "but Jane would be disappointed if I didn't invite you all."

Turning in at the Vicarage gate he added persuasively, "We're having Jane's own special vegetable goulash today, in honour of the Hog Roast tomorrow. I'll need some room for that!" he chuckled, ushering them into the Vicarage as Alex looked around curiously.

Sunday lunch was a huge success, Jane glowed with pleasure as they praised her culinary skill, and then nothing would have it, but Martin demanded company for coffee. By then they had moved into the vicarage's large untidy living-room. It was Sam's favourite room, overlooking a neatly trimmed lawn, where apple trees gently deposited that year's crop into the willing hands of Martin's three youngsters. The children were even now gathering their trophies into baskets, trundling them away noisily under the watchful eye of Mrs Thomas, (their cook cum housekeeper).

Sat on the long padded window seat, watching her brood Jane said comfortably, "That's our own Harvest Home thanks to Mrs Thomas. She's so good with the children; I don't know how we'd manage without her. She knew young Charlie's throat was sore before he complained, and I'm sure that if she hadn't separated the twins, they'd have both gone down with chickenpox together. Miranda was dreadfully ill and I'm sure I couldn't have coped if Maggie had joined her!"

She rested her head against the window, watching her family pottering about, and then asked absently, "Have you got a family of your own Mr Ford?", and from the depths of the huge sofa where he lounged cradling his coffee, their new friend chuckled.

"Not yet Mrs Short. We're pretty cut off raising sheep! I don't get to meet too many girls in the outback. I'm working long hours for weeks, only getting away rarely and might have to fly down half the state to socialise or conduct business. There are no fancy shops or hairdressers near Newlands unfortunately, and not that many girls to choose from either. Although it's growing rapidly, Australia is still a young country with whole areas the size of Britain unsettled as yet."

Jane nodded, but the thought of such a huge (relatively unoccupied) landmass seemed too alien to consider, in this quintessentially "English" setting, and that tiny break in conversation gave Sam the opportunity to ask questions of his own.

"You say that you are looking for family over here? Did they settle in Australia a long time back or have you just lost contact with them?"

He was pleased when his tongue-in-cheek innuendo was not lost on Alex, who grinned in high good humour.

"Oh, I've read that pamphlet about how Padways got its name Sam.", he said wagging a finger in mock severity before proclaiming, "None of *my* forebears were transported for being Forest footpads mate! Don't let your job go to your head, even if you've come to like shipping folk off to foreign parts!" he grinned amiably as he continued his story.

"I'm following a very faint trail that may lead nowhere. Until my Mum passed away last year, I believed I was entirely alone in the world. However, a few bits and pieces relating to my Dad's family came my way, which left me wondering if I could trace other relatives here. It may seem odd, but I just wanted to find out where I fit in, before I move on."

He sat forward a little, frowning with concentration as he marshalled his thoughts. Finally, he drained his cup, set it on the hearth beside him, and began to speak softly.

"It's a complicated story and to make it worse, I don't know whose story it is.", he glanced round to make sure he had their absolute attention, before pressing on, his accent perhaps just a little more pronounced as he spoke.

"My only memory of my father must have been when I was very little, probably no more than three. Someone tall, in uniform swinging me over his head is all I knew, then lots of tears, a long journey with Mum, and Newlands, which is where I grew up. Mum never told me much, but over the years I came to understand that Newlands was my paternal grandparent's place. Nan was certainly there when we arrived, and I had my Dad's old room. I was about four or five when he was killed. My Mum managed with the help of the hired hands who were too old or not fit for active service, and somehow we clung on, although we went through it a bit. A large sheep station takes some running, but they did it between them, my Nan and Mum until the shock of my Dad's death began to tell on Nan. She was born at Newlands, her own father worked there before the turn of the century. She died there, a sad woman, widowed during World War One. Losing her only son to war as well finally tipped the balance I reckon. By the time I was ten, my poor Mum ran everything, mothered me alone, coping as Nan withdrew into some world of her own. She died when I was twelve. Like most Outback farms there's plenty for a kid to do. I had to do school on air, then I went to

High School which meant boarding away from Newlands."

His face was alight with remembered joys; his hands sketched shapes describing his homeland, flat valley bottoms appearing in the sweep of a wrist, a ripple of fingers describing the slow flow of a river. They all leant back, seeing through Alex's physical interpretation, unusual landscapes, vast distances, great expanses of sky, and his love of his homeland in the creases of his eyes, the smile lurking at the corners of his mobile mouth.

The soft voice continued.

"I was one of the lucky ones. I liked schoolwork, studied hard and won a scholarship. Thought I'd make my mother proud, she worked so hard to make me the boy my father dreamed I'd be, even though he would never know what it cost her."

He sat up, looking around and commented as though surprised himself. "Wouldn't she get a kick out of this? Me, sitting down in an English Vicarage and behaving nicely too!" a wry grin wavered and fled before the next comment.

"I did well at school, got a bursary from some Trust to University and graduated last year. That's when things started to get weird."

His face and voice were drawn for a moment, a vision of pain so bleak in his eyes, that the small group drew together a little as Alex said rough voiced with emotion.

"I was away too long. I had a summer at home before I found out I had won a grant to attend University. I went off, never realising that the animal husbandry course and a degree in business management was Mum's way of making sure I could manage without her.", there were barely suppressed tears in his voice as he said raggedly, "I missed her at the degree ceremony, but Bill Andrews, our stock manager flew up and collected me and took me home just in time to say goodbye. She wrote me every week, shared all the jokes, passed on messages, gave me facts and figures to work on, yet she never told me about the cancer that was killing her! Not once did she hint that she might not be there to share in my success. Not once did she complain about the pain, all she wanted to do was to tell me about some box that went missing. It should have been sent to my Nan after my Grandfather died, but she never received it. My Dad was a newborn when his was killed in the Great War; he grew up believing that he had been cheated out of his father because of his war service and he would have none of the Old Country! He was Australian born and bred, but ironically we lost him the same way. My mother always said the only saving grace was that he knew about me, and that Newlands would eventually come to me, but apparently that isn't quite the case."

His listeners pricked up their ears, sensing something strained in the young man's voice as he added

"Which my friends, is why I'm here."

He gave his quick engaging grin as he continued.

"I need to prove my Grandfather's identity and marriage before any claim to Newlands can be made. There's no doubt that my Grandmother was the daughter of the foreman there, but he worked for a much older man than my Grandfather. After my Nan died, my mother was forever searching, looking for their marriage certificate I think, then, out of the blue months ago, I got this shoe box which some old friend of my Dad's had discovered. It was full of junk mainly, but a few pieces made me decide I'd start searching at the other end where my Grandfather may have originated, but I've mighty little to start with."

He reached into a pocket of his immaculately tailored suit and withdrew a small leather piece, which he carefully eased open. Sam held his breath, for the remnant of a Victorian luggage tag was painfully fragile in the young man's hands, but gradually Alex persuaded the hand stitched double fold of fine skin to separate. Inside was a handwritten card, torn or eaten away along the top edge, partially obliterating a name? The card, (almost illegible) had been badly water-stained right down to the last line which read "Padways", below that practically indecipherable, the address finished Great Britain, although only the top half of these words were visible.

By now the entire company were on the edge of their seats. Sam was hunched over the coffee table where Alex had gently laid the label. The Vicar, sat at his desk on an elderly rotating chair, had swung right round (eyes blazing with interest). Even Ellen slid forward, hands anxiously twisting round each other, as Jane peered over her shoulder, watching avidly as the young Australian took up the tale.

This was in an envelope containing a polished stone and a note from my Nan addressed to my father. I won't bore you with that, it's rather private but she basically made him promise that once he came home safely, he would pursue his British background for my sake. She said "James, when you can put this on your father's grave, and tell him I always loved him, then you'll understand what it is to be a father. I promise to look after your son and your wife, and I'll keep looking, so that what was denied him will be yours if you follow the path back to Padways."

The room was still with the pent up breath of Alex's audience as that long-dead promise stirred the air in the Vicarage living-room, and then he added quietly.

"Of course, he never got the letter. The envelope containing the tag and her note was still unopened when his few effects found their way to his friend, who'd lost contact with Mum. I only got them when the Newlands Trust advertised for anyone who'd known them to come forward. Anyway, after my Mum died I found myself at a bit of a loose end. The wool clip was over; the stock manager knows his job, having virtually run the place for the last four years, so I decided to pay my respects to my Grandfather for my Dad, who never got the opportunity. That choice has led me a pretty dance I tell you. I've left solicitors going through land registries, birth, death and marriage certificates to no avail, (which doesn't actually surprise me)."

The Vicar raised his eyebrows, then held out his hand for the intriguing luggage tag, as he joined the conversation.

"I have no doubt that you'll pull through my boy. Wool was a valuable export and war hardly conducive to business. Your mother along with every war widow must have had a hard time of it, cut off from many of the normal comforts of life, but you're doing alright now I take it?", and Alex laughed easily.

"O yes Reverend!" he exclaimed.

"My mother was well provided for. The Newlands Trust paid her a generous allowance, which enabled us to invest in prime stock, but where I fit in, is another story, dependent on finding those missing documents, which is not why I came. I came to trace the human story."

The Vicar nodded approvingly, leaning back, eyes closed, fingers steepled on his chest as he listened intently.

"My Mum and Dad married in 1937. I came along about a year later, so I must have been four or five when my Dad died. After that, Mum gave jobs to men who'd been in the forces, which worked out good, because they had a fair range of skills between them, including flying, which has really opened Australia up."

His attentive audience listened wide-eyed as Alex described his home with a real sense of what life must have been like for the boy who grew up taking school lessons on the radio, never meeting other children in the playground like his British counterparts.

Studying him covertly, Martin saw the loneliness beneath the polished façade, and heard the regret engendered by the necessity of leaving home to attend boarding school and higher education, and then the low voice stopped. Sam felt Ellen gripping his hand as they each silently studied the luggage tag, until the porter said briskly, "So here you are! Have you had one of those new-fangled laboratories look at that card, or has something eaten that wedge out of the name?"

Alex replied somewhat gruffly.

"Both actually. The Canberra University lab believe that the leather is British. It's fairly basic, probably written by someone unskilled. They thought a practised traveller would have printed the words in block capitals, in Indian ink on oiled card, which might have withstood damp and termites (the main cause of the damage). There's no hope of resurrecting it further I'm afraid, although they hazarded a date at the turn of the century."

He broke off abruptly, colouring as he realised how much he'd been talking, but he plainly had something else to say, so Martin (smiling) tried to put him at ease.

"...and there's more?", he prompted. Alex looked up, brightening as he saw Sam and Ellen's intent faces, the care and concern on the Vicar's countenance.

"Well, it seems that my search for my roots parallel another search by the Trust that provided my scholarship, then the bursary that got me through University. I don't remember the name of the man who called me, I've got his card somewhere, but in exchange for the use of a car and driver, they've asked me to simply copy them in on anything I find out about my family or the establishment of Newlands.", he patted his pockets disconsolately, adding the rider, "That's what I hate about living in hotels. You can never be sure of what you'll need out of the junk you have to leave in the safe every day. If I get any leads, I'll rent a cottage which would make life easier. However..." he continued (unaware of the sudden intake of Ellen's breath, or the exchange of glances over his head).

"That shoe box couldn't be the one my Nan didn't get. It was only produced around the nineteen-thirties, long after Grandfather died. I have no idea what this other box holds, or even what it looks like, although the solicitors hazarded a few wild guesses. It might be big, it might be small; it might hold the deeds to property, land registries, gold claims or opals! I am certain that it relates to something my Grandfather valued, but I'd be happy if it turns out to be his marriage certificate. My mother died believing we might find out my father was illegitimate, which would complicate matters pretty badly." he gazed at his audience silently before adding awkwardly.

"A piece of land the size of Newlands is a valuable asset. My mother always thought it should have passed to my Nan on Grandfather's death if he'd owned it outright, because he died when my Dad was a newborn Perhaps it should have been held in Trust for him, I know my Mum made some enquiries back here, but nothing was ever resolved.. My mother told me that Nan never inherited title because she couldn't prove their marriage. That's why my search is doubly important. It probably seems a bit old fashioned in the current climate of sex, drugs, and rock and roll, but Aussie's have high moral standards, and I just have to know, before I can get on with my life!"

His wry expression didn't mask either grief or anxiety, but the production of tea and cakes did a lot to brighten one young man's humour, and the thought of the Harvest Auction cheered them all up as they sallied out to place their bids. Ellen was keen to ask Alex if he wanted to rent her cottage, but Sam persuaded her to get his references checked before she mentioned it. Later however,, when they turned towards home, even Sam's concerns about his outfit for his talk melted when the Australian chuckled sunnily .

"Strewth mate!" He grinned up from the passenger seat as his chauffeur collected him, "You're too darn formal! Wear your uniform. It'll keep the audience focussed on the subject and lend you a bit of glamour as well."

It was so obvious that Sam chuckled out loud as he walked back from Ellen's, contemplating the next six weeks in a rosy glow of anticipation. He let himself in, ran light-footed upstairs, almost forgetting that not long after their marriage, Silver Street would only be part of history, its labours over, its story finally told.

That Monday (being a leave day), Sam took a leisurely soak in the bath (followed by lunch) then concentrated his efforts on his uniform. He carefully held his cap over the steaming kettle on his range, gently brushing the knap. Finally satisfied, he laid it to one side and checked the buttons on his jacket, relieved to find them present and correct. Having pressed his trousers, polished his shoes and ironed his shirt. He dressed, hanging his jacket over the door, putting his waistcoat on thoughtfully. His hands curved, fingers seeking for something missing, as he gazed idly at his reflection. Then he smiled, thoughts on his presentation solidifying as he ran upstairs to his father's old study, Reaching out for Charlie's antique silver fob watch.

However, as he lifted it on its chain (from the ticket lined biscuit-tin lid where Charlie had left it), something beneath the tickets "clinked". Intrigued he investigated, finding half a dozen thrupenny bits; a couple of keys and a harmonica nestled together. In the quiet room a poignant memory surfaced. Norman and Charlie, heads together, re-creating the hoots and whistles that had formed the soundtrack to their lives. Sam stared down at what most folk would have thought the pitiful remnants of two working lives, then looked up, caught in the moment as he recalled his Uncle deriding the harmonica, saying that its wail sounded like the American trains. Nevertheless, Charlie (who had received it from an American serviceman, just before his luck ran out), had stoutly defended it against Norman's uncanny ability to mimic the locomotives that they drove and loved.

Sam recalled saying, "I wish I could do that Dad!", as the old men nodded and competed with each other. He had practiced in private, not wishing to be laughed at, but had never had the confidence to demonstrate his own rapidly growing skill, (bar once), on the day after Norman's funeral. He'd come to regret the impulse however. Charlie, (mourning the loss not only of his elder brother but the end of their contests) had stared at Sam silently, white to the lips, laying aside his harmonica which he never played again. Now, greatly daring, Sam touched the instrument gently, then laying it aside, drew breath, and with his eyes fixed on the only photograph left, forced his memory to replay the sound of a particular train.

He could see his Uncle Norman's old Drummond M7 "Push - pull" locomotive emerging from the station, his father and Uncle visible on the footplate. He was never sure of the moment when sound, sight, smell and memory blurred to become the most extraordinary experience, but astonishingly he tasted coal on his lips, then Charlie's watch was in his hands and time wound backwards. Concentrating so hard that he didn't hear Ellen arrive, didn't catch Alex calling upstairs, Sam "remembered"...

First the hollow whine as the air compressed ahead of the train, the rattle and whirr of steel on steel. The memory surfaced, born on a thready whisper of sound that eddied around his mind until, growling with the pressure of a fine head of steam, it burst from his throat. Echoing uncannily, the accurate rendition filled his den, floated out into the landing, then screamed down the stairs, fading to a faint whisper, as memory and sound passed by, escaping out into the Forest to join the other sounds running free along Castleman's Corkscrew.

He didn't know who was more surprised; Alex, Ellen or himself, he coloured, embarrassed at his success, but the others, crowding in at the door were applauding seriously.

"Crikey mate! You need to get that loco out on a run!" was the Australian's awed comment. Ellen cried, "Sam! I had no idea you could do that! You should get recorded, it'll bring the house down tonight!", and so saying she said urgently, "Now, we've got masses to do, so come down and get organised dear, the evening will be here sooner than you think.", and so it was.

It was six o'clock when Ellen finished turning the collar on Sam's second best uniform shirt and folded it away. Alex, who had been listening to Sam's account of the impending closure at Silver Street with a frown, looked up as she rose.

"Time to go?" he enquired, and got to his feet.

"Come on Sam. Time to do your station proud and we've got to be there for the Auction results as well. I've put a bid on Emma Fleet's big marrow!"

"Is that her name?", Sam and Ellen spoke together, curiosity written clear across both faces as Sam reached down his jacket. Ellen continued thoughtfully.

"Poor woman doesn't get out much. She's welded to that shop, at the beck and call of that lazy lump she married, and her youngsters not much help either. Rory (the eldest) is in the Army, Harry is horse-mad and practically lives at the stables, and Dan is still in junior school. I wouldn't have thought she'd any time for gardening!"

Alex grinned over his shoulder as they stepped out into Sam's small porch.

"She tells me that young Dan brought home a few seeds from school.

They'd been working on some biology project, and he wanted to make a better drawing of them." They moved off together gathering the last pieces of Sam's display as they went, and Sam, setting his cap at a jaunty angle, followed, just in time to hear Alex saying cheerfully, "Apparently the seeds got wet on the way home, so Dan threw them out on the compost heap. Imagine Emma's surprise when they flowered. She didn't even know what they were. The Vicarage cook encouraged her, and she knows how to make marrow jam alright! I tasted some. I've bid for it and if I win, she'll make the jam so I'll get a jar for myself. The old folks place will get the rest!"

They trooped down to the gate together, as the Australian explained.

"That's where I first heard about you Sam.", he closed the gate carefully as Sam laden with books came through it and caught them up. "I was invited to talk there a few nights back myself. One of the chaps had a mate who saw me arrive at the station, and let it slip there was an Aussie in the locality. Seems that Matron has a shortage of speakers during the winter, and when I bumped into her secretary she asked if I would drop in and tell the elders about Christmas in Aus.", (which he pronounced Oz). I thought that I might get some pointers on the Ford family by talking to the "olds", but although I drew a blank there, I enjoyed dressing the part, and talking to them. One old boy (who's mentally very frail) reckoned your station is haunted. Ever hear of that Sam?"

He hopped forward, opening the gate into the Community Hall grounds as he spoke, and Ellen said sharply, "Alex! That's a horrid thing to say. I don't like talk about ghosts, hauntings, or weird stuff like that.", but Alex was laughing, unrepentant.

"You'd better not come over to Oz then." he exclaimed. "When the Aborigines hold traditional gatherings you'll hear stories that'll make your hair stand on end! It's one of the great pastimes amongst their elders. It surprised me when this chap came out with it, but then we had been talking about transport in the old days and the distances between towns at the time. He spoke of distance in terms of times; I distinctly remember him fumbling about looking for a watch and wondered what his connection was. He had an unusual name but I can't remember it now."

Sam sighed, heavy hearted as he supplied it quietly.

"I reckon you've been talking to Harvey Flaxman.", he ventured. "I'm glad to know where he is, but sorry he doesn't seem to have recovered much."

They had entered the Hall by a rear entrance and as Sam spoke Ellen was opening up the Committee room to Alex Ford's amazed view.

"Harvey was Station Master at Silver Street, right up to September last year. We've had a temporary in since then after Harvey was found on the up-line platform late one night. He was suffering a nervous breakdown the doctors said, so he was retired early." he carefully shut the door behind him and laid his precious book box down thoughtfully.

"I was on holiday when it happened.", he murmured, as he busied himself arranging books on the slopes he had made, aligning them precisely with the photographs and maps he and Ellen had prepared just three short days ago.

"I heard that they took him off to the hospital in a right old state, restrained from trying to stop a train that he claimed was heading for a crash!"

"Good Heavens Sam.", Ellen looked shocked as she asked, "Was there a train crash then, or did Mr Flaxman have it wrong? Do tell... I'm dying to know." she was shrugging off her jacket as she spoke and Sam, newly aware of her superstitious nature said carefully.

"Well, I don't think anyone knows what started it, or even why he was there at that time of night. Silver Street doesn't have passenger services after seven. Through trains, freight, but not passengers, for that you'd have to take the coastal line. However, Harvey was absolutely convinced he had to stop some train, but he was delusional, and now we'll never know what started his breakdown."

"That's a fact mate." said Alex Ford ruefully. "I had it pegged to some wartime incident, he seemed pretty fixated to me. Poor old boy, it's a shame we can't find out what the Station Master saw, because I'm convinced there was something that triggered that reaction. Hey Sam, why don't you and I try and find out what?"

Ellen's head lifted momentarily, but whatever she was about to say was drowned in the buzz of anticipation from the Hall, as Martin Short opened the door and glanced in.

"Well Sam, ready to go?", and with no time to follow the thread Alex had started, the porter was ushered out to face his audience, the others at his heels.

Smiling, the Vicar raised a hand for silence as Ellen and Alex took seats next to Jane in the front row of the audience. Ellen glanced around as the Padways Parish Council trooped onto the stage, joining Martin Short at a simple draped trestle table, groaning under the weight of trophies. The Vicar cleared his throat as they sat, then the results of the auction were given.

To Ellen's amusement, Emma Fleet's marrow was won by the

Australian, who seemed unabashed when his bid of five pounds was revealed. Mrs Castle stunned by the value of the sealed bid, whispered to Ellen.

"Five pounds! That's more than a week's housekeeping!", but subsided as Ellen whispered back.

"He's Australian." she hissed. "I don't think he ever met a vegetable marrow before, he just wanted to get his hands on a good pot of jam!", and the two women chuckled as Alex manhandled his strange prize back to his seat. Mrs Fleet (glowing with pleasure) collected the prize for "Best produce", traditionally awarded to a single fund raiser, then the sealed bids for the rest of the auction were announced, and prizes awarded. In no time at all, boxed entries were disbursed to winning bidders, cups, shields and plates were awarded, and the Vicar stood with a slip of paper in his hand. Solemnly he announced the value and distribution of funds raised, and then he turned to introduce Sam.

The night was drawing in; the light from the hog-roast (held in a barbecue pit behind the Hall) caused a little subdued flickering at the windows as the lights were lowered on a rapt audience. The stage had been darkened as the Vicar and his entourage departed, and only a single spot lit the table where Sam's precious maps were laid, along with his father's diaries. As the audience waited however, there was a sudden "chuff" of steam from somewhere, and the men in the audience visibly pricked their ears, leaning forward eagerly. Hidden behind the curtain, Sam held Charlie Smart's watch in his hand, gazing at the inscription steadily as he recalled being lifted onto Charlie's shoulders to see a special train go past. In his mind his father's voice said gruffly, "There Sammie boy, listen. You can hear "Lord John Hawkins" all the way from Ringwood. She's been diverted today, so Uncle Norman's going up to Paddington, with the passengers who normally go on the coastal line. Listen hard and you'll hear the rails talking to the loco; she's a powerful lady, some of that class pull the Bournemouth Belle".

He had encouraged young Sam to identify as many of the locomotives as he could, and even in the face of his young son's excitement used his own knowledge of the line to link the history of the engine to its sound. He didn't fail Sam on that occasion either As they'd turned to go back home Charlie had remarked

"That there was a Maunsell Lord Nelson class 4-6-0, it's a bit special, but not so special as some locomotives.." Charlie ruffled Sam's hair as he stepped into the "backs", a lane that ran down the back of their small row of cottages. .

"We had a Drummond "Bulldog" pull the Royal train with King George on board right through our station once". He sighed, and Sam recalled standing staring at the lines that the King had used.

Again Sam remembered, the harsh wool of his father's jacket against his legs, the steady hands that held him so high, then the thrum, (the song of the line his Dad had called it). A gentle far away rattle, a prickling sense of "Something coming", lifted his head, filled his mind's eye, his throat, and out across the hushed audience came the sound of a locomotive. There was the familiar chuckle growling at the back of Sam's mind, he concentrated, pouring all of his young memories into filling his auditorium with sound, cautiously allowing the volume to soar, eddy as if on the wind across Goatspen Plain, then narrow, sink, and with a shriek as his memory train flew past, to dissipate to a roar of applause, before stepping into the light, casually returning Charlie's watch to his uniform waistcoat.

"That was inspired!", murmured a greatly relieved Vicar to himself, stepping out to warn the hog-roast staff that they might have a long wait, but Sam was well prepared. His talk was to last an hour, but looking round the entranced faces of his audience, he gave them an hour and fifteen minutes, and the applause as he finished threatened to take the roof off the Hall. Martin Short was not the only one who saw a difference in Sam as he stood taking questions. His friendly Dorset burr seemed as intoxicating as Jane's parsnip wine, which was currently being dispensed to a stunned village. They gathered, respectful in silent contemplation of Sam's display, then circulating past the refreshments to pick up a plate by the roasting spit. They grouped, talking in hushed whispers, then returned to the Hall, bombarding Sam with eager questions.

Sam was stunned by the avid response as he spoke of the old fishing port of Bournemouth and the cost of opening up the routes to the west. Speculative investment brought about the building of Castleman's Corkscrew and the Forest lines during the nineteenth century, Silver Street also dating from that greatly innovative period. He had spoken with confidence, the knowledge he had gleaned embedded since a sickly childhood had seen him anchored in his books, and gradually the mantle of authority had settled comfortably on his shoulders as he related his beloved station's long history. He told his family's story, the young brothers forced to travel south to find work, an escape from the overcrowded mills of the North, to the peace and tranquillity of the forest. He reminded them of days gone past when Royalty (and its mistresses) had used the stations along this coast in pursuit of pleasure.

He recalled the years of privation following the Great War, the Slump, the General Strike and the cruel inevitability of the Second World War. Somehow he conjured the memory of forgotten faces from the names on War Memorials, exhorting them to continue this village community out of respect for those American Canadian,, British and Australian servicemen who had passed through en route to battle. Without him once mentioning Silver Street's impending closure, somehow John Oswald (who had slid in inconspicuously) found himself ostracised.

It wasn't obvious to anyone but the self-important Station Master, but the villagers crowded round Sam to the exclusion of the man who stood bitterly examining the bottom of a tumbler. This being filled with parsnip wine, proved a temporary bolster to John Oswald's crumbling ego. He had imagined that Sam, being a retiring sort of chap, would give a mumbling little talk and shyly defer to his seniors in an agony of embarrassment, but no! Sam had transformed (in front of him) into a raconteur, a mimic, a historian with a vast store of knowledge. He had expanded (in the increasingly intoxicated view of John Oswald), into the conscience of Silver Street. He abandoned his fantasy of being there to support his porter, dropped any idea of assuming the guise of a rail authority, and when the villagers joyfully escorted Sam and Ellen out to get their share of the roast, he "collared" the bottle of parsnip wine, emptied it into his tumbler, and went out into the night.

Draining the glass and depositing it on a table set out for the celebration, he shakily slipped on his bicycle clips and collected his bike from the stand, to begin wobbling his way home to Burley. He was very fuddled when the increasing gradient encouraged him to pull up, and push his bike over the road bridge that overlooked Silver Street.

His head whirled strangely as he glanced into a rising mist, which seemed to gather over the line, so he paused, leaning heavily on his bike for support, and rubbing his eyes blinked uneasily as a thread of sound encouraged him to lean perilously over the railing.

If anyone had been there, they might have seen John Oswald pale, sweat beading his forehead. They might have looked down-line to what appeared to be a ball of mist gliding slowly to a stop at the moonlit station below. They might have imagined for a moment that they heard the gentle clank of the wheel-tapper, a light "chuff" of steam, but in a million years they would never have believed the terror on the face of the man who had seen the gleaming locomotive (and the rail tracks that were clearly visible right through the engine!). There was a strange almost strangled cry of terror from the Station Master as he clambered into the saddle and lurched away moaning. The mist shrouded locomotive hissed contentedly, before gliding east, up-line into the night, emitting a thready whispered wail as it vanished around the bend leaving Silver Street to sleep under cool Autumnal skies.

Immediately following his talk, Sam was embarrassed by the wealth of congratulation. As the Harvest Supper closed, everyone that was anyone in Padways society vied for his attention. Eventually Ellen came to the rescue, clutching a neat notepad to take down names and telephone numbers. Drawing impressive ladies (with even more impressive bosoms) to one side, she explained their local historian would be more than interested in their late father's (husband's, uncle's or brother's) records. She systematically sorted the shy, blushing or confused into a line so that she could note anything of instant importance, filtering the wine infused bonhomie of a few parish stalwarts with tact and diplomacy, while Alex encouraged rail or ex-railway employees to leave their names and addresses with him.

No-one commented on John Oswald's presence (or of his abrupt departure), so it wasn't until the following morning that Sam became aware that the temporary Station Master had been in the audience. When Bert Credding told the shift during early tea-break that Mike Theobald was coming in to take over for a few days, that was the first time anyone missed the man (so well-oiled was the routine at Silver Street, but Sam (intrigued) bent his head to listen as the signalman explained further.

"Mrs Andrews said he ate or drank something that upset him badly." Bert announced with a grin and Sam, (coming in on the heels of the conversation) found out that Mr Oswald's landlady had been forced to call a doctor that morning.

"Mind you," said Mike Theobald later (signing off the morning crew's worksheet), "Don't you think about slacking off."

He grinned up at Sam, "I hear you did yourself and Silver Street proud last night. Mr Cuthbert came in this morning from Brockenhurst and tells me that the word went round almost before you'd stopped talking. It won't be the same without the line for any of us, but you seem to have hidden talents my friend. I'd brush up on those if I was you; keep the memory alive if nothing else."

He hung up the clipboard with his afternoon roster, before turning with a quizzical expression on his face.

"Have you thought about buying the old place once it closes?" he asked casually, and Sam (once again) felt a feathery tingle down his spine. He moistened suddenly dry lips, forcing his voice from a quavering treble down to its normal adult register, before saying dismissively.

"Don't talk daft man. How could anyone with no prospects afford a whole railway station? I'm not Royalty and I don't have millions!"

Mike Theobald chuckled dryly.

"That's where you're wrong Sam Smart! They're selling redundant railway property to ex-railwaymen at knock-down prices. I've got a list here somewhere. Do you want a gander at it?"

He lifted his briefcase onto John Oswald's desk and rummaged, finally producing a typed sheet which he offered with a grin.

"You could do worse," he advised. "Several of the Weymouth lads may try and buy some track and run it for steam enthusiasts. Seems to me that a man with your talents and knowledge could think of something to do with the old place, but I'd get in quick if I were you. Someone with the capital to buy land will be in before long. Developers don't give a toss about the history they'll destroy. If they can make money they'll throw up some of these modern places, leaving no trace of the station which would be criminal."

Sam gazed at him speechlessly, then turned and looked down at the notice he held. The words swam mistily before him as he tried to grasp the idea of such an impossible dream becoming reality, then they steadied as he traced the list swiftly.

There were station buildings, signal boxes, outbuildings, railway cottages from Dorchester to Brockenhurst on this page alone. He squinted at the values, and then shook his head trying to clear the muffled sounds which soon translated themselves into the anxious voice of the Ringwood under manager as he asked urgently, "Sam? Are you ok mate? Don't tell me that whatever took old Oswald out has got you too?"

Sam blinking at the line which read "Silver Street Station House, platforms and outbuildings from one pound apiece freehold." raised a shining face and said shakily, "I'm ok. Just a bit tired I suppose. Can I keep this please?" as young Mr Theobald turned back to his schedule.

"Yes, of course Sam," he waved Sam back to work, calling behind him. "Make sure you get your application in as soon as possible. The vultures are gathering!"

That afternoon in the guise of carrying out other work, Sam made it his duty to walk Silver Street as though he had never seen it before. He dutifully pumped water from the local spring up to the tanks and noted the rusty hue of the small river beyond with disfavour. He paced the platforms, checked out the sidings, and trundled a sack-barrow from one platform to the other and back again, measuring by eye how much land the old Station occupied. He surprised the earnest young clerk who'd replaced Harry Armstrong by spending half an hour sweeping the parcels office for no good reason. Trevor Steadman blinked earnestly over the top of a ledger as Sam prowled around the down line platform, totally unaware that if only in the porter's mind, this platform had already become the basis of a generous home, and this office Sam's smallholding chicken - coop.

Fred Cummins watched these casual manoeuvres with a knowledgeable smile, and over a cup of tea, (brewed illegally in the ticket office by shy Gerald Richards), he voiced an opinion.

"Well that's the old girl taken care of then." and the ticket clerk said hopefully,

"Do you think so Fred? Mike Theobald is a good man, but I'd hate him to push Sam into something he can't afford."

Fred smiled.

"Our Sam has his head screwed on Gerry. He's practically been brought up on Silver Street. Given a crack at it he'll do old Charlie proud. In fact, I reckon he's more wedded to Silver Street than he's ever going to be to his teacher. I just hope she knows what she's let herself in for!", the two men went back to work cheerfully, as Sam, contemplating all his recent dreams coming true, surreptitiously measured up the main waiting room, and worked out how to fit a kitchen into Gerald Richard's ticket office.

Thankfully, for the next few days both Ellen and Alex were busy about their own activities. Alex, having researched thoroughly, took himself off to Wiltshire to try and trace his Grandfather's last sad journey, intent on finding his grave or some memorial at the very least. Ellen, working hard on her intended transfer to the local authority school, locked herself in her cottage with Emma Fleet's sewing machine, for which Sam was pathetically grateful.

He busied himself, repatriating his property back home, but couldn't bring himself to confess that in all the excitement, Ellen's old tin box had lain wrapped in sacking under the trestles supporting the display. He kept his Uncle's photographs neatly wrapped in Charlie's tool barrow, thinking how appropriate they would look hung in the old station, and prayed for Alex to return. However, by the time the Australian (oddly pale and withdrawn) tapped on his door the entire world had something else to talk about, and the future of a redundant railwayman looked very bright weighed against the shock and grief of a nation as John F. Kennedy lay dying in the arms of his young wife. A President cut down before he could make good on the promise of a more united world.

That evening, after the Vicar called for the Church bells to be rung, the friends gathered to hear Martin Short pray for the stricken family so very far from their own everyday problems. With little thought of their own futures, the parishioners of Padways wished each other "Goodnight", as the Vicar quietly ushered Ellen, Sam and Alex into the warmth of the Vicarage kitchen.

The solemnity of evening prayers seemed to match Alex Ford's mood as they listened to his rough young voice describing what he had found at Fovent.

"There's nothing mate! No hope of finding out what happened to any single soldier. I don't know enough about my Grandfather, he was kind of secretive apparently. My Dad only knew, that his father was wounded at Messines in 1917, before he was born, but no-one knows where he died, or where he was buried. My Mum said that my Nan tried to find out, but got nowhere and I guess the Great War swallowed thousands like that. No amount of accounting could ever cover the number of men from every nation that fought. There's just no rhyme or reason for such a colossal loss of life. What I've heard and seen since I left here was on such a stupendous scale it seems impossible. Yet some of the sheer courage deserves more honour than it seems to recieve."

They sat, Jane and Martin, Ellen and Sam, listening to the awed young voice describing the Commonwealth memorial carved into the Wiltshire chalk downs above the site where so many men had been encamped en route to the killing fields of Flanders, and they saw how deeply touched Alex was.

"I walked up as close as was allowed." Alex said softly. "I thought I should try and do what my Nan wanted."

He touched a pocket of his sheepskin coat, and Sam knew instinctively that the shining Australian pebble entrusted to his father, had been laid against the slowly fading Fovent badge, and that at least one part of Alex's self-imposed task had been fulfilled.

As the Australian swung to his feet, Sam asked curiously, "Did you find many Fords Alex, or are you going to have to search further afield?"

Alex turned, (a rueful expression on his face.)

"Pages of them mate! Next to Jones, Smith and Brown I reckon Ford's the most popular name round here! Some folk land themselves a wild goose chase, I seem to have landed me a wild Ford chase, but that's small beer to the trouble the Yanks are in. I couldn't believe what I was seeing when the news came through, and of course that sort of thing is what sparks war. I was glad to come back to Padways somehow. Not quite home, but I feel safe here amongst friends."

He flushed self-consciously then Ellen asked impulsively.

"Alex? Would you like to rent my cottage? I won't charge much and you'd get a real sense of living in the village for a short while at least."

The tall Australian turned eagerly.

"I thought you'd never ask!" he said simply, and then raising his bush hat he turned and left the Vicarage, into a world that would dawn to a very different day.

Chapter 15 - Chance Encounter

It wasn't long before various items of interest began to find their way to Sam's door, and he despaired at the thought of what Ellen would make of his ever growing collection after their marriage. Quietly enlisting Jane Short's help, Sam began to relax as half the ladies of Padways were engaged in "cleaning Parties" by the redoubtable Mrs Castle. Soon rooms lon unused appeared after the "organising parties" found new homes for his Grandmother's vast repository of sewing materials, (not to mention Sam's precious documents) in the process and by the end of November, he could provide a decent home for his wife.

A week before their wedding, he stood on the platform at Silver Street, an indulgent smile on his lean face as he thought of going home after work to a wife, and John Oswald (much recovered but still unusually subdued) called out to him.

"Come along Smart do. Anyone would think you're some dewy eyed damsel dreaming of wedding bells! Standing around grinning won't get the post sorted. Get along with you man!"

This mild chastisement seemed out of Oswald's normal bombastic character, but Sam shrugged off the disconcerting suspicion that the temporary man was mellowing and continued his duties albeit reluctantly.

He'd privately decided not to worry Ellen with his intention to buy Silver Street, but could not keep the matter entirely secret from his close workmates (whom he swore to silence using the familiar blood-curdling oaths of their childhood days).

Taking especial care to ensure that John Oswald remained ignorant of his plans, Sam had quieted his basic instincts, working steadily through the program of clearing years of documents, boxing and labelling railway property for onward transmission to Regional Managers.

However, he'd taken advantage of a quick trip west to Ringwood only that morning when the Station Master asked for a volunteer, which happened rarely. John Oswald had seemed strangely uneasy lately, moods shifting between anxiety and elation, so Sam didn't hesitate to get out of the man's way for an hour, putting his own plans into action at the first opportunity.

He tucked the application forms into an envelope, picked up a suitcase for Lost Property at Ringwood, and swung himself into the guard's van as the 1.40 pulled out.

He made himself comfortable, sitting on the case and listening to an unusual syncopated chugging, as the train swung out of Silver Street. He decided that he liked the odd rhythm. It infused the traditional lickety split sounds he normally associated with this part of the track, so with his eyes closed, back to the carriage wall, he was soon engaged in adding this new refrain to his repertoire. Happily mimicking the sound to himself, he became aware that he had an audience when an awed whisper penetrated his fierce concentration. A child prompted enthusiastically.

"Daddy. Go on, ask him. He's ace!" followed by an adult's awed comment.

"Wow! That's uncanny, how long have you been doing that?"

Flustered, he looked up as father and son smiled appreciatively.

Sam explained ruefully, and as he did so, a speculative look crossed the young man's face.

"Look here," he reached for his wallet and extracted a card. "I'm Alan Harper (BBC Radio). You may know my programme Harper's Bizarre? I'm always looking out for people with unusual talents you know! I'm on holiday right now, but if I was to get the programme I've just proposed to the Big White Chief, then I could certainly find a slot for you. Interested?", but Sam was dumbstruck. Hadn't Ellen said he should get recorded? Hadn't Alex applauded that idea? Now a mere chance encounter was putting the opportunity in his way and he found himself thinking about Percy Adams (his father's gardening friend), as he decided to seize the day. As this short journey came to an end, he said slowly.

"Well yes Mr Harper. I've heard of your programme, even listen to it sometimes, but I'm not sure how I'd fit in. Can I think about it please?", and to his relief the young presenter nodded, made a note in a minuscule notebook and asked for Sam's name.

"I'm Sam Smart," he said guardedly. "At the moment I'm a porter at Silver Street Station, but Sam Smart, Church Cottage, Padways will always find me."

Alan Harper's eyes narrowed, "Ah yes, the line's closing isn't it. I'm interviewing a Mr Cuthbert for my new programme later tonight. It's a trial edition which won't be broadcast until they've made up their minds, but I'm very hopeful.", he switched tack, abruptly demanding as Sam rose, "Would you know the man the entire line is talking about by any chance? I haven't a name for him, but he works with you I think, and is some kind of historian. Someone at Burley tipped me the wink that I need to talk to this man before everyone else gets on his trail."

Shrewd grey eyes met Sam's burning face, then the young man nodded to himself.

"Yes, I thought so.", he murmured and clapped an astonished Sam on the shoulder.

"When you're ready Mr Smart.", he murmured gently. "I've a cottage down the coast at Keyhaven. Why don't you let me know and I'll talk to you there?"

Speechlessly Sam held out his hand and Alan Harper shook it warmly before instructing the silent child, who still gazed at Sam in wonder.

"Come along Robert. Time to go back to Mummy, Daddy has to go to work now."

He ruffled the boys hair, and they turned away chatting nineteen to the dozen as the train drew into Ringwood, and the most momentous decision of Sam's life awaited him.

In the end it was almost disappointing. The quiet scheming of the nights leading up to this faded into the mundane as Sam's application was receipted by the absent minded station clerk, (who seemed more anxious to reunite the missing suitcase with a frantic passenger than query the plain envelope carrying all Sam's hopes). He returned up-line bearing files for John Oswald, the precious receipt tucked into his waistcoat pocket.

The Station Master grumbled softly as Sam handed him the files, then quite suddenly said (as he pinned up yet another list to an overburdened schedule), "I don't suppose you'd care for a job after the line closes Smart?"

Sam (goggle-eyed) said promptly, "I'd consider it Mr Oswald, what are you suggesting?"

The man hemmed and hawed a little then said diffidently, "There might be a need for a night-watchman for a few months before the line's lifted. You know the station well, you live the closest apart from Credding and he's off to London once the traffic stops. I can't tell you exactly how long the post'll last, or even when it officially starts, but Credding's cottage will be vacant until it's sold so you won't be out in the cold. Think it over and let me know!"

He dismissed Sam airily and reached for his cap, turning out of his office on one of his proprietorial little walks as Sam pushed his cap to the back of his head. Addressing no-one in particular, he said in tomes of wonderment.

"Well if that don't beat all!"

He hadn't heard Fred Cummins coming up behind him, and was mildly disconcerted when his colleague enquired, "What's Pompous Percy up to now Sam?"

He listened intently to Sam's explanation (with a suspicious scowl on his normally placid features).

"Be careful Sam! He's up to something, and I wouldn't put it past him to try and upset your apple-cart. I heard him telling Gerry that you were too damn popular by half! Says you need taking down a peg or ten before you go getting ideas above your station in life!"

"Really?", said Sam with deep satisfaction, "Well Fred. My station is Silver Street, and in a month or two I should know if my application to buy her has been accepted. Then we'll see who comes off best. He can go on exactly as he is until they run out of rail to dismantle, and long after that Silver Street will still have a future if I have anything to do with it!"

Quite entranced with that idea, Fred went off to make tea and take bets on Sam's chances.

That evening, Ellen met the bus smiling, although her face was pinched with the cold of oncoming night. He sauntered off the conductor's platform, and bent his head to kiss her cheek as she dimpled nicely, then, tucking her arm in his advised him that she was now homeless, a mere waif of the storm waiting for her knight in shining armour to come to the rescue.

"I've moved lock, stock and barrel into Mrs Castle's guest room.", she admitted. "I had to get the cottage sorted for Alex before Christmas, so she suggested that several of the W. I. ladies would help with that, and I should go and stay with her. She's rather a dear once you get past that fearsome exterior, and her guest room is absolute luxury. She says I'm to tell you that she and Jane have finished "Dora's room", and have put some significant finds on your sitting room table."

They were walking up from the bus-stop as she spoke, and Sam (one arm round her shoulders felt her chuckle).

"Whose Dora darling?", she questioned lightly, then "Shall we have a sitting room Sam? Whatever have you been up to for the last couple of weeks?"

Sam (thinking rapidly that an early wedding present would come in handy right now), slipped the latch on his garden gate with relief and took Ellen's arm firmly.

"Now, you close your eyes.", he ordered gruffly and taking Ellen into the front entrance opened the door into what had been a junk room for more years than he cared to remember. With his fingers crossed surreptitiously, he clicked the light switch and ushered Ellen through into the modestly comfortable interior.

A large old-fashioned Chesterfield sofa lined one wall, decorated with plump new cushions that some nimble fingered member of the Mother's Union had fashioned from the limitless bales of material found in his

Grandmother Dora's room. Gleaming Benares-ware bowls stood against the tiled hearth, and a low table supported several small boxes, presumably left by the ladies of the parish for Sam to examine. However, all his attention was on Ellen who turned a glowing face towards him murmuring, "Oh Sam! It's beautiful."

She sank onto the Chesterfield and sat (one hand smoothing a cushion) as she examined the highly polished woodwork, the immaculately pleated curtains and the ready-laid fire in the hearth.

"What a day of surprises.", she continued, "Mrs Castle kidnapping me this morning, Emma Fleet buying up nearly all my mother's odds and ends this afternoon and then this!", she beamed happily, then Sam closing the door, revealed what stood behind it, and Ellen sat forward, two bright spots on her face as she saw her late mother's writing desk. He had worked on it for days after Alex had spotted the early signs of wood-worm and Ellen had dumped it in disgust. Now, treated and re-polished by one of the local men (more knowledgeable about timber than Sam), it had come back to Charlie's work-shed, where Sam had carefully re-seated hinges on the drop-down leaf, copied the tiny turned knobs on interior drawers and levelled the book shelves. It was never going to be a valuable piece for it had suffered far too much on the long sea voyage home from India, but Ellen's mother had loved it, and he'd seen Ellen weeping over its lamentable state, but he was thoroughly unprepared for the joy that she greeted it with.

Disentangling himself half an hour later, Sam went to the kitchen to make tea, reflecting that coming home to a wife was going to be a very good thing indeed, before discovering that it was very hard to whistle nonchalantly whilst grinning like a Cheshire cat!

He had taken Thursday and Friday off that week, and went with Alex Ford into the locality, looking for a gentleman's outfitters. He had discovered that Alex liked clothes, and where Sam had only been used to having a couple of choices outside his uniform, Alex revelled in "dressing the part". He waxed lyrical over his success at the old people's home, putting down the idea that his appearance in bush clothes had immediately fixed in elderly minds his nationality and background. He chortled joyfully over Sam's own appearance at the Harvest talk saying mischievously, "Think Sam. Remember how you mimicked that locomotive? You could hardly have wandered out on stage after that if you'd been wearing anything other than your railway uniform. I was on the other side of the curtain in the audience remember? It was perfectly staged. Half the audience wouldn't have been surprised if the locomotive itself had chuffed on-stage, the other half were forward on their seats, grinning like idiots because they knew what they heard was accurate. Now, imagine you'd wandered out in pink satin pyjamas and then tell me that clothes don't make the man."

He whooped with unrestrained laughter at the expression on Sam's face, then they amused themselves, suggesting one outrageous outfit after another, until Howard (the chauffeur) raised an eyebrow.

They were in a long High Street, a mixture of old established and modern shops falling into parades on either side. The car glided into a parking bay outside an imposing Post Office, and the chauffeur turned his head.

"New Milton sir.", he said deferentially, "May I suggest that you try Bradbeers? They have a tolerable range of "off the peg" suiting, and it struck me that Mr Smart would find them easy to deal with in the future."

Sam self-consciously whispered to Alex.

"I can't afford much Alex. I've sunk a month's wages into Silver Street already, and I only have about five months money to come."

His companion grinned cheerfully as they slid out of the car, (Howard officiating at the doors).

"Crikey mate! You don't think I'd bring you shopping just to blow every last penny you have do you? I've a few dollars set aside for this anyway. You need a present for your wedding gift, so don't take on like some dozy girl."

So poor Sam endured being measured and fitted. Shirts, underwear, trousers, followed a serviceable set of cavalry twills. Then Alex turned to the suits. Black was too stark, blue wouldn't do either, but his hand hovered over a fine charcoal grey lovingly. Sam shook his head.

"I can't afford it Alex," he protested mildly. "I couldn't wear that about Padways. It's no good choosing something that would do in Town, I don't go there do I?", and reluctantly Alex gave in. Sam on the other hand had spotted a suit in which he could imagine himself appearing at County fairs, it would work equally well for high days and holidays and he fingered it wistfully.

"Yes…" said the gentleman's outfitter thoughtfully. "Not quite olive green, not quite lovat, more bronzed should we say? Not everyone could carry that off sir, but your colouring could work with that. Shall we try sir?"

Finding it difficult to keep his face straight, "Sir" nodded and presently found himself staring into the mirror, while the fabric enfolded him as if made to measure. He sighed with pleasure then guiltily realised that Alex was talking to the salesman again. Returning to his cubicle, Sam eased himself out of the jacket as the salesman appeared with a waistcoat. Sam blinked as he was smoothly assisted into it, and stared in delight at the transformation in the mirror. Figured in matching tones of bronze and olive it turned the suit into a celebration of colour. The assistant's face took on an absorbed look as he conferred with Alex in the doorway before departing in search of something else. Sam stared at the slender brown stranger in the mirror, tentatively touching his unruly hair and wondering what he could do about that, as the salesman returned with a different shirt and what looked to Sam's untutored eye like a ladies scarf.

Seconds later he gaped in amazement as Sam Smart disappeared entirely, re-emerging in the mirror as the epitome of romantic heroes.

"Good Lord!", he exclaimed in surprise, and the assistant (who was deftly pinning the cravat in place smiled seraphically.

"Oh yes sir, indeed you'd make a very believable Mr D'Arcy.", he said to the chorus of Alex's,

"Cooee! Love's young dream!"

Reality refused to return as Sam took off his wedding finery and retreated. He found that Alex had settled the bill for everything, and no amount of persuasion, threat or even a scuffled arm-wrestling contest in the back of the Bentley was going to change that. A visit to the hairdresser and two smart pairs of shoes later he was still on cloud nine as they slid back into Padways with just enough time to squirrel away their purchases before the last rehearsal for Ellen's Nativity play took place in the Hall. They all went of course. Alex, Jane, Martin, Mrs Castle and the Mums, Dads and helpers. The senior girls from Pine Trees arrived in a gaggle accompanied by Matron, even a few villagers popped in, drawn by the sound of Ellen playing the piano. It had been a good day or two Sam considered quietly as he stood (back to the wall), listening to the woman who would be his wife before that weekend was out.

"A very good few days indeed.", he thought with conviction, suddenly aware that he could count on more of those as he stepped into a new life with Ellen at his side forever.

They were married quietly the following afternoon, between the school choir practice in the morning and the dress rehearsal that evening. The day was cool and clear, no-one seemed to take any notice of the unexpected finery, and by now Alex and the Bentley were such a common sight in the village that no-one paid the slightest attention as his chauffeur drew in to Ellen's cottage. He gravely handed her into the rear, then took the passenger seat beside the chauffeur as they set off for the Church.

Ellen (dressed very simply in a buttermilk suit) looked calm, but nevertheless Alex said quietly and (he hoped) reassuringly, "Everything alright?", as her face lit up in a smile.

"Yes Alex, I'm fine. I was just thinking that my parents would have loved Sam's sense of fair play. Of course my father never met him, but my mother always said he was very knowledgeable, and the kindest person she knew. I don't know what they'd have made of our marriage, but I remember them telling me that friendship is a strong platform for love. Sam has always been a rock solid friend to me, and I am very sure that this is the right thing for both of us."

"That's alright then isn't it?", said Alex with satisfaction, "I'm sorry you haven't more family around, but I'm proud you asked me to give you away. I've found real friends since I came here, as well as a place I feel at home, so this is the icing on the cake for me!"

Ellen chuckled at his earnest young face, then said apologetically, "Well, we're here, and now you'll have to brave my Matron of Honour."

The car had glided silently into the small bay outside the Church gate, and as the chauffeur opened the door, Jane Short greeted Ellen with a swift overall glance of approbation.

"Ellen, you look wonderful. That buttermilk wool suits you perfectly, just let me check you over."

She bent to tug the hem of Ellen's suit down, helped her re-pin the small hat into place, then handed Ellen a cream prayer book, into which a ribbon holding a spray of cinnamon coloured silk roses had been stitched.

Just as she stepped into the porch, a bright shaft of wintry sunshine touched the honey gold of her hair, then she reached out a slim hand and found the crook of Alex Ford's arm. He smiled down at her, brushed the curtain aside and took her up the aisle to her husband to be.

Sam, strangely certain about this day, smiled at himself in the mirror, carefully adjusted his hair as he had been advised, then ran lightly down the stairs where Gerald Richards waited for him. The ticket clerk, wearing a sober grey suit stood as Sam entered his homely kitchen, and literally gaped at his colleague.

"My, my!", he exclaimed impulsively. "That's a terrific suit Sam. You look so different, younger for certain. I hope you and Miss Armitage have booked a photographer?"

"Never thought of that Gerry. We've got to save the pennies you know.", Sam paused then added gently, "I shan't need photographs to mark the day mind you. It just so happens that my Mum and Dad got married on the 13th December too, so I'm following family tradition. Now Gerry, have you got those rings?"

Gerald Richards nodded, touching his left pocket, and they set off for the church a few minutes later, but as Sam entered (expecting to find it empty), he was amazed to find the entire congregation of Padways waiting. They had arranged themselves neatly, all Ellen's W. I. friends together (in lieu of family) then he caught sight of Fred Cummins!

He paused, whispering urgently, "What's going on Fred?", and was amazed and touched to discover that half the staff at Silver Street had arranged to take unpaid leave to attend. Fred grinned happily.

"Mr Oswald won't know what's hit him!", he chortled. "Mike Theobald is taking my shift, Paddy Burnett has been giving him hell since Wednesday when he took over your duties, and we shunted Phil Thomas into the ticket office. He's high and dry, surrounded by bolshie Ringwood men who only answer to Mike. Long live the revolution!"

Scandalised, Sam grinned uncertainly straight into the eyes of Emma Fleet who'd dressed for the occasion. She dropped him an enormous wink, then Martin Short appeared and Sam and his best man made their way to their appointed positions.

He remembered his father bringing him to his grandmother's funeral. Then to Norman's obsequies, but he couldn't remember coming to a wedding here himself. He looked at the choir stalls, his eyes following the glimmer of candle, the sheen of creamy blossoms cascading from ornate holders, glints of ruby and gold shimmering from stained glass, glinting off pews, then the door opened behind him, and Ellen was there.

He remembered the depths of her eyes, the fragrance of her skin, and the fragility of the hand she so trustingly placed in his. Martin Short's calm presence, his own clear voice ringing with sincerity, Ellen's gravity as she took her vows. Then, in a peal of bells, the tenderest of kisses, as they walked out together in a blizzard of confetti.

They hadn't planned a reception, but they were swept into the

Community Hall, where Mrs Castle, Mrs Thomas and the rest of the Women's Institute waited, tables groaning. Surrounded by friends and colleagues they drank parsnip wine, cut the cake that Mrs Castle had so proudly made for them, and were eternally grateful when Alex rescued them some time later.

Howard (the chauffeur) appeared holding an envelope, in which they discovered a note. Ellen let Sam read it, then as Sam pressed her hand meaningfully, she rose and they followed Alex out into the Committee room, where he explained.

"Time to escape.", before turning and taking them out to the side entrance where the Bentley stood waiting. Howard opened the doors for them with a deferential murmur.

"Mrs Smart, Mr Smart.", then as the young couple gazed at each other in delight, he slipped the car into gear and swept them off to Burley Manor.

Alex's room was at their disposal, the receptionist explained, so they ran upstairs with their suitcases, and changed back into ordinary clothes. Sam's hand lingered over an envelope for a moment, but before he weakened, he turned and hugged his bride, leaving the official looking letter alone.

He thought "Better not ruin the start of our life together, there'll be opportunities later.", then laughing he followed Ellen out, as they were spirited away to the path that led to the back of Sam's cottage, where a couple of hours of peace and tranquillity awaited then, before the all-important dress rehearsal began.

They curled up on each side of the range in Sam's kitchen, utterly oblivious of the village revelry as cheerful voices left the Hall. They were too full of their new life together to talk, until Ellen yawned, rubbed her eyes ruefully and announced her intention of sleeping on the Chesterfield before they went out again. Sam, (too weary to argue) gently lifted out his grandmother's footstool, and lifted Ellen's legs onto it.

"It's warm in here sweetheart, let me make you comfortable where we are."

She smiled up at him as he took Dora's hand crocheted blanket and covered her lightly. He kissed her nose, then curled up in Charlie's chair, covering his legs by sliding them under Ellen's blanket, and having set his father's watch to strike, dozed alongside his new wife.

They woke about an hour and a half later, Ellen first, then Sam, who opened half-dazed eyes to see her watching him. He grinned at her.

"Well Mrs Smart. Shall we put that soup on to warm before we go to rehearsal, or will I slip back once proceedings are under control?" He took her blanket and folded it as she stretched.

"Come on trouble," he pulled her to her feet. "Time to get your face made up, you've smudged your eyes in your sleep you know. I'll get us a cuppa, then we can head over to the Hall. If we get in before everyone else you can set up the costumes as you like."

Ellen gave him a fleeting smile and fled into the bathroom, staring into the mirror in dismay. She looked like a panda. Great smudged eyes, mascara stained eyelids, whatever would anyone seeing her think? Sam tapped the door, and as she opened it, gravely handed her the wash-bag she'd put into her overnight case, and her own peach coloured towel.

"Thought you'd need these love.", he said anxiously, "Do you need your make-up or anything else. I haven't organised properly yet, I hope you can manage?"

She saw his worried face crease in a frown and laughing grabbed her bag and towel.

"Don't you worry Sam. I've managed in far worse circumstances than these. Imagine trying to keep clean in an air-raid shelter, when dust, soot and debris are liberally spread all around you. Provided you've a damp flannel, and a means of washing that out later, most women can work miracles."

Thus reassured, Sam went away and made tea.

Ellen was right about miracles, he realised two hours later as a hushed audience listened to the choir singing around the Hall. A lump came into his throat as he watched Ellen adjusting angel's wings, tilting haloes, and reassuring those stricken with stage-fright. He spotted the Indian silk drapes amongst the cloaks of the three Wise Men, noticed the elaborate treasure (largely made up from Ellen's mother's beads by Emma Fleet, and wondered if there was anything his beautiful, talented and courageous wife wouldn't turn her hand to. Briefly he regretted the impulse that had prevented him sharing the news that Mike Theobald had handed him, but perhaps it would be better to let Ellen get over the next three days of putting on the play before he broke the news that they were about to become the proud owners of a railway station!

Saturday dawned sullenly, but Ellen and Sam (waking for the first time together) could not bring themselves down to terra firma. Ellen reached for her dressing-gown and grinned at Sam as he shot out of bed, then self-consciously grabbed his trousers and shirt before running downstairs to the bathroom.

Ellen took her time descending the stairs, and had put a kettle on the range, then set about laying the breakfast table before he stuck his face round the door. He was still drying his face and had his shirt open to the waist when a discreet tap sounded at the front door.

"It's nearly seven Sam.", the new bride remarked helpfully, "Do you think that's Alex? He can't have burnt my cottage down surely?"

She sounded rather less than anxious about that prospect, so Sam simply pulled a wry face and went to answer the summons. Ellen reached for the bread-board and calmly cut two slices of bread, inserting them into a cunningly hinged wire rack. She closed the two halves, lifting it by its handle onto the hot-plate of the range, lowering the hot-plate's lid onto the contraption. A few minutes later, Sam returned to a kitchen filled with the enticing aroma of toast, a broad grin on his face.

Ellen watched him fasten his cuffs and tuck in his shirt, then poured his tea and passed him the toast-rack before he commented on their visitor.

"That was Dougie Jones love. I got word about a week back that he might have something of interest for us to look at, if you're still minded to part with Lady Jane. We can go over to this new place he's got out at Hordle if you like. At least over there no-one in Padways will notice what we're up to, until we're good and ready to go."

For a moment her hand hovered over the Marmite while she tried to grasp what he was saying, then she squeaked with excitement.

"Sam! Are you saying that he has an old ambulance for us to convert? Heavens, with all that's been going on I'd almost forgotten that idea," then she looked stricken. "We can't go for the next three days Sam. I haven't the time with the Nativity play being so important this year. Today is First Night. Tom Collier's coming over this morning to check the lighting for me. He's a Wellworthy maintenance man you know, and two of his nieces are in the play. He's volunteered his expertise, mainly because he used to do theatrical lighting for the Amateur Dramatics Group when they lived in Winchester. He's a cricket man like you apparently."

Sam stared at her, astonishment written clear on his face. He'd known the Burley wicket keeper for years and yet in one conversation, Ellen had told him more than he would ever have known about the man. His mind drifted to Silver Street, and he cautiously wondered if Tom would check over the station's wiring once it was theirs. Then Ellen reached out and caught up his hand smiling with those beguiling brown eyes of hers, and his heart thudded suddenly.

"Time to go to work my love.", she reminded him, "Don't be late home now. I've a casserole of lamb to go into the oven at three. We have only just enough time to eat before the curtain goes up, and I find out if my crew can cut it in Show Biz."

She bent forward kissing the startled porter seductively, then clapped his cap onto his head and opened the back door. Framed in the doorway, she struck a theatrical pose, declaiming mournfully in a startlingly realistic Scots accent.

"Och, ma dear one, will you no pass this way again? Am I to be abandoned to ma fate?"

Sam's face creased in appreciation as he brushed her forehead with his lips remarking dryly, "Abandoned hussy more like. See you later alligator!", and departed with a spring in his step to find his next best girl in total uproar.

Market days at Silver Street, saw the early shift start a little later, but provided twice as much chaos. In the car park farmer's vehicles (complete with trailers), transported local produce to the train for onward transmission to Ringwood. From trays of eggs, to live chickens the west bound platform heaved with vendors and their wares. The bicycle racks outside the platform were full, prospective customers clutching empty shopping bags thronged through Gerry Richard's hands, over the footbridge and queued, chattering like a human rookery. Sam, who always walked to work one day of any working weekend, smiled as he slipped in through the wicket gate, and went to check that his best man had everything he needed, but Gerry's absorbed face and cheerful nod showed him nothing amiss in that department, so he risked a peep into the main waiting room.

"Everyone ok?", he enquired cheerfully, and was greeted with a chorus from the few who gathered there.

"We're alright Sam. Just getting sorted before we go over and join the queue. Didn't expect to see you today though.", Mrs Long (mother of the paper-twins) as Tommy and Tony were known smiled cheekily, and Sam felt his face burn.

He turned from the cheerful banter, but couldn't help grinning as Steven Carter joked, "Poor lad looks exhausted ladies. If you've anything to carry perhaps I'd better help. We can't work the poor man to the bone after all he only married yesterday!"

Soon enough the loco drew in, and Sam, plus every free hand on the station set to with a will, loading bread trays, straw bales, boxes and bags ready for the weekly commotion that followed the market Special down the track. Every week this ritual repeated itself with only minor variations on the theme. Once a month livestock proliferated, overtaken by many more consumables for the other three weeks. Every duty weekend accompanied by the shrill cries of children, mother's seeking children and excitable shoppers en route to market, Sam supervised the loading of passengers and goods as the doors were closed, and the guard put his whistle to his lips.

Today was no different. As pandemonium peaked, the curious upward inflection shrilled out over the gentle chuff of the engine, echoing a little in the chill morning air, then with a staccato rattle of closing windows, the long shudder of pent-up power, and the familiar pant of the locomotive, the guard called out, " All aboard now! All aboard!"

Sam watched the train draw out with a satisfied sigh, enjoying its business like "chug" as it rounded the bend, gathering speed. He finally turned away and found Fred Cummins at his elbow.

"Your day went ok mate!", Fred stated simply. "Your missus looked absolutely smashing, and my Molly asked me to invite the pair of you over for Sunday dinner once you've got yourself sorted out like."

He shifted shyly and then said in a low voice, "You know Molly works up at Robin's Way (the old folk's place). She tells me Harvey Flaxman seems to be a little better. They had some Australian chap up there a week or so before you gave the Harvest talk, and the old boy seemed to come out of his shell a bit. He gets confused still, but he's well on the way to recovering from that breakdown of his. Molly reckons he was pushed to the end of his strength trying to make the freight line pay, he should have retired ages back."

Sam, (thinking about Alex's odd comments) said cautiously, "Well Fred, that Australian chap is trying to trace his antecedents, who seem to have come from Padways around the turn of the century. I'd like him to meet Harvey again, he's renting Ellen's cottage at the moment, but I know he intends going back to Australia at Easter next year, so we haven't long. Could Molly find out if it would upset the situation if I bring Alex up to Robin's Way over Christmas? Failing that I could ask Matron on Monday when they come to the Nativity play?"

Fred seemed uncertain but said he'd ask, then added as they drifted back to work, "You know Sam, once the lines are lifted, there's a huge amount of land round the station buildings. I know you're a grand gardener, but what are you going to do with it all? It struck me that a few animals wouldn't go amiss, and there'd be plenty of good rich Dorset soil for growing veg. Molly and I only have a little rented flat with no garden, but I've worked outdoors all my life and can't bear the thought of being cooped up inside all day. Iffen you needed a handyman, or a bit of digging done, I'd take it very kindly if you'd bear me in mind. I've still got ten years work in me, Molly won't retire for another three after that, and we're looking for anything that'll provide a bit of food on the table."

Sam felt very reluctant to speak all of a sudden. He thought about his fellow railwaymen, those he'd called friends for more years than he could remember, and dismay flooded over him as he realised he couldn't help all of them. He cleared his throat, then decided to confide in Fred.

"Look," he said urgently, "I haven't got the foggiest idea how I'm going to fund it, but my Ellen wants a small-holding. I want her to have the opportunity to try her dream out, and I think we can make something of the place. During the war years, the local girls and the boys from the airfield used to meet up at local stations and even created their own tea-rooms nearby. Of course, times have changed, there's nothing like the amount of traffic or local use now, which is why our lords and masters deem it necessary to close the line, but answer me this. It is going to be essential that some sort of transport continues to connect Ringwood to Burley, Holmsley, Silver Street and Sway. Those passengers could do with a stopping off place, a tea-room, a place to buy plants, vegetables and home-made produce. It's not guaranteed of course, but I reckon we might get some interest. Mind you!", his voice took on a severe tone.

"Ellen doesn't know I put in for Silver Street yet. It's kind of a Christmas present and I'll wring the neck of anyone who talks out of turn."

He stared into Fred's face, deliberately letting his face chill until Fred said hastily.

"Mum's the word Sam. Definitely! However, I reckon you've hit on something right enough.", his blue eyes twinkled for a moment, then he turned away, lugging a sack barrow towards the end of the platform, before pausing to call back.

"There's no point doing things by half Sam. You work on your plans and remember what your old man used to say!"

There was a sudden gust as Fred jumped down to the barrow crossing, and the line hummed unexpectedly as Sam, startled, looked down the line, half expecting to see a train, but there was nothing. He waited until Fred stood the sack-barrow against the Station House wall, then called over the track.

"What's that then Fred?" as the other porter turned, touching his hand to his cap in mock salute.

"Fortune Favours the bold my lad! Now go ye ahead, and don't forget that!"

Was it just Sam's imagination, or could he hear Charlie's voice echoing that sentiment? He stood gazing west, looking into the distance where the lines curved and disappeared from view, an odd expression on his face, absolute determination in his heart.

Ellen bore the next two days with barely concealed excitement. First Night was as any first night of performance, a mixture of wild elation, deep despair and indulgent giggles, provoked when the youngest angel fell asleep in the manger into which she'd crawled unseen.

Sam, (bursting with pride) watched a dumbfounded Miss Silversmith edged out of the conversation with the Regional Education Manager on Monday afternoon. He'd wangled a half-day for the final performance), and used his time wisely, (cornering the Matron of the Robin's Way Home for the Elderly, as she followed some of her more active residents out to their coach. He asked her permission to visit Harvey Flaxman over Christmas, but she'd seemed doubtful until he mentioned Alex Ford, which was a different matter altogether!

"Aah," she cooed happily. "They liked Mr Ford. He gave them a lot to think and talk about you know. Long after he came to tell them about his home, many of the old boys who seldom mix, started coming to coffee with the other residents. They were all sympathetic to the young man's search for his Grandfather's grave. I'm sure they'd like to know how he got on. Old Mr Godwin is a hundred years old this Christmas Eve you know, we're throwing a party for him, and so if you and your wife would care to bring Mr Ford along for tea, you might find out some more. He's very frail of course, but his memory is clear, and as he was the local farrier cum ironmonger he knew everyone in the district hereabouts. Yes, do come along Mr Smart. It'll be an occasion to remember!" She moved off after her party, leaving Sam re-stacking chairs for the evening performance.

Ellen was brimming with excitement as she joined him to close the doors.

"I think I've got a part-time job on offer.", she announced cheerfully. "Apparently Martin made a special plea to the School Governors and because we are comparatively isolated with no upper school in the village, the Area Education Office decided to look at a plan. I can teach English Language and Literature here for two days a week, then transfer to Ringwood High to teach Drama on the third. Both posts have been advertised for over a quarter with no response so now they are thinking of combining them. What do you think Sam? It would keep us going for a little bit longer, give us time to get our feet on the ground, but there will be a problem Sam, to do the two jobs as one, I'm going to need Lady Jane."

Sam picked up Ellen's basket and sewing bag as they left, catching hold of her hand in the process. They walked home, sobered by the decisions they had to make, Sam feeling his guilty knowledge weighing him down. However, all that disappeared almost as soon as they went into their cosy kitchen and prepared for tea.

Ellen's basket contained a neatly labelled pot of blackcurrant jam, half a dozen home-made scones, and a box of eggs. Sam brightened as Ellen produced the haul, then she said cheerfully, "They're from Liz Collier Sam. Tom dropped her off to gossip with Mrs Castle when he came over this morning to fix something he'd spotted on Saturday. They are really nice people, despite being involved with Burley cricket team! Tom's brother has a small-holding and his sister Joan works on it with him. They've got chickens, bantams, bees and loads of vegetable plots, but he's quite keen on going in for this idea of "Pick your own", possibly concentrating on soft fruit. They started a little shop last year and already he's thinking of doubling it the response has been so good. Now, do you want one egg or two with your tea?"

Sam gazed at the enormous brown egg she was offering, then said faintly, "Oh, only one I think love.", as he began to realise that he had nothing to feel guilty about. It seemed that the idea of a small-holding worked for others too. Undoubtedly there were problems to solve, they might run into difficulties from time to time, but nothing was impossible. If Tom Collier could hold down a full time job and take on private work as well, he could do better than mourn the loss of his job. Silver Street wasn't dead or even dying. The old station was simply emerging from a chrysalis and becoming a full grown butterfly.

"Yes," he thought joyfully, "This isn't the end of my life as it was! It's the beginning of an adventure. Dad said "Fortune favours the bold", and look how far I've come in ten weeks. I've made new friends, got married and if Alex can travel half-way round the world looking for something he may never find, then I can certainly face up to more local issues. I had one chance and took it, now what's wrong with that?"

He reached out and hugged his startled wife as she put his egg cup in front of him. She giggled in mild protest.

"Now Sam don't you start getting ideas! We've got twenty minutes to have tea in, then I've got to put a stitch in a robe which is a little long for my third shepherd, then we're off for the last time. Today's been particularly tiring, but once tomorrow's over and everything has been cleared away we can talk about our own dreams. Just fancy, it's only a week until Christmas and I've got no shopping done at all!"

By Christmas Eve, Ellen had taken herself off to shop so often that Sam despaired. He heard muffled giggles as Jane and Ellen wrapped parcels for the forthcoming festivities, ducked through unexplained garlands adorning his bathroom, and commiserated with Alex as they and Martin Short were evicted from hearth and home, so that the necessary decorating could be completed. They had made for the Church, Martin ostensibly to check on the vestry preparations. However, Alex had paused looking at the memorial plaques, so they joined him, commiserating over the singular lack of Fords named on the memorials, Martin watching curiously as the young man lingered below a brilliantly back-lit stained glass window. It depicted a man, woman and child knocking on the doors of Heaven, with attendant angels hovering around as Saint Peter conferred with the recording angel. The tall Australian looked up at the window for a long time, then asked curiously, "What's the story behind this then Vicar?"

"I'm afraid that's before my time Alex," Martin smiled, he had a fondness for the window himself, and was intrigued by the visitor's interest.

"I believe that before the Second World War there was a brass plate explaining the story, but when that end of the Church took a direct hit in 1943, most of the original window, certainly the brass and a great many pews, not to mention the roof and other masonry were completely destroyed. It was some time before any repairs could be made, we had neither the money nor the man-power until the end of the war. Then it turned out that the Church commissioners had lost a vast number of records during the Blitz and so we had very little to go on. Villagers helped out with photographs, we had kept residual glass so that it could be matched and we were extremely fortunate that we received a grant from the Fullingford Trust (who represent substantial local landowners), or we might never have been able to repair the glass. Now, if you'll forgive me, I must go and check the choir's laundry has been done. What with carols at Robin's Way tonight, followed by midnight Mass, then all the services tomorrow I've a lot to get on with."

He left Sam and Alex and disappeared in the direction of the vestry. Alex pulled a rueful face.

"He's got a hard routine. It never occurred to me how hard until last night when I was taking a turn round the village late, and saw him coming down the hill from that nice old cottage with the creeper growing on it. He looked absolutely devastated. I've never seen a face that bleak, so I invited him in for a cuppa, and he jumped at the opportunity. Seems like the couple up there lost their new baby to this cot-death syndrome last night, and poor old Martin had been out to comfort them. Apparently the child was kind of frail having been born early, but for it to happen at Christmas must make people wonder about the nature of their faith. How that bloke stands by for every tragedy there is and maintains his own belief I don't know!"

Sam unaccountably thought back to September and how Martin had supported him through the shock of sudden redundancy, and nodded solemnly.

"Yes, he's a good friend, a marvellous Vicar and an example to us all," he had just had a wonderful idea. "Hang on there Alex," he spoke urgently, "Perhaps I can cheer him up."

He turned and went to the vestry door and tapped cautiously. After a moment Martin's puzzled face appeared, and Sam went in to join him.

"I wondered if you'd like some news Vicar?" he asked diplomatically, adding the rider. "Ellen won't know till after Christmas but as this might concern you, I thought I'd tell you now."

He paused for a second (as though steeling himself for an adverse reaction), then said in a rush, "They've sold Silver Street Station you know. Seems as though they couldn't wait to settle the matter, but let it go to the first bidder."

Martin's face was a picture. His cheek's flushed, he bit his lip, and then he turned a sympathetic eye on Sam.

"My dear boy!", he exclaimed in dismay. "No doubt one of these wretched developers? It'll bring mayhem if they throw up some modern estate so close to Padways. The roads can't take it, we're already stretched to the very limit with school-places, we've only a part-time surgery, no shops or employment…", he rubbed his face wearily as Sam grinned at him.

"Martin, stop it. I only meant to bring you good news, not a heart-attack my friend," he said as the Vicar looked at him in bewilderment. "I have it on very good authority that the station has gone to someone who is sympathetic to the village, wants none of this development business, and who intends to put the land to good use."

"Oh?", said the Vicar disbelievingly, "and where is this paragon of virtue Sam. Will we be consulted in any way before the development starts, and who will get employment out of it exactly?"

Sam took a deep breath. "Everything will be put to the relevant authorities before anything happens to Silver Street believe me. The Parish Council will be invited to inspect every inch as the land is cleared, and to begin with there'll be jobs for all ex-railway staff that fit the bill."

Martin stared at Sam, who seemed to the Vicar to have grown taller in the last five minutes.

"But Sam," he protested vigorously, "You have to tell me who's bought the place, you know don't you? For goodness sake man, put me out of my misery!"

Sam grinned, reached into his pocket and withdrew the precious letter he planned to share with Ellen later. He opened it carefully, then handed it to Martin with a wry expression on his face.

"I may come to regret it, but you're looking at the new owner of Silver Street Martin. Nobody else seemed to want her, and I'm planning on making her pay her way by opening a small-holding at least. There's a lot more in the works, but I thought that Christmas might be rather wearing this year, so I came to cheer you up."

Slowly Martin's eyes ran down Sam's letter of acceptance, then he straightened, took a step back and raised a hand.

"God Bless you in this endeavour Sam," said his smiling friend, and his shoulders lifted as he said solemnly,

"I won't say a word to anyone until you're ready my friend, but that's the best news I've heard for months."

Greatly reassured, Sam withdrew, leaving Martin setting out hymn numbers on a wooden board. He was humming "Silent Night" placidly, caught up in planning the annual outpouring of faith from his flock, his own never more certain.

They left the church still sobered by the news from Daiken's Cottage. Sam (without realising the effect on his companion) spoke harshly.

"Alex, I don't want you saying anything about that child's death, do you hear me? Ellen isn't to know until it becomes inevitable. I don't want her hurt just when life is beginning to turn round for her. Nor are you to let the Silver Street cat out of the bag! I decided not to tell her until we've settled this Harvey Flaxman thing. She's superstitious, frightened of things she can't control I suppose, and I can always sell it on if she hates the idea! I'll go and get her shall I? We decided to walk up and come home with the Carol Singers afterwards. We can go to midnight Mass, then have a lie in tomorrow. We've a spare bed, so you're welcome to stop over. Go on, give Howard the day off man, or did you intend eating at Burley Manor?"

The young Australian grinned.

"Too right I hadn't!", he said ungrammatically, "but crikey mate, you two only just got married. You don't want a bloomin' gooseberry around.", but he was eventually persuaded to slip back to Ellen's cottage (where Howard awaited him), to get some "gear" together, (as he put it).

Sam walked up the steep path to Church Cottage, sighing as he surveyed the winter-dressed flower beds whilst considering the sale of the only home he'd ever known regretfully. Squaring his shoulders, he tip-toed into the sitting-room, and paused, amazed to find it richly dressed with decorations, packages laid beneath a small spruce tree in a bright red tub. Ellen, (dressed in all her wedding finery) glowed with excitement as she stood before the tree, a glittering silver star in one hand. His heart leapt into his throat as she turned and smiled up at him expectantly.

"What do you think Sam?", she demanded handing him the star to top out the tree.

"Isn't it pretty? I love Christmas, it really cheers me up when everything is so dark and gloomy!"

As delicious in cream and gold as any Christmas tree fairy, she nestled against him, and he caught his breath, hardly daring to believe his luck as he found himself praying that his own present wouldn't go amiss.

He positioned the star dutifully, then went hastily to put on his suit, approving of Ellen's plan to let the residents they knew share a little of their wedding, returning to help pack boxes of wedding cake into a basket.

They had only just completed this task when Alex returned, gleefully sliding into what had been Sam's bedroom, carrying all sorts of parcels. He was absent for only a moment, then came downstairs complete to a touch in bush hat and jacket, joining them in the sitting-room.

The brass Benares bowls gleamed against the flickering firelight, the fairy lights twinkled on the tree, even the Poinsettias glowed jewel bright from the table where Sam had placed them after lighting the fire. Alex placed two bright red packages on the Chesterfield, accepted the small sherry glass that Ellen handed him, and toasted his hosts gravely.

"Here's to you and your future my friends, here's to me and my search, and here's to Christmas."

Ellen dimpled as Alex insisted they open at least one present before going out into the cold December night. He was suitably delighted with the hat and gloves that Ellen gave him, then stood grinning as Sam undid a wonderful sheepskin coat.

He remembered touching one wistfully during their shopping trip to New Milton, and flushed guiltily as Ellen liberated its partner from her parcel. She swung it over her wool suit, and luxuriated in its warmth, as Alex assisted Sam into his.

"Well chaps, best bib and tucker on, now let's go see the elders and sing some carols.", the tall Australian laughed, "Although I must say I'd rather swap bush clothes for what I was wearing last Christmas Eve, and get a bit of sunshine to go with it."

He caught sight of Sam's puzzled face and said cheerfully, "I know you can't picture it mate, but last Christmas I was with a crowd of folk from University, and we spent all day on the beach. Australia being in the southern hemisphere gets December during our summer. It's hot, dry and sunny so most families have picnics, beach parties or barbeques. I spent Christmas Eve in swimming trunks and a towel!" He laughed as Sam shuddered at the idea, clapped him on the shoulder and said cheekily,

"Mind you Sam, it's a good way to get the girls!"

He turned away, studying the sky as Sam and Ellen picked up torches and collected their baskets, keeping a weather eye on the clouds gathering as daylight faded. Ellen told Sam softly, "He's looking out for snow. It's comical really, and he wouldn't enjoy it if it happened, but he's only seen snow in the mountains, or from the plane. I think traditional Christmas cards give an entirely unrealistic image of our weather, but I hope it doesn't rain!"

In the end Howard ran them up to Robin's Way, meeting them half-way down the village with the reminder that they had to pick up the jam from Emma Fleet's before they departed. This being accomplished swiftly, they were soon swooping through the twilight, passing Pine Trees, a darkened bulk against the trees from which it got its name as they drove out of Padways. The chauffeur cleared his throat suddenly at this point, and Alex looking up said instantly, "Something up Howard?", as the man said deferentially,

"Not really sir, just something occurred to me as we came past that odd narrowing as we leave the village."

Three pairs of eyes swivelled in his direction as the chauffeur continued.

"I have been privileged sir, to drive Lord Montague from time to time. He has a great estate at Beaulieu, with high walls and lodge gates. Although well out of Beaulieu's period, I notice the remnants of a high wall where the road narrows, and something in the set of that wall makes me wonder if there was in fact a lodge there once. The natural sweep of the road brings the car close to the school building, but if I was building a public road between the village and the main road, I could make it shorter and a lot cheaper by taking it to the left of that farm we passed back there, rather than bringing it past the school."

Under their combined stares of interest, Howard's neck turned quite pink. "It's just an observation sirs and madam, but I wondered if that school wasn't once quite a grand house. It goes back a long way and the walls that enclose it are certainly an earlier addition. At the moment we are in what might have been planted as an avenue approach which has been named Robin's Way, from which the Home for the Elderly takes its name. It occurs to me that some of the history of the place might be approached by finding out about that name. Of course it might be the choice of the local Council, but it might be an interesting line for Mr Ford to pursue."

They were still taking that in when the car slowed as they approached a junction. Howard continued smoothly, "At the cross-roads ahead, we'll turn right, through another walled area, and into the courtyard fronting the Home for the Elderly. However, it's my contention that it may once have been the stable-yard to the Manor from which they've created that school?"

They all looked at the high wall running down the right hand side of the road. It apparently followed their course until Howard indicated and turned the Bentley to the right. They purred in through open gates, and came to a halt in a courtyard car park, as Alex let out a hiss of surprise.

"Well, I'll be jiggered!", he exclaimed, glancing at Sam. "I wonder if you're not on to something Howard. We'll certainly have to look into it.

Now, we are here until the Carol Singers collect us. You on the other hand can take the rest of the day off. I shan't need you tomorrow either so it's up to you to have a good Christmas. Got plans?"

The chauffeur's face creased in a smile as he said happily, "Well sir, I have family in Christchurch whom I haven't seen for months. I bumped into them the other day and they gave me to understand I'd be welcomed over there. I have their telephone number here sir, the car will be at your disposal day or night if you care to call."

He held the door for Alex, came round to assist Sam and Ellen, then opened the boot and produced a large box carefully wrapped in Christmas paper. He saw them into reception where Molly Cummins was waiting to greet them, then carried the precious cargo through into a lounge positively hopping with excited residents as the birthday party began.

It took only the appearance of Alex in his bush-hat to attract a phalanx of elderly ladies, and soon the rangy Australian was surrounded by earnest enquiries. Sam and Ellen found Harvey Flaxman and settled down to gossip about their wedding. Sam was suitably impressed however when the clink and rattle of tea-cups approaching on a trolley created some sense out of chaos. Very quietly three enormous doors had been folded back to reveal a buffet table laden with food, at the head of which was a giant birthday cake, crammed with candles.

"Wow," Alex exclaimed, to the delight of his flock of followers. "Who's the lucky chap who gets to eat all that by himself?"

"Now then young man!", Molly Cummins chided him gently. "Matron and I have enough to do without you leaving us to pump someone's stomach out. The cake is for Mr Godwin, he'll be along in a minute. He's just collecting something he wants to show us."

Sam smiled as Harvey spoke up.

"Ollie Godwin's an interesting chap Sam. He knows more about this area than most. If you want to know anything about horses, shoeing, running a forge or the like, he's your man."

Sam eyed the sprightly little figure that was being ushered to the guest of honour's place. He didn't look anything like Sam had imagined, and for a moment he was doubtful, but soon conversation drifted in the right direction and he leant forward listening as the centenarian chuckled with pleasure and a telegram was revealed.

"That's from the Queen you know," the dry voice rustled, "Fancy that. Old Ollie Godwin got a telegram from the Queen herself!"

The old man seemed highly taken with that idea, then remarked apropos of nothing in particular.

"I met plenty of Royalty in my time. Coming and going they were, sometimes shooting, sometimes taking the air," his voice lowered dramatically, "sometimes up to no good at all. They came and went you know, that Lily Langtry and all. I did pick them up in the old Squires carriage from time to time. Aye, I see'd the foreign blighter too. Him what came to Highcliffe Castle for talks. He went in a car of course but his servants came along o' my dog-cart."

Sam was fascinated, and listened entranced as the old voice reminisced, then he found Ollie Godwin's bird-bright eyes fixed on his.

"I were born here on Padways Manor you know lad. My pa taught me all about horses. I got up winter mornings to break the ice in the troughs, fetch the feed and then start the furnace in the forge. Man and boy I've worked this yard, and now I'll end my days here too! Now wasn't that well-arranged? One hundred years, born here, worked here, breeched three boys here, and soon I'll be buried here too!"

His voice died away as he nodded to himself, and Sam straightened up, feeling the past brush him as Alex whispered in an awed voice.

"Jeepers that's awesome. He must be able to remember Queen Victoria. He's been around since 1860 Sam. Do you think there's a hope in hell that he'd remember my family? Obviously this is not the time to ask him, the local press want to take a shot of the old boy blowing out the candles on his cake, and he's already tired, but I could ask Matron later when the fuss has died down."

Sam shifted to let Alex sit between him and Ellen who was actively engaged in talking to Jeff Stubbins, the local reporter who was edging his way round to talk to Ollie if the occasion presented itself. He watched as a sturdy red-haired man (festooned with cameras wriggled into the gap, and heard Alex offer to dim the lights for the all-important shot. His mind drifted over the past century. Ollie must have been leading the carriage-horses round to hitch them up when cameras were the latest novelty. He studied Alex, who'd shrugged off his coat and hat, and slid over towards the light-switch, consciously aware that Ollie Godwin had his head on one side, eyes fixed on Alex as if considering some idea.

The moment passed of course, as with a flourish the Matron started to light the cake candles. The residents listening to her soft voice counting soon joined in, and Jeff scribbled his impressions as the chorus chanted the last ten candles, bursting into spontaneous applause as they quivered and flickered beneath dimming lights.

Sam, sitting with an unaccountable lump in his throat, suddenly became aware that Ollie was staring up at Alex, whose face (under-lit by candle-light was in a sort of dusky relief against the wall where he had just operated the light switches. Ollie's lips moved (cautiously as though trying out an idea once or twice to make sure), then the ancient voice proclaimed.

"No…Ford's not right! I'd know your face anywhere boy, I see'd that face every day of my life until he went. You can't live a hundred years without knowing whose face you bear. You're no kind of Ford lad. You're the Fullingford boy returned!"

Chapter 20 - Slow Trains and Planting Platforms

They kept their counsel until the carol singers had performed, and Ellen was forced to borrow Sam's handkerchief to blot away the tears that sprang spontaneously as the quavering but true voices of the residents echoed the choir. Even Ollie Godwin joined in with God Rest Ye Merry Gentlemen, but his old eyes lingered on Alex, and he whispered urgently to Molly as she steered him off to bed.

"Now do be a good girl Sister, ask that boy to come back and see me, and tell him not to take too long about it. There's something I want to tell him privately."

Molly relayed the message as they left to walk back to Padways, but sadly the planned meeting was not to take place. A solemn voiced Vicar announced the passing of the oldest and youngest members of his congregation at Evensong the following day.

Ellen wept bitterly over the baby, but Alex persuaded Sam to let her curl up in bed and have her grief, his own face sombre as the porter joined him by the range.

"I'll brew up mate," the young Australian said shakily, "I need to do something with my hands. It's so bloody unfair. That baby didn't get a chance at life, the poor old boy only needed a little longer and he might have halved my problems. Now he's gone, all those fabulous memories with him, and I'll have to start over if he was right, but was he? It's crook Sam, I don't know where to begin or what name to search for.", he dragged the kettle onto the hotplate as Sam put out three striped mugs on the table and thought about the problem.

He leant his elbows on the table, folding his hands under his chin and surveyed his guest, a remote idea forming as he spoke hesitantly.

"I wonder…", he cleared his throat self-consciously as the kettle came to the boil and Alex leapt into action. "I wonder! Suppose for a moment he's right and you are related in some way to this "Fullingford boy" he mentioned. There's a possibility that Parish or County Records offices have some mention of the name. It's a long shot, but we might find a trace of that name in regimental archives. Ollie said he'd seen your face every day as he grew up. Now that could indicate someone else who worked in the stable-yard, maybe a man who'd seen military service. There was plenty of that about when we had an Empire, and you already know that your grandfather died in 1917 just after your Dad was born. Have you got, or can you get a copy of your Dad's birth certificate by any chance. If it's a full one it could have your grandfather's profession on it which might also help. This isn't the end of the line Alex, I'm going to be free to help do more research now I don't have that wretched talk hanging over my head. Ellen is a whiz at knowing who to ask about stuff like this and remember, the search can go on even when you have to go back to Australia. I'll be unemployed soon enough, Silver Street can go on the back-burner for a while, and you need my help!"

There was a slight sound at the door as Ellen came in wrapped in her dressing gown, and Sam swivelling round met bewildered eyes.

"Don't mind me, carry on chatting.", she invited, "I just came down to wash my face. Sorry about the miseries…", her voice drifted away as she went through to the bathroom. Alex gulped and whispered covertly,

"Hell's Bells Sam. You haven't told her yet have you?", busying himself with the tea-pot.

It was Boxing Day before Sam got up the courage to spill the beans. They decided not to "do" Christmas presents in the light of their news, but to prepare a mysterious meal Alex called Christmas Stew. Claiming that this had been handed down from his grandfather's days, he set about chopping vegetables, carving meat, and chuckling over Ellen's spice cabinet.

Gradually an enticing aroma filtered through the cottage, until Sam and Ellen (who'd been banished to the sitting-room to relax), could bear it no longer. They crept in to the kitchen as Alex placed a steaming casserole on a rope mat and lifted the lid. "Ham, chicken, diced carrots, potatoes, parsnips, cabbage, cauliflower and runner beans bubbled merrily in a broth which seemed to indicate the use of mushrooms as well as a plethora of tinned stuff that Sam didn't recognise.

"There," announced their practical guest proudly. "Christmas Stew, all the left-over's, loads of variety in whatever's available, served with spuds or rice or pasta. Eat as is on Boxing Day and save mother cooking, have it curried for supper or lunch the day after, and garnish with salad if you fancy a change. Every year the same meal, every year a different taste. If that ain't psychedelic enough I don't know what is!"

They drew up their chairs and watched in awe as Alex ladled the meal into bowls, cut great slabs of bread then devoted himself to tackling the concoction.

"That was delicious!", Ellen spoke for both of them as Sam sighed with contentment and stretched back in his seat, murmuring "Wow!", to himself as much as anyone else.

They drank coffee, hot from Charlie's old percolator then stacked their dishes in the sink to soak.

Alex peered out of the window hopefully, but there was no sign of snow, so he turned back suggesting that they should walk off their meal without further ado.

Ellen had a strange look on her face, but agreed easily enough and went upstairs to fetch her coat. Alex pinned Sam with a meaningful look and hissed urgently.

"Now's your chance mate! You've got to tell her sometime and sooner rather than when she finds out by chance. Act your age Sam. It's not a secret that's safe anymore. Just the minute Southern Rail decide to publish any of the detail you'll be dropped in it anyway. Have the courage of your convictions man, and go get your coat. She's coming back!"

In the end they walked up to Robin's Way and left their condolences, writing short messages in the Book of Remembrance that the Matron had opened. That done, they went back to the road and (one eye on the weather), walked through the path that led up to Silver Street. They stood on the road-bridge overlooking the empty platforms (much from the same position as John Oswald had on the night of Sam's talk), and looked west, following the line that Sam's father had driven, with their eyes tracing the line of the forest as it enclosed Silver Street.

Ellen's voice sounded small as she asked softly, "What will become of her Sam?"

She had given him the opening, but again Sam declined the offer, side-stepping the issue neatly as he described the plans for the final passenger departure.

"I've no doubt that there'll be a contingent following all the way to the railhead at Brockenhurst."

He turned, leaning his back against the railing and staring eastward up the line towards London.

"Dr Ruddy Beeching won't know or care about all the grief and trouble this'll bring in its wake.", he said morosely. "There'll be hell to pay. The scooter boys are bound to tag along, we know the bikers aren't amused, and even old Oswald has plans afoot to counteract vandalism."

"Then what?", Ellen demanded. "Is the station simply going to be absorbed back into the forest again? Are they going to demolish it, break up the platforms, and drag out the rails?"

"Now, now!", Alex's eyes screamed at him silently. "Tell her now!", and Sam turned and caught her hand up in his.

"What would you say if I told you that someone wants to turn this into the most fabulous smallholding you ever saw?", he asked gently, with relief noting Alex slipping away into the shadows gathering under the trees. Slowly Ellen nestled against him, her gold head resting on his shoulder.

"I was just imagining ducks waddling down the platform," she said indulgently, pointing to the end where the trolley crossing hugged the west-bound lines. "I can't imagine it without rails but with the track as a path, I could have a couple of goats grazing up there, perhaps a vegetable plot and a hen-house, and we could grow mushrooms in the signal box.", she sighed soulfully. "However, there's nothing doing Mr Smart. We simply haven't got the sort of money that kind of project takes, but it was a nice dream Sam, a wonderful dream."

Perhaps she sensed him withdrawing from her, girding himself up for the inevitable disappointment as her practical voice continued, muffled now against his collar.

"You know I'm right Sam. Dreams are for dreamers who can afford such luxuries. Reality is a hard task-master but we're better off helping Alex set enquiries afoot, than wasting what we've got. What can't be cured, must be endured as Mother used to say. My dear man, there's no future in slow trains or planting platforms, we couldn't even afford to rent the land let alone buy it!"

Silently Sam drew back, taking the Southern Railways envelope out of his pocket. He forced himself to be calm (feeling the prick of disappointed tears) as Ellen started to read the letter. He watched her mouth as she bit her lower lip, then heard her whisper painfully.

"Darling? How on God's sweet earth did you finance this? Sam Smart! I knew you had a bee in your bonnet, now we've room for hives, honey-making, a shop, a tea-room, main crops, special crops, glass-houses, goats, pigs...", he caught her in his arms as she burst into excited tears, kissing her up-turned face tenderly.

"Never mind my dear one," he murmured gallantly, "Just remember that the parcel's room has already been measured up for the chickens, and we'll be alright!"

She was chuckling when Alex re-joined them, and noting the questioning lift of an eyebrow, she remarked tartly.

"I might have known you two were in cahoots. How much are we indebted to Alex, Samuel Smart?, she demanded, then was suitably astonished when Sam showed her his receipt for payment made.

"It's no wonder that the Government can't make ends meet if they're prepared to let railway property go for such ridiculous prices.", she exclaimed, before adding more thoughtfully, "There's bound to be a catch in it somewhere."

Alex (walking on the other side of Ellen) nodded cautiously, then spoke up in Sam's defence.

"Yes, of course there's a catch Ellen. The railways have become so run-down that a lot of the buildings are beyond any form of maintenance. The Government couldn't afford to invest in new building, and Silver Street is older than Ollie Godwin was for Heaven's sake. I gathered from Sam that your old buildings come under special protection in some cases, can't be altered or adapted without all the expense of using original materials and building methods. However, that's not all, is it Sam?"

Sam groaned as he felt Ellen pause in mid-stride.

"Thanks mate!", he growled softly, internally, but to Ellen he said cheerfully, "Of course there's a lot to put right. The electrics have to be checked and replaced where necessary. There's no running water even to the Station House, which hasn't actually been lived in for years. General maintenance isn't a problem, I can do that myself, but roofing's a speciality trade and that does need attention. It'll be a long term project love, Rome wasn't built in a day, but we've got the potential rent of two cottages to fall back on. I've got two allotments to plant on which we can survive, and if we keep Lady Jane, you'll be able to make ends meet."

For answer she hugged him impulsively, then stiffened and almost shouted her next words.

"Sam! The moment you mentioned two rents to fall back on, I realised where we know the name Ollie put to Alex. He said Alex was "the Fullingford boy returned", didn't he? What about the Fullingford Trust? I know it has offices in Bournemouth, Winchester, and probably all over the south, perhaps we can enquire there about the background to the name. It's worth a try isn't it?", and with that comment she walked briskly down the hill to Padways, ignoring the greying sky until Alex gave a whoop of delight as a few white specks whirled out of the late afternoon sky and touched his face icily.

"Sam, Ellen…" he capered exuberantly, "It's snowing, look at the Hay Rack's sign!" They paused under the light illuminating their local inn and watched the snow pouring out of a leaden sky.

"Marvellous…"said their friend in deep satisfaction. "A clean white page for the New Year. I so wanted it to snow too, it feels right somehow. Strange, different to home, but right in this setting."

So it was, that Alex had the last word as Christmas 1963 ended and an era of rail travel drew inexorably to its close.

The New Year dawned with terrifying speed. Sam found himself working all hours as he started planting seed trays in Ellen's cold frame, broke the soil on his allotment and turned his compost heap. The snow had come and gone, leaving muddy puddles in its wake, and after ten days of enforced idleness, Alex took himself off to London, saying that he needed to contact the trustees that were sponsoring his trip, and pay a call on Australia House. He hadn't been gone more than three days when Ellen and Sam had their first row.

It wasn't over anything much, just that Sam noticed that Ellen was looking rather tired and decided to intervene in what had become a never -ending ritual of late night studying.

She was deeply engrossed when he took her book away, flipping it neatly over, and asking cheekily, "What's a chap got to do around here to get some attention Missus?"

He hadn't been prepared for her to snap at him nor was he sure of what escalated the argument, but suddenly she was sobbing, furiously collecting her note-books and reference materials and storming off into the sitting-room.

He waited for a while, then put the kettle on and made tea for both of them, wondering what he'd done to provoke this. He thought about the lectures Charlie had given him about "giving girls a bit of room" every now and then, and decided that this must be one of those times. However, tapping on the sitting-room door only produced the muffled instruction to, "Go away Sam."

He went back to the kitchen, drank his tea moodily, then went up to his den and started to sort through a box file of railway memorabilia that had recently come into his hands. He heard Ellen go into the kitchen, then out to their bathroom, and idly wondered if he should get a plumber to look at the cottage with a view to moving the bathroom upstairs, then he heard Ellen's low voice.

"Sam? I'm sorry I got mad at you. I'm going to pop over to Jane's for a while. It's not your fault love. I'm just fed-up and disappointed."

Sam leapt to his feet (spilling several things in the process) as he clattered downstairs and caught his wife's hand.

"Disappointed darling? What's happened to disappoint you Ellen, you've only got to tell me and I'll do anything to put it right!"

She leant her head against his chest and whispered shakily, "Silly boy. There's nothing you can do, it's just that there won't be a baby this month, I haven't heard anything about that job, and this came today." She sniffed inelegantly, put her hand into her pocket and withdrew a crumpled envelope. Sam looked at her wan face and decided to draw her out of the chilly hall and take this into the kitchen before they went any further.

He persuaded Ellen to let him lift her onto a stool, put the kettle on with one hand, and tip her chin up with the other, so that their faces were level. He adopted a stern face and said meaningfully.

"One, it isn't very smart to fight when one side doesn't know what's wrong! Two, it isn't very smart to fall out, if the matter doesn't warrant us falling out. Three, it won't be very smart for us to fall out right now because you've got a tenant and nowhere to go to and I've got to get this place up together so I can sell it. What's more, if we fall out there's no chance of babies, this or any other month. Now repeat after me. If it ain't smart, Smart's don't do it!"

Hearing Charlie Smart's family motto for the first time, Ellen didn't know whether to laugh or cry, so she did both while Sam made the tea. He brought hers over and leant against the worktop as Ellen mopped her eyes and waggled the envelope at him.

"What is it love?", he asked her gently, and she bit her lip, then invited him to open it for himself.

Puzzled, he did so, noting the name of a well-known publisher as the headed notepaper unfolded. He read slowly, running the words through his mind without really taking in the meaning and looked up into Ellen's clouded face.

"It's a rejection slip.", she said perfunctorily. "They've looked at my manuscript and "It doesn't fit their current needs". I bet they never even read it!"

Sam was astonished. He had no idea that Ellen harboured dreams of writing a book, however, she had suggested that he might, so she knew something about the process. He cleared his throat and found his voice, but what could he say to someone whose hopes had just been dashed so cruelly?

"I still love you sweetheart.", he managed weakly, and thankfully Ellen's sense of humour was touched.

"I didn't want them to love me Sam. I just wanted them to publish my work, but I think the subject is quite specialised, so the appeal might be too limited. So, I've just got to pick myself up, dust myself down and start all over again!"

He was relieved as she sang the well-known line, and decided to add his own comments.

"So long as that applies to making babies too!", he ducked laughing as she threw a tea-towel at him, escaping upstairs to pick up the spillage he'd ignored earlier. Having restored a bunch of photographs to the box file he'd scattered, Sam spotted Charlie's tin-lid upside down under his desk. He groaned and crouched retrieving the conglomeration of ephemera into the tin again, thrupenny bits, springs, screws, keys and old tickets were shovelled in willy-nilly as Ellen called up to him.

"Sam love, it's too late to bother Jane now, and I've got to fetch my stuff from the school tomorrow. I'm going to lock up and go to bed if you don't mind, I think we could both do with a reasonable bed-time don't you?"

Peering blankly at Charlie's keys, Sam realised he was too tired to pursue the stray thought that had crossed his mind, and let it go before reaching down a technical manual with which to bore himself to sleep.

He followed Ellen's example, slipping into bed beside her before asking curiously, "What are you writing about love? I caught the fact that you'd offered the book to an arts and crafts outlet, but I thought your interest was mainly historical?"

She answered him gruffly, her voice muffled beneath their eiderdown, which she had lovingly quilted herself.

"I'm interested in looking at the development of soft toys.", she mumbled, then turned guiltily to face him, busying herself in plumping up pillows and retrieving the soft toy elephant that she customarily left on the floor.

Sam propped his book on his chest and said quietly, "Go on!", hoping to encourage her, but it seemed to have the opposite effect.

"That's it really!", she snuggled the elephant under her chin, and Sam suddenly saw her "inner child". He grinned at her sleepy face, then said encouragingly,

"Well...I don't suppose these lasses in short skirts want to stitch or knit toy elephants any more. They'd prefer to buy the new baby a toy that's washable, brightly coloured and available from all good High Street chain stores like Woollies!" He parodied the ATV advertisements wickedly, then said slowly.

"Don't they have toy manufacturer's Fairs love? Something like those Ideal Home Exhibitions they hold at Olympia? I still get free travel for a few more months, so why don't you find out? I can get you a ticket, only it occurs to me that books like the one you're considering are often sold at events like that. Train enthusiasts buy books on all sorts of obscure subjects, and they are sold at museums, steam Fairs, county turn-outs etc."

He turned his head on his pillow, studying her limpid gaze as her brown eyes flickered and closed dreamily.

"Night-night sweetheart.", he murmured, switching out his bedside light, "We'll sort it out in the morning.", said Sam drowsily, as Ellen curled protectively around her childhood companion, one-eared, one-eyed and yet an elephant for all occasions.

January slipped past with all the attendant troubles of winter. Passengers grumbled incessantly about the cold, John Oswald came and went to 'important meetings, and Sam had to draw on every scrap of Charlie's perpetual reminder to stop himself losing his temper at the smallest provocation, (of which there seemed to be all too many).

About half-way through February, he noticed that things were going missing far too often for it to be a coincidence, and decided to talk to the crew himself before raising the matter with the temporary Station Master. He started with Fred Cummins who (slowly transferring a toffee from one side of his mouth to the other) nodded shortly.

"Yes," the older man agreed readily, "I told Awkward 'Arry about that last week when my fire-bucket disappeared."

He jerked a derisive thumb back down the platform to where John Oswald was winding up the station clock. Sam frowned and asked quickly, "Didn't he do anything Fred? Other than get you a new fire-bucket I mean. He certainly didn't ask if I'd seen it, there's no missing items listed in the book, and I'm a trolley short."

They watched John Oswald check the station clock against the prestigious silver fob watch he customarily sported, then as the man adjusted the minute hand a fraction, a curiously proprietorial look crossed his face as he closed the glass and patted the top of the Station clock. The two porters looked at each other warily.

"Do you think...?", Fred started to ask, a speculative look on his face, at which Sam said abruptly,

"Not out loud if I want to keep my job," as he noticed the Station Master's glance falling on them.

"Tell you what Fred," Sam continued smoothly, "We all know Harvey's drill for getting senior advice without letting the public know there's anything wrong. Let's put that to work while I check something out. I'm over t'other side iffen you need me, conducting a stock-check of my own. Get word back to Gerry and cover for me by delaying anyone coming over the footbridge. Gerry will advise Ringwood at tea-break if my suspicions are correct."

He ran up over the foot-bridge and went to the parcel's office, engaging young Trevor Steadman's attention as soon as he arrived.

"Now then Trevor, I've got a particular favour to ask.", he said (with a subtle jerk of his head towards the opposite platform. "In a few minutes Gerry Richards will step out of the ticket office as he goes to the gent's.

He'll give you a thumbs up or down as he does so, which is where you come in.", he grinned infectiously as the young man nodded uncertainly.

"It's very important that we carry out a check on everything that belongs to the station without causing Mr Oswald any more headaches.", he said diplomatically (not knowing young Steadman's allegiances), "So, rather than bother him at the moment, the troops are going to do it themselves. Gerry is just going to cover our backs in the usual way by advising Mike."

He needn't have worried. Trevor's eyes gleamed maliciously as he murmured (out of the corner of his mouth in an admirable mid-Translantic accent).

"Ok. I get you 007. The CIA are happy to mind your back."

Sam chuckled, picked up a broom and thoughtfully went out to sweep his platform and litter-pick the verge where the bus stopped.

Gradually, he worked his way out into the station yard, an anonymous figure carrying cleaning equipment from place to place. He spent less than five minutes in the large store shed where deliveries of consumables were made to the station. Here, (he reckoned grimly) there should have been cleaning materials for about six months, but he could only find three cases of light bulbs, an open drum of commercial cleanser for the wash-room, and a few broom handles. He hissed in disgust, made a note in his pocket book, and then carefully locked the evidence in place, using a spare padlock (to which only he had a key).

Moving back into the yard, he walked purposefully over to the bicycle store, which had at one end a locker containing emergency equipment. He opened the door and gaped paling. Where there should have been hammers, axes, crow-bars and every manner of equipment to rescue passengers from a disaster, there were only hooks and clamps which had once secured them in place.

Sam felt light-headed as the wash of righteous rage shook him. Forcing himself to breathe,(and to look anywhere but at the pompous form) as Oswald paraded out onto the up-line platform, he evaluated the situation clinically. It didn't matter that he was personally sick with loathing and fearful of the consequences of this spur-of-the-moment search, he had to do his duty, regardless. Straightening his shoulders, he took his locker padlock out of his pocket, re-securing the emergency store after taking a reading from Charlie's watch and noting the time in his pocket book. Then, careful not to draw attention to himself, he slipped out of the gate on the first leg of the emergency response plan.

Ccrossing the road bridge quietly, he returned via the up-line entrance, before he had time to regret his actions. Gerry Richards was waiting, and slid off his stool, shutting the ticket window and putting his "Temporarily Closed", sign up smartly. He lifted the phone, dialled the outside line and was presently connected to the Ringwood under-manager's office. Handing Sam the receiver, he left the office, sliding through the half-door in a practised wriggle, before going to Bert Creddings signal box and bringing him up to date. It had only taken one glance at Sam's notes for him to know what to say, then Sam was on his own, tersely giving lists to the outraged man on the other end of the line.

"Fred noticed fire-buckets, Trevor's missing a sack-barrow, I've lost a large trolley, and both the stores and the emergency locker are almost bare!", he acknowledged. I deliberately didn't check the sidings or any of the up-line storage because to do so would only draw attention, and as yet I can't name names, but I have my suspicions. Some fat blighter likes wandering around as if he owns the place, so it wouldn't be hard to imagine that he has some responsibility, but I can't point the finger Mr Theobald. We close soon enough but we still have to consider the safety of our passengers and ourselves. The emergency locker is checked daily as you know, but since Christmas, he's taken over a lot of those duties, so he can't say he isn't aware.", he listened for a moment, then said deliberately,

"I have replaced the official padlocks with my own and Fred Cummins's locker ones. I noted the time I did that in my pocket book, noted the numbers off the others, and have got Gerry to lock those in the Ticket room safe. I've got to go now, I'm likely to be missed soon enough, but I'll keep an eye out for you."

He replaced the receiver, swapped places with his look-out, then leant against the ticket clerk's window and spoke swiftly.

"Mike's alerting the railway police. They'll come into the freight yard and take over. All you have to do is tip Bert Credding off. Mike says three rings on the box line will do."

Gerry flashed him a broad grin and said (sotto voce), "The King is dead. Long live the King!"

Sam stared at his friend in bewilderment as Gerry explained.

"Come on idiot. Who do you think is going to run this place for its last three or four months? Everything on this line is being run down before it closes anyway. I bet your bottom dollar that Mike turns up in uniform. He's well qualified, and we need him here. It'll be a great chance for him too, I can't see it not happening. Anyway, get you gone before we're accused of wasting valuable time.", and his scandalised friend went about his lawful duties.

Fred Cummins perched himself near the wicket-gate on the up-line, assiduously re-filling fire buckets with sand. He had a brush and pan half-filled with rubbish, three cleaned buckets, and was busily attacking the fourth when a freight train slowly entered the sidings, men dropping silently from the far side of a wagon.

They swiftly re-appeared at the doors into the Station, where two of them lingered smoking. These two wore dark civilian suits, but Fred knew that even as he stretched and yawned, a very wide-awake clerk was handing over padlocks, keys and Sam's pocket book to their uniformed companions.

Sam, seeing the pre-arranged signal stepped out of the parcel clerk's domain, and walked down his platform towards the trolley crossing, busying himself with a stiff brush as he went. Across on the other platform he watched two officers enter the Station Master's office, followed by Mike Theobald, who was very conspicuously wearing his uniform jacket and cap. Shortly afterwards a white faced man was led away to a plain unmarked car that had drawn up silently into the parking bay hard by the main doors. Feeling strangely uncomfortable, Sam waited until Mike Theobald came over the footbridge with the plain clothes men in tow. They greeted Sam politely, then followed him as he showed the Ringwood man what he'd discovered. Mike clicked his tongue impatiently at the service stores.

"That's insane.", he exclaimed with marked irritation. "How on earth did he think he'd get away with it Mr Smart? I grant you that there's little enough draw on these stores anyway, but they would have been missed, and surely he knew that. The line is closing in May, and every item that isn't nailed down will be shipped off to fill other orders from working lines.", he scratched his head in bewilderment as one of the railway police said brusquely,

"It's money sir. Real money. If you realised the true cost of petty thieving from employers, you'd be amazed. Silly things like envelopes and paper from offices, toilet rolls and tea-bags from rest-rooms. The employee sees them as "perks", but they represent a real cost. In this case, ticket prices go up to cover the losses, the lines start to lose money and honest men lose their jobs!"

However, the entire contingent was silenced when the emergency locker was opened. Mike Theobald said sharply, "Hell and damnation!", as the taller of the two policemen said urgently,

"They'll have spares at the railhead. Get your signalman to phone through, they can come down-line on the three-thirty."

He examined the padlocks that Sam had replaced, suggesting that they hadn't been tampered with, but said he'd get the locker dusted for prints anyway. Sam breathed out in relief. He hadn't touched anything since his suspicions had been aroused. He'd only touched the padlocks to open them, hadn't even gone into the service store over the last three months, so it was unlikely that he was implicated in any way, but he had to admit he was unsettled by the mere presence of the railway police in his station.

"I hope I did the right thing," he remarked as Mike Theobald drew his attention to their railway duties, leaving the police in charge.

"Is he likely to come back before we close Mr Theobald?", Sam couldn't help asking, aware that in some strange way he'd known that John Oswald represented some sort of threat, ever since Reg had opened his eyes on that fateful trip to Lymington. Mike shook his head.

"I don't think so Sam. A clever lawyer will get him off I suppose, but the police want to push the fact that he has "knowingly endangered the lives of the travelling public", and they have a point. Some of the tools he's taken are specialised and then there's the detonators!"

Sam stood horrified as he realised how serious the loss of such things could be. Rarely used but essential, detonators were deployed only in extreme circumstances to warn oncoming trains of potential collisions ahead. In the wrong hands they posed a danger in themselves, and if they fell into criminal hands! He closed his eyes grimacing as Mike said, "Exactly!"

The police interviewed Sam a little later, but essentially he had done his bit, they said.

"Of course it was a serious offense.", said one. "Oswald is not thought to be a danger to the public, but his mental health was certainly not all it could be.", said the other, and Sam's spine tingled as they both chuckled.

"We've been talking to Detective Superintendent Gold at Boscombe where milladdo is currently entertaining himself.", they grinned amiably across John Oswald's desk.

"He's got the idea that the trains are out to get him," they chortled, "says he went to some talk in the local village, but didn't have a very happy time of it. On the way home however, he stopped off at the station where he saw a "ghost train!"

They rose, putting together their statement sheets, and went off to interview the others, but as they departed one said thoughtfully.

"Wasn't there someone else a year or two back that went off his trolley round here?", as Sam followed them out.

"Not really," he protested. "Mr Flaxman had a nervous breakdown.

He's well recovered now and has retired locally. So you think the same thing happened?", his fleeting sympathy for John Oswald's plight must have shown, for the officers said briskly,

"Never can tell. However, ask yourself this. Would your old boy have stolen railway or any other kind of property because he'd seen a ghost train? I'll tell you the answer before you bother. Going off your trolley is unfortunate, but it isn't a criminal offence (yet). Obviously you might do something unlawful while the balance of your mind is disturbed, but that doesn't include stealing enough cleaning products to stock the average household for two years and packing it up for sale, all neatly labelled. That didn't take long to find, chummy has very little imagination in that respect!"

They turned towards the footbridge as the senior man spoke. "However, taking the means to save life in an emergency and making damn sure that passengers and railway employees are put at risk is an entirely different matter, and will be looked at in an entirely different light!"

Sam (still chilled by the realisation that Oswald put his own importance and comfort before the lives entrusted to him) shivered as the tall detective said bleakly.

"I shouldn't trouble yourself feeling any sympathy for him. We have a strong suspicion that chummy was prepared to fit you up for the job, should he be in a position to do so. Now then my dear chap, don't you worry about your late Station Master. We'll take very good care of him, never you fear!"

Sam was economical with what he told Ellen, leaving the matter of the ghost-train severely alone. She was as happy as a lark because the job she had so longed for finally materialised unexpectedly. Her letter from the Area Education Office offered her three days at Saint Jude's local primary school, and two days teaching Drama at Ringwood High. She was ecstatic, Sam was relieved, and became more so when the doctors advised Southern Rail that John Oswald was too frail mentally for them to proceed with any real chance of securing a conviction. Neither the courts or the papers would get excited by John Oswald's strange claims, Silver Street was safe, he would watch over her as Mike Theobald put on a Station Master's cap for the last months of her working life. All was well in his world, with no need to protect Ellen or himself from "Ghosties and ghoullies or things that go bump in the night!", he could even forget his occasional "awareness" of strange coincidence, he smiled relaxing…then Alex Ford returned.

PART 3 - CALL IN THE CAVALRY

If Sam harboured any illusions about hard work, Mike Theobald promptly removed them. The young Station Master happily rolled up his sleeves joining every shift as the station entered the last phase of its current life. Sam, as enthused as the others by the sight of Mike as he tackled the windows of his new office (declining all assistance), thrilled as a new smarter, cleaner, more cared for look began to emerge.

Every member of his team grew proud of their joint endeavours, as the atmosphere changed for the better. Even the disillusioned up-line porter commented favourably when Sam discovered him carefully brushing dust off the Station sign.

"Got to treat the lady right haven't we?", the older man grunted as he worked a cloth over the words Silver Street. Given us a living hasn't she, so I agree with Mike. Let's keep her right and trim to the last day, let's not allow old Beeching to look at this station and say it failed from obvious neglect. We've only got three and a half months left, but Mike's got us some paint from down-line somewhere, so we're coming in as the evenings get lighter to fix her up good and proper."

So, as each day stretched eagerly towards spring, Sam began to walk into work, remaining behind each day to sand, varnish and paint interior walls along with his team. Bert Credding (boxed up and ready to move), re-puttied the windows of his signal box, and attended to his cottage maintenance, as Fred, Gerry and Mike took care of the up-line buildings, and Sam and Trevor worked the west-bound platform.

Ellen, whose comings and goings were governed by her unusual working week, got into the habit of cooking huge meals, then splitting them up over two days. She hankered for a bigger fridge, yearned over a freezer she'd seen at an Ideal Home exhibition, and generally worked so hard on her own projects, that Sam was glad of the distraction when Alex invited them to dinner "at his place".

Ellen grinned amiably as Sam went into their kitchen with the simple note in his hand.

"What's that love?", she looked up from a picture she was examining in the pile of reference books she'd brought home. "Why are you looking so pleased with yourself eh?"

He handed her the invitation, and Ellen read it swiftly, lifting her head to comment sharply.

"His place? Cheeky blighter! Still, he's been a bit low-key lately, it would be good to catch up with him and find out what he's been up to.", she poured tea absently, returning to her book with an indulgent smile on her face. Sam (replenishing the kettle), leant over her shoulder peering at the reproduction of the front page of an American newspaper.

"More schoolwork?", he questioned lightly, and Ellen blushed, surprising him as she caught his hand, lightly resting it against her hot cheek.

"Not exactly darling," she confessed, "I've been doing some research lately and I've got some news to share myself. Can we wait for Alex's dinner-party before I tell you? It's not going to be a secret for long, and I'd like to share my news with Alex too." She asked curiously,

"Does he say what his plans are? Do you think he's giving up his search and going home?"

He looked down at her glumly, suddenly aware of how much he'd grown to like the young Australian and how much he'd miss him.

"I haven't seen him about since he came back from London," he admitted slowly. "He's been caught up with some business matters I know, Howard told me that much when I bumped into him at the shop the other day. I don't know what his plans are to be honest sweetheart, perhaps that's what he's going to tell us, anyway, I'll drop a note in accepting his invitation on my way to work tomorrow, then we'll find out."

The following morning, Sam walked in to work via Ellen's cottage. Taking care not to disturb Alex at a quarter-past five in the morning, he posted their acceptance through the letterbox and walked on past the last cottages, before the road swung into the bend that took it past Pine Trees School.

Although dawn was breaking, the light was too poor for him to see anything which would give credence to the chauffeur's expressed opinion regarding lodge-gates, so he picked up the pace a little, jogging along the road cheerfully whistling as his path wended up alongside the Old Home Farm. Here much more activity brightened the day. A herd of Friesians stamped and bellowed, two of the farm hands wrestled the gate into place, calling out friendly "Good morning" greetings as he passed.

Sam lengthened his stride, full of the thought that within the year this idyllic lifestyle could be achieved at Silver Street, and diverted by the consideration that soon enough he and Ellen might start the day milking goats, he entered Home Farm wood on the shortcut up to the station. He was comfortably on time for work, the day was lightening until he could see his path even through the over-grown coppice when he became aware that he was being followed. It wasn't much, just the odd crackle of a step not quite in time with his own, yet the hair on the back of Sam's neck bristled alarmingly as he stopped to glance back. He was sheltered by a large oak at the time and was never more grateful for that, when he saw John Oswald staggering along in his wake, muttering to himself.

"Good Lord, he's drunk," he thought inadequately, then realised that the man was dirty, dishevelled and looked as though he'd been sleeping rough. He'd certainly lost weight and for a moment he actually entertained the idea of trying to find out if he needed help. However, the stream of slurred threats (uttered in a chilling monotone) froze every good intention in their tracks, as the man stumbled along wildly brandishing a stout branch.

He stood shivering for a moment, grateful for the shelter of the tree, then cautiously, he turned back, making for the farm and safety in numbers. At his shocked and incredulous face, the farmer was only too happy to let him warn Bert Credding, whose cottage was connected to the phone.

"Right-ho Sam!", the signalman responded easily. "Jack'll let you come up to the station on the trailer with the churns. I'll call Fred in early, and tell Mike before he gets on the train. Drunk you say? It's a good thing his landlady never suspected that! Very anti-alcohol Martha Andrews.", he chuckled as Sam thought back to the disturbing figure that was still out there waiting.

He found himself stumbling over his words in horror as he thought of the consequences had he decided to approach his former colleague, and fear for his friends sharpened his voice.

"Bert, listen," he ordered. "If he's either drunk or drugged, he's a risk to himself, to staff and passengers. He absolutely must not gain access to Silver Street. Whatever the cause, he's in a hell of a state anyway. Looks as if he's sleeping rough but he's threatening to kill someone. I heard him, clear as I hear you now, so be a good lad and call the cops, they know him, and will pick him up safely. Don't for God's sake tackle him on your own, and try and stop him getting onto railway property. We can't protect passengers if there's a mad man on the loose! Tell the police I'm coming up with the milk; that I saw him in Home Farm woods above Padways, but he's all over the show and I'll probably beat him to the station anyway!"

He jumped as the farmer touched his arm.

"Got that Sam, I've told the men to keep the cattle in while I get you up to Silver Street, Beryl's riding shot-gun.", announced Jack Sherrington and to Sam's everlasting shame, Jack's sprightly mother was doing just that!

Sat on the front of the trailer with her twelve-bore tucked under a jacket, the pugnacious septuagenarian gave him the impression that she was actively looking forward to the possibility of armed combat.

As they sallied forth from Home Farm (tractor towing trailer), the Silver Street rescue party comprised determined farmer, his warlike mother and a very confused porter propped against the milk churns. Jack revved the engine as they went out onto the main road, then they were swinging up the short incline onto the road bridge, before swooping down into the main entrance. Jack made a practised turn of the wheel, which brought them neatly into the main up-line loading bay, where they came to a stop. Sam (getting out to unlock the doors) was never more relieved to reach work safely and turned to help the farmer unload the churns, rolling them onto a trolley and straight out onto the platform where the milk-train waited.

Glancing at the Station clock, Sam was amazed to see that it wasn't much after six, and relaxed a little as he thanked Jack and his mother awkwardly, querying if Beryl would really have used the shotgun.

"I most certainly would have had that man threatened you.", she said briskly. "Drunk or drugged, mad people are entirely unpredictable. I didn't like the look of the fellow at the Harvest Home either. It's my belief that he probably drank most of a full bottle of Jane Short's parsnip wine that night."

There was a short awed silence as the men took that information on board.

She continued blithely unaware of their reaction.

"He was sitting at the bar, muttering and moaning under his breath in a very ugly fashion. Based on my experiences out in Africa, I'd say the booze will put him in his box if the police don't restrain him pronto! His eyes are quite yellow. Liver shot to hell I should say!"

Sam grinned involuntarily, the clipped "County" voice was remarkably at odds with Mrs Sherrington (senior's) appearance. She was small, fragile looking, with a short mannish hairstyle. Bright blue eyes twinkled up at him, an absolute match for the fine sweater she sported beneath a working jacket. She wore tiny gold ear-rings, a Paisley scarf, and jeans (as well as the most combative scowl he'd seen in a long time). Jack Sherrington laughed at Sam's uncertain expression.

"I warn you Sam, Beryl's a top shot, stands no nonsense, and could easily bring down an elephant charging if she needed to. She's had plenty of experience in Africa. Still never mind that, we got you away right enough, and if I'm not away before long myself, life will become complicated by officialdom. You know where we are if you need us Sam. So long."

He climbed up into the tractor, watching as his mother nimbly hopped up behind him, pausing only to let her drop a tarpaulin and his jacket over her shot-gun. Then, as a police-car slipped into the parking bay where Sam still stood shivering, he pulled out, turning in a wide arc before returning the way they'd come.

Sam directed the sleepy-eyed constable who approached him, but the man shook his head, explaining that others were taking care of the matter, he just wanted to assure himself that no-one had come to any harm. He jerked a thumb over his shoulder towards the departing tractor as it turned out on to the road.

"Right you are then sir.", he said evenly, "No-one hurt, but a nasty experience all the same."

He took out his note-book, took a few details and chuckled when Sam (trying to be diplomatic), said that the farmer's mother had come along so she wasn't alone at the farm.

"Mmmm…", said the constable in a disbelieving voice. "When I was at school, Mrs Beryl Sherrington came to talk to us about her home in Africa. She brought the house down telling us about the native uprisings, going on safari and shooting the rhino that killed her late husband. I'll bet this little adventure was right up her street. You shouldn't believe that all little grey haired ladies with cut-glass accents are entirely innocent Mr Smart. Yon laddie will give the doctors more than enough headaches with his problems though, so I'm grateful that picking buck-shot out of him won't add to their woes."

His car radio crackled suddenly, and telling Sam to wait he hurried to answer it.

"Reception's terrible," he grumbled five minutes later, "but they've got him. He's as drunk as a lord, cold, hungry and sorry for himself. However, he's not fit to be out either, making wild threats to kill all of us, so we'll give him a lift into the Royal Victoria at Boscombe and see what their trick-cyclist can make of him. He'll be out of circulation for a few days anyway, so I'll catch up with the paperwork later."

He made a quick note of Sam's duty times, promised not to get in the way of work, and left Sam where he'd found him.

That was the odd start to an even odder day. Around ten-thirty before he could regale the others with this story, a slender pale-eyed man in a city suit arrived on the down-line platform. He carried a briefcase and stood for a moment as though deep in thought, looking around the station. Sam was just thinking of coming to his rescue, when a Bentley drew in, and Howard, resplendent in full uniform approached the gentleman, touching his cap deferentially. The visitor turned, a smile on his face, and Howard picked up the small suitcase Sam hadn't noticed, and led the way back to the car. He opened the door, the man got in unselfconsciously, and Howard, nodding to Sam, got in and drove off towards Burley, as Sam polished a door-handle unnecessarily.

Mike collared Sam shortly after tea-break, (now made quite openly in the men's locker room off Trevor's parcel office). The new Station Master had looked critically at the space allowed for his crew, and suggested some changes would benefit everyone. He had pointedly turned a blind eye as they came and went, going out of his way to let them get on with it by themselves, so that once they'd reorganised, they were more than delighted when he invited himself over the line for tea.

"My word!", he'd exclaimed over their rearrangement of lockers, which incidentally provided a snug but ample changing area for those coming on duty during inclement weather. He walked behind the banked lockers, noting the regular clothing hooks (each neatly named), then stopped at the table bearing the electric kettle that Sam had donated when Norman died.

"I'll settle for mine being strong and sweet, and I'll bring in a flask so that Gerry gets his on time, even when he's busy. We've a few market days to get through before we close.", the crew gave a subdued chuckle, but they had come to recognise the wisdom of the man, as their duties became easier, more friendly, and even Trevor came out of his shell and proved he had a mature sense of humour, previously unsuspected by the regular team.

Today, leaning back to the wall, clutching an empty cup, the young Station Master asked Sam what he was doing about getting a supply of water sorted.

"Without running water and sewage connected you'll not get the place registered as habitable Sam", he warned. "You'd better get over to Burley and talk to the Collier's. One of their part-timers is a dowser. I have it on very good authority that he can find old water courses, springs, lost wells, just about anything you want tracked. He's bloody good Sam, and quite cheap I understand."

Fred screwed up his face thinking, then after a moment he asked doubtfully, "Do you mean Paddy Flynn Mike? Little Irishman, odd bloke but great with horses as well?", all eyes swivelled as Mike burst out laughing.

"Yep, that's the man. About four feet ten, green eyes, looks like (and probably was) a blooming jockey? Used to live in Burley, but I haven't seen him in ages. Someone told me that he went travelling a while back, he's generally in the Forest through spring and summer though, and failing that, I may know someone over at Brockenhurst who can dowse a bit, but Paddy Flynn's your best bet."

Sam went home that night with his head in a whirl. He didn't like it, but he had to confide the latest round in the John Oswald saga to Ellen for her own safety, and did so, fearful of her reaction, but she was surprisingly unperturbed.

"How horrid!", she'd exclaimed, more fascinated by his description of Beryl Sherrington than distressed by the danger her husband had been in.

"I wonder if I can get her to come over and talk to the school again?", she'd murmured quietly (an acquisitional expression on her face). Sam retreated in high dudgeon, putting his mind to sorting out Charlie's workshop, which he literally hadn't entered since the day before their wedding.

He went out into the back garden, unlocked the shed, and stood peering at the dim benches where Charlie's tools nestled alongside his own. He soon realised it was still too cold and dark to be working out here late at night. Going back into the house, he abruptly decided that he would go over to Burley, talk to Tom Collier about getting some light and warmth out to the workshop, and then he'd see about finding Paddy Flynn. Thus cheered, he made up the range, refilled the coal scuttle and made tea for Ellen and himself. This weekend he would be off duty, they could go to the Library, collect his spring seeds, and talk to Tom Collier before going to Alex's dinner party. He made up the living room fire ready for Ellen to light after school tomorrow, and went up to bed contentedly.

He woke abruptly wrenched from dreams of running horses along the beach, and found himself trembling, agitating over something he'd forgotten. It hovered, just outside his reach, teasing him until he drifted back to sleep uneasily aware that whatever had wakened him, was important. Very important indeed.

Chapter 24 - Bedevilled by Night

Saturday dawned brisk and cheerless in the way of early spring days. Ellen, eyeing Sam's programme doubtfully, made him go down to Emma Fleet's and contact the Colliers by phone, telling him that he'd be lucky if they could spare the time at such short notice.

However, Tom was delighted with the idea, greeting the pair of them at the door with a huge grin.

"Well then Sam, how's tricks?", he ushered them through into a spacious kitchen, where his wife was seated sorting seeds.

She looked up, her hand hovering over a packet of Swiss chard, and Sam (seeing the bright white stems and dark green leaves asked curiously, "How well does that perform on clay rich soil? It's something I've looked at, but never actually tried."

"We do well with it," she said smiling up at them, turning the packet over, scanning it for further information, as Sam shrugged off his jacket, and Tom took Ellen's coat.

"I can't see anything specifically against it." Liz Collier added, "Here, have a look for yourself.", she passed the packet to Sam, and made way for Ellen to sit at the table beside her, saying brightly,

"Tom's sister would be able to tell you more I expect. We just grow a bit for our own use. I'm very partial to a drop of spinach and that hasn't got a bitter flavour. It's easy to germinate, grows like a weed, and provides enough iron in the diet so that we never worry about anaemia!"

Over her shoulder, Ellen had already noticed the dark blue of a nursing uniform drying on the line outside, and asked Tom's wife, "Where are you nursing?"

Before Sam knew what had hit him, Ellen had found out that Liz Collier was a midwife at the Royal Victoria Hospital in Boscombe.

With both women chatting, heads together over the table sorting seeds as the kettle came to the boil, Sam was able to detach himself and follow Tom into the workshop, where all his electrical wizardry was on display. Strangely reluctant to voice his plans, Sam gazed around him. On one wall a bank of cable reels was suspended, spilling light flex from one drum, armoured cable from another. A workbench held boxes of switches, light sockets, even silent radios waited Tom's attention, and Sam watched as the electrician deftly replaced a plug before going to collect two mugs from Liz at the door.

"I don't let her out here.", the man said with a shy grin at Sam. "I'd hate her to hurt herself, and when I'm in the middle of a project I'm an untidy blighter. Sit yourself down Sam, that stool will be fine, but watch your hands. It doesn't take much for a piece of wire to pierce a fingertip. Liz is always on at me to clear up, but a man's got to do his work somewhere!"

They sat, swigging back their tea in comfortable silence for a moment, Sam appreciating Tom's skill as the electrician deftly stripped old flex from a table lamp while he waited for Sam to tell him the purpose of his call. Eventually, Sam took a breath and began to explain.

"Remember that day you told me about the Royal Blue coach courses?", he asked awkwardly, remembering how he had virtually choked off his host in mid-stream.

"Yes I do!", Tom answered gruffly, "Sorry. I should have handled that more sensitively. I didn't realise you took not being able to drive so much to heart."

Sam (who'd just been about to offer his own apologies), grinned sheepishly, then said (equally gruffly), "Well, no matter now. Besides, I have something to tell you, which might put quite a bit of work your way if you're interested. It'll be ongoing, slow and steady work. It's a big project and it'll start at my place. Interested?"

Tom nodded, "Anything that gives me a little boost toward retirement interests me.", he said firmly putting the conversational ball back in Sam's court again.

"Right," said the porter gravely, "I need my workshop put on mains power Tom. It's close to the back of the house. I think it's possible that I'll need the cottage re-wired fairly soon, then you can start on Silver Street!"

The silence that greeted the last statement was deafening. Tom Collier, perched on the edge of a bench with his cup half-way to his mouth, was completely taken aback. He blinked, shook his head, then said uncertainly, "Silver Street Sam? What do you mean, Silver Street! What's an old railway station got to do with my rewiring your place?"

Sam grinned, heartily amused at the electrician's reaction.

"It's easy Tom. You start with my workshop. Then while you're doing that, you can look at the cottage, get it up to standard like, then, once we're ready, if I like your work, (and you've maintained a level of discretion over my plans), then I'll let you play with my railway station. Only by then it'll be a smallholding, mine and Ellen's home, and quite possibly other employment for a few close friends as well."

Never (on or off the cricket field) had Sam enjoyed such a reaction. Tom Collier went pink, then he started chuckling "fit to bust", as Charlie would have put it. He sniggered, caught his breath, and then giggled helplessly, tears running down his face as the two women appeared to see what all the hilarity was about.

"By Gum. That'll set a few folk back on their ears!", he finally crowed, then sobering, he spoke solemnly.

"Well done Sam! There's nothing like turning a local disaster into something positive. Now then let's fresh up the teapot Mother, I've a fair bit of work to sort out with Sam here."

He waited for the puzzled women to disappear into the kitchen before speaking, then said sternly.

"Don't let the news out too soon Sam. You're too kind hearted a chap to turn hopeful folk away, and Silver Street won't even support you and Ellen for a while, let alone the hungry hangers-on. I'll keep Mum, never you mind, but once we start work you're going to need a project manager. I'm quite happy to help in that department as far as I'm capable, but it's not my trade, and besides that, I retire next year, and I've got plans of my own."

Sam said darkly, "They'd better not interfere with you playing cricket Tom!", and an odd expression crossed the Burley wicket keeper's face.

"Believe me, if some fool set me rewiring Paddington Station, I wouldn't miss stumping your bails for all the tea in China!", came the rude reply, and both men roared with laughter as they entered a new phase in their relationship.

The rest of the day went past so quickly that Sam could hardly believe Ellen when she pointed him in the direction of the bathroom, and told him to "Smarten up Mister."

He shaved carefully, splashing on after-shave with abandon, then went into the kitchen whistling, as Ellen folded something into her handbag, and lifted down Sam's neatly ironed shirt. He eyed her doubtfully, glowing jewel-like in a dress of deep green linen. Her amber eyes were warm, honey-gold hair shining over her shoulders, and suddenly his heart was full. He pulled her into his arms, lingering over her lips as he kissed her, then raising his head he whispered gently.

"You are the most beautiful, talented, intelligent woman. Why for Heaven's sake are we entertaining the idea of a dinner-party invitation, when we could stay home and make love?"

She gurgled appreciatively, then tucked his shirt under his arm, instructing him lightly.

"Through that door my lad, upstairs and fix yourself up nicely please. I have it on good authority that Alex wants us to meet someone important tonight, so best bib and tucker and no more nonsense!"

He obeyed swiftly, wondering who Alex was entertaining alongside them, unaccountably disappointed that he wouldn't be able to tell their friend about their own adventures in front of a stranger. He glanced in the mirror, pleased with his appearance, then as natural curiosity took control, he caught up his jacket, and went into the evening with his wife, both intent on a night of discovery.

Ellen's cottage glowed a subdued welcome as they tapped on the front door, and she whispered quickly, "This feels really odd," before Howard appeared. He was soberly suited this time, and Sam raised an inquisitive eyebrow as the chauffeur-turned-butler showed them into a radically altered sitting-room. The blue carpet had been tenderly rolled and stored in the loft Howard informed them quietly, as they took in the expanse of highly polished wooden flooring.

Ellen's piano had been moved into the bay window, deep chestnut curtains reflected in the polished lid of the instrument. At the other end of the room, a large Indian carpet in tones of bronze, chestnut and cream warmed the area beneath a gleaming table laid for four, and Ellen gaped as she saw the elegant setting.

They were still marvelling when Howard suggested that they move through into what he referred to as the "snug", and led the bemused couple towards the double doors (opposite). These led into Ellen's mother's study, and she followed with interest, dying to see what Alex had made of it.

She wasn't disappointed. The overbearing bookshelves had gone, replaced by a collection of easy chairs separated by small occasional tables here and there. Deep blue curtains covered a narrow window, and the same colour was revealed in the light given off by table lamps dotted around the room. As they entered, Alex's infectious chuckle rang out, then he was cheerfully hailing them from the depths of an armchair.

"Sam, Ellen, come on in and meet Colonel Robertson."

Sam barely had time to take in the plaster-cast encasing the Australian's left ankle, when the slim, pale-eyed man he had seen Howard collecting at the station, rose to his feet and greeted them warmly. He was a little older than Sam had expected, a lot thinner, but his grip was vigorous, and his eyes danced merrily.

"How do you do?", he asked in a cultured voice as he took Ellen's hand. He smiled at Sam easily, true warmth flickering in his eyes, but his face remained watchful and Sam noticed that he held himself a little stiffly, as he turned to offer Ellen a seat.

"Sorry, we're both a little crocked at the moment," he apologised as he sank back into his armchair. "Damn fool thing really, but we got caught up in an incident in London, and I forgot I'm not as young as I'd like to be."

He seemed disinclined to complete the story, but Alex let out a hoot of laughter, and began to explain as Howard entered with a tray of sherry glasses.

"Too right he forgot his age!", the Australian commented. "There was some sort of demonstration a street or two away, I had just come off the train and was crossing the road when all hell broke loose. I could hear shouting, then a clatter, after which I took no further part in the proceedings.", he grinned at the Colonel who said laconically, "Poor blighter didn't stand a chance. Stood right in the middle of the road when something spooked a police horse. The noise was diabolical. Women screaming, whistles blowing, you know the sort of thing? Riderless horse came out of nowhere, galloping down the road and young feller-me-lad looked in the wrong direction, probably fooled by the echoes off the pavement."

Sam leant forward, fascinated by the clipped regimental speech, but Ellen said faintly, "Good Lord Alex, you might have been killed outright. What have you done to your foot, is it broken?"

The Colonel grimaced sympathetically, continuing the tale (as interesting smells filtered through from the kitchen).

"Well, if half a ton of frightened horse bolted towards you down Oxford Street, would you attempt to catch it my dear?"

Into the pause that followed Ellen exclaimed in shock.

"Alex! You didn't did you?", and Colonel Robertson coughed and looked embarrassed.

"I'm afraid I did Ellen.", said the abashed Aussie. "There were women and kids around, the horse could have hurt itself as well. How was I to know that the darned thing was trained not to let people grab at reins, saddle or rider?", he asked sorrowfully. "It reared up, I fell down, and Dobbin landed on my outstretched foot, at which point in time I went to sleep like a good boy, and left the round-up to the real experts!"

This virtuous statement was greeted by a subdued giggle, followed by a sympathetic murmur and the wry lifting of the Colonel's eyebrows, as Howard announced that dinner was served.

The tale emerged as they sat to table, expertly waited on by Howard (who had apparently done all the cooking). The pot-roast melted in the mouth as a spell-bound couple heard how Colonel Robertson had emerged from his office, taken one look at the scene and realised that his cavalry training was needed and ran to help. A passer-by had assisted by cupping their hands under the Colonel's foot and throwing him up into the saddle, whereupon the horse (after cavorting for a few moments), had calmed down enough for the police to catch up and take-over. Alex had regained consciousness in hospital, stayed in overnight, and had then been swept off to a hotel courtesy of a trustee from the company that he had been about to visit.

As Howard served a wonderful compote of fruit for dessert, Sam could no longer restrain himself and asked curiously, "I thought you went up to London to make enquiries at Australia House?", and Alex blushed guiltily.

"Aah…Australia House! I was going there initially. However, having pursued another line of enquiry over the phone, I changed my plans and went straight to meet the Colonel at his London office, the rest you know. I've been stuck kicking my heels until the doctors let me go. Colonel Robertson spent two days getting over his exertions, then went walkabout looking for some information, now he's here, or rather up at Burley Manor, and I'm dependent on Howard to keep things running for a while. I'm due to go into Boscombe to get the plaster checked, then I should be able to walk on it. I didn't want the results of my enquiries to pass you by, so once we've had some coffee, we can listen and hope that some good comes of it all."

They took coffee in the snug again. Alex leaning painfully on Howard was helped back into his chair, groaning involuntarily as he sank into its depths. He smiled somewhat wanly as Ellen lifted his leg onto a footstool, and placed cushions to support his back.

"It's rotten luck you being laid up like this Alex," she exclaimed sympathetically, "Does it give you a lot of pain? We have a good doctor who'd almost certainly take a look if it keeps bothering you."

The young Aussie frowned, deep lines scoring his forehead as he admitted with an ironic smile, "Ellen dear, it's badly bruised, quite possibly not broken just crushed. It's murder by day, the absolute devil by night, but I'm alive, the cavalry came to the rescue, and I can't wait to hear what he's going to say. So be a good chum, shut up do, and let's get the Colonel's story right away!"

They all chuckled as Ellen poked her tongue out at him, then they settled back and waited expectantly, as Colonel Robertson deliberately finished his coffee, placed his cup and saucer on the tray and took an envelope out of his inside pocket. Sam, waiting with bated breath felt a frisson of energy run down his spine. Somewhere in the dark a dog barked, a breeze carrying the sound across the village sighed and a passing train called up the track. It was a distant desolate cry in the night, and the porter shivered apprehensively as the Colonel began to speak.

Chapter 25 - Tying up Loose Ends

The neat figure of Alex's other guest sat very upright in his armchair as all eyes swivelled in his direction. Sam could imagine him dressed in uniform and masked a smile as he considered the dry, almost pedantic manner in which the Colonel had reported the incident in London. Instinctively, Sam had taken to the man's straightforward approach to Alex's search. Over the course of dinner, he had made it abundantly clear that he appreciated Ellen and Sam's position in Alex's life, so as the older man cleared his throat and looked down at the paper he held, Sam prepared to give him his full attention. He settled back in his chair, ran a swift glance round to check on Ellen and Alex, unaware that a flicker of keenly intelligent eyes rested on his own face as he looked away from the Colonel, then the man took over.

Well-spoken, his innate air of authority came over clearly as he addressed the assembled company. Neither brusque or indifferent to others, he easily commanded respect as he launched what must have been the most unusual after-dinner speech of the decade.

"Right-ho then.", the Colonel began, "It's still a bit of a tangle, but these are the facts so far as I have them."

His eyes shone as he confessed shyly.

"You'll have to bear with the history class first, the rest is a bit of a Boy's Own story, but I've barely had time to scratch the surface and we certainly won't get through it all tonight!"

He grinned boyishly, as Sam (realising that quite possibly most of the Colonel's life fell into the category of "Boys Own" stories), watched him put on a pair of rimless spectacles and glance over the paper he held, before returning it to his pocket as he began.

"Right.", he said briskly, "In the eighteen seventies, Australia was beginning to shake off the reputation of a penal colony. Enormous deposits of minerals had been found, land was being opened up and the country was ripe for investment. Along similar lines, the African interior was beginning to show potential as the Empire's influence reached its peak. However, although land was comparatively cheap to buy, there had to be a reason for buying it, and in those days (from such a distance), it was impossible to assess the potential use or risk without an agent on the ground."

He looked around the avid faces watching him, and went on.

"The journeys undertaken by explorers are legendary, and don't need repeating here, but the men, women and children that followed the trailblazers took as many risks as those who opened up the continents. They my friends were not going home to live on their laurels in peace and comfort. No, they were in it for the long haul, no return tickets, just their hopes, courage and the arrogance of youth.", he paused as Howard entered, wheeling a small trolley, and set about refilling coffee cups. A few minutes later the cheerful chuckling of an electric percolator ensued as their cups were replenished, and Colonel Robertson began again.

"During the entire nineteenth century, as much of our own countryside depended on private investment, as the development of the Empire under Victoria. Great wealth had been generated by an explosion of technical and engineering expertise, and there was a great responsibility to re-invest the resulting wealth in further developments such as mining, transport and land. Some invested heavily in areas of our own country. Take Castleman's Corkscrew itself and the enterprise of the rail engineers as an example that Mr Smart is familiar with. A careful investment by a local solicitor, made it possible for travellers to push out westward and by so doing created the potential for mere fishing villages to develop into resorts such as Bournemouth. Villages served by the railways attracted development and investment. Half the towns in Britain owe their current prosperity, if not their existence to the forethought of those entrepreneurs.", he nodded to Sam, who sat head on one side taking this all in, then turned with a smile to Ellen and Alex, who maintained expressions of polite interest to cover their mutual bewilderment.

"Imagine.", the light dry voice continued.

"If Bournemouth as it currently exists, was valued property by property against its value before the railways arrived, what do you think the difference would be calculated in? Thousands? Millions? Or...", his voice died away speculatively as the others contemplated the problem.

Sam broke the silence with a whistle. "Phew!", he declared, shaking his head. "It's actually impossible to calculate.", he mused thoughtfully.

"You'd need to prepare a mathematical model that would allow you to constantly update the value of each piece of land, alongside its changing use. Towns evolved slowly, some are chains of villages that have spread out, others develop around a focal point, but all of them include areas that have supported residential, commercial and industrial practices, many of which have overlapped or encroached on each other. That's where the same land can change in value very rapidly, and not all in a beneficial manner."

Ellen's eyes glazed over as she glanced at him, face furrowed as he tried to grasp the magnitude of the problem. Then his eyes brightened as he suggested hopefully, "If it was possible to have one group, possibly a family pass the property on in an unbroken line from the beginning to current times, you might just hazard a guess as to the growth in value, provided that somebody could apply all the attendant data, like devaluation due to war damage, hikes in property values and the cost of living. However, such a group can't really exist outside of the landed gentry can it sir?", and Colonel Robertson's lips twitched in amusement.

"I hope so Mr Smart.", was the astonishing return, then he said with a perfectly straight face, "Now apply that analogy to the African and Australian continent, alongside a fair slice of Southern England.", he chuckled at Sam's astonished face and added simply,

"From Victoria's time to the present day, land owners have invested in property all over the world. Their faith followed the thousands heading out of Great Britain to explore, expand and settle the Empire. We didn't just sally forth, knock over a few natives and move on you know. We developed country after country, ruled some of them, lost some of them and made friends and investments out of the rest. That took feet on the ground, chaps who were prepared to run our business overseas, out of which I must say, they also carved new lives in places they may never have dreamed of visiting."

Alex sat forward suddenly, shifting his foot uncomfortably as he asked.

"Do you think my family belonged to one of those land traders sir? Is there anyway of tracing who worked in that capacity after all this time? My Grandfather's records seem to be non-existent as you know, so there's impossibly little to go on. I don't know anything other than that he lived at Newlands with my Nan, fathered my Dad, but died over here, from injuries received during World War One before Dad was born. I don't even know if my own father was legitimate."

His voice had risen with anxiety and fatigue as Colonel Robertson grimaced.

"Alex my dear chap, hold on a minute. What I'm about to tell you might be impossible to prove, but despite that, I'm going to tell you anyway. This story can quite likely be repeated through many families, over many centuries. We, like so many others, may just have to be patient a little longer while I set about tying up loose ends. Now, before you get too tired to take this on board, I'll show you where I think I fit in. Tomorrow's another day, and we have all the time in the world to prove or disprove our connections, however tenuous they may be."

Well pleased with the effect this had on his listeners, Colonel Robertson's lips quirked before he admitted freely.

"To a certain extent I'm exceeding my authority in this matter, but I have a personal interest to pursue alongside your own bid to improve your tenure at Newlands, so I may as well come clean."

He patted his pockets absently, withdrew a business card and glanced at it briefly before he continued quietly.

"I'm afraid I haven't been entirely honest with you Alex, but please give me a chance to explain. My name *is* Robertson, and I carry the rank of Colonel of Horse (Blues and Royals). After leaving the services, I applied myself to a family concern, and was lucky enough to achieve my current standing quite some time ago. However, I have always been drawn towards the historical background of the family, so having been made aware of your existence by our Australian agent, I took an interest in your education to begin with. Your mother was an exemplary tenant, and I heartily endorsed her plan for you, when she made us aware of her illness and the likely prognosis."

Sam sneaked a look at Alex, who sat very still, his lips firmly compressed into a thin, bitter line, as his guest continued gently.

"Part of the Trust I work for has always promoted education, training and qualifications amongst tenants, employees, or fellow investors, so, when you wanted to go to University we found a bursary straight away. With great reports coming out of New South Wales, I was more than satisfied that we'd done the right thing when your mother died, leaving you a bit of a mystery to clear up."

He held up a hand as Alex frowned, and said peaceably, "You'll see why I'm so interested in a moment my dear chap, but I must put my cards fully on the table so to speak.", then with a courteous bow, he handed Alex the business card. Alex took it, staring white faced at the inscription, then read aloud for the benefit of the others.

"Colonel Robertson Fullingford (Trustee to the Fullingford and Newlands (Africa and Australia) Trust."

His voice died away as he turned bewildered eyes on his surprising visitor.

"I was sent down to check you out, then submit a report to the Board.", the colonel said placidly, "However, if I'm even half right Alex, you and I are definitely related. If it goes further than that, I'm afraid we'll truly set the legal cats amongst some very fat pigeons. Some parts of the story you brought to me aren't very clearly established, but I'm beginning to get the feeling that this may get a whole lot weirder yet, so I hope you're prepared for one of my wilder flights of fancy!"

He looked around the little gathering and said quietly, "I'm sorry chaps but this isn't for public consumption. My principals have demanded that I swear each of you to secrecy because what I'm about to reveal has major implications for not only the distribution of wealth amongst our investors, but would quite possibly create a precedent in law. Nothing that is discussed in this room must go out of it, I trust I make myself clear?"

The dry clipped voice sounded so severe that they all nodded involuntarily, as the Colonel fumbled in a pocket and produced a Victorian calling card with a photograph of a highly sophisticated gentleman on it, besides the legend "Anthony Fullingford Esquire General Manager (Australia) Newlands Trust.

Alex stared at the smiling face and instinctively turned to check his own in a mirrored panel near his chair.

"Jeepers mate!", he spluttered eventually, "That's uncanny. He's got my face hasn't he Sam?", and the astonished porter found himself blinking as Ellen whispered softly,

"Ollie was right Sam. Alex might have been this man's twin! He is his "Fullingford boy returned", but who was he and what made him go in the first place? I do so wish the poor old boy could have told us more before he died."

The Colonel's mouth quirked in appreciation of that point as he laid the returned cards on the occasional table beside him and sighed.

"I couldn't agree more Mrs Smart, but family breakdowns, money problems or private scandals often aren't recorded. Millions of people experience that form of dislocation. Children leave home in protest and never return, or can't return. Brothers and sisters fall out over minor matters, each are too proud to reconcile their differences and time rolls inexorably forward. Of course, nowadays I can write to Australia, Africa, and South America in the knowledge that my letters will arrive safely. I can send a telegram and get an answer in twenty-four hours. Goddam it, I can fly to anywhere but Australia inside that period, but those who preceded us took weeks, even months to get anywhere, and many lives are a testament to poor communication. Which is why I'm afraid to speculate further, on the grounds that I might just be imagining a situation that didn't exist? I'm not just afraid of disappointing Alex, I'm concerned that any of our findings might tip the balance of business adversely, and of course I don't like the idea of upsetting the Board, sacking myself and of losing the one family member I'm ever likely to meet in the process."

Alex's face was a picture of misery as Howard arrived shortly thereafter, and began to clear away the coffee things. He said awkwardly, (as Howard departed frowning), "Sorry blokes. He's a good scout really, works bloody hard every hour of the day, and he's going to be livid if I don't follow the doctor's advice. Perhaps we can re-convene tomorrow when I've had some sleep and got my head round this?", he eyed the Colonel doubtfully.

"I don't really know how to address you now sir...", he shook his head, squinting at the Victorian visiting card covertly, as the Colonel absorbed the comment with a wry grin of appreciation.

"Yes...difficult.", the older man mused then suggested blandly, "Try Rob. I use my rank only when it's useful anyway. I'll try and sort out the family connection for you tomorrow, but we're still uncertain if your name is Ford or Fullingford aren't we? That's key to our enquiry by the way, but if your ancient blacksmith was right you and I would be cousins, and the last survivors of the Fullingford family."

They surveyed each other shyly as Howard came back to assist Alex to bed. Ellen turning to Sam said brightly, "Why don't we take Rob over to Burley with us Sam. If we go by Silver Street, you can show him your baby by moonlight, and tell him all our plans. That way poor Howard doesn't have to turn out again, and Alex will be safely tucked up for the night."

They drifted out into the village, collected Lady Jane from the parking bay below their cottage, and sallied out into the Forest with Alex's exhortations ringing in their ears.

"See you all tomorrow, but for God's sake Ellen, don't spook any Forest ponies around Rob. He's the very devil on horse-back!"

Sunday dawned bright and breezy as Sam and Ellen woke. They lay, savouring (for a change) a day in which neither of them had to leap out of bed or race downstairs to get ready for work. Sam turned his head, lazily surveying his wife's sleepy face, and then said conversationally, "You know Ellen, I'm beginning to see what drove Alex over here to try and locate his family records. You and I were both on our own, but we had the luxury of having known our parents and their extended families. My memory doesn't include my mother of course, but my Nan, my Dad, and even Uncle Norman constantly referred to her, keeping her memory alive, so much so that it feels very odd to realise that I was only weeks old when she died."

He propped himself up on his elbow, gazing down at Ellen who responded drowsily.

"I was even luckier than you." she stretched cat-like, laughing as Sam tickled her nose with a strand of her hair.

"I have adult memories of Mother (head constantly in one book or another). Dad, grumpy and dictatorial (when Mother was looking), the provider of so much wisdom (and too many sweets) when she wasn't."

She plumped up her pillows, half-sitting up as Sam swung his legs out of bed asking, "Morning tea and toast in bed love?"

She wrinkled her nose at him considering, then threw back the bed-clothes with a wry chuckle.

"You were on to a winner until you mentioned toast my lad." she remarked severely. "I may be getting so old I can't remember when we last had a lie-in, but I do remember what you did with those biscuit crumbs last week! Besides, we have to get up and get going or we'll be late picking up Rob from Burley Manor."

In a mood of playful exuberance she turned as Sam departed for the bathroom.

"I was thinking last night, that we really ought to sort out those seeds you got at Scat's yesterday." she called after him. "We'll run out of window-sills to put our seed-trays on soon. I looked at the old lean-to yesterday. It's only tiny, but it has windows. If you moved the timber store somewhere else we'd have plenty of room."

Sam turned back.

"I'd forgotten Charlie's potting shed sweetheart, there's only enough timber to make a couple of starting shelves, but I'll sort it out later. It could come in handy once we start work at Silver Street."

His thoughtful expression changed to one of outrage as Ellen slipped past him grinning, and made for the stairs. Her voice floated back up, taunting lightly.

"Ho! Beat you Mr Slug. Last one in the bath's a donkey!" Grinning, Sam chased her downstairs with an encouraging "Hee-Haw!"

They ate breakfast in high good humour, making a combined "Things to do" list as they worked down a pile of toast and marmalade.

"After Easter, Pine Trees will re-locate to Boscombe." Ellen swept up her plate and surveyed her husband as he lingered over his coffee. She cleaned the table absently as she mused.

"It's come round so fast I can hardly believe it. By that time, I shall have been at Saint Jude's for two months, you'll only have a month before passenger services stop, and then we'll have to get on with the allotments as well. We should I suppose think about relinquishing those once we've settled at Silver Street, but I'm reluctant to do so while we still have a foot in the village."

Sam, gathering his own crockery, paused en route to the sink and asked doubtfully, "Do you see moving to Silver Street as leaving Padways?" relaxing as she shook her head. He continued seriously."

"I suppose we'll have to dream up a name for the small-holding, get horrid things like post redirected and we'll need to be on the telephone as well!", he sighed as Ellen asked curiously,

"I often wondered why the station is called Silver Street?", as she hurriedly dragged a comb through her hair, applied lipstick and hunted for car keys.

Sam smiled.

"Dad told me that the locals saw the line as the road to wealth and opportunity, like similar road names in medieval jewellery quarters. I believe that the name was intended to salute a journey of high expectation (in either direction) when the station opened during the mid-nineteenth century."

Ellen looked up into his earnest face, saw the concerned expression in his eyes, and said lightly, "Then let's not go troubling trouble! I don't want to change the station's name. Silver Street smallholding sounds perfect to me and I don't think the locals will mind either. We may not be able to change the name even if we wanted to, don't you forget the Royal Blue has secured pick-up services for all the villagers who used the station regularly. School buses will operate from the same pick-up point. Our local traders all know the station, re-naming it will just cause confusion and unnecessary expense. Besides, what would we call it?"

Sam opening the front door as he reached for his jacket stared at her in surprise. He hadn't even considered this point, but he tipped his head on one side, a quizzical expression on his face.

"Padways Halt?" he suggested slyly as he locked the door behind them, turning to follow Ellen down their steep little path, "Beeching's Defeat?", she countered as they reached the parking bay where Lady Jane waited.

"Teacher's Terminus?" he offered gallantly and yelped as she swatted him lightly.

"Porter's Pottering!", she said firmly, adjusting her rear-view mirror, and chuckling at Sam's widening eyes, before bursting into laughter as she started the engine, and backed out into the road to Burley Manor.

They didn't even have to get out of the car and enquire for Colonel Fullingford. He came smartly down the steps, a small briefcase in one hand, and came to the rear door of the car as Sam opened it towards him.

"Good morning." he greeted them briskly, "Lovely day. There's quite a feeling of spring in the air isn't there, and no, before you ask I haven't been out chasing Forest ponies either!" His brief bark of laughter caught them by surprise, but he sat happily unaware of this as they swooped down the hill and out towards Padways.

By the time they had parked and filed into Alex's "snug", they had discovered that when Rob let down his habitual guard, he was quite amusing, and they quickly responded to his less than flattering view of government decisions, as Alex arrived with Howard's help.

He looked better, Ellen decided, and wasn't that surprised to hear that Howard had already spoken to the local doctor.

"I'm getting a visit later." Alex confided with relief. "He has to see one of the Fleet boys apparently, so he'll drop by afterwards. He didn't think much of actually plastering my foot if there isn't a confirmed fracture. He's of the opinion that rural doctors know more about horse related injuries than London teaching hospitals and I hope he's right!" He sat upright in his arm-chair and looked longingly at the assorted paperwork Rob had assembled on a low table.

"What's all this then Rob?" the Australian questioned cautiously. "Does it get us any forwarder?"

Rob chuckled. "Not precisely, but it may give us some leads."

Sam, recognizing a family tree of sorts, rolled up his mental shirtsleeves and said abruptly, "Shall I take notes for you?", as Howard pulled out a nest of tables and served coffee.

Rob Fullingford looked at Alex, observing the glint of excitement in his eyes and warned.

"There are frequently gaps in family histories that one could drive a double-decker bus through, however, when enough dates tallied to piece together an outline story, it made both your mother and I decide to take a proper look. Unfortunately, as her illness was quite advanced, the situation wasn't conducive to doing much research, so we still have this intriguing dilemma to solve."

Noting the grim turn of Alex's mouth, Rob said simply, "Your mother didn't want to keep her condition secret Alex, but you were too young to understand. I deliberately brought her letters with me, so you can follow her progression into the past yourself, as we journey through your history. It would greatly assist your understanding of the situation I feel, and Sam can take notes as we go, if he doesn't mind. I'd like to get another amateur historian's take on this, and Ellen can provide us with the feminine angle as we talk."

They gathered around the table as Rob put on his glasses and began to explain.

"You'll remember that we spoke about the nineteenth century and land development in Australia yesterday." he stated flatly. "Well, about three generations ago, there seems to have been a series of events which apparently caused a rift between the Fullingford brothers, who were the principals behind the Trust I work for. Around 1895, my father (Anthony Fullingford) disappeared off the social scene, only to reappear very briefly before his marriage into the Newland family. He then re-emerged in Australia, before disappearing again, this time permanently. I hit a stumbling block, trying to follow his tracks, and having discovered that the other half of the family were wiped out in some disaster, I finally accepted that I was the last of the Fullingford line. Being brought up by my mother's family, all my cousins are on the Newlands side, so when the speculation started regarding the ownership of Newlands, you can imagine my being intrigued. So, let's start with me. I'm the only child of a short - lived marriage between Anthony James Fullingford, and Julia May Newland. I was born in 1897."

He smiled engagingly at the stunned trio in front of him and added with a despairing shake of the head.

"That only makes me sixty-six chaps! Not precisely Methuselah."

"Jeepers mate!" Alex burst forth. "If I can vault into the saddle of a rearing horse, settle it down and walk afterwards at your age I'll reckon myself fit." Rob surveyed him down the length of his nose.

"Pipe down in the ranks young man.", he suggested mildly, and carried on laying out more documents, amongst which was a marriage certificate.

Sam picked it up, noting that the marriage had taken place in Southampton, and made a swift note of the parties involved before replacing the certificate with a nod at the Colonel, who carried on talking.

"My mother (it seems) was unable to accompany her new husband out to Australia. My maternal grandfather Giles Newland (another founder of the Trust), owned the shipping line on which he travelled, but it takes skilled reading between the lines to discern the possibility of a scandal. For private reasons, my father left Britain, although there's no hint of estrangement between my parents. It seems my mother remained at home waiting for word which never came, until I was born, (during the course of which event, she died). I have no idea why he never sent for her. The family simply closed ranks about me with devastating consequences."

Rob absently took a sip of coffee as Alex leant forward and tapped the marriage and birth certificates with a long forefinger.

"How come your grandfather didn't try following the Fullingford connection?" he asked seriously. "He obviously knew Anthony well enough to permit your parent's marriage. In those days, strict rules governed who was socially acceptable so this wasn't a hole in a corner relationship or a holiday fling. They'd known each other a year or two at least before marrying. Then there's you. Even if you came along straight away, surely the Fullingfords would have been involved?"

"Yes, in the normal scheme of things," Rob agreed solemnly, "but it's my contention that Anthony Fullingford left this country to avoid total disgrace. Shortly thereafter, his brother's entire family was wiped out in an accident, which I believe may have led to my father becoming a bit of a recluse. He seems to have founded Newlands not long after his arrival in Australia, taken himself there, abjuring the kind of social scene he'd previously enjoyed. Did guilt for some action we don't know about play a part in that? Or was he simply happy to reinvent himself?" he squared his shoulders, met Alex's gaze with a humorous twist to his lips, and in that moment, Sam saw the likeness between them for the first time.

The older man continued speculating, voice soft as he sketched the era firmly in their minds, covering every eventuality. He sighed resignedly, "I've come to suspect that with most of the key players either beyond these shores, or dead, it was easier for the Newland family to assume that my father had adventured too far and fallen foul of that adventuring. Under those circumstances, absorbing a fatherless baby into a well-to-do background was less likely to bring whatever disgrace Anthony was in to light, thereby avoiding scandal." Alex leant forward as Rob casually placed the photographic calling card down on his parents' marriage certificate.

"Could he have had a second family with someone else in Australia I wonder?"

He picked up the calling card, gazing at the debonair features (so very much like his own) and sighed, relinquishing the card reluctantly.

"There's one queer thing I do know. My Grandfather's name was Robert, and my father's full name was James Robertson Ford. It's why your name startled me a bit to begin with. I wonder if there's any mileage in the fact that my Great Grandfather may have also been a Robert." he screwed up his face in disgust.

"Sounds like the way Americans use Christian names. Robert Ford senior, followed by Robert Ford junior, followed by Robert Ford the second, followed by..." he tailed off uncertainly as the Colonel leapt to his feet, pounding one hand into another.

"By Jingo!" he exclaimed out loud, "Out of the mouths of babes and sucklings!"

He stopped dead in front of Alex, who stared up at him as a broad grin split his visitors face.

"That's another part of the jig-saw obviously. Not Robert senior and junior my boy! What about Robert and Robert's son? I always wondered about that." Sam cautiously raised his head. "That's all very well my friends," he said gravely, "If we know who Robert was in the first place. Up till now we've only heard about Anthony. Now if we are to presume that he dropped out of sight when he founded Newlands, we have nothing to go on. If he left Newlands to this Robert, it might show up in a death certificate or a will. In the absence of either, I might be persuaded by the property name and registration documents. However, that still doesn't tell us who Robert was does it?"

There was a forlorn expression on Alex's face, which coupled to the mutinous twist of his mouth gave him an astonishingly pugnacious look.

"Whoever he might have been, he was my grandfather!" he insisted stubbornly. "It might cost me the only home I remember Rob, but I'll have you know I won't hear a thing against him! He left home before he knew he was to be a father, and still a young man, went to the trenches and gave up his future for Britain, just like his son was to do later."

Sam heard the depths of the sigh that came from Rob Fullingford, who looked back at the younger man steadily.

"I'm merely pointing out that whoever he was must be established before your position at Newlands can be confirmed Alex. I am merely pointing out that Robert poses a mystery, which we should solve. Whoever he was, he gave up his life so the rest of us could come home, and yes Alex, I was eighteen when I went to the trenches in nineteen fifteen. I'm old enough to be your grandfather myself. I certainly never intended to imply any lack of respect; I hope you'll accept that!"

There was an awkward silence in the room, and then Ellen leapt to her feet decisively as the door knocker fell.

"That's the doctor." she announced swiftly. "Now, while you have your mind set on family name formulae Sam Smart, don't you even consider something similar should we have children!"

She assisted Alex to his feet as she spoke, leaving Sam staring as they moved towards the dining room.

"Oh my!", commented the Colonel admiringly as they departed.

"Sam, followed by Samson! What a combination!"

"Huh!", remarked the porter disdainfully. "Beats the heck out of John, Paul, George or Ringo!"

Chapter 27 - The Turn of a Corkscrew

They re-convened after lunch, with a very relieved Alex (sans plaster-cast), his foot expertly strapped with adhesive tape. His toes had been covered with a loose sock, but he proudly displayed the violet discolouration to an admiring audience.

Rob said severely, "You'll have to keep off that now Alex.", but his host was grinning cheerfully.

"Doc says the bruising will disperse nicely providing I keep it elevated for a few days. After that, he wants me to get it re-X-rayed and see a physiotherapist. I can have crutches from the practice tomorrow. He reckoned it will still need support for a while, but at least I'll be able to get about by myself. Now, are we getting anywhere chaps? I thought that maybe we'd go round to the Vicarage and ask Martin if he can dig through the Parish records for us. Perhaps we can follow the names back?", at which Rob said softly,

"We might even consider the other part of the Fullingford family, particularly as your Mr Godwin had such a strong reaction to seeing your face. It's true that you appear to resemble my father strongly, but how that comes about I can't see. There's no previous marriage, no known children (legitimate or otherwise) and your mother told me that he is buried at Newlands, having died when I was about nineteen."

Alex, who had endured Ellen lifting his foot onto a pile of cushions, ran his mind over the problem before saying abruptly, "Whoever he turns out to be Rob, my grandfather couldn't be your half-brother from a subsequent marriage. I hope you don't mind me shooting that theory down in flames, but if Antony only left Britain in eighteen ninety-six, he couldn't have fathered my grandfather who died in nineteen seventeen in his late twenties. We're years adrift somewhere, and yes, I have considered the chances that this Robert *is* the scandal he was exiled for, but it doesn't ring true somehow."

His young voice sounded matter of fact, but Sam, stealing a glance at his friend saw his brows drawn together in a scowl of concentration as he continued, "I think we'll find out that unless Anthony legally adopted himfrom somewhere, my Grandfather wasn't Anthony's son. So who the hell was he?"

"How do you know how old he was when he died Alex?", was Sam's question, and Alex explained ruefully.

"My Nan was a great cross-stitch fanatic. I remember her working samplers for just about every wedding, birth or death amongst her friends. Anyway, there's a sampler on the chimney-breast at home which she worked for her own wedding. When I had measles, she got it down and showed me one day. It had doves on it, holding a wedding ring and their names as well as their birthdays. I thought she'd made a mistake because his birthday was one day different to hers, but she explained that he was one day older than her until her birthday, when they were both the same age. It stuck in my mind because she used to say that she stopped having birthdays on her twenty-fifth. She didn't want to have birthdays without her Robert. Of course, after they married he left to come back to claim some sort of inheritance and she never saw him again."

"My dear chap!", exclaimed Rob sympathetically seeing Alex's composure waver, as the childhood memory surfaced. "I can't think that anyone could make that up, it's too personal, too poignant. Besides, samplers are valuable dating tools, materials, stitches even the layout demonstrate their authenticity. I've studied a few in my time, which makes me feel particularly helpless! If only I could get out to Australia myself and check all this out!"

Alex raised blazing eyes. "Why don't you Rob? You know that we'll have to take that step anyway. Let's go, find out what we can and come back. I'm sure the Trust would see the point of the exercise, after all, we might think of someone like Ollie Godwin who could remember my grandfather's time."

Almost immediately, an odd expression crossed his face, his eyes glazed momentarily, then he said in a strangled gasp.

"Strewth! I just remembered. My Nan told my Mum to take care of old Jim Kennedy. He's a rum sort, ancient as the hills and part aborigine I think. Anyway, he's about eighty now, still cooking up trouble near Newlands! Oh yes! Rob, if he's alive he'll know more than anyone about this. Why didn't I think of him before?"

There was little more to say at that point. Alex was quivering with pent-up energy, and fairly tore through his mother's letters, picking up points to hammer home with enthusiasm. Rob made copious notes, resting a pad on his briefcase and guardedly agreeing to pursue the matter of a trip out to Newlands, once they'd scoured the County Records Office in Bournemouth. Sam and Ellen took themselves home for tea, and passed on the request for Parish records to Martin after evensong, before returning home to prepare for the working week.

Still restless, Sam stared pensively towards his father's work-shed, (dimly visible now the lighter nights were beginning). He complained to Ellen.

"Well, that's us out of the picture love. Those two will take themselves off to Australia chasing phantoms, and we'll just have to get on with life here. It's just as well we're going to be too busy with the mundane matter of converting a railway station into a smallholding to worry about who that boy's grandfather was, 'cos the answer lies far beyond these shores."

She smiled at his wistful expression, reminding him that he didn't like travelling at more than fifty miles an hour.

"Go on with you Sam," she remarked crushingly, "You're just jealous! I wouldn't swap our nice well-behaved station, nor all the work to convert it, for hours of flying, foreign places and strange dinners. I don't like some of the things that fascinate Alex you know? We aren't meant to know some things, and this grandfather of his sounds quite sinister in a funny sort of way. I don't like mysterious people, and there doesn't seem to be any rhyme or reason to this Robert does there? I'd want to be sure that he wasn't just some itinerant who moved in on a lonely ageing man, far from home, cut off from his family. Oh Sam.", she shivered, "What if he turns out to be some dreadful crook after all. Alex will be so hurt, he's so proud of the man's sacrifice. No I'm glad we're not stepping into the middle of an ancient mystery! Give me old railway stations, old porters, and closing railway lines anyday rather than mysterious men, and the possibility of resurrecting some ancient scandal. Thank God nothing weird ever happens round Padways!"

"Oi!", said her husband sharply. "Who are you calling an old porter madam? I got plenty of life in me yet!", and proceeded to demonstrate.

That last month and a half positively shot past. Passenger numbers fluctuated wildly as commuters with cars took to the roads, or took advantage of sharing transport and (as one was heard to put it), "Getting into practice for the new routine."

The car-park on the down-line side of Silver Street got County Highways attention. A team of workmen widened the entrance, a proper coach bay was painted and a timetable fixed to a Royal Blue sign was erected.

"Looks more like a bloody bus stop than a railway station.", Fred grumbled, but brightened up when he saw the accoutrements being installed.

"Cor!", he said reverently, as Sam and Mike encountered him cutting across the newly laid gravel. "There's going to be a proper shelter, toilets, large bins and a job for a maintenance man as well. I just put in for an interview. They want someone to lock and unlock the toilets, clean and litter-pick the car park, and keep the ponies out. It's only part-time see, but it's all gris to the mill!'"

Mike smiled encouragingly.

"Well done Fred, I hope you get fixed up with that. It'll run in nicely for the last few weeks, then you'll be able to browbeat Sam into giving you a bit of land to grow some veg and Molly won't have to worry about where to find you!" He chuckled as he walked back along the newly painted railings, clipboard in hand, checking the boundary of the down-line platform. Fred eyed Sam dubiously, then said brightly,

"Now don't think I'm pushing Sam, but he's right. Iffen you could spare me a little patch about the size of an allotment I could be occupying myself with the car park mornings, digging and planting afternoons, then locking up afterwards in time for Molly to collect me on her way back home. She doesn't work shifts at Robin's Way, it was one of the things that attracted her. We like our weekends and evenings free, and now young Trevor Steadman is courting a Padways girl, he's interested in covering for me when I need him. What do you say?"

Sam thought about it for a moment, then nodded.

"We're still clearing for Southern Rail till the line is lifted.", he reminded Fred. "I don't anticipate there being any objection to my getting on with marking out once traffic stops altogether, and besides that, I've two cottages and two allotments on the go myself. Whatever or wherever is all the same to me Fred, just don't expect me to pay you wages when I don't have any myself.", and so Easter passed in the usual flurry of flowers and egg hunts. The days lengthened, the hours and minutes passed, and May shook her blossoms on the hedgerows as the last passenger service drew in to Silver Street.

There had been a staff party of sorts the night before, bunting hung from the canopy, tubs and pots of flowers decked the trolleys, but Sam saw significance in the presence of two passengers who prepared to board a train bristling with reporters, protestors and those carrying a petition to Whitehall. Alex, (now restored to full mobility was clearly torn between wanting to support Sam and Ellen, and his own impatience to be off, back to Australia.

It took the suave dignity of Rob Fullingford to control the impatient hopping about of his protégé, and Sam was glad of the older man's influence as he turned to the sound of the rail's low humming.

"Cooee! Here she comes!", said the exuberant voice, as the last passenger service steamed into view. Sam's throat clenched, stifling him temporarily, then he was swinging heavy suitcases off his barrow, as she glided to a hissing expectant stop, the guards van almost opposite the

Station Master's Office.

They boarded silently, the young Australian, Colonel Fullingford, followed by Sam, who lifted the first-class passenger's luggage on to the racks then took Alex's hand.

"Keep your chin up mate!", his friend exclaimed impulsively, "Don't forget what your pa's mate told you. This door closes, but a whole raft of others open. You just keep your chin up and look for the openings!"

Rob Fullingford shook Sam's hand warmly.

"I'll look after him Sam. We'll be back as soon as possible. Don't forget to wire me your telephone number once you get it sorted and we'll let Howard know once our flights are booked."

The train jolted and clanked, a powerful "chuff" of steam made Sam think that it was impatient to be out on the track, and he retreated back to the platform where he belonged. All the staff were lined up in front of the station clock, a photographer was kneeling by a large box camera on a stand, and Ellen touched Sam's hand, pushing him into place beside Fred Cummins.

There was a band playing somewhere as the wheels rattled and jostled under the restraining hand of the engineer, camera's clicked and whirred, photographers exhortations to "Look this way chaps", and "Hold up the petition sir!" rang out, but Sam's eyes were too full of tears to see as the station began its familiar chant.

"Clear the doors now! Clear the doors!", to the accompaniment of slams, and the clack of descending windows.

"All aboard now! All aboard!", followed by the ascending double blast of the guard's whistle as photographers scrambled into the guards van, and Mike Theobald stepped forward to salute the train and her precious cargo.

The steam billowed along the platform, the engineer building it deliberately before losing the voice of the locomotive in a haunting salute.

"Woo-hoo", it called down the generations of its kind as Sam's lips moved, locking this memory, the sounds of this memory deep in his heart forever, then she was moving.

"Chuff, chuff, ker-churr, chuff ker-churr, chuff, chuff, ker-churr!", she sang to the London line, and even if she wore a banner proclaiming R I P, there was nothing dead in the steam that wreathed Silver Street as its last passenger service reached the turn of Castleman's corkscrew, and passed out of sight.

Summer 1964 was one of those periods that Sam preferred to forget. Somehow, the loss of his daily routine, coupled to the sheer slog of transferring the ownership of the old station, completely robbed him of his happy-go-lucky nature. Overwhelmed by responsibilities, he worked his allotment, silently unapproachable, reading late into each night, attempting to forearm himself against an uncertain future, depressed by his lack of confidence in anything. In the week following Alex and Rob's departure, Ellen kept her distance, going over to the Vicarage to plan her own allotment with Jane and her gardener, but eventually she could stand it no longer.

She found Sam, sitting on an up-turned crate near their back-door, steadily working his way through his tools. Eyeing his progress as he sharpened and oiled chisels, she took a letter out of her pocket and said abruptly, "Before Alex left, I was going to share some news with everyone, but somehow it didn't seem appropriate. I'd much rather share my news with you alone, but if you're too busy I can tell you later."

Sam caught the note of uncertainty in her voice and looked up puzzled, then he seemed to shake himself out of his "brown study", and came alive to her enquiry.

"News missus?", his flippant reply didn't fool Ellen for a moment, as she settled down on the door-step facing him.

"Yes darling, news and good news at that. I eventually discovered that there are specialist toy fairs, where various publishers take stands. A number of them produce books about toy-making, some of them even run business courses and one of them promotes interest in the history of toys. I eventually plucked up the courage to send them a synopsis, and this is what they propose. I'm to send the first four chapters so that they can get a feel for style, any additional illustrations or photographs that go with those chapters, then they'd like me to go to London and discuss a contract!"

She smiled up at Sam happily, and he grinned back, saying, "Wow! I knew you could do it my girl, but where are you going to find the time to write, teach, and help me get settled at Silver Street? I could do with forty-eight hours a day myself, and I'm sure we can't manage if you have to give up teaching!"

Undeterred by his obvious concern, Ellen said promptly, "Well, there are changes at work after the summer holidays Sam. I've been asked to go full-time at St Jude's. Don't get me wrong, I love teaching Drama, but my first loyalty is to the village, and Martin. He tells me that he's getting numerous requests for school places in September, which ironically seem to come from mothers having to give up the family car so that their husbands can continue to work. As you know, our initial fear was that young families would move away once the station closed, but that doesn't seem to be the case. Driving into Ringwood takes up the hours I need on the allotment. Our plans come first this time Sam, besides it'll pay better and I won't have the expense of travel."

Sam closed his tool-box thoughtfully, nodding as she continued, "Emma Fleet wants to give me a hand on the allotment as well.", she smiled as Sam said enthusiastically,

"Yes, I heard about that. Seems she's got some idea of repeating last year's marrow prize, she's already popped in to borrow a book or two, though what she really wants is her husband to give her a hand. I can't fathom the man, he's got no hobbies, no job, and never stirs himself to help in the shop either."

Ellen glanced up, it was unlike Sam to be so judgmental, but seeing the puzzled expression on his face she decided to confide in him.

"I think a lot of people have got Bert Fleet wrong dear.", she patted Sam's knee. "It's not all his fault. Rory tackled him head on when he came home on leave last week, Emma told me all about it, but this has to remain confidential, or it could wreck whatever chance I can give him."

Sam's head came up as she explained slowly, "It seems that the poor man has been trying to hide the fact that he can neither read nor write, although he's far from stupid. I've got some colleagues looking into the cause of his difficulty while I've promised to help him, so he can begin to lead a normal life in future."

"Good Lord!", Sam said, remembering the avid interest Bert had shown in his photographs of the railway at his Harvest Home talk.

"That would exclude him from nearly every job going. Poor blighter, yet all their kids are clever with their hands. Perhaps Bert is too, but hasn't got the confidence to find out!"

His shock and pity were genuine and furthermore he seemed to have come out of the place into which he'd retreated recently, so Ellen well pleased with the effect of her news made "bangers and mash" for tea, and went into their small sitting-room to begin work on the book she planned to write. They soon settled into a new routine, and Sam began to feel better. He'd undertaken to clean and restock Ellen's cottage, which was once again ready to rent, and if he felt the gap left by his exuberant Australian friend, the little changes he had made to Ellen's cottage more than made up for that.

Alex had expressed surprise when Ellen had asked how much she owed him for getting the floors sanded, and for the equipping of the kitchen with luxury items, but Alex just grinned.

"You'll have to talk to Howard about that. He simply wasn't going to revert to his previous calling as "butler cum general factotum" without the right equipment. He'd been spoilt by some film star or another, and working in London, he was always talking to someone's valet, someone's butler or worse still Lord somebody's cook. You take anything you want with you and Sam up to Silver Street when you go. If the cottage isn't let before we return, we'll talk about taking it over again, but Rob's overdue for retirement now, and it's likely the Trust will have found his replacement by the time we get back. He's got a service flat in London, hates it with a vengeance, and is determined to settle in the country. He's a wealthy man, and I have my suspicions that he'd look in this area if he had a base to work from."

"What about you?", Ellen had said, wondering if Alex would ever settle for one country now he had the taste for travel.

Alex simply smiled and admitted, "I don't really know Ellen. Home is where the heart is, and while my family were alive that was Australia. However, when Rob and I go up to Town, he's going to gather up the story of how the Trust was founded. We're going to take a look at that, see where Newlands fits into the picture, and evaluate it carefully. We'll let you know the minute we arrive, and write regularly. Don't worry, we won't forget you!", and to her great surprise he'd swept off his bush hat, leant forward and kissed her cheek.

She'd relayed all this to Sam at the time, but he was drained with the emotion of closing day, and she'd been forced to repeat it again when he questioned the use of a huge Kenwood mixer one evening. He'd brightened under the influence of a slab of cherry cake however, laughing as she described Mrs Thomas's envy.

"Honestly Sam… she was nearly green when I told her what I'd been given. She came over and watched me using it, now I don't suppose for a minute that she hasn't passed on all its merits to Jane, the Vicar, or Uncle Tom Cobley and all! I can see that I'll be asked to make cakes for the W I next, and I just don't have the time. Still, Alex bought it for Howard, so even a man can use one!"

Sam, (resisting the obvious temptation she was throwing in his direction) remarked gloomily that he didn't think the Men's Institute had such a commanding ring, and went away laughing when Ellen suggested he start one up and ask Bert Fleet and Fred Cummins to join.

Over the summer he'd gradually recovered his sense of humour, found himself getting excited over their forthcoming move, then the vandals struck.

It was late afternoon at the end of August when he became aware of running feet and a panting voice calling his name.

"Mr Smart, Mr Smart. Come quick, the station's on fire! Mum's called the Fire Brigade, Dad and the Vicar are calling in everyone who's on the phone, but we've got to hurry!"

Young Dan Fleet vaulted the gate and ran up Sam's path, his face white with fear. He came to a quivering stop, as Sam grabbed a spade, thrust another into his hands and said tersely.

"Well done Dan, tell me later, just run now!", and pounded past, long legs stretching as they hit Padways main street.

A tractor and trailer were turning out of Home Farm as they ran towards it, Jack Sherrington driving, his two sons riding in the trailer. The farmer slowed to a crawl shouting back over his shoulder as one of his boys leant out to steady Sam, grabbing his spade as the farmer's voice rang out.

"Hop up Sam. Dave saw the smoke and went to investigate. Some of those stupid young blighters on Lambretta's just thought they'd have some fun, but it's backfired badly. Beryl's applying first aid to the one he caught, the others rode off towards Sway. We'll leave the cops to catch them, we're heading up to Silver Street."

By now Sam had leapt into the trailer, but Dan Fleet hesitated.

"Should I run around the village and turn everyone out?", he asked, and noting the grim set of Sam's mouth, he handed up the spare spade, saying,

"Right, I'll go to the Hay Rack next. Meet you in the coach park."

"Oh my God!", Sam burst forth. "We'll have to evacuate the coach stop.", then the tractor was racing up the incline, and all he could do was to grasp at the bar on the front of the trailer and pray.

Jack Sherrington's face was grim as he blocked the road. Sam, Dave and Mike Sherrington running towards the billowing smoke that poured up from the station climbed over the railings. Throwing old potato sacks from the trailer over first, they headed (without a glance up or down line) over the trolley crossing to where the water tank stood. Knocking the pumping handle into place, Sam prayed that he'd left water in situ, pumping as he assessed the extent of the blaze.

From the outer edges of the west-bound platform, encompassing the coach-park (that fronted the old station car-park), greasy smoke billowed. It hung heavy in the atmosphere, wreathing the coppice of willows that stood beyond, out and into the typical gorse and bramble strewn thickets, where Forest and heathland met.

Eyes stinging with smoke, Sam bent to his task, shouting directions as the water began to flow reluctantly from the overhead tank onto the ground where a steady pile of potato sacks had grown, (courtesy of the Sherrington boys).

The water was warm, brown and stank to high heaven but it was wet and plentiful. Soaking sacks, and grabbing fire buckets which he'd found stacked beside the parcels office Sam grimly advanced off the platform and into the dried undergrowth of the nearest thicket, where flames flickered in the shadows under the trees. They heard shouts ahead of them and found Fred Cummins pounding a smoking bush to the ground.

"Wretched scooter gang.", was his only comment as they fought what at first seemed a small blaze into submission, but it wasn't over by a long chalk. Gradually a working party assembled in the far side of the loading bay where smoke hadn't penetrated, and teams were equipped with potato sacks to wet, and runners to take them to the fire-fighters. Out of the corner of his eye, Sam saw Molly Cummins arrive for Bert, then taking in the situation, park her car and set up a first-aid post on the up-line platform.

A fierce crackling told Sam that flames had caught something dry, and he turned to see them licking greedily at the gorse bushes close to the back of the storage sheds along the rear of the sidings. Only dimly aware of a clanging bell (as the fire-brigade arrived), he let out a roar of fury and leapt into the fray, as the fire encircled his Silver Street Station, and threatened all he had worked for in his life.

It took hours to bring the blaze under control. Weeks of dry weather, the proximity of the Forest and nearby heathland, and the fact that the culprits had started the fires in several places, left men sweating and exhausted and still beating out and dampening down until early the next morning, but Silver Street survived.

Sam sat on the up-line platform. Jeans ripped, face blackened with smoke, and grinned hugely as the firemen crowded around rolling up hoses, surveying their handiwork.

"You were very lucky my friend.", Martin poured Sam another cup of tea from a thermos flask as he spoke, grey hair plastered to his scalp with sweat, clerical collar beyond salvation, but a beatific smile on his face.

"Indeed we were.", Sam agreed solemnly, "What's more, I just realised that I've saved a fortune as well. I'd just decided to clear that thicket ready for planting, now I shan't have to! What's more, there's enough potash to treat that ground ten times over. Natural fertiliser always works best, though I wouldn't want to go through this to produce it."

There was a little chuckle from the firemen standing nearby, then out of the blue, a gentle Irish voice broke in.

"Mind your hands sor! The skins are still a bit hot! Mind your hands gents!", and both the Vicar and Sam found themselves (along with most of the firemen) clutching hot baked potatoes in both hands. Laughter broke out as Jack Sherrington shook his head and accepted potatoes with a wry grin at the slight figure with the brogue that cheerfully ran back and forth to where one section of smoking ground was still being guarded from re-igniting.

"Well sor! I'd take it kindly if you'd agree to donate those few tatties so I would.", announced the man with the piercing green eyes as he conversed with the farmer who towered over his slight form.

"Well...Mr Flynn", the farmer retorted cheerfully, "I'd take it kindly if you'd find me another spud like the last one! Fire-fighting's hard work, and as you wouldn't know about that, you may as well do something useful!"

"Now I'd call that really unfriendly!", protested the Irishman, heaving a hugely theatrical sigh. "Where's the sense in having half a trailer full of spuds, perfect baking conditions, and not putting the two things together?"

There was a ripple of laughter as he scampered off to collect more "tatties" from the edge of the smoking ground, and so it was that out of the disaster that never was, Sam met Paddy Flynn, and found out about dousing for the water Silver Street needed so badly. However, that was not the only thing that Sam learned that summer. One of the firemen spoke to him as they began to pack up. He was a tall, serious faced individual who said solemnly,

"I understand from Mr Sherrington that you are the new owner of Silver Street. Now, I'd advise you to cut back along the edges of the property line. Take stock of where your land has trees and bushes and make sure there's a well maintained gap between raw Forest and your property. When the two things get intertwined like those gorse bushes along the sidings, we can't expect Fire to know the difference. I'll send someone along to advise you on creating a firebreak along your boundaries, but remembering that your buildings are largely timbered, I'd do it sooner than later. The police will catch up with the lads that started this lot, but that's a twin edged sword, because the moment this hits the papers, some idiot will try to copy them, we see it all the time. What's the state of your insurance cover?"

Sam eyed him squarely, feeling slightly sick as he realised he didn't know, and the fireman nodded seriously.

"Check your buildings and contents cover mate, and remember, while this stands empty you're a sitting target. I'd say Home Farm is your nearest neighbour, so you need a night-watchman. Set up a fire patrol at weekends so that coach parties using the Royal Blue don't get onto the station with unfortunate results, and I'll get someone out to advise you further."

Sam watched them depart morosely, wondering precisely how he could afford to insure the station as things stood.

Notwithstanding that particular concern, he busied himself about Silver Street for the next few days. Mike Theobald arrived one afternoon, and found him steadily ripping out gorse along the sidings with a mattock.

He surveyed the singed ground all about the station seriously, then called out to Sam, who was thoroughly engrossed in the operation.

"Sam? Can you spare a minute? I've something for you from Southern Rail, and a present that I think you'll find useful.", he turned towards the large van he'd arrived in, and almost as Sam came over the rails and up onto the down-line platform, he went to the back doors of the van, and let down the tailgate. Sam gaped as he saw (sitting just inside) a sturdy looking machine, with huge wheels and long handles which were canted up at an angle. The whole thing was resting on its "nose", a large metal loop at the front, then he became aware of other attachments in the back of the wagon. Something that resembled a ploughshare, another with tines, then bundles of hand tools were revealed as someone fixed back the doors.

"Hello!", the ex-porter said admiringly, "What's all this Mike? Why aren't you at work? I thought you'd gone to Brockenhurst to understudy Mr Cuthbert."

He was peering into the van as he spoke, and Mike grinned as his companions came round to off-load the intriguing machine, carrying a length of timber to create a ramp for the strange mechanism.

"Well Sam," said Mike comfortably, "I'll hold you to account for my becoming assistant Station Master at Brockenhurst. As a result of which, I no longer have the time to look after my old Dad's allotments He's too old to manage them himself, so as I have moved into my own place over there, he gave me our Trusty tractor. He's going to Eastleigh to live with his sister, so we have absolutely no need for it, or for all the tools in the back there. Mindful of the good turn you did my career, I thought you'd like the permanent loan of the old Trusty. It runs like a dream, will make short work of clearing the fire-breaks that should have been maintained here, and it's simple to use. We'll put it into the large storage barn for now, along with the tools, and I'll get one of the Sherrington boys to show you how to use it."

There was a shaking as Mike's two companions rolled the fearsome looking two wheeled tractor down the ramp, then one of them bent to the starting handle and it roared into life.

While Sam paled at the thought of controlling such a throaty machine, the beast placidly chugged along towards the storage barn, steered into place by Mike's driver, (who seemed utterly casual about handling it). The two men emptied the van, carefully placing two jerry-cans, a funnel, and other incidentals into a cool, dark corner, then returned to the van as Mike locked up for the night, while Sam gaped in disbelief.

He eventually found his voice.

"I don't know what to say Mike.", he stuttered, "I've never driven anything in my life mind, so I hope I can manage your Trusty!", at which Mike grinned.

"Not mine anymore mate!", he reminded Sam cheerfully, and "Yours truly has given up being towed round allotments by a mechanical plough. Just don't come off the platform in either direction and you'll be ok. Their lifting the line shortly, but I'd hate to see you trying to outrun the Bournemouth Belle if you come off the up-line platform!"

They watched Fred locking up the coach park, then Mike said suddenly, "Good Heavens Sam, I almost forgot.", he reached into his jacket and produced an enormous envelope which chinked as he handed it over solemnly.

"Here you are mate.", said the last Station Master at Silver Street. "The keys to the kingdom. You are now master of all you survey, and may I wish you and yours the very best of luck!", and smiling he handed Sam the package formally addressed to "Mr Samuel Smart, (The Owner), Station House, Silver Street Station, Padways, Dorset."

Chapter 29- The End of the Line

Autumn was colouring the trees when Ellen rushed into Church Cottage excitedly. She habitually stopped to hang up her coat in the hall cupboard (where her neat nature had banned such items), but today she scurried into the kitchen, and threw her arms round her bemused husband. With no specific routine, Sam usually got home ahead of her to serve tea, so when she arrived, they could share news, plan their evenings, or work on individual projects until bedtime.

This evening, he smiled down at her, then returning the unexpected embrace with enthusiasm, enquired guardedly, "How much is this going to cost me?", but she dimpled mischievously and waived two letters at him.

"Nothing silly!", she exclaimed happily, "I just heard from Annette Julian. Sam, she's working for a French exchange student organisation, and she's bringing ten students over with a male tutor, and they'll be in the area for at least three weeks. She wants to know if we can put her up here for a few days, but better still, she wants you to show off Silver Street, then give a talk to the group. She says...." She scanned the flimsy air-mail form and said breathlessly,

"Oh, it seems that Jane and Martin are hosting Monsieur Gilbert (the other tutor), they'll be using the Hall for classes, and the rest of the group will be staying *en famille* round the village, with the parents of the reciprocating students. If this idea takes off, a lot more will happen in the future. They are even contemplating non-exchange students who will pay for their stays."

She beamed at Sam, and said happily, "We get paid for hosting Annette of course."

"I'm not bothered by finding room for one extra mouth love," he said gallantly, "she's your friend, but we don't lead a particularly interesting life, and things are a bit basic round here you know."

She surprised him by kissing his worried brow, then waving the second letter at him.

"This will take care of any of those sort of concerns my lad!", she handed him the letter. "That's money in the bank.", she chortled, "I've got to get my head down now though and I need a title for my book!"

She passed him the letter headed "B. Bathson Limited (Publishers)"] and Sam stared at it blankly as words swam before his eyes.

"Pleased to offer you a contract....", and "secure your presence at the launch....", followed by "signings at Hamleys of London!" He struggled to clear his mind, listening to his own voice commenting briskly.

"Right then. I'll have to get on and set up the back-room as a study cum sewing-room for you won't I? I've put it off for far too long, but if I can get Fred to help me out it won't take more than a week. When do you expect Miss Julian's crowd to arrive? We'll do the spare room at the same time. It'll be two more jobs off my list, and it'll keep Fred occupied as well. How much do you reckon we can spare?"

Ellen gaped at him, unused to this new decisive person she was married to, then she gurgled with laughter.

"I can't see Fred Cummins decorating.", she chuckled. "Have you seen the size of his hands? I need more than a bucket of whitewash slapped on station walls darling.", but Sam grinned benignly and said,

"Just you hold on young lady. You can't castigate a man for short - comings you don't know he's got. He's neat, knowledgeable and likes decorating. He's done rooms at Robins Way for the old folk, helped no end of youngsters get set-up in their first homes as well. Let's go see him before casting any of those "nasturtiums" about !"

So, (for the sake of domestic peace) Ellen agreed.

Several evenings later, they were shown into a beautifully proportioned living-room which looked out over a neatly trimmed box hedge to the upstairs neighbour's garden. However, when Molly appeared (trying to be hospitable) her puffy eyes told Ellen that something was badly wrong. While their hosts busied themselves in the kitchen, Ellen said wretchedly, "Sam! I have the horrid feeling they're in trouble. I don't know what's wrong but we're decidedly *de trop.*"

He grinned, touched her nose with a finger and said lightly, "Don't let our French visitors make you talk funny my girl. I get the meaning sometimes but I'll speak plain Dorset thank you!", then turned to see Molly mopping red-rimmed eyes.

Before Ellen could prevent him, Sam rose, took Molly's hand and said gently, "Molly, we can't help noticing that something's wrong. Whatever it is, would you two be better off if Ellen and I took ourselves back to Padways? We won't starve I can assure you, but you've obviously had some sort of upset, and you need time to sort it out.", but Molly shook her head, and said gruffly,

"Sam, I'm only grateful that you're here! It'll stop Fred going off his head and punching someone. Perhaps he'll talk about it to you, I can't make him see the wood through the trees, he's so darned mad about things. Just let me dish up, and we'll talk over dinner."

As they filed into the small dining room next door, Ellen cast a surprised glance around the room. Whereas the living room had been a gentle blend of greens and creams, in the dining-room someone had given way to a more romantic approach. The slender legged dining table (more commonly set for two) had been fully extended to accommodate all of them, and the rosewood gleamed against the deep rose of the walls. From swagged curtains to cream rugs this room was fit to display in any woman's magazine, and Fred blushed becomingly as Ellen declared impulsively, "Oh, how lovely. Molly you lucky thing.", as their hostess passed a basket of warmed bread through a serving hatch and her husband helped his guests to seat themselves.

They ate a vegetable soup with the bread and Sam didn't need to ask if it was home made as he tasted carrot, onion, courgette, mushroom and barley in an intoxicating blend of herbs and wine. There was silence until Sam said reverently, "I reckon there are some of those top chefs that couldn't cook like that!", and to his immense surprise Fred blushed again, and Molly said proudly,

"Don't look at me Sam. I can't boil an egg and I've far too much to do with my career to bother about it now. Fred is the frustrated chef, who could never afford the training. He spends hours following cooking programmes, goes to all the exhibitions, spends half my wages on kitchen gadgets, and can be relied on for parties and barbecues if ever you're throwing one. It's just unfortunate that he can't get a full-time job in that field, and that we're going to lose our lovely home!"

Her voice faltered for a moment, but as she hastily rose, clearing away dishes to hide her tears, Ellen looked up and found herself staring right into Sam's eyes.

As Fred and Molly clattered about serving up their main course, Ellen thought frantically.

"Alex hasn't let us know when he's coming back yet. He wouldn't hold it against us if we let the cottage would he?", as Sam frowned, thinking along similar lines.

Tender loin chops, fresh garden peas and crisp roast potatoes with a garnish of finely chopped vegetable (in shades of red, yellow and green) followed, then as dishes were cleared, Molly said apologetically, "Neither Fred nor I do puddings folks, but we've biscuits and cheese and coffee to follow if that's ok?", and they settled to listen as Fred cleared his throat.

"I'm sorry Sam, it's not been the evening we planned but the post was a bit of a shock. We didn't have any time to take it in before you arrived.

He opened an envelope, looked at the contents, and then thrust the single sheet into Sam's hands, saying abruptly, "It's not fair. They haven't given it any time before giving up.", and with mounting apprehension, Sam saw that the thick white notepaper was headed "Royal Blue Coach Services." He bent over the page reading out loud for the benefit of the women.

"Due to the lack of bookings and the fall-off in established routes, we regret that as of 31st December 1964, all but the 7.30 am service to Brockenhurst, and the 8.00 am (weekday only) service to Lymington bus station will cease to operate.

Passengers using the Lymington service will have to return via the standard Hants and Dorset service departing Lymington Bus Station at 5.25 pm (weekdays only), terminating at Burley. There are no current plans to upgrade this service which is currently under review.

New Forest Coaches (Brockenhurst) will continue to operate a school bus to and from Brockenhurst (pick-ups unchanged), and will also run (additionally) a return service from Brockenhurst to Silver Street Station meeting the 6.05 pm London train (weekdays only).

Wellworthy employees can board a dedicated service from Silver Street. (Pick-Ups unchanged).

As a result, Royal Blue Coach Services are unable to continue employing maintenance staff at Silver Street, or Holmsley Halts, and must therefore (regretfully) give you notice that the six months trial period of employment initially offered, will cease as of midnight 31st December 1964."

Imagining how helpless Fred must have felt, Sam switched his attention to the other missive, now clutched in Fred's large hands.

"It gets worse mate!", Fred exclaimed dramatically. "not only do Royal Blue want to get shot of me, this smarmy blighter wants our home "for his own use!"

He blushed, aware that Ellen was watching him, and mumbled an apology.

"Sorry Mrs Smart, I've come to the end of the line I'm afraid! I don't usually call people names but honestly, this one takes the prize. ".

The mere flicker of a plea in Molly's face inspired Sam to suggest they air the problem in Fred's neat front garden, getting out his pipe to encourage his friend to accompany him. They sat on the low brick wall, contemplating the four square feet of grass that comprised Fred's only access to the outdoor life, as he thrust his hands into his pockets and spoke morosely.

"Mr George Randall, our esteemed landlord, has a small property empire stretching from here to Winchester. He owns at least six properties in Burley that I know of, but he's come badly unstuck in London it seems. As a result of which, he has decided to return to this area. He stresses (or rather his solicitor stresses), that this is not a matter of his choosing. However, both Mrs Hill (upstairs), and I have been told that as a result of his current situation, our leases which we were due to renew next month, won't be renewed at all, and the legal magic lies in the following sentence. "My client therefore advises you that he requires the property for his own use." I've got to go over to Lymington and get it checked out, but our solicitor seemed to think there's nothing we can do. We'll get our deposit back alright, we won't lose our references, but a months' notice? We'll have to move, after fifteen years. Molly's frantic over her job, she's in-line to step up to Deputy Matron next year, which affects her pension prospects substantially. I thought losing Silver street was bad, but Sam, this takes the biscuit. I can't help recalling how he said our flats were "the pick of the bunch", when he did a surprise inspection back in January."

Sam nodded sympathetically, an idea growing swiftly as he knocked the dottle of tobacco from his pipe and returned indoors, gravely noting that in their absence Ellen and Molly had gravitated to the living-room, where they sat side by side on the sofa, Molly's eyes suspiciously wet. Sam beckoned Ellen urgently, and whispered to her as Fred put a kettle on to boil.

She heard Sam out, grinned and nodded in agreement.

"It's exactly right Sam. Yes, if you hadn't suggested it, I certainly would have, although I'm sorry I can't help the lady upstairs."

Sam only waited for Fred to put down a tea-tray before broaching the subject directly.

"How would you two like to move to Padways?", he asked, watching the colour ebb and flow in Molly's unguarded face.

Ellen picked up the offer, "My last tenant was only temporary, and my cottage needs someone living there permanently, or at least until you two find your feet again. I don't need deposits immediately, I don't need references (though I'm not going to tell his solicitor that). Just a simple agreement suits me fine, and I'm not going to raise the rent anytime soon.", she caught Sam's quizzical gaze and explained that had Fred or the other tenant protested, their landlord would have nearly doubled their rent in order to provide himself with income sufficient to rent a house for his own use.

"That's despicable!", cried an outraged Sam, but Fred had the last word on the subject. In a mixture of relief and frustration, he stated (to the amusement of the others),

"Well, I daresay I shouldn't speak like this in mixed company, but some men have the misfortune to be born bastards. However, Mr George Randall is what you'd call "a self-made man!""

By the time he had finished chuckling they'd spoken to Mike Theobald on Molly's phone (a necessity of work), persuading him to lend the use of his van with no difficulty, matching Jack Sherrington's efforts with the trailer. Ellen wrote a stiffly formal letter terminating the couple's tenancy, relieved to discover that their upstairs neighbour had other plans and was returning to Birmingham.

Fred and Molly finally made the move over one bright October weekend, calling in at Silver Street to leave two large bookcases, a set of kitchen chairs and a small table they didn't need, as well as a large map of the line. Sam raised an eyebrow at Fred, but the older man just grinned admitting gleefully, "Old Oswald couldn't believe that had gone!", he chuckled, "Gerry swiped it that day you went up to Ringwood with that bloke's suitcase. Sir was wandering round as usual, so while he had his head in the store sheds, Gerry nicked it and chucked it up to Bert Credding in the Signal box. He rolled it round one of the levers and secured it with rubber bands. Pompous Percy stood chatting with his hand six inches from it, bewailing its loss and moaning about the thieving gits that would pinch the tail off a dying donkey! The nerve of the man. You know he's right off his rocker don't you mate? He's ended up in some Institute apparently, for which I'm truly sorry, wouldn't wish that on my worst enemy, but I'd have cheerfully seen him sent down for his own dishonesty. Now, about that decorating...", he referred to his last week's work cheerfully.

"I know you said you'd pay the going rate but you supplied all the wherewithal, so I don't want any money. I've got a great little cottage out of it, Molly's over the moon, and that's good enough for me. She already found me some paid work at your shop. Seems that Mrs Fleet needs a regular maintenance man, and I've agreed to stop by later and give her a quote. Her husband's a nice chap isn't he?"

Sam's mind reeled. Fred had clearly taken to Bert Fleet, one of the surliest individuals Sam had ever met, and his expression must have surprised Fred, who said cheerfully, "Oh, I'll give you he's a bit quiet like, but he's a bloody good cook!", and Molly interrupted giggling.

"We were over at the cottage with Ellen, and she was showing us her little cold frame when Mrs Fleet popped up on the other side of the hedge. They were on the allotments watering, when they saw Ellen and came over to introduce themselves. We offered them tea while Mr Sherrington offloaded Fred's toolbox into that shed, and straightaway Bert Fleet skipped off and brought back a slice of his chocolate cake!"

Entranced, Sam watched Fred as he waxed lyrical on the subject, eyes glowing with reflected pleasure.

"Light, even constituency, not too sweet and moist right through to the last crumb!", he breathed in awe. "Now, there's a bloke after my own heart, and friendly too. He's going to pop over and show me how to work your good lady's Aga properly, and I'm going to decorate their place and learn about baking! Strikes me I'm quids in mate."

His long (normally mournful) face broke into a grin, as he trotted away to Mike Theobald's van, to join in what was to prove the best move of his life.

That week, Tom Collier and Sam started clearing Charlie's work-shed in preparation for installing electricity. Much against his original desires, Tom had persuaded Sam to let him begin in Silver Street (which he had completed during September) winning him over with the single comment, "Light her up boy, light her up. Nothing quite repels a vandal so much as the thought they might get caught. A few judiciously placed lights (inside and out), wired so that you'll be able to switch on from a single switch should do the trick. Paddy Flynn tells me that you're a great douser! How's he settling in by the way?"

Sam had laughed holding up hands that had tried in vain to restrain a simple hazel twig from twisting furiously in his grasp, and considered the strange sensation.

"Great douser indeed! I can't even control the blooming withy, let alone that Irish blighter. He's a real oddity, but I like him, and I don't think he'll do me a bad turn. He's happy enough camping in that little clearing beyond the river. His pony is no problem, he's keeping the grass short, and he's been a blessing getting those ruddy fire-breaks ploughed. I've nearly got the hang of the Trusty myself, but I'll never throw it around with the gay abandon Mr Flynn uses. I'm scared of turning it over or losing it down a ditch. Did I tell you the story of the silencer that nearly killed the Vicar?"

Intrigued, Tom stood rigging his test equipment, following the cables in what had been Gerry's ticket office as Sam regaled him with the latest turn of events.

"That Trusty is a noisy beast.", he began, "I'd kind of bothered about it when I realised that I might help the allotment owners in the village clear their land for over-wintering. Well, Paddy took a look at those drawings

Mike left me so I could get it serviced, and just after that, Ellen brought one of my Dad's old friends over from Lymington, so that he could see what we've taken on.", he grinned, took a swig of Ellen's homemade lemonade, and took up the story again.

"Well, old Percy Adams is in his eighties, but there's nothing much horticultural that he hasn't handled one way or another, so I left Paddy and him hunched over some arcane contraption constructed from an empty baked bean tin stuffed with wire wool."

Tom collier's brow furrowed, his eyes widened and a grin began to emerge as Sam continued the story.

"They'd decided to clear some of that potash off the back level behind the car park, so off they went, and like a fool I let them go while I fetched sacks from the big store, so I didn't see all of the action. However, Martin had just arrived to fetch Percy down for lunch when Paddy started the Trusty. It ran true, and a lot quieter too, but as Paddy told me later, they hadn't thought the fastening out very well, and the compression built up until the tractor back-fired. Honestly Tom, you should have seen it! The Vicar was crossing the car park towards the silly pair, I'm coming through the edge of the spinney behind them, and there was an incredible bang, and Paddy starts screaming "Duck!" Their "silencer", shot off the exhaust like a smoking missile, aimed straight at Martin Short, who simply flowed out of the way neatly and called back, "I say Umpire, I think that was a jolly old wide don't you know?" I've never been so relieved to see he hasn't forgotten how to play cricket!"

Tom chortled, then turned his head as Paddy Flynn appeared in the doorway.

"Good morning Mr Collier, morning Boss. I found your spring this morning, and I've marked it up for you. It's nice and handy to the Station House so the water people should be able to test the quality and tap into it. If you're happy for me to stretch my legs, I'd like to get those spuds in before winter, then I'll be off to Home Farm to help with the milking."

He sketched a salute and disappeared outside again as Tom said seriously, "He's a hard worker Sam. God alone knows how old he is, but he's the fittest bloke I'll ever know. He's worth keeping if you can persuade him to stay. He worked on my brother's self-pick place, helped him set up, tracing water supplies and making himself useful. He kept on as night watchman for six years until they were well established, only leaving a year back. Mark is always saying that he'd be nowhere if it wasn't for Paddy Flynn, but he's never stayed in one place since he left Ireland. I suspect he'll drift back there one day, but he's a good judge of people and he's paying you a huge compliment by stopping over."

Sam stared at Tom contemplatively, then asked, "Are you suggesting that he's some sort of good luck charm Tom?", and the electrician grinned shame-faced and admitted, "Well, my brother swears by him, and he didn't kill your Vicar after all. I think he's in tune with things we might not see, and haven't you noticed how his eyes change colour? They are particularly green when he's "in touch", and I know you've heard of people with sixth sense. I'm sure he's one of them."

A stray breeze stroked Sam's cheek, and he got to his feet remarking tartly, "Yes, I'm sure he's one of the little people Tom, but don't you breathe a word to Ellen. Paddy may not have killed the Vicar but I wouldn't give you one chance in ten if you scare a superstitious woman!"

Chapter 30 - Next Stop Adventure

When the small coach arrived in Padways, Ellen was the first to greet their French visitors. The driver, busy letting down the side-doors to the luggage compartments touched his cap hopefully, as Ellen approached, obviously looking for someone in authority.

"Sorry we're late.", he apologised, "They've had a rough crossing, then their coach broke down in Dover, but I reckon they'll be no trouble at all. They're too exhausted to get up to mischief!"

He handed out rucksacks, then the coach door opened and Annette Julian descended in a rush, flinging both arms round Ellen enthusiastically.

My dear," said Ellen, shocked by the dark circles under her friends eyes, "Give me your clipboard.", and mounting the steps took a roll-call in French ticking off listed names, identifying each host family as she went.

"Please remain with your tutor until I call your name, then come and meet your hosts, who will take you home with them.", she instructed, glad to see that Monsieur Gilbert had taken her lead and was helping to sort out hand luggage at the rear of the coach.

She returned to the pavement, where Annette was distractedly signing the driver's sheet, and making arrangements for him to park his coach overnight in the Hall car-park, sending him to negotiate his own accommodation at the Hay Rack Inn.

Ellen turned to the group of host families, and started to pair them with their students.

"Ah, Mr and Mrs Groom," she called out, spotting them hovering uncertainly. "I'll call.", she consulted Annette's clipboard rapidly, "Philippe Dubois for you, I have no doubt you'll want to talk to Monsieur Gilbert as well.", and turned back to the coach. The young tutor (by this time), seemed to have marshalled his faculties (as well as the two boys on this trip), and with relief Ellen introduced him to the host family and left them to make their own arrangements, while she called the next host forward.

For the next half-hour, she packed off sleepy teenagers with host families, and then there was just Annette and the young tutor left.

"I'm so sorry you had a bad trip.", she exclaimed as formal introductions were made, "My husband will help with your luggage Annette, and here comes Martin for you Monsieur Gilbert."

She was startled to see Annette blush as the gentle velvety voice swept over her.

"Thank you Madame Smart, but I can manage for both of us.", and as his burning gaze flicked up to Annette Julian's lips and lingered, Ellen thought immediately,

"Oh my goodness! They're head over heels with each other. How lovely, I've got Sam and she's got Francois, who would have believed that? As Sam says, there's a pattern to life that we can't see, and perhaps that's as well."

She turned to follow Sam and their visitors, totally unaware that another pattern was unfolding, one that would encompass her in the most amazing experience of her life.

For the next two weeks the daily routine was commanded by their visitors, then, just as they had become used to people that rose with the sun and poured forth, coming home (like a flock of noisy starlings at sunset), they were gone.

They left before dawn, Sam and Ellen assisting the driver to load luggage while the teachers directed yawning children into seats. Finally, Annette and Francois smiled from the door, as Sam (after enduring a familiar kiss from both of them), recovered his equilibrium, while Ellen squeaked joyfully over a small solitaire engagement ring on Annette's hand. The newly engaged couple boarded reluctantly, as Sam raised his eyes to the children (whom he'd enchanted with his renditions of steam engines), and grinned as he put his fingers to his lips.

The sound of a guard's whistle shrilled out, the breathy pant of the loco echoed round the deserted green, then as the coach driver started the engine a voice rang out.

"All aboard now! All aboard. Next Stop Calais!", then Padways with its sadly depleted population, shook itself and turned to the prospect of oncoming winter.

Harvest Home was a quieter affair that year. The village was adapting to life without its station, the initial strength of feeling had dissipated under the daily exertions of driving to work or making other arrangements, and only the spirit of competition fuelled the allotment owners. Emma Fleet had abandoned the idea of growing giant vegetables, but glowed with quiet pride as once more she raised the single largest donation, by the sheer volume of her produce. Under Fred's influence, Bert Fleet had cleared and planted Emma's modest back garden, watered Ellen's allotment and hoed and weeded Sam's alongside his new friend.

Fred (now master of the Aga), had learned to bake, and suddenly Emma had started selling home-made pies, cakes and bread, and planned to introduce a cold cabinet for cheese and other perishables previously unavailable. Sam surprised himself (and everyone else) by entering some of his own vegetables for judging, and cheerfully bore off second prize for his cauliflowers, then he learned to drive.

He kept it secret, swearing Jack Sherrington to a total blackout on the subject, as the farmer built up his confidence. They used Beryl's old Ford Poplar, going out as far as the abandoned wartime airfield, so that word wouldn't get out, and as Ellen had promised, Sam suddenly realised he could coordinate, and he was a fast learner. Eventually, around mid-November Jack said deliberately, "Well then Sam, I can't teach you anymore. There's nothing for it but to go into Lymington and book you a test. It's quite simple really. You go to the testing centre, the examiner just sits with you like I do when we're out, and you do exactly as I've taught you, and he'll either pass you or not. I've got the forms, let's go for it," and they had.

Three weeks after Christmas, Sam had stared shaken at the examiner who had to repeat himself twice as he handed Sam the form that told him he'd passed his driving test first time.

"Late perhaps Mr Smart, but I'm sure you'll be a careful considerate driver, not like some of these young things in souped up sports cars. I understand you've a small-holding, so your licence will be very important to you. Watch out for these new speed limits coming in and make sure you keep to them!"

Sam had re-joined Jack (who'd accompanied him) grinning like a Cheshire cat.

"Oh well done Sam! Well done, I knew you could do it. Now for the best bit!", the farmer went round to the front grill of the Ford and untied the L-plate, returning with the second and inviting Sam to "Rip them up lad, then get you behind the wheel, you're driving back home!"

Nothing would have it but Jack insisted that they drive into Padways and honk the horn until curious friends and neighbours clustered round. Proudly parked in the lay-by reserved for Church Cottage, they waited until Ellen arrived, on her way to fetch Sam home from Silver Street, where she presumed he was still working.

She stared incredulously at Sam's "pass" form, took in Jack Sherrington's guilty expression, and chuckled.

"Well done darling. I'm glad I didn't know, I'd have been out of my mind with worry, but passed first-time? It took me three attempts so you can do the driving just as soon as you're insured to use our car."

Jack grinned, "He's already insured on this old thing. Beryl doesn't drive anymore. She'll be eighty next year and she can't cope with poor light, she gave me the car so I could teach the boys. They're both fixed up, so Sam is free to use the Ford whenever he likes. He may as well, it's sitting idle on the farm, and he's paid for the insurance."

So Sam carefully reversed out, and drove Jack home, but his mind was on another Ford thousands of miles away as (unexpectedly weary), he returned to Church Cottage, his next step taking him closer to Silver Street.

Having persuaded Jack to lend them a trailer, Sam and Paddy took the Trusty down to the allotments, and helped the Committee clear a few poorly maintained plots for redistribution. During one heated exchange with a disappointed member of the association, Sam learned that a number of increasingly frail gardeners needed help, and mentioned this to Ellen during their Christmas break.

"I don't know what to do about it love.", he confessed, "Ideally younger family members would take over, but there aren't enough young men to go round. I do worry that the allotment Association might find themselves with more allotments than members, and that won't do, but how do you engage the interest of those who never learned about self-sufficiency from their parents, or make them connect with those who don't have family to teach? Then again, this goes beyond allotments. Just take a look at Fred and Bert, there's a match you could never have predicted, and look what's come out of it! Bert just finished redecorating Dan's room I hear, and Fred's cooking cakes for the Vicarage tea party next week! Takes a practical partnership like that to prove my point, but if it can be done anywhere, Padways is the place for such things. I just hope the allotment Association can match a few members to save us having to redistribute allotments next year, even if I won't be involved anymore."

Ellen's head shot up at the last statement, but Sam grinned equably and reminded her that his term on the Allotment Committee was coming to an end.

"Darling, I've far too much to do at Silver Street to be worrying about Committee meetings.", he protested mildly, "Don't you forget that now we have water laid on, electrics signed off and the builders ready to put in the kitchen, we've only weeks to go and we're moving in."

She'd stared at him owlishly over the rim of the reading glasses she'd been forced to wear for close work, and he saw with interest that she was stitching something made from some furry material.

"More practice pieces, or something for the book?", he enquired, as she blushed laughing.

"It's a Teddy Bear kit!", she said mournfully. "You know I went to that exhibition last week? Well, I saw this, and thought that as I'm engaged in writing a history of soft toys, I'd better get some hands-on experience of making a bear. They form the last section in its entirety, but it's not as easy as I thought. I could do with one of those workers that formed the backbone of the industry to show me the tricks of the trade!"

She had paused in mid-sentence then said thoughtfully, "Sam? Would you mind if I pinched an idea you've given me? I want to launch a "Practical Partnership Club."

He remembered her face, absorbed and hopeful bent over her sewing, and how he had encouraged her, little thinking that he too might benefit from the plan. However, Ellen's idea put forward at the first Parish Committee of the year had been greeted with enthusiasm, Emma Fleet getting to her feet to volunteer to host a request book.

She said firmly, "We only need to provide an introduction to people who want to join in, we don't need Committees or officers. There's no money involved, no property required for meetings. Let's just create a means by which partners can be introduced. We can host that at the shop, we only need a notice board or a book, whichever people would prefer. A board on which post-cards could indicate an interest from which anyone can get the information, or a book which is a little more secure for both parties."

Eventually, after much wrangling, it had been decided that Bert Fleet would keep a book. Divided into sections by interest, prospective partners could lodge their names with him, and he would pass on the details. Sam was suitably stunned when Bert asked to say a few words, but the reception of his speech was instantaneous.

The man rose to his feet, and said quietly, "I'd just like to explain what this means to me. I never used to play any part in Padways. Didn't like being cut off from my mates in Christchurch when Emma first took the shop, but there was another reason too. I only found out about it recently, but I've got a condition that makes it difficult for me to read and write." There was a concerted murmur of sympathy as Bert continued huskily,

"Mrs Smart got Rory to take me to see someone in Winchester, who confirmed I have dyslexia, but that only tells me what's wrong, it doesn't cure it. What's made a difference was discovering that I had skills that could help someone else."

He grinned around the room, then announced softly what had obviously become some kind of mantra.

"My friend Fred wanted to learn to use an Aga and bake. I needed to learn how to maintain our property, and take better care of my family. So, we swapped skills. My Dad never had any time for me and thought I was thick. Poor Em has put up with years of my being helpless, angry and unable to work, but 'my friend Fred' taught me to read and write, while I taught him how to bake in an Aga, and I know who gained the most."

There had been utter silence as Bert spoke, but immediately spontaneous applause rang out, then Emma Fleet hugged her husband until he blushed and sat down.

So, the Practical Partnership Club was born, and to Sam's utter amazement he found himself the target for loads of requests.

"Could the Women's Institute have the occasional meeting at Silver Street? In exchange they would make curtains for Station House. They would also like Sam to give a talk on how a station functioned."

"Could Mr Smart take a series of guided walks along the track once the rails were lifted? The Padways ramblers would happily give one afternoon each walk to help with hedge-trimming, or other outside maintenance work."

"If Mr Smart could allow the Cubs and Scouts to use Silver Street for wood-craft training, Jim Southall (Burley and Padways Group Scout Leader) would give him some assistance with plumbing or building as required.

So the momentum built, then the letter came from Australia.

They had been up at Silver Street, over-seeing the final touches being put to their kitchen and bathroom. The day was cold, there was no heating installed and they had clutched their sheepskin coats closely, huddling into them as the plumber had discussed progress on that front. Even the mug of tea provided by Paddy at his caravan did little to warm them, and they were only too glad to get back into Lady Jane and make the short hop back to Padways, running up the path, jostling through the door, almost missing the airmail in their determination to get into the warmth.

Sam picked it up, glanced at the unfamiliar writing, then saw the return address, and grinned. He sat at the kitchen table, slitting the seal (with Charlie's small penknife), as Ellen reached for the kettle, and slid it onto the hotplate to boil. She had just placed their old metal teapot onto a trivet to warm, and was still spooning tea-leaves into it, when Sam sat up, coming from a fireside slouch to full alert as he scanned the last line of the letter again.

"Cor blimey!", he exclaimed inelegantly. "No wonder Rob was a little economical with facts when he was here. They've made contact with Alex's old chap, in fact, Rob says they moved him lock, stock and barrel back to Newlands and got a doctor to give him a check-up. He can't tell us much at this stage, but there's some inference that this Robert they're chasing is anything but some drifter that moved in on Rob's father. If they can prove the link, Rob says Alex is in line to inherit substantially more than Newlands, however, they'll have to come back here to continue the research! They anticipate leaving Australia next week...can we put them up if they get here by March?"

Ellen gulped thinking of the piercing cold at their new home, then saw Sam grin as he quoted directly from Rob's letter.

"He's aware that they're imposing on us, but the Trust will contribute a sum not far short of a brand new heating system, if they can lease the cottage again for at least six months."

His eyes glazed, rapid calculations taking place, then he said firmly, "Yes. If I can get the bottom half of Station House completed by the time they get here, we'll have our lounge, dining and kitchen ready. What I'd planned to use as holiday lets next year, will have to be our bedroom albeit on the opposite platform."

He continued to muse later that night as they prepared for bed, sliding gratefully into warm, sweet-smelling sheets as he confessed.

"I've never slept anywhere else that I can remember. I never thought of it before. We'll have to adjust our ideas but I can bear that, so long as we're together. Alex and Rob can move in here, our next stop is adventure!"

Ellen yawned and switched out the light.

"Listen to the man who's never left home!", she mocked gently. "Adventure isn't necessarily all that it's cracked up to be my lad, besides, I only agreed to move to Silver Street, if it's adventuring you want, you're on your own."

"Yes love.", her husband agreed, snuggling into her drowsily, only half listening, his thoughts whispering down the lines that would soon no longer be there.

PART FOUR - A PROMISE FULFILLED

Chapter 31 - A Flock of Fullingfords

When the gleaming Bentley slid into Church Cottage parking bay, Sam was mortified as he compared it to his workhorse. Jack's Ford had become Sam's runabout, making it possible for Ellen to go to London from Brockenhurst (a situation frequently demanded by her publishers) now the launch of her book was imminent.

Closing the front door behind him, he went down the path to relieve Howard of two large suitcases, and winced as he swung them up onto his trolley, his back still protesting two full weeks after their move.

Rob gave Sam a weary smile as he left the car where Alex still slept, then Howard raised an enquiring eyebrow, as Mrs Castle came to the door.

"I'll serve tea in the sitting-room Mr Smart.", she said as Sam lowered the cases to the hall floor, standing aside to let Rob enter. She continued thoughtfully looking over Sam's shoulder (as Alex tottered to his feet).

"That boy looks exhausted." she observed, "It's just as well I've warmed their beds. Mrs Smart tells me they won't be going far until they acclimatise, so I've left Mr Howard some milk, butter, bread etc., and if he needs anything else, I'll be happy to pop a list over to Emma's for him. The telephone people only just finished connecting you up in time didn't they?", and Sam nodded, giving Mrs Castle the new telephone number while he remembered it.

"Yes, thank goodness, Ellen's in London for two days, and I wouldn't want to be at Silver Street and have to run down to the shop to keep in touch with her!", he beamed at Ellen's friend as Rob wearily plodded in, a subdued Alex at his heels.

Sam opened the sitting-room door as they entered, leaving Howard to take the suitcases upstairs, as Mrs Castle brought in tea.

"Hello Martha, how's tricks?", enquired the incorrigible Australian, and a bemused Sam watched the matriarch of Padways W I melt.

"Goodness me Mr Ford!", she protested, adding a huge slice of Victoria sponge to his plate.

"Whatever will Mr Smart think?" She pressed tea and cake on both weary travellers as she spoke, smiling directly at the younger man..

"Well, I'm not coming home to ignore my best girl!", Alex murmured, but it was obvious that both men were on the point of collapse, so with promises of more cake when he wanted it, and the excuse of "a brief word with Mr Howard", Martha Castle fled in high good humour.

Sam spoke swiftly.

"Rob, Alex, I'm glad to see you home, but I'm short-handed. Ellen is in London on business for two days, we only just moved in. Her cottage had to be let in emergency I'm afraid, so we've advanced some work here to give you a home."

He led Rob upstairs, pausing in the doorway of what had been his den.

"Here's one room Rob.", he said diffidently, "I think it'll suit either of you. The other single is next door. We are still working on the place, but not for a few days at least." he explained.

"My work-shed is going on mains power after the weekend. In the meantime, we've put Howard in Ellen's study cum sewing-room. The bathroom etc. is on the ground floor, through the kitchen."

He took Rob on a brief tour of inspection, received assurances that they were happy, and left them sleepily transferring themselves to bed.

Cheerfully, he drove round to the allotments to pick up Fred and the trailer that they'd built for the Trusty. It was filled with panels from the small shed Sam and Fred had used, which they were transferring up to Fred's new vegetable patch at Silver Street. Tying them in place, Sam remarked that he hoped it would go back together again, laying garden tools in the back of the Ford as he spoke.

"You could use a pick-up truck Sam.", Fred said helpfully, "Something like the builder used when he delivered the pipes for the heating. He was playing around with that back-boiler when I walked down earlier. Reckon you'll be nice and toasty soon. The old place has come on a treat!"

Sam tested the ties on the panels, and then lifted the trailer's tow-hitch connecting it to the car. He spent a few minutes firmly tying the obligatory red flag to the rear of the load, and then they set off to Silver Street.

"I'm glad Ellen wasn't home when Alex got back.", he remarked as they off-loaded the small shed into Paddy Flynn's keeping, "She'd have talked the hind leg off the donkey, and both Alex and Rob are going to need care and protection for a day or two. She'll have to wait to give them her news until they recover their land-legs.", but it was Rob and Alex's news that was to overtake their lives.

Ellen came home a day later, clutching the hand-printed announcement of her book launch. Sam gazed at it admiringly, and said he would pin it up where they could see it every day. She swatted him lightly.

"Fool!" she exclaimed indulgently, and leaned against the kitchen counter, looking out through the newly inserted window across the gap where the lines had been lifted.

"Do you know darling, it might be a bit hit and miss round here, but now I know that the rustlings and shufflings are just Mr and Mrs Badger taking the little ones for a walk, and the squeaking and squawking are just bats and birds, I sleep better here than I did at the cottage? Are you and Paddy really going to plough up the siding bed today?"

Sam nodded, mouth full of toast, as she demanded, "What are we planting there Sam, and don't you dare tell me spuds. That Paddy will drive me round the bend if all we get to plant are potatoes. Surely not all the soil needs a crop of potatoes?"

Sam grinned. "I'll tell him what you said if you like?" he offered, and Ellen groaned, protesting.

"No. It's alright dear. I don't need another lesson in crop rotation; though I thought he said something different could go in the fire field?"

Sam chuckled, "Yes, that's already had a good yield of spuds so once those are up, we can really start working out what goes where, and the first thing will be Fred's plot. It's amazing how well he and Bert have done with my allotment. Emma is so thrilled that we passed on yours to her, and mine to Bert and they'll both be fine additions to the Committee, but Fred wanted his plot up here with us. It suits me, I hope it suits you, and I'm hoping that once we're really going, Gerry Richards will do the books."

Ellen continued to gaze out of the window towards the down-line platform, but she was smiling as she said cheerfully, "Oh, I don't have any objections to any of your workmates coming to play Sam, only please make sure they understand that I won't have muddy boots tramped through the house."

Sam watched her go out of the door; past the cunning serving hatch he and Fred had created out of Gerry's ticketing window, and pass from the dining room they'd created out of the main entrance hall, through into the living room that now occupied the space where he had once stoked the fire in the up-line waiting room. He smiled fondly after her, and then froze as a peculiarly familiar thrum passed through his day-dreaming mind.

He blinked, abandoning the vision of Ellen surrounded by fans clutching her book, and went out of the door onto the up-line platform to investigate, but there was nothing to see, except his squirrel friend, making a brief foray out into the pre-April sunshine, so he turned away, dropping lightly onto the empty rail-bed, as the telephone purred on Ellen's desk.

Paddy and he had a good morning, marking out the boundaries of what he had known as sidings, and which Ellen had dubbed "the growing ground". They'd already raised and stacked the ancient sleepers, using them as bulwarks against casual intrusion from what was to be a public footpath following the line of the Corkscrew. This set Paddy off on another tack, and they were engrossed in conversation regarding the benefits of planting a screen of willows around the old sidings, when Sam saw the Irishman's nostrils quiver, his eyes glaze, then, as though he consulted some inner memorandum, the man said confidently,

"Well Boss, I figure on moving those last two sleepers over, and then I'll pack up, and pop over to Bashley. I've seen some large water butts advertised, and iffen they happened to be the right size, we could organise a static water supply for the nursery end. Your visitors will be here soon!", and to Sam's amazement, he'd melted into the coppice beyond which he'd parked his traditional horse-drawn caravan.

Thoroughly confused, Sam rolled up the drawings he had worked from, turning away as the Bentley glided into the car-park, depositing Alex and Rob, as a thrill of presentiment touched Sam's cheek with a familiar whisper.

Five minutes later, Alex stood staring down into the bare rail-bed grimacing. "Jeepers mate! This is different to what it was when I first arrived here.", then he dropped down onto the trolley crossing and strode down-line, sheepskin jacket flying as he hugged Sam fiercely, then as Rob caught up with them he declaimed dramatically,

"We've been kicked out. Tom Collier wants to cut of the electric power, Mrs Castle has finished the cleaning and doesn't want us mucking things up, and Howard thought we'd be safer here. He's phoned Ellen already, and they're going shopping in Lymington, so we've brought lunch to share with you, then Howard's going to create a dinner-party at your place. Can we bring the car round to the parking bay at the back? It'll be easier for Howard to offload the hamper and fetch Ellen."

Sam grinned at Rob, who said curiously, "Yes. Mrs Smart was very mysterious, telling me she has some news she is anxious to convey. However, we have fairly monumental news of our own, so we've agreed to wait and share it over dinner."

Sam allowed himself to be dragged up onto the up-line platform, only half listening to Alex laughing exuberantly, as Ellen departed with Howard. Then, as he invited his guests to inspect his neat new kitchen, Sam felt that sudden thrum of anticipation as Silver Street started to reveal her secrets.

They explored eagerly, after which Sam prepared lunch, while they washed and brushed up in the small cloakroom off the entrance hall. They ate in the kitchen, admiring the skill with which Sam (and the builder) had created a glass and timber panel to separate the front lobby area from the new dining room.

"There's some great features here Sam.", rob commented as they attacked the pork pie and salad that Mrs Castle had provided. "I reckon that if you're careful to keep the finish to really high specification, you and Ellen will have a valuable property in no time. What's upstairs?"

Sam picked up a pencil, sketching the floor plan of Station House on the back of an envelope as they shared a wedge of cheese for dessert, and Rob said approvingly, "I think your builder is probably right. It makes sense to use what is already up to standard, but my dear chap, it must be very strange crossing the track to go to bed."

"Hellishly inconvenient if you leave something one side when you're on the other." added Alex with a brilliant smile.

"We're used to that!"

Sam grinned, putting plates in the sink and leading the others out along the up-line platform to show them over Signalman's Cottage (where the builders stored their materials). They crossed backward and forward, looking at the rail bed curiously, then he showed them round the old signal box, only returning to Station House as a flurry of closing doors and cheerful calls announced the return of the shoppers.

Ellen was bursting with excitement, and Rob glanced up at her, as she carefully removed her hat, and escaped to the cloakroom, shedding her coat as she went.

The minute she returned clutching her handbag, she announced in thrilling tones, "Sam, you'll never believe what happened in Lymington?", and Sam smiled as he used the tried and tested riposte to such a declaration.

"I have no doubt you're going to tell us love!", he suggested wickedly, but she took no notice of the wry grins, and reached into her bag, withdrawing a bright poster filled with photographs depicting antique toys.

She kept her eyes on her husband as she continued to unfurl it, eventually opening it out to reveal a large Teddy bear, reclining against a pillow, apparently clutching an illustrated book in a reading position.

Sam's eyes widened as he caught sight of the book title. "The Bear on My Bed by Ellen Smart", then as Rob and Alex looked up grinning with genuine pleasure, Ellen burst into happy tears.

"It was on the wall in King's Library." she confided. "I had arranged to meet Howard there, so I took a little walk down onto the quay to get some fish, and coming up that side of the High Street, I just looked in to see what was new. To my utter amazement, that was on the wall over the cash register. I had to tell them who I was to get them to give me a spare, but I actually got a book signing out of it Sam. What a peculiar feeling that was, perfectly ordinary people behaving in a most extraordinary way, because I've written a book. It isn't out till September, but the manager at King's assured me that I'd chosen the most opportune time to publish. As if I had anything to do with it!"

She laughed a little shame-faced at her own excitement, then disappeared into their sitting-room, as Howard appeared carrying the kitchen table.

To Sam's astonishment, the next thing to appear was an old hoarding that he'd planned to use as a divider upstairs, but Howard blithely produced a small occasional table of the same height, laid the board over both tables then covered them with an enormous paper tablecloth, transforming their bare dining room into a salon, fit to grace any restaurant.

"Good man!", said Rob approvingly, "Now then Sam, what about us beating the bounds, and getting out of your good lady's way while Howard continues to turn you upside down. He's rather a 'no holds barred' man when it comes to entertaining, and this is my shout, so we'd better get out of his way."

They walked over the road bridge, and lingered on the footpath, looking down on the empty rail bed, listening to Sam telling them snippets from Silver Street's wartime history. Rob listened carefully, remarking only now and again as the porter enthused..

"I was reminded of catching a troop train during my teens when I came through here the first time," the colonel said softly, as they finally turned back, and Sam remembering that bleak expression he had seen in Rob's eyes, shivered.

Later that evening, they talked lightly through a wonderful dinner, amazed by the fluid dexterity by which Howard conjured meals fit to serve a king, then they retired to the living room, admiring the furniture that Sam had picked up at auction, as they settled down to hear the news.

At Alex's request, Howard joined them, and then Rob spoke severely.

"We still don't have written proof of half this story, but things are moving along nicely, however, I do have to remind you that we are still in confidential waters. Now, gentlemen and lady, security is paramount as you'll soon see, but in the interests of pursuing local enquiries, you had all better know what we are looking for."

He paused as coffee was passed around, took a sip, and then said very deliberately, "We are looking for the marriage certificate of Robert James Fullingford. We also need to find his will or any documentation that relates to him after 1905, when he was reported dead along with my Uncle and the rest of his family."

As bewildered silence filled the room, Rob sighed, put his coffee cup down on the tray, and spent a moment crossing his legs, twitching the creases in his trousers into place, and looking both pensive, yet excited as he finally said quietly.

"I have organised a thorough search of all records relating to that tragic event, but if my suspicions are correct the Royal College of Heralds has a headache on its hands!"

Straightening his shoulders, Rob smiled affectionately at Alex's woebegotten expression, and began to explain.

You'll hardly have forgotten Ollie Godwin's comments which resonated with me particularly. My private indulgence in family history, comes from being brought up on the story of how my mother was deserted by my aristocratic wastrel of a father, so when Alex started to research his Grandfather's background and we discovered several co-incidents, I began to wonder if we weren't researching the same story from opposite ends?" He shifted, sighed, then said simply,

"It begins with one of those family breakdowns we spoke about. I don't have the full story yet, but it appears that the Fullingford brothers were unable to resolve their differences. This eventually led to my father being advised to leave England before some scandal broke. Alexander had apparently decided that he could no longer support his wild escapades. I suspect the schism goes deeper than that, but we may never know what drove them apart. However, we know Anthony disappeared with no notice, reappearing at Newlands, leaving my mother and me behind. We also know that after a period of time a British stranger arrived, a boy of about fifteen, and according to a living witness, was greeted as a relative.

He smiled faintly at their bewildered expressions, and then continued softly,.

"We found out that my father became very reclusive at a time which coincides with my birth, and my mother's death. I attribute this to the fact that he may have been made aware of his wife's death. He then apparently threw himself into establishing, a successful business, employing men who for various reasons could not find other work. He had a stock manager and so on, but no relatives ever visited him until this young man arrived out of the blue.

He was little more than a teenager, and according to our witness came specifically looking for him by name. For several months no-one ever saw this chap, but gradually he was installed at Antony's house and our informant says he believed him to be a younger relative, which of course was news to us at the Trust."

He drew a long breath, then held out his cup pleadingly for Howard to refill, his face extremely guarded for a moment, then he almost slyly slipped in the suggestion, "What if plain "Robert", turns out to be Robert James Fullingford Son of Lord Alexander Fullingford, my father's cherished nephew, and heir to his twin brother's honours and titles?"

The air bristled with expectation as without turning his head to look at Alex, Rob continued softly, "

"If that much is true, did that "Robert" father James Ford legitimately?, As natural grandfather of Alexander James Ford, should a valid marriage have taken place), Alex automatically becomes fourth Earl of Padways."

Oh my Lord! exclaimed Sam, as Ellen whispered simultaneously, "Oh Alex, that's unreal. It makes me think that the Fullingfords are flocking, from the far corners of the Empire, through time and war. How wonderful Rob, you've found your family at last, and so has Alex."

"Yes, indeed." their friend agreed seriously. "I rather think we've found each other, now all we have to do is prove our theory beyond a shadow of a doubt!"

Chapter 32 - A Key component

Once they'd accepted that Rob wasn't pulling their legs, Sam and Ellen stared helplessly at Alex, and it seemed that he'd read their unspoken thoughts. He sat very still, trying hard not to meet Sam's quizzical gaze, until he finally blurted, "It's so bloody unfair. Rob denied a father through family strife; grandfather denied a life because of war. My Dad brought up believing he'd been robbed of his heritage, and I still don't know who I am for sure. We talked to Jim Kennedy; he's as sharp as a razor and knew precisely who we were talking about. He was sworn to secrecy about the lad who'd come to live at Newlands, long before "the old Boss" died, however, he accepted Rob as his "old Boss's" son without question."

He grinned affectionately at his kinsman, who said firmly, "Alex, my father doted on Robert. Remember that piece from Lord Alexander's diary?"

He pinched the bridge of his nose as though unbearably tired, then explained briefly.

"I set the Trust quite a task, turning out archives etc. in search of anything that would connect the two of us. A diary came to light (amongst thousands of private papers still unread). I discovered one telling passage saying that his younger brother would do well to follow his own example, marry and have his own son! Alexander obviously didn't see how a child could adore his Uncle in preference to himself, but in those days affluent parents had very little contact with their own children. They belonged in the nursery or the schoolroom, to be visited when the mood took them, and otherwise seen but not heard."

He slipped a hand into his pocket and withdrew a slim volume, and opened tissue thin pages, filled with copperplate script. He ran a finger down the page, adjusted his glasses and read slowly.

"Anthony goes too far! Not only has he set the nursery by the heels, he's upset Godwin with this blaze-faced pony! Completely ignoring my wishes in this matter, he has taken Robert from his letters, dismissed the protestations of his tutor, and spent most of the afternoon running alongside the boy, whom he mounted (without my permission) on this sway-backed beast."

Now we seem to have a new entity in the household. Robert insists his name is Robin, (and like the Shakespearean creature of that name) has thrown the household into disarray. He is wilful, declares his Uncle more to his taste than his father and refuses to attend his classes unless he is allowed to ride his pony up and down the bridle path to the stables, which Anthony has christened Robin's Way!

I despair of Robert! Anthony needs a good whipping, but he's my brother, although I pray not the changeling I suspect him to be!"

"Poor man!" said Ellen with a depth of understanding that only a teacher could bring to bear on the subject.

"The Fullingford brothers obviously had a difficult relationship. How much older than Anthony was Alexander?"

Rob looked up amused by something, then answered gravely, "It's difficult to tell, records of that age are nothing like as accurate as those kept nowadays, but we believe it was a matter of about ten minutes! They were identical twins."

"Aah!" Ellen breathed understandingly. "Sometimes there's enormous rivalry between twins. Social acceptance of the devotion of twins to each other is often far from the truth. Two people who are perceived as identical are often left unhappily struggling to develop independent identities, which may have led to your father eventually deciding to step out from his twin's shadow and leave the country, but how did Robert come to follow him, and why didn't anybody explore what had happened to that child?"

Rob winced, then said earnestly, So far we only have a theory. I didn't know anything about my Uncle, until my request for the details of the establishment of the Fullingford Trust resulted in this diary appearing. It's quite hard to read, some of the more private confidences are very painful, particularly those that touch on the death of Alexander's first wife, when Robert couldn't have been much older than four. She died after a horse bolted, and Alexander seems to have gone off his head. He ordered all the horses destroyed, forbade Robert to ride, and after substantial trouble in the schoolroom, sacked the boy's tutor and sent him to boarding school as soon as he could. He remarried when Robert was eight, but Leonora Woods was not a sympathetic stepmother. She doted on her daughter, but this diary goes no further than her birth, so I don't know what provoked the rift between the brothers. And I still have a lot of reading to do."

There was a sudden silence, and then Alex glanced up at the clock and said in tones of astonishment, "Jeepers. It's nearly ten o'clock Rob. We'd better break up for the night, or Ellen and Sam will be breaking their necks trying to get over to the other platform in the dark!"

Sam was delighted to show off Tom's outside lighting, and judging by the reaction, Rob and Alex were impressed, and so the party ended. Ellen and Sam wishing their visitors, "Good Night!"

Waving them off from the parking bay outside Station House, then hurrying across the trolley crossing under a brilliant light, and waving from the wicket gate on the down-line platform, as the Bentley glided over the road bridge, leaving the Smarts to consider the remarkable tale they'd heard.

Sliding gratefully into bed, they clung to each other for a little while, reassured by mutual warmth, then they sank into sleep. Sam was troubled by occasional dreams of soldiers in First World War uniforms crowding onto the platforms. One of them with Alex's face asking him plaintively, "Porter? Have you seen someone just like me? I'm sure he was here a minute ago, but I can't find him."

Rather horridly Sam awoke in the wee small hours, gasping from the exertion of looking into everyone's face. They had all been identical, but none of them had answered to the name Robert and the chilling thought struck him that unless they could complete some strange circular journey, they were trapped at Silver Street, destined never to travel onward.

He kept those feelings (and the dream that had provoked them) to himself however, content to watch his squirrel's family growing through early summer. Ellen pottered about their "growing ground" in the evenings after school, Sam researched the drawings of the station, building up a picture in his head of what could be done to maximise his profits, and the days turned lazily as Rob and Alex constructed a theory based on family correspondence, Lord Alexander's diary, and the memories of the older generation.

About six weeks after their dinner-party, Rob and Alex walked up from Padways and having presented Ellen with a bunch of flowers from Sam's garden demanded his whereabouts.

"He's on the growing ground I think", she said brightly, "They're weeding and thinning out today."

"Good, good…"

Rob seemed distracted, but Alex, sticking his head back through the living-room door as the older man departed, said (in a conspiratorial undertone), "Don't worry about Rob. He's a little off the beat today. The Trustee's want to start advertising his position, and they reminded him of his retirement I suppose. They certainly sent him a hell of a lot of paperwork."

He twinkled at her, swept her a bow, and trotted after Rob, who was already striding down the woodland walk towards the growing ground, now almost unrecognisable behind a greening screen of willow.

The two men strode along the path that separated distinctly different growing areas, noting where the wartime sidings had not quite swallowed all of the long gardens that had once supplied fruit and vegetables to the railwaymen who had previously occupied cottages along that edge of the Victorian track. They soon spotted movement up ahead, and looked with approval at the nursery end, where Fred and Sam bent over cloches protecting tender plants. A third man slowly wheeled a barrow of manure to one side, and stood staring after them, as they approached, heading directly for Sam.

"Good Morning!", Colonel Fullingford was at his authoritarian best, and Sam stood, easing his back and stared, not at Rob as he made his business-like way toward him, but at Paddy Flynn (who frozen where he had come to a halt), was stood at attention, one hand raised in a military salute.

Coming to a stop in front of Sam, Rob became aware of the direction of his gaze and turned to see the little Irishman.

In the next moment Rob had spun on his heel, and was pumping the little man's hand vigorously.

"Good God Flynn! You horrible, disreputable, Feenian horse-trader …Where on earth have you been man? I've tried everywhere to contact you since your demob. How the bloody hell are you?"

Alex's eyes crinkled as he took in the obvious signs of reunion, greeting Sam himself.

"That's a relief," he announced cheerfully. "He's been as cross as a bear since the Trust landed him with enough paperwork to sink the Titanic. He's only opened the top letter, and that was enough to set match to blue touch-paper. I wonder what the story is here?" he said innocently, as Rob reappeared, Paddy in tow.

"Well Mr Smart," he said in mock severity. "Harbouring one of the most disreputable persons to escape Ireland has to be the charge! How do you plead sir?" Sam laughing decided to plead guilty, and stood listening as Rob and Paddy reminisced over their Cavalry years.

"Colonel is it now?" Paddy enquired cheerfully, "Well, you look well enough, but not riding anymore? What nonsense. You always used to hack round the park, what's stopping you now?", and in between whoops of mirth, the story of Alex's introduction to the Colonel was told.

Paddy looked at Rob admiringly, "For a desk-jockey you acquitted yourself mighty well, but you'll need to keep it up if you aren't to cripple yourself at the next event." he observed, watching the interaction between the two men closely.

"Would you be my Major's grandson?" he asked Alex, accepting the qualified acknowledgment of relationship with a shrug, saying happily,

"Aah. Well sir, if you decide to settle here, I'd be happy to seat you on a good hunter.", and Rob roared with laughter, all traces of his former pique lifted.

"Once a horse-trader, always a scallywag!" he said with a satisfied air, adding ruefully,

"I've been summoned to London Sam. What I came to ask is, can we (by any remote chance), get that shed you were removing, up here while I'm gone? Alex wants to stay, as Mrs Short is entertaining young relatives over the next three weeks, so he won't be lonely. I was also hoping that you wouldn't be averse to my putting a properly built summer-house where the lean-to is now? We've done as Ellen suggested, using the double bedroom as both storage and dressing room, but with Howard in the back room, I need somewhere to work, away from phones and the television that Alex wants.", he smiled at the Australian talking to Fred, saying (sotto voce),

"He's a long way from home, and even further from his ultimate destination, but the Trustees confirm that they have launched a full investigation and I think that the more normal relaxation that young man can get, the better."

He touched his breast pocket lightly, murmuring (almost to himself), "Perhaps I should never have got him involved, but who am I to appoint myself my cousin's Keeper?"

If Sam hadn't heard it before, the sound of a passing train teased the edge of awareness and fled, hard on the heels of the departing Colonel, who was persuaded to let his company groom drive them back down to Padways in his pony and trap.

A busy fortnight later, Fred, Alex, Sam and the Vicar congregated in the garden of Church Cottage, having planned the move with less than military precision. Paddy was due to collect whatever remained in the potting-shed by cart in half an hour, so Sam (with no clear memory of its contents), had arrived early with many hands to assist with the clearance, but was now staring dumbfounded as he opened the door.

"They're here Alex!" called a girl's voice as Melanie, (Jane's youngest niece) appeared on the path. "Mr Flynn is putting the pony's nose-bag on; Aunt Jane's making tea, so we can get started now."

Alex smiled in acknowledgment, and then Sam groaned in dismay.

"Good Heavens, it's full. Whatever did Tom put in here?"

Fred chuckled, "Everything but the kitchen sink I reckon." he heaved a few things aside, helpfully suggesting, "Let's get those two sets of staging out first. We can use them as tables for the other stuff. You know it was all under that right hand workbench where Tom ran the electrics?"

Sam stared at him blankly.

"That lot never fitted under that bench!" he said disbelievingly as boxes and bags were hauled out into the light of day.

They dragged, carried, and wheeled Sam's "junk" (as Ellen was to call it), down to Paddy's trap until it was full. Under Martin's bewildered eyes, half of it was taken to the Vicarage for Mrs Thomas to sort.

"She'll find uses for all that rag", he said, coming to the door of the lean-to, and looking inside with interest, as Sam hauled coverings aside.

"What's under that sacking Sam?"

As the mysterious tin trunk reappeared, Sam heard, no…felt the train passing and froze. Old memories of a terrible fright resurfacing as the gust drew him, sucking greedily at his body, trying to overwhelm him. He trembled blindly as the hum of a non-existent line dizzied his senses, then the Vicar was saying urgently, "You've stood in the sun too long Sam, you'll be alright in a minute. Great Heavens, you're shaking my boy. Steady the Buffs!" and the moment passed as they gaped at the box that the trader had given to Ellen more than a year ago.

The Vicar grinned.

"Gotcha!" he exclaimed gleefully, "You just don't fancy lifting that brute round to the cart! Sam Smart! I was convinced you were about to faint."

He grinned, assisting Sam to take the unusual tin trunk into the garden, then glanced round the lean-to as Sam (thankfully recovering his equilibrium) came back to dismantle his father's potting shed.

"Hang on a minute Sam! There's something up on that ledge." the Vicar (speaking from a good head taller) backed out, letting Sam run his hands round the narrow lintel, to emerge clutching a key.

Slightly larger than the average, beautifully finished in a strange bronzed metal. It warmed to his touch, as without any question or doubt, Sam's eyes sought the lock of the mystery box.

"Do you know what I think Martin?" he asked curiously. "Dad was always finding odd things; he had the knack of it he said. A hundred people could sit in a railway carriage and not see the umbrella, bag, or wallet. Charlie only had to walk down the carriage, and things folk had left leapt out at him. What if that trader came here by train? He didn't say he had, but it's possible. If he dropped the key at the station, or in the carriage Charlie could have found it, but I'm not at all sure I want to investigate until Ellen comes home!"

The Vicar nodded solemnly, "Why don't we wait for the weekend Sam? You take it up to the station with you, that'll give Jane and I an excuse to escape love's young thing! By the way, if you hadn't noticed, I suspect that Alex and Melanie are fast becoming what my wife tells me is inelegantly termed "an item"! Perhaps he won't be going back to Australia after all. Or we could be exporting a niece!"

He patted Sam consolingly and said, "My dear chap, buck up do! We've got this shed to take apart and Rob's new summer-house to install before then!"

In the end, Alex, (his self-appointed shadow Melanie), Bert Fleet and Fred Cummins turned to with a will, and the concrete base was cleared and cleaned in time for the purpose-built retreat to be bolted together. Martin stood back admiringly as two large, and enthusiastic men primed and coated the panels then made the roof weather-proof.

Sam watching closely, was reminded of the beach huts at Hordle Cliff on his first trip with Ellen, at which, a gentle "toot" made him jump, as he registered the fact that it wasn't a car! Into his mind came the oddly syncopated sound he'd been caught emulating as he went to hand in his bid for Silver Street Station.

Deserting the gaggle of helpers, he went back to his workshop, found his rucksack hanging on the door and looked for the card he'd casually dropped into it. A breeze stroked his cheek as his fingers encountered a corner and he looked at it for a moment before going into Church Cottage and lifting the phone.

A quick light voice answered promptly. "Harper's Bizarre, how can we help you?", and Sam started to explain, but was silenced in mid-flow when the voice said incredulously,

"Oh wow! Of course I remember you. I was talking about you only this morning. We're utterly desperate at the moment. My planned programme (due to go live on Monday) might have to be cancelled. Another guest has been taken into hospital and I'm out on a limb. However, I expect you could provide some local colour, although the chosen topic wasn't aimed at trains,! but at people who have deliberately chosen to make a home from their workplace. We were to interview a Vicar who ended up converting his church into a home when it was decommissioned, except that the poor man had a heart attack last night. We've possibly got one fall back in a pub landlord who's just converted his pub, but Mr Smart, why are you laughing?"

Ten minutes later he emerged and buttonholed Alex, who was just paying for the summerhouse.

"Sorry Alex got to go!" he said hastily, "I have to get back; I'm about to get a visit and a sound test from the BBC. See if you can tune in to Harper's Bizarre on Monday evening. With any luck it'll be broadcast from Silver Street. Iffen I'm any good at all, we're going to put the place on the map!", and he left his bemused tenant, explaining to a rapt audience that Sam Smart, well-known railway historian had just departed to appear on radio.

Chapter 33 - Ghost Train

Back on his own territory, Sam had one moment of horrified indecision, then the peace and tranquillity of Silver Street enfolded him as the young presenter began the broadcast.

"The BBC welcomes you to "Lost Locations", a series based in the rural heart of our community, visiting favourite haunts lost to modernisation. Tonight in a change from our advertised programme, we bring you to Silver Street Station, near Padways, Dorset. Once the thriving heart of its community, carrying passengers and freight down the recently closed line to Dorchester".

Sam's eyes were glued to Alan Harpers assistant as he nodded and gave a silent count-down, then it was Sam's turn. Dressed for the occasion in his porter's uniform, he touched Charlie's watch for good luck, and remembered. The radio crew stared in disbelief as the thin thread of sound grew, a subtle growling down non-existent lines filled the main entrance where they had set up their broadcasting equipment. The room echoed that familiar sound back, deft fingers turned dials and slid switches, augmenting the astonishing volume that Sam was creating by himself as the memories crowded in. He conjured the thrum and whir of descending windows, the hiss of escaping steam, then, forcing his voice down, a muffled announcement instructed, "Mind the doors", as he re-created the shrill of a whistle, before allowing himself to draw breath, launching it immediately into the chuff of a locomotive "on the roll".

Alan Harper sat enthralled as Sam sent his imaginary train off, integrating the "clack" of the descending signal arm with the sound of the train as it rounded the bend out of the station, and drew further away.

There was a ripple of spontaneous applause from the listening technicians and then Alan Harper said gravely.

"You are listening to the greatest living exponent of steam train mimicry I have ever heard. Mr Samuel Smart, last head porter at Silver Street Station, and now its proud owner, was brought up on the sounds, tastes and smells of an era of steam railway that is passing far beyond our recall. This modern age with its rockets and jet transport has left behind an age where men challenged the very contours of the land in order to provide passenger and freight services from the capital and ports to every county in England...", and so it went on.

Sam was encouraged to tell the story behind the birth of the line, its wartime contribution, and all the while, he too was listening, awed by the seamless continuity of the young presenter, the perspicacity of his questions, and the easy manner in which he assimilated Sam's knowledge. He encouraged Sam to tell the daily story of the old station, weaving (with skilful counterpoint) a picture of that lost world of steam. When the programme drew to a close, Sam re-created the sounds he had filed on closing day, allowing his own sombre sense of finality, to colour his voice, as Alan Harper played him out to the sound of Flanders's and Swann's "Slow Train".

He sat back exhausted as Alan Harper's team congratulated him, and then the young presenter shook his hand firmly and said (in tones of deep satisfaction).

"Thank you Sam. You've not only rescued "Lost Locations", you've probably well and truly put it on the map. Our producer is going to have his socks knocked off, and it's to be hoped that you'll do well out of it yourself."

Sam's air of mild bewilderment must have shown as the presenter said sharply, "Don't tell me you haven't realised what this could mean for you Sam? You're an amazing mimic. Recording studios will be lined up trying to secure your services to give authenticity to plays, books, film and TV. Now the steam era is over, they need those sounds. If I was you, I'd invest in a good session, lay down some tracks while the memories are fresh, and then you'll be able to use those to finance your work here. Your knowledge is phenomenal, and it's first hand too, you've experienced all of it yourself, or listened to those who have. You could write for radio or television, provide talks, or write a book…" he broke off astonished as Sam began to chuckle.

"Oh no, I daresn't go there Mr Harper. One author in the family is quite enough!" he declared, then groaned as he saw Alan Harper register what he'd said.

"There you are Sam," he shot back swiftly; "You could do your wife's career no end of good if you'll ride the shirt-tails of this programme. You see if I'm not right!", he challenged, and then they were gone in a flurry of outside broadcast vehicles, leaving Sam and Ellen wondering what would happen next.

They were picking, preserving, and bottling soft fruit and vegetables now. Every day more of the same, every night Ellen's despair rising as she viewed her rapidly diminishing ability to cope. They were begging, borrowing and buying Kilner jars, reduced to re-using any suitable glass jar for jam when a large car arrived in the down-line car park.

A dapper looking gentleman appeared, took out then spread some sort of drawing on the bonnet, then started pacing out an area. Having watched him for a moment, Ellen wasted no time in going to the fire field, where Alex and Melanie were helping Sam and Paddy pick runner beans.

"Sam, I don't know what's going on, but there's a man parked in the coach park, where I think he'll get in the way if a coach pulls in. He's looking at drawings and I'm not able to deal with him if he needs help. Could you spare me a few minutes? I've got lunch sitting in the kitchen for anyone who wants some quiche and salad."

Having delivered this news, Ellen turned away and went back to sterilising the last of her precious jars. She had just slipped them onto an oven rack in their Crag range and twisted the dial on her clockwork kitchen timer, when she saw Sam and Alex greet the stranger in the coach bay. Five minutes later, a shy tap brought Melanie to the door, so she carefully cut a wedge out of the quiche she'd made that morning, added some salad to two plates and suggested that they could eat on trays in her living-room, leaving the men to fend for themselves. The girl dimpled, opening doors and asking enthusiastically about the progress of Ellen's book. Ten minutes later, Ellen and Melanie, heads together were comparing favourite toys, as unbeknownst to either of them; the fortunes of Silver Street took a turn for the better.

They heard the men returning from the other platform. Alex enthusiastic, Sam guardedly optimistic, but stayed checking Ellen's galley proofs over, letting the men go into the kitchen, then Sam stuck his head round the door, a bright expression on his face.

"That was James Marshall from New Forest Coaches. Apparently his board of directors heard "Lost Locations", made some calls, and now they're taking over the coach stop and all the services in their entirety. Come into the kitchen love, you need to hear this. I can see them being of benefit to both the community and us."

They collected trays and went to listen as Sam sketched out plans for a shift system of coach park attendants, proper maintenance, and routes that included bi-monthly shopping trips to Lymington and Christchurch. The mere suggestion that proper facilities would have to be provided had amused James Marshall, who had viewed the lock-up provided by Royal Blue with contempt.

"I should think we could do considerably better than that." Mr Marshall had concluded, "We want to keep our passengers healthy and happy. Our maintenance crew are properly equipped to service several halts through the Forest. We want to provide not only regular local transport to and from remote villages, but attract tourists as well. If we set up a picnic area, keep it clean and serviceable, would you be prepared to accept a nominal rent for the use of your car-park during the day when coaches are loading or discharging passengers. We'd obviously insure you against accidental damage, including fire caused by careless smokers, and there would be an opportunity in the future to resurrect the concept of the old war-time tearooms should your missus be interested."

Sam related how he and Alex had restrained themselves from disappointing Mr Marshall over this idea, but Ellen said sweetly, "I'll phone Bert and Fred, Sam. It's ideal for them, and if this company want to provide a picnic area, they could do worse. There's not enough work for both of them in Padways, and given that they'll need some extra facilities, they could make a Forest tea-room work well."

Like an echo in his mind, Sam felt the feathery touch of a breeze stroke his neck, caught the whiff of coal-scented steam and found himself thinking "are you telling me this is a good idea?"

He held his breath against disappointment for the split second it took for his ghost train to reply, then it came to him and in his mind's eye he was stood on the platform, wreathed in steam. His father spoke clearly, from that place in between waking and dreaming, "This here's a "Greyhound" Sam. The work-horse of the line. They're very big, strong, and fast too. They're like an idea really, you need to catch it quickly or it'll be gon, up the line and only a whistle to remind you what you missed., Uncle Norman's going to show Daddy how to drive this one. You'll be safe with Grandma and Aunty Mary until I get back. I'll be on Uncle Norman's locomotive for a while, but when I've got my own train, I'll take you up on the foot-plate one day.", but he never had, and for a moment Sam's face clouded, that chance gone forever.

"Sam? Oh you are a dreamer love. Come back from wherever you've gone." Ellen was tugging his arm indignantly, as the plaintive request for another slice of quiche was voiced by Alex. Sam shook himself, looked about absently, as Ellen cut the additional quiche, but Sam had the last laugh.

Watching the young Australian take an enormous bite from his second helping, he said mournfully, "Bang goes my supper!" gathering a pile of punnets as he went back to work grinning.

Not long afterwards, a contingent of ladies arrived, hot on the heels of the programme, determined to buy fresh vegetables regularly. With amusement, Sam sold pounds of Paddy Flynn's despised spuds, pulled carrots and lifted beetroot, then, after allowing bemused customers to set their own prices, reported back to Ellen. She gazed at the pile of notes and coins he handed her, then said faintly, "They're mad! Do you realise they've paid nearly double the going rate Sam Smart?" giggling as he demanded performance fees when he explained that they had also wanted to get the "train-man's" autograph.,

He hadn't told her everything about his ghost train; he hadn't told her how often he heard it either, having too much on his mind to deal with Ellen's superstitious nature. Besides which, Church Cottage was let, and he wasn't leaving Silver Street, even if wild New Forest ponies were involved. Certain in his heart that the train meant no harm, he rode the wave of success, worked sun-up to sun-down, and waited for Rob to return to the fold as eagerly as the others did..

When at last Howard drew in to Church Cottage parking bay, Colonel Fullingford stood, breathing in the evening air in quiet satisfaction. He took his briefcase from Howard, then said awkwardly, "Howard, this is going to be a tough evening. I don't think we'll need you, but would you stand by just in case?"

"Of course sir." the chauffeur took Rob's suitcase from the boot, locked the Bentley and opened the gate for his passenger. They went in to a suspiciously quiet cottage, Howard disappearing with the suitcase, Rob going alone into the sitting-room where Alex sat reading.

The older man put his briefcase down, shrugged off his coat, and all the time (it seemed to Alex) the air in the room stretched as taut as his nerves, then Robertson Fullingford bowed his head briefly and said very softly, "They only need the marriage certificate Alex. They've found his enlistment papers. They've a copy of his death certificate, and we've got your father's papers. The only thing left is to prove your Grandfather's marriage, and find out why he changed his name. In the meantime, I have to look for my father's will, if he died without one, I get Newlands. If he left it to Robert, you get it. Whichever way it goes, you are already a wealthy man, but I'm so tired of hearing about family estrangements. It really hurts me".

Seeing fatigue line his cousin's face Alex stood hugging Rob affectionately saying, "You're tired. Are you hungry? Mrs Short left a supper for us. I'll just check in with Howard." he scooped up Rob's coat, went into the kitchen and found Howard preparing to serve.

They ate in the kitchen, listening to Howard's description of the latest gadgets he'd discovered at Olympia, promising him a large freezer once they had the room to accommodate it. Then, over coffee, Alex recounted the emptying of the potting shed, and Sam's reaction to the discovery of the tin trunk.

Rob listened abstractedly at first, but when Alex explained what the Vicar had told him and Melanie about its questionable provenance, he sat up and demanded a description of the box. Staring at Rob's sudden animation, he replied.

"Heavy, old, a bit battered with an unusual locking system. I didn't see it too closely, besides, Mel and I were off to the pictures, so I didn't hang around."

"It sounds remarkably like an immigrant box I saw being auctioned." Rob said seriously, "but if they're right about its origins, what in hell is an immigrant box doing here?"

"We can find out tomorrow Rob." offered Alex brightly. "Martin and Jane plan to be in on the opening if the key Sam found fits it. I know they were abandoning Mel and me, but she's had to go home early anyway, because her brother has just won a place at University. They didn't expect him to succeed the way he did, so much shopping is planned, and Mel wasn't going to be left out of that expedition!"

They made two phone calls then went to bed pleased that when the box was opened, two more interested bystanders would be present, little dreaming that Sam's strange "awareness" would inexorably link them to his theory about the pattern of life.

Bright and early that Saturday morning, the Bentley carrying Jane and Martin Short, along with Colonel Fullingford and Alex, purred through the village, swept over the road bridge, and turned left into the old loading bay outside Silver Street, as Sam unlocked the front door.

Jane stepped out, took one look at the flowering shrubs fronting the old station, and smiled appreciatively, as Sam welcomed them, showing them through into the dining-room.

He gravely busied himself, hanging jackets in the cloakroom, displaying their new appointments to his visitors, and then took them through into their living-room where Ellen and the mystery box waited.

Sam had carefully lifted the tin trunk on top of an old blanket chest they used as a log-box. They stood by the hearth, the matt blacked surface of the log-box contrasting strongly with the dull metallic gleam of the tin trunk, a carefully positioned light reflecting off its unusual curved lid and the lock and bar system as it faced the room.

"Good Lord!" exclaimed Rob catching sight of it, (then apologetically) "Sorry Vicar...but I meant it most sincerely. Alex, yesterday that seemed a remote possibility, but today I can tell you, that shape and style of box is known as an immigrant chest. They were designed to carry the worldly possessions of thousands headed for new lives all over the Empire, but they are rarely seen here."

"I'm glad I'm not expected to cram my worldly goods in a box that size!" exclaimed Jane in surprise, but her husband said placidly,

"My darling girl. Most immigrants left their country of origin because they had nothing to stay for. Often the poorest, unable to afford such a box, left home with only a few scraps of food, and the clothes they stood up in."

Sam glanced at Ellen and said curiously, "Well darling, this is your shout I think. You and Martin hold that box in trust. Who wants to open it?"

The Vicar grinned, but Ellen seemed oddly reluctant, drawing her cardigan around her shoulders despite the late August sun pouring through the large window where she sat, gazing at the platform from where so many had travelled to an uncertain future.

"I wonder if the immigrant whose box that is left these shores and came back safely?" she mused. "Perhaps this box belonged to someone emigrating to England?", and turning impulsively to Sam, she said thoughtfully,

"My parents came back from India to retire, their old friend owned Burley Manor. He'd been in India too. It's why they bought the cottage here, so the two old boys could play chess."

She turned decisively and held out her hand to Sam, who placed the key he'd found in her palm. She walked over to where Rob was crouched in front of the box, looking at the lock and the way the bars across the front worked, then she silently handed him the key.

He stood, frowning at it, and then she pointed to the mere suggestion of scratched initials she had spotted, as Rob's eyes lifted to hers.

"I thought I was dreaming when my fingers encountered those." she said softly, "but I'm not, am I? Those letters are an A and an F aren't they?"

She crossed to her desk, lifted a magnifying glass and they all crowded around anxious to see what Ellen had found, then Rob said quietly, "There's one man with those initials present, and with its provenance, it could be the property of a relative. As to what might be inside, that affects his future far more than mine. So would you mind if I ask Alex to open the box Ellen?"

She paled visibly, crossing her fingers, then whispered self-consciously, "I wish I'd never heard of Pandora!"

They gathered around as Alex accepted the key, slipped it into the lock, watching closely as the curious bars dropped away and the hasp released.

There was a concerted gasp as he lifted the lid to reveal an ancient revolver on top of a pile of papers. Then Alex gripped Rob's arm and moved away, pinching the bridge of his nose to stem the tears that sprang to his eyes. Sam gently moved the others back, as Rob gazed down on the miniature portrait of a beautiful woman, nestled against a dried rose.

He whispered haltingly, "Mother! I'd know her face anywhere. This is the portrait she sat for just before they married. My Aunt Madeleine (who brought me up), used to tell me how good she was. I remember saying my prayers every night under that picture, but I never knew there was a miniature. Perhaps we all misunderstood my father; it looks like he really loved her".

He gulped suddenly, turned on his heel and walked out through the dining-room and stood, gazing blindly across at the platform where he had first arrived, before slipping his hand into his pocket and extracting a slim box. Sam watched as the Colonel lit a cheroot, and turned back saying quietly, "That's hit him hard Alex. I didn't even know he smoked!"

The Vicar was carefully sorting papers from the top section of the trunk onto a side table, and to do so, had lifted out a cedar-lined compartment. Sam stared as Alex reached into the lower compartment, then saw his friend's jaw clench. In a strangled voice, barely recognisable through emotion he said huskily, "The things in the top section are Rob's, but these papers were my Grandfather's. I just found a photo of my Nan. She was gorgeous.", then his body stiffened, and his voice came out as a harsh whisper.

"Can someone call Rob? I just found their marriage certificate! Oh my goodness! There's even a snap of the happy couple!"

Colonel Fullingford simply inclined his head and followed silently, as Sam told him Alex needed him. He seemed more remote than Sam had ever seen him, but as they entered the comfortable retreat, Martin looked up from the table, and said courteously, "Colonel, I can see this is very sensitive territory. Would you prefer us to withdraw? Jane and I can easily wander back home by ourselves.", and something unfroze in Rob, lending him warmth and renewed vitality.

"Not at all Martin," he reassured, "We could do with an independent witness, besides which right now, both Alex and I need a family around us. We have been privileged by our adoption into Padways, so I (for one), appreciate you and Jane being here." he turned to Alex, who sat rigidly gazing down at the contents of a plain white envelope for a moment longer, then he said raggedly,

"It's ok Rob. They married on August 27th 1916. That's the certificate and a picture as well. So what's with the name thing? I don't get it. If Grandfather was a Fullingford, then my Dad should have been a Fullingford too, but my name is Ford!"

Jane and Ellen's eyes met, the Vicar looked up, and then Sam remembered. When Ellen had been widowed so tragically soon, she had reverted to using her maiden name, returning to her father's household and picking up the threads of her old life where she had left them. He held out his hand to Rob who was scanning the marriage certificate blankly, and checked it. On that far-off day at Newlands, a visiting pastor had indeed married Robert James Fullingford to Emma Ford, daughter of one Edward Ford (foreman of Newlands), who witnessed the marriage, along with another employee. He braced himself against the sudden celebratory sashay of his ghost train, closed his ears to the wild cacophony of toots and whistles, and said solemnly, "Ellen sweetheart? Could you explain this to Alex? It comes better from one who has been there, and suffered much the same way.", then he followed Jane Short into the kitchen and put the kettle on to make tea.

After ten minutes they carried tea through to the rest of the company, where Martin was conferring with Rob over a letter. They set the tray down for Ellen, then they turned to Rob, who plainly had something to say.

"My friends.", the older man said gently. "I cannot think of a better company or a better place to celebrate. For some time, Alex has been trying to prove his late father's legitimacy, in order to secure his family's business in Australia. I, on the other hand, have been researching a generation earlier, for any clue as to why my father emigrated, leaving my mother and me behind. Today we have found ourselves holding the opposite ends of the same piece of string, and although we still have much to learn, we have established one, no, two valuable things. We are first cousins twice removed, my father and Alex's Great Grandfather being brothers. We are also able to establish a firm familial link with Padways, from which our paternal heritage springs."

He raised his tea-cup to the company then indicating the box with his free hand he announced solemnly, "Ladies and gentlemen, I give you the Fullingford Legacy.", and to resounding acknowledgements Silver Street embraced them once more.

It was clear to Sam and Ellen that there was a wealth of family documents to go through, but neither Rob nor Alex seemed inclined to proceed immediately. Spent by emotion, they sat happily listening to Martin and Jane's simple pleasure at having been part of such a remarkable repatriation. Alex had reluctantly surrendered the precious certificate, and under Rob's instructions, the Vicar had listed everything they'd touched, created a brief statement relating how the immigrant chest had come into their possession, and signed it, along with Ellen. They laid it carefully on top of the contents, then Rob asked if they had any sealing wax.

After investigating a small drawer in her desk, Ellen eventually produced a sorry looking remnant with a cry of triumph, as Rob and Sam re-locked the chest. Rather self-consciously, Rob dropped the key into a manilla envelope, added a statement outlining that morning's activities, (signed by everyone), then melted a large blob of sealing wax onto the closed flap of the envelope. To Alex's obvious confusion, he impressed the warm wax with a heavy signet ring, until the initials (R F) stood out as the seal hardened, uncapping a fountain pen, to add the address of a London solicitors in a flowing script. Alex watched this in silent dismay, before protesting.

"I thought we'd go through that together Rob. What's the point of paying solicitors to do it? Those blighters have cost me a mint back home, but never found anything."

Rob chuckled dryly.

"These particular solicitors work exclusively for the Trust my boy. They have been moving heaven and earth to find these documents ever since the question of Newlands was raised. We already pay their fees, so do be a good chap, and let them earn their keep for once!", so highly tickled Alex had given in to the idea of taking the afternoon off.

Ellen, having already prepared lunch for all of them, was unusually quiet as they congregated in the dining-room, but when she laid out her best china, and Howard swung into action serving slices of bacon and egg pie with freshly picked salad, Jane said appreciatively, "This is wonderful Ellen. How do you do it all and write books as well?"

Immediately, the tension lifted. Away from the box and its potential, Rob lightened up, and Alex relaxed, once more his uncomplicated colonial personality shining through. Ellen smiled as Howard loaded their plates, then turned to stare wistfully out onto the woodland walk as a group of ramblers went by. She sighed, and Jane (catching the direction of her glance) said softly, "I know its hard work Ellen, but once your book is out, things will settle down. I'd like to put in an order for Mrs Castle. She's going to show the Mother's Union how to bottle beans and spinach, so we need a quantity of those. Mrs Thomas wanted us to order for the Vicarage, and Emma and Bert want Sam to set up a wholesale account for them. I hear that you are going to get a picnic stop organised? Mr Cummins is like a dog with two tails, and Emma tells me that 'my friend Fred and his partner in crime', are on course to launch the Forest tea-rooms. Now Alex is satisfied that he can keep Newlands, Mel will stop bothering me about what he's going to do, and things will settle down nicely, you'll see."

Ellen smiled wanly as her friend enthused, then she rose abruptly, murmuring urgently, "Jane, please cover for me. I feel sick!", and fled.

The Vicar looked up at his wife sadly. "Just reaction I hope? She never handles excitement all that well!", he offered, having known Ellen for some time, and Jane nodded reassuringly.

"She's tired more than anything I think. Coping with all the results of Sam's labours, on top of finishing her book and teaching, isn't a good mixture for anyone, and she's had to relive a rather exacting emotional experience today, on top of Rob and Alex's finds. All she needs is a good nap, and she'll be fine!", but although her words had the desired effect, and the party continued cheerfully, Jane's eyes had narrowed in speculation.

After their orders had been satisfied, the chest and their friends had been spirited away, leaving Sam and Ellen with a long hot afternoon on their hands. She had immediately retired to finish the last few pages of her galley proofs and type a letter detailing a minor alteration to her publishers, and Sam, left to his own devices, decided to take a walk. He went down to Home Farm, arranged to look over a few of Jack Sherrington's chickens the following day, emerging from the five barred gate looking towards Pine Trees just as Rob appeared on the steps of the property.

The Colonel came straight to the point, crossing the road and buttonholing Sam purposefully.

"I secured the keys about two weeks ago," he announced cheerfully, "but I'm a blithering idiot. I forgot what they told me almost as soon as it was out of their mouths, now I can't work out which set refers to what. Is your good wife likely to know Sam?"

Intrigued, Sam had been on the point of suggesting he come over and try, when a dry cough behind him interrupted them. Beryl Sherrington smiled up at him, her fine aristocratic nose almost quivering as she took in the two bunches of keys that Rob was holding.

"Good afternoon Mr Smart.", she said briskly, "Can I be of assistance?", as she took in Sam's companion in a single inquisitive glance.

Sam made introductions, cautiously interested in her reaction to Rob's name. She looked into his face searchingly, then said firmly, "Fullingford? Well, Colonel you come from an illustrious background. It's a long time since any of the family lived here. I quite thought all of you had died out during the war years."

As Sam heard the sly "shush" of an idling engine, he realised that Rob was holding his breath as Beryl observed sharply.

"You're not so very like the man I knew, although you have the same air as the older generation, so where do you hail from eh? Are you any kin of that Australian chap I keep missing? Harry Godwin called in after clearing his father's possessions from Robin's Way, and says poor Ollie thought he was seeing a ghost!"

She gave a brief bark of laughter, then turned her attention to the keys.

"Simple!", she said dismissively ten seconds later. "The ones on the magenta key-ring are for the main house. The silver fob holds the stable-yard keys.", she eyed them challengingly, "Shall I show you around, or do you know the building?"

Rob found his voice (though he hardly recognised it) and said humbly, "I'd be very glad of your company Mrs Sherrington. If you could spare me the time, we can talk as we go, although you are likely to know more about my relatives than I do."

Sam, (silencing the excited panting of his spirit train), followed, wondering whether he had suddenly turned psychic, or whether his next call should be to the Vicar to arrange an exorcism?

Chapter 35 - To the Manor Born

A brief inspection soon dispelled Sam's expectations of a gloomy vestibule festooned in spider webs. As Beryl began opening the shutters on the far windows, she revealed an entrance hall, utterly devoid of character. Outside, beyond a paved terrace, a wide expanse of lawn sloped gently away, fronting a single wing to the left of the main building. Sam stood staring curiously, noting the tennis court, beyond which a high wall blocked his view.

Rob's amused voice broke into his thoughts chiding gently.

"Come along Smart do. No casting envious eyes on that lawn either. Flynn is not having a yard of Padways Manor for his spuds!"

Obediently they followed Beryl, as she assumed the role of housekeeper conducting a tour of the house, listening as she told little anecdotes as they went.

"The Manor has had a few uses since the Fullingfords left." she remarked, leading the way into a beautifully proportioned hall, which had clearly doubled as a gymnasium.

"This room was originally a ballroom with a sprung floor. Then it was split into two wards for injured officers returning from Flanders. I came here in service when I was about fourteen, but that didn't last long!"

She grinned amiably adding, "That house was intimidating. So many places servants couldn't go, and I was a flighty thing then. There's no getting away from it, I wouldn't have lasted ten months. Not long after I was told, (in no uncertain terms) that the butler (Hopkins) and the housekeeper had their eyes on me I met Johnny Sherrington. He and I hit it off straight away, so, when his Grandfather died, we took the money he left and out to Africa. His younger brother Harry took Home Farm, but never married. After my Johnny was killed, he gave my boy a start, eventually leaving the farm to him."

She led the way into a library, opening shutters on tall windows that gave a glimpse of the pines beyond.

"Nasty dark things those trees," she commented acidly. "They're a blot on this corner of the house. The Forestry Commission say they're too tall for their proximity to the building, and need to be felled." she sighed.

"This room used to be lovely all year round but it's dark and gloomy now."

Empty bookcases dominated walls painted in a deep forest green, and even though the woodwork and plaster mouldings were picked out in white (like the Regency room it emulated), it felt chilled and unloved.

"This was Lord Alexander's library back in the day!" she flung open another shutter. "He used to work in here." she commented, and Rob shivered, touching his breast pocket over the precious diary as he turned to leave. Sam closed the shutters behind them, and followed, wondering exactly as the Colonel had, if Lord Alexander's cry of outrage against his twin had been written in that very library. He shut the door softly, clattering down a staircase behind their guide, through a swing-door and into a corridor leading to well-lit classrooms.

For an hour or more, they wandered back and forth between the school conversion and private rooms, listening to Beryl's confident identifications.

"This was the old housekeepers room, where she conducted the business of the household.", followed by, "Officers Mess for Bomber Command during the last war, which became the prep room once the school took over.", ending with the return to the entrance hall.

As a thoughtful Rob pointed out, they hadn't looked at the attic rooms (once the domain of servants), glanced into outhouses or explored cellars, but it became obvious that Rob's brain was engaged in planning. Beryl eyed him sideways as she returned the keys, and said suspiciously, "Why did I think you were only distantly related to my Fullingfords Colonel? You're plotting something and I know that look. What can we expect next hey? A lot of builders is it?", but Rob chuckled easily.

"No Mrs Sherrington.", he said firmly, "One or two at the most, but I don't think you need worry. I'll have the Forestry Commission deal with those pines though, so perhaps you'll warn Jack."

By this time they were out on the steps, and he locked the doors with a steady hand as she stared up at him.

"Are you fixing to move in then?" she queried with a smile, but he shook his head.

I don't know yet, although that might be one solution. Incidentally, just to put you in the picture. My father was Anthony Fullingford, and I am the principal Trustee of the Fullingford Trust. What happens to the Manor is subject to a Board meeting, but as valued neighbours, you and Jack will be the first to know. Now I must cut along, thank you for your guided tour. I'll look forward to seeing you soon."

He gave his stiff, almost military bow, and walked briskly away towards the village.

Beryl Sherrington gave a low unladylike whistle. "My Heavens!" she said appreciatively. "Wouldn't that be something Sam? A member of the old family back in Padways? I rather like the look of this one. If ever I saw a real gentleman, he's to the manner born!", and with that she went away whistling cheerfully.

During August there was a sudden influx of visitors. Sam lined the old weighing room with shelves, setting out a display of Ellen's pickles, preserves, jams and chutneys. He made a serving counter, traded honey, eggs and cheese with the Sherrington boys, stacking boxes of vegetables ready to be weighed below, and stood cogitating where to put the shop sign.

Trevor Steadman and his girl sauntered in from the car-park grinning from ear to ear at the sight, as Trevor made introductions shyly.

"Belle's looking for a job Mr Smart. She knows about plants and shop-work if you need someone. I'd be grateful for a few hours too. I got my certificates in book-keeping this year, but I've only got a few hours keeping the picnic area clean, because I need to keep my options open if I'm going to get into accountancy. I hope you don't mind my asking?"

The young voice was anxious, but Sam smiled inviting their opinions on his layout. Belle suggested placing his sign on the back wall of the building and sent Trevor up to the newly erected picnic benches to test her theory.

"People picnicking should be able to see the sign." she argued, "Ramblers or cyclists on the track can see you have a shop by the display on the platform, but you have to maximise passing trade!", as Sam gave in and took them on!

Eight log tables of the type that have integral bench seats had been erected under Paddy's critical supervision as they were set up in the old car-park. A temporary tea-room was erected, parking bays marked, as under Sam and Ellen's astonished gaze, Silver Street began to regain her place in the heart of a thriving community.

Ramblers arrived with sandwiches, and departed into the distance munching Silver Street apples. Picnic parties appeared, filled their stomachs (and the boots of their cars) as Trevor trotted over, clearing and cleaning the area for the W I. Ellen (returning to school after the Summer holidays), arrived home at four-thirty, put dinner in the range, went and did some marking, then at five o'clock, helped Belle put away plants and cash-up. Trevor filled in the sales ledger, and then re-stocked what they'd sold before he and Belle roared out of sight on his motorbike.

Paddy and Sam planned and planted as summer ended, and the Forest turned crimson, gold, and copper, then the train began to tease Sam's conscious mind. From time to time it was possible to hear traffic on the main coastal line, but now, the majority of locomotives were diesel electric. What Sam heard was different. Even the approaching experience prickled along his nerves like the song of the line. Some days it got so bad he'd jump out of his skin if anyone spoke to him, then (just to be doubly annoying), when he thought he might be able to identify the engine, it didn't come at all. He grew distracted, taking himself away from the popular hurly-burly that he'd worked so hard to reclaim, and Ellen, facing the oncoming launch of her book in London, watched him with worried eyes.

She was sensitive to atmosphere herself, but sunk in her research she'd been ignoring odd sounds, until the weather turned wet. One evening, (convinced she could hear a child crying), she got up, left the comfort of her living-room, and opened the door onto the platform, calling anxiously, "Is anyone there? Don't cry, just come to the door, we won't hurt you."

For answer, there was a gust of rain-sodden wind, and then a tabby cat appeared through the shower, sneered at her disdainfully, and shot off towards the signal-box, where it disappeared from view. Sam looked out from the kitchen (where he had been working), as she retreated crossly.

"Problems love?" he enquired as she passed him, crossing the room to make tea, avoiding the table where Sam had been poring over the plans again. She shook her head, but took the opportunity to ask him,

"We're doing alright aren't we Sam?" and he looked up surprising a shadow in her eyes.

"We, my dear love, are doing superbly." he said promptly. "I've got builders starting upstairs, as soon as we close for winter. We got a good price, so you can have your sewing-room, plus two large and one small bedroom."

He stood, drawing her back against him, bending his head to nuzzle her neck, aware that she was as taut as a bowstring.

"What's wrong darling? Didn't you realise how well we're doing? What made you ask?"

She relaxed against him, and then said with a shaky laugh. "Oh I don't know Sam. It's probably the weather, or more likely me! I thought I heard a child crying, but when I looked out, it was only some darned cat. It took off towards the signal-box, but I certainly don't want it trying to get into the chickens, if it's gone wild a cat can cause as much harm as a fox."

"I'll go and take a look in a minute love." he reassured her, "but at least we know it isn't a child!"

However, she seemed somehow unsettled still, and then the dreams began.

It was dark and foggy when she arrived on the up-line platform, and she had the oddest feeling that the porter hadn't seen her at all. The damp air penetrated her coat, hung visibly in the light of the one lamp swinging above the entrance, misting the face of the station clock and preventing her from seeing the time. However, there was activity across the line in the bay outside, and as she watched, people began to appear. She relaxed, then time seem to jump forward, there was a train in the station, her train possibly, but there was no-one there to clip her ticket. She began to run, thrusting her ticket into the faces of the staff, the passengers boarding, but everyone ignored her as though she wasn't there.

Then, she saw the boy through a rising curl of steam. He was only about fourteen, rooted to the ground, staring at her as if he couldn't believe his eyes. As the guard's whistle shrilled and last minute passengers boarded, he seemed to be looking for something, peering into trolleys, hunting along the platform. Ellen felt sick with anxiety. The train was leaving, the mist was thickening, she couldn't see clearly, and then the train began to roll as the boy called out in despair. "Ellen, I've got him. Don't cry Ellen, he's safe and I'll get him back to you. I promise."

The boy was running alongside the train, running into a wall of dense fog, just a dark figure wreathed in mist. The night echoed his voice dully as it repeated slowly, "I'm sorry Ellen. I know I promised to be good.", then the train tooted and passed out of sight, and the mist descended, and the boy was gone.

She woke crying, sobbing inconsolably, frightening Sam who could make neither head nor tail of her story, and so it went on. Once, twice, even three times a night, until Sam insisted she see the doctor a mere two weeks before her book was to be launched. They had just recovered from the stress of the animated discussion following this (not unreasonable) demand, when the knocker dropped on the front door. Silenced (for once) by Sam's implacable attitude, Ellen said shortly, "For you I suppose! I had a call about half an hour ago, but you were too busy beating your breast and aping Tarzan for me to tell you about it. It's Alex, and he's in a real state! May I wish you joy of him? I'm not playing silly male games; I've got a speech to write!"

He went to the door as she stalked past, headed for her desk, and he knew better than to try and get any sense into her while she was in that particular mood.

Alex was on foot, dressed in jeans and jumper but still managing to exude his own air of affluence. However, he seemed furtive, glanced hastily around, then slid into Sam's dining-room as though pursued.

"Jeepers mate!" he exploded wrathfully, "You took your time answering! Didn't Ellen tell you I'm on the run? When a fellow needs to go walkabout, you don't need to leave him hung out in the cold for the press to find!"

Sam steered him into the kitchen, settled him on a stool, and fixing his friend with a stern eye, said levelly.

"Ellen is in the middle of writing a speech for her book launch. I don't think she'd notice if the Queen rang and asked for shelter, she did tell me, but it consisted of a disjointed mutter, and I caught nothing outside your name. What on earth is up?"

For answer, Alex miserably held out a London paper which proclaimed in headlines, "Lost heir to millions found!", and Sam, (feeling weak at the knees) sat and ignored the drawn-out hoot of a steam train exulting as it thundered through his blood.

Alex, (very pale and vaguely tearful), said direly, "I should have gone up to London with Rob. He took a call this morning, quite literally stood at attention while he listened, then he said (and here I quote verbatim).

""Yes sir! I understand completely sir! At two-thirty pm sharp sir! Thank you sir!" Then he packed (or rather Howard packed), and when he couldn't persuade me to go with him, he told me to stay close to the house, not to speak to anyone I didn't know and to contact you or get myself here if anything strange happened. Howard got all huffy when I told Rob I intended to do what I liked, and told me that if I still wanted to retain his services, I should do what I was told. They took off at a hell of a lick. I was called by Rob's office at about twelve, and he told me he had important news, and that he'd call about four. Well, he never did, but I heard an odd noise, lifted the receiver and was convinced someone was listening in. I went to the back door, just in time to see what I took to be a phone engineer up a pole, and then Bert Fleet walked in, cool as a cucumber, carrying a tray of pasties. He tells me the shop is full of press men, and persuades me to pack up an old jumper and jeans, change clothes with him and take the tray back to that van he and Fred use."

Sam was staring as the young Australian said happily, "I don't know who let the cat out of the bag, but we're going to have to get out of the cottage Sam. I've just changed into my own clothes, put Bert's bakery things in a bag and sent Fred down to rescue him. Can I stay here until the heat dies down or Howard rescues me?"

Ellen was finally persuaded that Alex was serious when Jane called her, bursting with questions. "It's on the news Ellen. Martin has talked to the police because the blighters are trying to bribe the children to tell them where…" (and here she drew a shaky breath and said firmly) "Where some poor chap called Lord Alexander Fullingford is hanging out?"

Sam stared as Ellen crowed in delight, then he smothered his mouth with both hands as Ellen dropped Alex an enormous wink and said coldly, (in the broad Scots she imitated so well).

"Och Jane. I told you that blighter was a con man didn't I? Seems he looks like this poor chap who's just surfaced, so he's trying it on with as many folk as are daft enough to fall for it. Seems to me that the Press would be better investigating when this Lord High Muck a Muck entered the country than wasting time and money chasing phantoms round country villages. You know me, ah'm so careful I wouldn't trust anyone who said he was a Lord until I saw his coronet!"

She replaced the receiver, and said vulgarly, "and anyone listening in can shove that right up their kilt!"

From astonished outrage, Alex was suddenly in hysterics. Sam let him laugh, until his composure shattered, sending tears running down his face, then Ellen said consolingly, "Come on silly. It's been rather a shock to the system, but you can do it. This Lord thing is only a ten day wonder, you've got a bolt-hole in the Outback if you really can't stand it, but more importantly you've got the breeding, the education, and (if the papers are to be believed) the money to make a difference to so many people. The strength, wisdom and purpose of Lord Alexander, tempered by the ability to love (however unwisely) is not something to be squandered on just anyone. You are the right man for the job, the only man for this job, so hold your nerve, while I phone Rob's office, then we'll get you out of here."

Twenty minutes later Ellen drove into the yard at Home Farm in Lady Jane, followed by Sam in the old Ford. Beryl greeted her enthusiastically, wearing a pale pink cardigan over white slacks. Ushering Ellen through the normally unused front door, the conspirators gathered in the kitchen as Sam parked carefully, close to the milking parlour that ran down the right hand side of the yard. He got out, went to the right-hand rear door, opened it, then shook his head (and leaving that door wide open) went to the boot to retrieve a heavily laden basket. Meanwhile, Alex made his way (at a crouch) into the milking parlour on the right, unobserved by the disconsolate reporters gathered on the Manor steps.

Dave Sherrington, leaning on the farm gate watching, sent his brother Mike to fetch in a few young calves so that suspicion was diverted when the gate opened five minutes later for the two ladies to leave the farm in Ellen's car. Sam deliberately took another five minutes, chatted with the boys casually, then returned to Silver Street as Alex (very self-conscious in a pink cardigan and white slacks, complete with pink and white headscarf) was whisked away to Mike Theobald's care.

Shortly thereafter, a smartly suited figure waited with the Station Master for a fast train from Brockenhurst to London. However, thinking about the swift cloak and dagger operation of Padways, the young Lord Fullingford felt his confidence return as he prepared to leave anonymity behind.

Chapter 36 - The Last Passenger

Once the excitement over Alex died down, and the inexorable march towards winter began, the Smarts saw a change at Silver Street. Gradually, the seasonal decline in casual shoppers accelerated. The temporary Forest Tea Room was removed on a huge lorry, and the winter coach timetable superseded the familiar summer routine. By the second week of the month, only the hardiest or the out-of-season holidaymakers came through, and reluctantly, Sam found himself locking the wicket gates and hanging up "Closed till Christmas" signs.

Supplied with a stock of railway memorabilia from books and place-mats, through model trains, plans and postcards Belle and Trevor (whose brainwave this was) disappeared giggling to turn the weighing room shop into a fabulous Christmas grotto, dedicated to the line.

When Ellen and Sam were invited to inspect the result, they could hardly believe their eyes, with a corner for Ellen and a full shelf to hold her books, and a place for the porter to entertain the children, the Silver Street Christmas shopping event was set up in advance. When it was done, all the crops had been lifted and stored, autumn planting was finished, there had been no walkers for a week, and Silver Street snoozed, while Sam fretted, more than aware that something was about to happen.

He had spent a few days wandering back and forth, drawings rolled up under one arm, clipboard and notepad in the other, pencil behind one ear, and Ellen (who had taken a fortnight's holiday to prepare for her book launch), was getting increasingly irritated. Once or twice she'd heard the "chuff" of a steam train, caught the strange ululating quality of a passing locomotive's whistle, and surprised herself (and Sam) by snapping at him.

"Unless you've been in touch with Alan Harper and are in the middle of rehearsal, do give over playing at Southern Rail!"

She'd leant out of the kitchen window as she spoke, and Sam turned from where he'd been placidly entering measurements on his clip-board, and seeing the ruler he gripped between his teeth, she'd withdrawn confused.

A few minutes later, she'd opened the dining-room door onto the platform, gruffly apologised and invited him in for tea.

"Don't worry about me!" she'd announced wryly, "I'm clean round the bend. That bloody speech has finally done for me. I'm making tea unless you'd prefer coffee?"

Rather perturbed, Sam accepted tea and slowly followed her back to the kitchen, so engrossed by his measurements, he never noticed a stray shaft of sunlight that turned her hair to gold. She'd already cleared her own work away, piling her reference books back on her desk, leaving only the notebook with her speech and her sewing at one end of the table, making room for his roll of drawings. Now, pouring mugs of tea as he sat down, she surprised him by demanding suddenly, "What's the matter Sam?"

Realising how badly her superstitious nature would rebel at the mention of "ghost-trains", he prevaricated.

"I don't rightly know love." he muttered, (dropping into broad Dorset), unaware that this only highlighted his own apprehension.

She hooked out a stool and perched there, notepad in hand as he struggled to come to a decision. Should he tell her what he'd found yesterday, or should he keep quiet and investigate when she went back to work? He frowned sighing, as he reluctantly acknowledged he couldn't deceive her but he held his peace until she hugged him fiercely.

"Sorry Sam. I'm letting my nerves get to me lately. Look, I'll trade with you. If you'll listen to my speech and tell me honestly if it bores you to tears, I'll help you sort out whatever's bothering you, no matter what it is. You've put so much into this place; we both love it to bits, so I'll trade you a speech, if you tell me what's wrong!"

Sam's resistance crumbled, he cleared his throat to speak, found he couldn't, and buried his face in his mug instead. At that precise moment, his train solved the dilemma for him. There was a distinct "chuff", followed by the sighing release of steam (almost as powerful as his own anxiety), then the cheerful salutation of a train coming in on the growling wave of compression, as the lines vibrated beneath the wheels. Ellen staring straight at him blanched, and Sam (local burr intensified by strain) found himself blurting, "That's what's wrong! I'm 'aunted, and I know by what! Now do you want to trade missus?"

She bit her lip, her new fashionable bob swinging forward to hide her face but eventually she sighed, shrugged, and said brightly, "There are no such things as ghosts Sam Smart, and it isn't Smart to tease a desperate woman. However, you tell me what's haunting you, then I'll practise my speech, and that will see any ghost off the premises I can assure you!"

He drained his mug, put it down slowly, and then took a deep breath, feathering it to the back of his throat. As if prompted, in his mind the picture of a locomotive rose, he caught the tang of hot coal on metal, the gentle all-pervading hiss of steam, and touched his father's watch where it nestled in his dungaree pocket. This time the train spoke through him, he felt the trembling ululation of a time long past as the sound rolled and echoed round a room that knew it down to the last rivet. He heard its call in his blood, felt its pain in his soul, and down the long years since it had prowled these lines, the plea for a champion to argue its case thrilled in his throat.

Ellen stared as though she too had seen the train, then she raised an interrogative eyebrow.

"That there's a Drummond T9 "Greyhound." Sam announced.

"Common enough 'ereabouts, often used for excursion trains. Norman and Charlie used to drive them occasional like, I even watched my Uncle Norman take one through on "Special" when I was little. ..." he paused, face screwed up in fierce concentration, They was in service from the 1890's so whatever , it's looking for could 'ave been 'ere more'n 'alf a century."

The soft voice continued thoughtfully, "It just goes to show that poor old 'Arvey wasn't barmy either. He loved this place too you see!" at which Ellen said soberly,

"I know, but look where it got him. You don't really believe in the supernatural Sam Smart. Messing around with things we don't understand is dangerous. I'm still waiting for one of those satellites they keep putting up to come down with a bang. You mark my words Sam; we're better off taking care of our own world before we start mucking around with spirits or space!"

Sam grinned and relaxed as Ellen opened her notes and said sharply, "Now, I've been good, heard you out, so it's my turn. Thank goodness my interests are in dolls and teddy bears and there's nothing out of this world about those!"

She bent her head over her speech, and began, accentuating her 'h's, gently teasing Sam until he blushed. As she got into her stride however, he listened with awakening interest as she spoke about toys excavated from Egyptian tombs, medieval puppets, then moved to Victorian dolls. As she followed the course of her book, ending with the birth of the modern Teddy bear, he was thoroughly impressed by her confident approach.

She was speaking about Clifford Berryman's sketch dramatising an event back in 1902, and Sam leant back, wondering what the relevance was as she turned the last page, glanced down at her notes, and answered his question.

"In conclusion, the phrase "Teddy's bear" (coined by the Washington Post on 16th November 1902) referred to Clifford Berryman's sketch "Crossing the line". This depicted Theodore Roosevelt's refusal to shoot a disabled immature bear. In adopting President "Teddy" Roosevelt's well known commitment to fair play, the paper unintentionally engendered an affection for toy "Bruins", renaming them "Teddy Bears" in the process. Subsequently, the last minute purchase of three thousand Steiff bears at the 1903 Leipzig Fair, secured not only the future of Steiff, but the future of soft toy manufacturing and the happiness of children everywhere."

She broke off, colouring as Sam clapped appreciatively saying, "Bravo! You'll knock 'em dead." his eyes shifting to the poster as he read out loud.

"Book Launch at the 1965 International Convention of Toy Manufacturers; Ellen Smart's book "The Bear on My Bed" launches at Alexandra Palace, London, on 27th September 1965."

He chortled, "Cor, it'll cost me two bob to talk to you soon!", as Ellen looked up.

"Sounds good, but no-one's bought a book yet, and it'll soon disappear into obscurity if they don't! You on the other hand Mister, deal with people face to face. You've been on the radio, got half the inhabitants of Dorset eating out of your hand, so perhaps I'd better cough up first!"

She hugged him suddenly, and for a moment everything else faded into the background, then she asked soberly, "What are you doing about this haunting stuff Sam? I don't want to feel frightened in my own home, should I get Martin to come and advise us or what?"

His face creased as he agonised over his next sentence, but she prompted him gently sighing as she spoke.

"Go on Sam. There's more isn't there? You'd better tell me the worst; next week will be too late. Rob will be back (Alex already phoned). I've got a dress fitting, a photography session, and an appointment with a publicity man! Let's get it over with, and then we can forget it."

His hand touched the bib pocket of his dungarees as he considered his next move, then it became irrelevant as his train cried out sorrowfully, and Ellen held out her hand unsteadily.

"Show me!" she demanded, and he passed her a yellowing fragment miserably aware that if they stood any chance of staying in Silver Street, this matter had to be resolved.

She glanced down, eyes narrowing as the vintage type sprang into focus, but as she murmured "Dear Lord!", Sam stood, looking out where almost sixty years before, the dreadful tale began.

Ellen read out loud, her voice quavering just a fraction as the details became clear.

"September 16th 1905 - Fullingford Flyer Derailed."

Her pallor increased as she read the following lines.

"Reports of a fatal accident involving a privately chartered locomotive, outside Silver Street Station, west of Brockenhurst, Hampshire. Breaching the Viaduct above a junction, the train derailed. Fatally injured: Lord Alexander Fullingford (45); second wife Lady Leonora (26); heir Robert Fullingford (15) a Winchester pupil; and daughter Ellen (6). Still to be identified are; a number of household staff; employees of Fullingford Factors; and the usual LSWR employees. There were no survivors."

Shocked, Ellen murmured, "It's the other half of Rob and Alex's story Sam, but if he survived why is Robert named as a victim? I've wondered from the beginning how could a boy of fifteen disappear so effectively, but they obviously thought him dead! I know Rob said he'd tell us how everything happened once he's pieced all the facts together, but we ought to involve them straight away shouldn't we?"

Sam shook his head decisively. "This 'ere' is railway business." he stated flatly. "They're not the ones being 'aunted, we are. It's my place to make sure Silver Street don't 'old no more secrets do you see? I'm not worrying about things long past, if there's something we can do about it now."

The train panted softly, steam gently rising round the corners of her memory, as Ellen asked, "What are we going to do then?", and a hopeful look dawned on Sam's face. He wrinkled his brow, speaking hesitantly, "Well...I found that cutting yesterday, half underneath a door off the Station Master's office. I didn't know it was there, just stumbled as I tried to pick the cutting up, and fell against it. Proper papered over it is! Real mysterious, like no-one wanted it found."

Ellen questioned him fearfully.

"What's inside that door Sam? I couldn't cope with skeletons, but that's silly isn't it? Only bad lots keep skeletons in their cupboards...", then having delivered this particular piece of nonsense in a monotone rush, she burst into tears. "It's all ruined, all spoilt. Our lovely home is haunted and...."she sniffed inelegantly and wailed, "I'm scared Sam, promise me you'll get Martin and make it go away."

Sam was so shocked he swept her up in his arms, holding her close and murmuring endearments until she settled wearily.

"There's only one way to find out about skeletons sweetheart," he said gravely, braving himself for another uncharacteristic outburst, "and that's to open the cupboard."

She sat up indignantly. "Do you mean to tell me that you didn't look to see what's behind that door?" she demanded, "Why not?", but Sam avoided her eyes.

"I was that startled when I read that cutting." he acknowledged shame faced. "It were already dark, and we haven't put a light bulb in there yet, so I left it."

She chuckled indulgently; "Scaredy cat!" she taunted, then before her own nerve deserted her she followed that up with an offer.

"It's nice and light today, so come on Sam, there's no time like the present!"

That afternoon, Sam and Ellen entered the Station Master's Office. Only a desk and a few cheap prints hinted at its previous life, as Sam dropped his toolbox, wedging the door to the platform open. The evidence of his discovery (in the right hand wall) was revealed by three slashes of a broad knife, where a faint *darkness* appeared under the cracked and peeling plaster. As Sam said, it felt enticingly mysterious and with childish bravado, they started stripping it bare, bundling three layers of paper and large pieces of plaster waste into old potato sacks as they worked.

The door gradually appeared, and Sam exclaimed in delight.

"Lost Property Office.", running a finger over the faint inscription above it.

"Well it were certainly "Lost" behind all this." he announced, gesturing at the waste that had concealed it. "It weren't 'ere in my time.", he continued thoughtfully, "but then, neither were the sidings. There must 'ave been a load of changes during the war, rooms knocked down, sheds put up, but it's odd. Lost Property were always with parcels on t'other side. Nobody mentioned this, so I reckon nobody knew about it either! It's old...very old."

She observed him silently, so, after a moment, he turned the door handle (pulling), meeting no resistance as the door swung open. He peered cautiously into the darkness before entering, and then she heard him calling back in mild disappointment.

"It's just a cubby hole!"

Then, before Ellen could reply, his voice (charged with excitement) floated back to her.

"Hallo...? What have we got 'ere?"?

Goose bumps stood out on Ellen's arms as Sam emerged carrying a thick book and a large package. He laid them on the desk and they stood silently, looking at the waxed brown paper, tied with hand twisted twine. A large blob of red sealing wax covered the knot, where a label proclaimed, "Miss Ellen Fullingford. Left behind 16th Sept 1905."

"Oh!" said Ellen wretchedly, "That poor little girl. I wonder what she lost."

Sam reached for the parcel, and Ellen, seeing that he held his trusty penknife, caught his arm.

"Should we?" she questioned in a whisper, "By rights I suppose that belongs to Rob and Alex!", but Sam replied stolidly.

"Silver Street has waited for sixty years to return this to an "Ellen". Better it be my Ellen than leaving it here, in the dark waiting. I got no reason to believe we wasn't meant to find it love."

He carefully cut into the cord holding the parcel together, and the paper parted to an intake of breath and a whistle of surprise, as Sam lifted into Ellen's arms a large Teddy Bear, with strangely elongated arms and legs.

"I don't reckon he's "Lost Property.", said Sam Smart dubiously, "I'd call him the last passenger wouldn't you love?"

Ellen stroked the bear in rapt adoration.

"Oh Sam, this is Steiffs, 'Bar PB 55', but I thought there were no known examples outside the Steiff collection!"

As her voice trembled tearfully, her expertise came to her rescue.

"Richard Steiff's first *jointed* toy bear. Full plush fabric; innovative glass eyes, no button in the ear, so definitely pre-1904…", her gaze narrowed as she gently pressed the bears limbs, examining the visible clues to his manufacture, as she declared in rising excitement.

This is wool stuffed. It must be a prototype. Worth an absolute fortune mint condition. I think he came directly from Steiffs. Sixty years just waiting for me! Sam, do you realise what this means?"

The bear warmed under her hand as Ellen, thinking of the child who would never return for him, gulped, blinked, and hugged him to her.

However, Sam, far from picturing their dreams coming true, listened to the distant toot of an old steam train, wondering privately if this story was actually over yet.

As Ellen reluctantly confided, she had been unable to remember her strange repetitive dream in any great detail, but when (after two restless nights) it reoccurred, Sam decided to tell Rob and Alex about the find. He didn't know what to expect, but it certainly wasn't a visit in person, he'd assumed that they would be busy settling their own affairs. However, they arrived the following day, and after taking in Ellen's wan face, Rob came straight to the point.

"My Uncle was constantly looking for new outlets for the natural products that Fullingford Factors sponsored." he shuffled through the paperwork he'd brought with him.

"He seemed a remarkably dedicated character, sourcing work for those who had been crippled or widowed through their service to the Crown. Anything made from wood grown on the estate, anything made from the local twine industry, he got orders for. Men, who would never work again in the normal way, were enabled to support their families. He'd have no dependent widows or orphans, he drove hard bargains and everyone worked for their living, but they loved him all the same." he reached forward and stroked the bear thoughtfully.

"He could have secured sales of wooden toys, or twine at some exhibition in London, which might fit the reason behind this excursion special and his taking household and work staff with him. However, it's purely academic now. Although I'm sorry your lives seem to have been turned upside down by Bertie Bear's arrival."

There was a thundering roar in Sam's ears as the night train went through! The door to the dining-room which opened onto the old up-line platform crashed open, and steam billowed in on the back of a gust of wind. Alex stood up shakily.

"Jeepers mate!" he cried involuntarily as Ellen gripped Sam's hand, and Rob gathered the letters (scattered over the floor).

He held one out to Ellen with a rueful expression on his face. "My fault I believe," he said gently to Ellen, "but I think we're on the right track. That represents the only clue I have to this whole sorry business.", and Ellen found herself looking at the rounded hand of a youth.

"Sir, I have quarrelled with my father and have earned my sister's disapprobation for doing so. My family are attending an Exhibition tomorrow, so I plan to apologise in person, intercepting them en route. The boot-boy is coming with me for safety. R F".

Ellen raised her eyes from the page and whispered, "Sam, this is to do with my dream. I saw a boy running alongside a train. I don't know what he referred to, but I remember a promise. Do you think he's still trying to fulfil it?"

Sam looked straight at Rob and said shortly, "Well Colonel? It seems that there's as many twists and turns to your family's fortunes as there were bends on the old Corkscrew. 'Owever, iffen me and Ellen are to get a nights peace, this particular problem 'as to be solved."

"Point taken.", the older man replied laconically, then turning to Alex he suggested.

"If I read this right, our presence on the 16th is called for, but in the meantime, you and I have a lot of reading to do."

Sam solemnly saw them off the premises, and then crossed over to join Ellen, who shivered in his arms despite three blankets, a hot water bottle, and the comforting presence of her childhood elephant.

She whispered sleepily, "We're caught between a child's dreams told to her bear and the desperate promise of a frightened boy. What welds them together seems to be the glue of love, death, and that bloody train." this explanation satisfying both of them, they slept in each other's arms.

By unspoken consent neither Ellen nor Sam referred to that strange evening the following day, both of them being too distracted to consider the odd invitation that they had extended to the Fullingfords. They seemed to be inundated with visitors that morning, all wanting to get their reaction to the latest rumour.

Beryl Sherrington had been the first to call, bringing with her (as an excuse to gossip) a jug of cream to go with the last of the gooseberry crop she'd picked only that morning.

"You've a great little pocket of land." the older woman told a surprised Ellen. "I can remember my Johnny saying it was one of his favourite memories, scrumping apples from the Station Master's garden.", she turned wistful eyes on Sam's growing ground as she spoke, both of them watching Sam and Paddy wrestling the Trusty tractor round the new patch they were opening up.

"We were in Kenya quite a long time and poor Johnny used to hanker after apples. He especially like the old varieties of course, but we never solved the problem of growing those in a hot climate. I wonder what this Australian chap is going to make of the Manor," she continued in a ruminative voice, "It seems odd to us that they should overlook that Colonel Fullingford, and give a title and absolute millions to a chap who wasn't even born here. I like the boy, but Colonel Fullingford is a perfect gentleman. British to the backbone, distinguished military career, yet the younger chap gets the title!" she paused to accept Ellen's hand as they stepped back onto the old up-line platform, her tone mildly scandalised.

"Do you know they're up at the farm with Jack, and he's talking farm business as though he knew it inside out, and when Jack showed him the plan of Home Farm, pointing out that as the largest farm in this area he was hard pushed to manage without outside help, do you know what he said? I was never so mortified!"

She grinned all the same, a wickedly humorous expression on her face. Ellen, busying herself with the kettle, screwed her face up contemplatively, and then it came to her. She parodied Alex's accent reasonably well as she suggested, "Jeepers mate, don't struggle by yourself. Give us a shout and we'll pop up and give a hand. It's not like we live too far away."

The farmer's mother gave a brief bark of laughter, and then she said brusquely, "There'll be no 'popping-up' for that young lordship, and as for Jack calling him to help get the hay in! I expect farming's a bit of a novelty to him, but its hard work and often poorly rewarded. Both Jack's boys want to go to agricultural college, but we just can't spare them and turn a profit."

Ellen was shocked into silence, then she remembered Alex's own story, and spoke cautiously.

"Beryl," she said as she poured tea for both of them, "you are totally wrong about Alex. He never knew a title existed and believe it or not, he's totally genuine. He's also a farmer, has a degree in animal husbandry and business management, and forgive me if you think I'm talking out of turn, but I think a nicer thing couldn't have happened to Padways.", she warmed to her theme, telling Beryl Sherrington that although Alex didn't conform to her idea of a lord, she couldn't ask for a more considerate neighbour.

Mrs Sherrington's eyes brightened, and then she elaborated.

"Well, that Colonel went over the Manor (with your man in tow) the other day." she confessed. "I was there, and he seemed quite happy, although that school left it as plain as a pikestaff, all the character stripped out of the place. Anyway, since then, we've had a visit from the Forestry Commission and at long last those ruddy pines are coming down. Your Colonel says they were planted after the Lady Rowena's horse bolted during a thunderstorm and killed her. They cover the ground where poor Godwin had to bring the horses so Lord Alexander could see them shot."

Her voice faltered for a moment as both women saw the dreadful finality of a man's grief, Ellen picturing the implacable face staring at the destruction of his dreams, while Beryl (who'd known Ollie Godwin), remembered the weight of his sorrow at the needless results. Then, simultaneously recoiling from the contemplation of so much pain, the subject was changed, but not before Ellen made a mental memorandum to talk to Alex about the Sherrington boys.

Next to arrive was the Vicar. He provided Ellen with an excuse to post some letters, while he kept Sam (and his nauseating coffee) company. Martin accepted a Bourbon biscuit, and leant back with a quizzical expression on his face.

"I've come to get the low-down on Rob's plans." he announced as Sam hitched up a hip, and perched on the edge of the table. The porter wrinkled his brow, saying innocently,

"I don't know Rob's plans Martin. What's the latest?" and Martin laughed.

"Why, he tells me that they're opening up the Manor again, but better still, the Fullingford Trust (having decided to move out of London), are relocating their offices and will occupy the school wing of the Manor. He says that they'll have plenty of room, will be able to accommodate their own archives and better still, it will provide a lot of local employment."

He grew positively animated as he discussed the changes, outlining secretarial positions, clerical posts, and the fact that Bert Fleet had made the suggestion that he and Emma would consider opening a sub post office if that was the case.

Sam considered this, saying brightly, "Well, that'll provide for young Rory, he gets demobbed next month, and Mr Carter wants to move back to Lymington. As you must realise, the two shops could be knocked through very easily, and once the Carter's have gone, their flat would make a good home for Rory. They're a Trust property aren't they?", and so it went on.

Fred Cummins arrived hot on Martin's departing heels.

"You know the Misses Searle who run the Bay Tree?" he asked seriously, "Well, they've decided to retire. They've got a brother in Bournemouth (just widowed), so they want to move over there, to take care of the poor old blighter. Anyway, they came over to see me and Fred, and the upshot is that I'm going to have a full-time job. Mrs Castle is going to help out three days a week. We're going to offer lunches and evening meals, instead of morning coffee and tea only, and Bert is going to run the Forest tea-room taking on additional help through the summer."

Sam grinned, "You won't need your garden plot any more then?" he suggested wicked teasing lights dancing in his eyes, but Fred wasn't so easily put off.

"Huh, says who?", he answered rudely, and they were still in the middle of an animated wrangle when there was a knock at the door, and Trevor Steadman appeared smiling.

"Sam, I've landed a place at college, studying accountancy." he announced proudly, "but it's left me and Belle with a bit of a problem. I was hoping to get into somewhere this side of the Forest, but I've ended up with a grant that takes me to London. Now, that's fine, I can manage digs and so on, but Belle hasn't got any family that counts, and she desperately wants to stay here. Do you think you'd consider renting Bert Credding's cottage to her? She'd only have to walk down-line to work?" and it was in the light of this question that the whole business turned back to Sam and Ellen's dilemma.

"We can't let them know until we've worked out what to do about our ghost and this bear love." Ellen argued cogently. "We can't help being involved, we already live here. Alex and Rob have chosen to involve themselves because of their family links to the whole affair, but we can't bring in outsiders until after the **16ᵗʰ**. It would be like adding non-combatants to a battlefield don't you see? Good Lord, do you think if I wasn't involved I'd be sitting here myself? Tell them we've got to consider their idea, get someone to look at Signalman's cottage, and then ask them to wait until the 22ⁿᵈ. By that time it might all be over!"

She didn't need to tell Sam how fearful she was herself, so he accepted her advice, and sent Trevor a note, telling him he'd have an answer the following week, and prepared himself to withstand whatever Silver Street was about to throw at him.

The weather turned cold that week, Paddy Flynn kept a bonfire going, muttering mournfully about November nights and how he reckoned space-flight had altered the seasons. Sam chuckled to his face, but privately he eyed the rolling vista of gloomy grey] and worried about it clearing to frost. Ellen meanwhile had carefully measured Bertie Bear, using an ancient set of callipers and dividers to create a rough pattern, determined to follow the genius of Margaret Steiff, in some strange desperate need to know what it was about their creations that had endeared them to children for so long. Occasionally she just sat and stroked him, delighting in the way he seemed to respond to her touch, as if he would communicate with her, if only she could talk "bear".

She was sat, day-dreaming on a sofa (with the bear on her lap) when the Fullingfords arrived on the 15ᵗʰ. Her hair gleamed gold against the upholstery, her skin glowed against the burgundy sweater she'd chosen, and the bear nestled against her breast in an oddly childlike attitude.

Sam, bringing their overnight visitors through stopped in the doorway and thought he'd never been so reluctant to wake her, but she opened dazed honey flecked eyes, smiled sleepily and poked the bear in the middle saying lightly, "Come on sleepyhead, time to wake up, we've stuff to do before you're on your way again.", and the Colonel bringing up the rear with Alex's bag asked easily,

"Is that what you think we're about to do Ellen?", and she stared at him, biting her lip. After a while she swung her legs off the sofa, handed the bear to Sam and said slowly,

"I think this whole thing is about an interrupted journey Colonel. In fact it's about many interrupted journeys. There is only one good reason for a train, and that is to pick up passengers, then convey them safely to their destination, before picking up the next lot. In this case, it seems to me that our bear missed his train, he could simply be looking for another connection."

They moved through to the dining -room, where Howard was setting out the supper that Rob and Alex had insisted on providing. Plainly intrigued by her turn of conversation, Rob pulled out a chair for her, as Howard glanced at Alex then pulled out his chair with a graceful inclination of the head and a murmured "My lord?"

Sam seated himself warily, frowned as Howard shook his head reprovingly, then succumbed with gratitude to the trivial conversation during supper. He couldn't help having one eye on the station clock that now had pride of place on the wall of the dining-room. However, Howard's paté served on hot toast, followed by the most delicious pie, accompanied by their own fresh greens brought an end to all thought except the one that persistently chugged through his thoughts.

"If I die tonight, let it only be me.", as the thread of fear tugged at his mind and refused to let go. However, even the best attempts to indulge in small-talk died away, as Howard appeared in a pair of jeans and a sweater, the complete antithesis of his normally impeccable self.

Wordlessly Sam watched him hoist two sleeping-bags over his shoulder and carry them into the living-room. Colonel Fullingford waited until Howard returned, (then over coffee), he reopened Ellen's previous topic of conversation, while Howard washed up in the kitchen.

"Please continue Ellen, I was interested in your theory, because it links rather well with ours. Do you want to explain Alex, or shall I? This incidentally clears up another facet of the mystery Sam, which I have no doubt Martin will be happy to learn about."

He turned to the young Australian, who took a deep breath and began.

"We rather focus on my Grandfather it seems, but that is where the missing link is. A great deal of this is speculation, but from early letters we can see that he had a kind of hero worship of Rob's father Anthony." he glanced at Rob, and the Colonel sighed, taking up the tale.

"Well, my illustrious parent seems to have been a thoroughly bad lot," he remarked cheerfully, "but he had charisma in spades! He could charm the birds out of the trees, got shown the door of the Manor for clandestine relationships with servant-girls, and entered Society with panache. He gambled away the fortune his mother left him, betting on horses, cards, and which of two flies in a room would land first, and eventually his brother got wind of what was going on, and hauled on the filial reins bringing his twin to heel, or so he thought.", he slid a finger into his breast pocket and withdrew another diary, very similar to the first, but with a black leather cover.

"We found that in amongst the Trust's deed-boxes.", he observed grimly, "It doesn't show my father in a very good light at all." he remarked, as Alex took up the story.

"My Great -Grandfather found out that his twin was deeply in debt. He paid those debts off, brought him home, tried to set him up with a responsible position within the Trust. Anthony simply refused to respond. Claiming boredom, he joined a particularly "fast" set, and let his brother down badly. Time after time Alexander forgave him, but Anthony insisted on the greatest folly, and finally broke Alexander's heart by that stunt with the pony. Less than a year after Rowena (his first wife) was killed in a riding accident, Anthony got drunk, bought the pony off a gypsy, and staged the final scene, while Alexander was at Court."

Rob said softly, "Everyone tried to stop him, poor Godwin received a wicked slash to his face, trying to take Robert out of the saddle, and the tutor lost his job when Alexander came home to find Robert had been turned against him. I can only surmise that Anthony did it to punish his brother for being such a paragon of virtue."

The silence that fell was only broken by the sigh of a light wind that had risen, and the ticking of the station clock, then Rob rose and walked over to the door which opened out on to the platform, and stood staring out, rocking back and forth on his heels, before answering Ellen's unspoken question.

"From what I could find out, Alexander finally approached Giles Newland. They were both members of the Trust, and Giles had already offered to take Anthony on, telling Alexander that a year at sea would cure him. However, it didn't come to that because Anthony fell in love with Julia, and they decided to give that love a chance. However, Anthony had to take one last throw of the dice; he embezzled a huge sum of money from the Trust, unknown to Julia whom he'd persuaded to start a new life in Australia. He'd bought tickets, but when Alexander found out, he intercepted Anthony, took the money back, and virtually shanghaied him. The Newland family would never have been told the truth of it, and thought he'd simply abandoned his wife."

He looked down at the diary and said quietly, "This is what he said…"

"Today I have crossed a line I never thought to cross, and I have sent Anthony away for good. I thought my heart would break, for next to Robert, he is my only living kin, and he is me, or part of me. How can he have dreamt that I could forgive his deceit? I know he pleaded, said he would go willingly, but he would have stolen the bread from the mouths of my orphans to do it. No! better his own child be brought up an orphan than to have a father so criminally irresponsible.

I have not cast him adrift completely. I have given him work as a land agent, but he will never again have his hands on Fullingford funds. He must go, out of my life, out of any place where he can exert his influence over my son. Let him send for Julia if Giles will let her go, but let him go, slipping out to sea where I pray most sincerely he comes safe to dry land where he can hurt nobody but himself. I am resolved to strike his name from the family bible, but tonight, after that ship weighed anchor, I could not. O my brother, what have you made me do?"

The low voice ceased, and yet the sound of that ancient anguish filled the room as they silently checked their watches and went to bed, waiting for the call of the train.

Chapter 38 - The Fulfilment of Dreams

Sam's head reeled, his eyes gummy, tongue thick, even his skin felt oddly rough as he stirred, teeth chattering. He didn't remember getting out of bed, but found himself lying on a bench, cold, hard and in the wrong place. Shaking his head in a vain attempt to clear the fog from his mind, he staggered to the water-trough to break the ice and splash his face, but found himself in pitch darkness with everything about him wrong! He whirled as a shadowy figure lit a lantern, hanging at the tunnel-like entrance, where he was used to seeing their own front door.

Dazed, he watched it swing, then desperate to break the nightmare, he plunged his face into the water...

...and re-woke, staring at the unguarded alley through which he could see the platform. He stood between the ticket office and the first class waiting room, where there should have been a dining-room. There was a low mist rolling up the line, and as he stood bewildered, wondering how on earth he'd arrived on the up-line platform when he'd gone to sleep in his own bed on the other side, a gruff voice bellowed.

"Oi get those lamps lit you!", and without thinking Sam put his hand into a trouser pocket looking for his lighter.

Just then, a harried man passed him on the run, muttering wildly, "Get the lamps lit, open the gates, and let the Quality into the waiting room! What more does he want?", and he rushed off, clanking two old-fashioned bull's eye lanterns, struggling to hook them into place. As Sam watched fascinated, two boys (wearing uniforms out of the ark), sidled onto the platform, making for the waiting-room where the dull glow of a well stoked fire flickered invitingly.

As they hovered at the door, a gruff voice challenged.

"Oi, you young varmints, where d'you think you're going?"

This was followed by a more ingratiating flood of.

"Yessir, sorry sir. They'll be here shortly.", then everything shifted again, and he was being swept along in a throng of cheerful chattering folk carrying cushions, blankets, baskets. Unable to resist, he was borne on a well wrapped tide, anxious to board the train panting gently behind him, until he got as far as the Station Master's Office.

Here, an irascible figure erupted from within, (stalking past, as though he didn't exist), shouting orders as staff fled to obey. Coming level with the door he changed course, sticking his head into the waiting-room. Adopting a greasily avuncular manner he announced.

"His Lordship has just driven up in his motorcar." withdrawing as one boy fled towards the second carriage, and the other muttered disconsolately,

"Oh my hat! Now I'm for it!"

As the train reacted to this unconscious prophecy, there was a shuddering chuff, a billow of steam, through which a dignified gentleman swept into view, escorting a slender unsmiling woman, together with a small girl clutching a Steiff bear.

Dismissing the attentions of the Station Master with a curt, "I'll conduct this interview in private Higgins," he addressed his companions in a gentler tone.

"Go and make yourselves comfortable my dears, this won't take more than two minutes."

Glancing at a plain silver pocket watch, he opened the waiting room door to demand brusquely, "Well Robert?" followed wearily by, "How many times must I bear your alarming propensity for shattering my plans with your wilful inability to conform!"

Sam, (shivering in sympathy with the hapless youth) crouched blatantly eavesdropping, as the irate man launched a blistering attack which lasted all of one minute before he snapped out abruptly, "No you cannot accompany us. Until you have redeemed yourself making good your worthless promises, you are no son of mine. When you understand the meaning of respect, inspiring it in others, then I will call you son, but not a minute sooner. Like my unlamented brother you enmesh others in your toils without considering the consequences to them, or to you. Your current companion will be removed from your sphere of influence by remaining with us. He will benefit as a direct reward for ensuring your continued safety, after which, I will decide your fate!"

The door crashed open, the figure stalked past in silent condemnation, and the train shuddered as icy rage enfolded it, drawing out silently, as a wave of dizziness rolled down the track like a living entity and swept Sam away, thrusting him down, down, down into sleep again.

It was the voices that woke Rob Fullingford. He eased his stiff hip (a service legacy), then lay, cautiously listening. Somehow, those others in the room couldn't see him, so (taking a leaf from his military training manual) he kept perfectly still and listened.

The young voice, shrill with protestations, said urgently, "Father, you're not listening to me. I only came to apologise for upsetting your weekend shoot. I shouldn't have taken the Vicar's cob for a ride, but he's easy to handle, Mr Redding has broken his leg, and the animal needs exercise. If I'd known you were shooting Home Farm copse I wouldn't have gone that way! I'm sorry I disobeyed you, but it's hardly a hanging offense!"

Then the other voice, low, cultured, bitter, broke in, its owner somewhere close. Rob stayed agonisingly still and listened.

"Robert, since you were a child, I have specifically forbidden you to ride. You know the reason, and I refuse to elaborate further. You are my only heir; I cannot risk everything I have worked for on a childish whim. You will do as you are told for once. Now, if I am not to risk this entire excursion, I must go, and that is my last word on this subject."

The speaker had moved by this time, and Rob felt the bitter blast as a door was opened and closed firmly behind the older man.

"I won't.", said the adolescent defiantly. "He can't risk everything he's worked for? What about me? I don't want his stuffy old title, or his rotten causes. I want to go outside with the other chaps, ride, hunt, shoot. Maybe I'll join the Army, or go to sea. Maybe I'll find Uncle Anthony, at least he loves me!"

Those anguished comments were delivered in a fierce mutter, but as the youth opened the door running out onto the platform behind his father, Rob lifted his head, and stared in amazement at an immature version of the man who slept on the opposite couch, unaware of what was occurring. Then a sort of mist descended, Colonel Fullingford lay back wearily trying to make sense of what he'd heard as the old Station clock ticked monotonously, a gentle hiss of steam billowed around him, then he slept as the train pulled away from the echoes of emotional disaster, tooting dismally as night closed in again.

Alex stirred sleepily, and then came fully awake to find himself sitting on a trolley full of kit bags as a number of men unloaded an old fashioned military van, under the dreary drip of British weather. He blinked, and this time the van was pulling away, the men quietened by shouted orders from the rear, closing up into ranks, ready to board as a light locomotive made its stealthy approach.

He turned, looking about him, noting the number of Australians gathering, listening (with unconscious relief) to the ribald humour bandied about as his countrymen shuffled forward, ignoring his presence completely. It was dark, only the fitful moon passing behind a bank of cloud illuminated the station yard, yet nobody talked, nobody used a lamp, and a shivering apprehension seemed to have fallen on the soldiers as they boarded.

The swift clatter of approaching feet startled him, then a group of officers appeared, one of them looking about him as if waking from some walking nightmare.

"Good God!" he exclaimed as they came level with Alex, a very light enthusiastic, but undeniably British voice declaring in tones of awe.

"I'd know this place anywhere! I'm home! How bloody wonderful is that?" his slightly hysterical chuckle drew a frown from a senior rank who said sharply (in broad Australian).

"Pipe down Fullingford, there's no need to spook at the station. No-one's shooting yet!" and a ripple of mirth ran through the other ranks as they marshalled nearby.

"That's our Pommie officer," one man declared affectionately. "Can't seem to get his mouth in gear round the brass, but he'd do anything for his blokes. He's got a place back home, a kid on the way too, poor bastard. He won't be there when it arrives, but he can't wait to be a Dad. Still, he'll learn after two or three!"

There was a muted rumble of laughter, as Alex found his feet and followed the officers towards the waiting room, but on the brink of entering he stopped. Lieutenant Robert Fullingford hadn't gone in, he was standing at the door, his face sickly white and withdrawn. Alex stared at the man he'd so wanted to know, so wanted to know about, as the young officer muttered harshly.

"No, that's not right. I can never go back, never go home again. They're all gone; there is no past reaching out to weigh me down with useless titles, unwanted responsibilities."

He walked forward very deliberately and remarked (almost as if he could see Alex), "What would you say soldier? Stick with what you love and let the rest go hang, or take the world on your shoulders for no love at all?"

Alex choked at the bitterness in his voice, then the train shrieked its call to arms, and the world exploded.

He was running, dodging, falling, and struggling in the stinking mud. Then he was hurting, his world shrinking to a pin-prick of light in which an angel hovered, hands carrying something horridly clinical, but her eyes serene, calming the thunder of blood in his ears.

"It was strange," he thought, languidly drifting in the void, he wasn't frightened, just regretful as he thought about Silver Street and its part in the journey that had brought him here. He knew he was dying, but there was no pain, just regret. He would never again see Emma, or their unborn child, see Newlands, or keep his promise to his sister. Silly really, but he'd like to return her bear to her, but he'd missed that train a long time ago…"

The light was fading, silence descending, broken only by the tick of the old station clock. He slept.

Ellen woke clutching the bear, somehow aware that she'd been summoned. She stumbled upright, forcing stubborn eyelids to open, and gasped. She was in her dream again but this time it was different. A large woman in the outdoor garments of a nanny regarded her thoughtfully.

"You're fagged to death my girl! Seems to me you'd be better off sleeping than sweethearting!" she announced brightly, as Ellen took notice of the people gathering, ready to board when the train arrived.

The friendly woman continued briskly.

"You want to think yourself lucky getting into post just before this trip," she enthused, "His lordship always makes it a good outing for us. We have the whole of this carriage for household staff, and we don't have to do anything for the whole journey. His works people are in the middle carriage so he can talk business on the way up, and the family are in the front carriage. First Class is how they travel, only her maid and Mr Nugent (his valet) to look after them, and Lady Leonora looking after Miss Ellen. I'm sure I never saw such a devoted mother, though she doesn't care for Master Robert above half, but then that's his own fault. He cannot abide her, says she's the reason Lord Alexander sent his uncle away, for it's true, nothing from before her time with Lord Alexander pleases her ladyship, but I daresay that's natural enough, although how she can blame him for having a twin I don't know."

"Stand back ladies and gentlemen." a porter's voice called. "Stand well back, the Fullingford Flyer's coming in.", and there was a gentle thrum from the line, a blurring of reality, and she was standing wrapped in her old overcoat, just inside the doors of her dining-room as her dream came to a stop.

Sam was staring at the clock, his father's pocket-watch in his hands, water dripping off his old sou'wester] although it wasn't raining. Rob (clad in semi-military pullover and jeans) sat looking out across a mist shrouded station, as Alex woke, started, and rolled out of his sleeping-bag, hastily pulling on plimsolls.

"Crikey mate! You should have woken me.", he hissed as Ellen "shushed" him, "I had the most horrid dream…I think I'm dead…", then catching Rob's bleak expression he lapsed into silence as Sam replaced the watch in his pocket. There was a faint whirr from the Station clock, the hands jerked round the last second to midnight, as from the wreaths of rising steam the train crept in.

Ellen stood frozen as she realised belatedly that she had no idea where the bear had gone, and her face betrayed her distress. Sam caught her up, sliding one arm round her as she made the first move towards the door, and then he pointed, holding her firm as she saw the bear, sat on top of a trolley, back supported by the post of the Victorian canopy above. She turned glowing eyes up at him, then Alex was saying urgently, "Where's Robert?"

They stared blankly, and then his half angry, half bewildered voice said irritably, "Don't you see? He's trying to fulfil his promise! His sister dropped the bear, he promised to return it to her, but something went wrong and the train pulled out before he could. He was thinking of that missed opportunity when he died! I know, I was there!"

Sam stared, recalling the scrap of information he'd gleaned when he'd dreamt of that departure sixty years ago to the night. He pulled out his watch, glanced at the clock then stepped forward and unlocked the case. Ellen suddenly caught the drift of his mind and said urgently, "Sam, it's always two minutes early. Mike told me that when we took the station over.", and Sam grinned as he turned the key, adjusting the clock to match his watch.

"I know," he murmured, "but the repair man said the spring hung on by a thread, and refused to deal with it for Southern Rail. They weren't paying his bills it seems."

He closed the glass thoughtfully, then, as midnight struck, everything seemed to jump and lock into place.

The locomotive glided forward, porters carrying lamps opened doors, the mist rose across the platforms, but all eyes were on the forlorn figure on the trolley. Then just as Sam thought he would burst with pent-up anxiety, he heard the unmistakable sound of a squad of soldiers approaching, and before he could restrain Alex, the Australian was outside, on the platform.

They stood irresolute, then Ellen said quietly, "I think we're all meant to be there Rob. Alex needs our support, as does your unhappy cousin, in life or death.", and so saying, she took Sam by the hand and stepped out bravely.

Through the mist the passengers were obscured, but the scene was identical to her dream, except that she couldn't see the boy. However, as Robertson Fullingford stepped briskly behind them, a running man appeared from the rear of the silent platoon drawn up along the platform.

"Robert!", Alex exclaimed, stepping forward and holding out Ellen's bear. For a brief moment in time, it seemed to the onlookers as if some arcane relay race was taking place, but as the running man came abreast of

251

him, Alex saw the man with his face smile, relief flooding from his body in a nimbus of light as the baton of the bear was handed on, then he was running again, towards the first carriage and his family as a guard raised his whistle towards his lips.

There was a deadly struggle going on. In Sam's ears the Station clock whirred towards the quarter, his father's watch pulsed, then a door in that first carriage opened, and a man stepped out. The Edwardian coat swinging from his shoulders billowed as he opened his arms, the running figure seemed to be moving in slow motion, then a voice called sharply.

"Hold the train. That's my son!"

As they watched, the soldier seemed to diminish with every step, shrinking from adult to youth as he ran, until he was in his father's arms.

There was a long sighing ripple which pulsed the length of the train, a low click, then time stopped.

Sam and Ellen leant together in helpless relief as the boy was helped aboard. Rob and Alex gripped the edge of the trolley as the same voice called back, "Thank you Porter!", then for the last time, for the last passenger, a green flag was raised, and to a faint hiss of steam, a gentle shudder ran through the train as it began to pull away.

Sam held his father's watch, listening to every note, and all the familiar sounds of his life as they disappeared forever, then locking them away as he closed the unadorned watch case, he bent his head, and very deliberately kissed his wife.

A long time later, they gathered silently sipping cocoa in the living room. An apologetic Howard, (who had blissfully slept through the entire process),had withdrawn, and only the four of them remained.

"There's a few things we need to sort out.", Ellen suggested looking round the table at her three exhausted companions. Soon they would be going their separate ways, soon Silver Street and Sam would come back to her, but for now, she needed, no *they all* needed to know that everything was alright.

Alex looked unbearably sad, Rob seemed to have aged, and Sam seemed somehow diminished with no more mysteries to solve. She drained her mug of the best cocoa Howard had ever made, and that simple action seemed to perk their interest.

"Let's get everything chronologically.", she invited, but Sam said defensively,

"That'll be difficult considering we all seem to 'ave ad different dreams!", at which Rob nodded in agreement, saying,

"Let's start with the original episode then.", so Sam set the scene, his sympathies patently engaged with young Robert Fullingford. Rob took up the tale.

"I suspected something of the sort from Robert's note to his house-master," he spoke sombrely, "Let's face it, a crash that leaves no survivors in a rural district would make identification of the victims virtually impossible. There was nobody left to identify the Fullingfords. Anthony was long gone, senior servants were all on board. Understandably, the authorities thought the boy in Winchester uniform in the First Class compartment was Robert. He may never have known what happened to the boot-boy, but the psychological damage to my cousin shaped the rest of a short unhappy life. Despite my Papa's best attempts, I don't doubt Robert believed his destiny was irreparably damaged."

His voice was very soft as he related the interview he'd "overheard".

Alex interrupted bleakly.

"Well, he died longing to put things right, and he'd certainly earned the respect of his men by then, even if his officers didn't appreciate him. What I want to know is did we make a difference?"

Sam sighed, then Ellen said firmly, "Yes Alex, we did. If I'm right, something caused the Station clock here to send the Fullingford Flyer off two minutes early. We may never know if that contributed to the crash. However, it is certain that your namesake told his son he would not recognise him, until he'd learned the meaning of respect, engendering respect in others. *We* know he achieved that, but he didn't. He thought the only way back, was to find the bear and return it."

Three pairs of eyes turned to her as she endeavoured to put into words what she meant.

"Sam's affinity with the train summoned it. Once it was here, we were almost steered into finding the bear. Sam was wrong on one account only. He thought the bear was the last passenger, but of course, the last passenger to board that train was Robert. The bear was his ticket!", she frowned concentrating, and then Rob said abruptly,

"Of course, and they needed Sam to be the physical empowerment of a time change. Because he trusted his father's watch and altered the clock, they finally caught up with each other."

Sam was staring at his father's simple retirement watch. He had it in his hand and Rob asked if he could see it as Ellen wearily got to her feet.

"I don't think it's very valuable.", Sam held the pocket watch out, and Rob looked at it closely.

"It's a very fine watch actually Sam. You say the men bought it second-hand? You're lucky it wasn't engraved with the previous owner's initials.

Obscurely, I'm rather glad my signet ring was. I came by it in a backstreet market in Southampton just after my demob. I couldn't believe I only had to have it resized. I reckon some lad or another had pawned it to raise money…", then the penny dropped, very much like Rob's jaw.

"To buy a ticket to Australia.", he whispered, but there was no hint of a question in his voice. He stroked the ring as Ellen remarked softly,

"You've always loved it Rob, you were meant to find it.", her eyes had filled with tears, but Rob was turning Charlie's watch round in his hands, pressing something, then the back sprang open.

She stared down, then her eyes lifted to Rob's tired face as he held out the watch to each of them.

Sam read the tiny inscription.

"Geo: Fullingford. In gratitude for permitting the construction of Silver Street Station 1847."

Alex groaned.

"That's enough to make a psychic superstitious!", he exclaimed, (adding poker-faced), "From Ghosties and ghoullies and long-legged beasties.", as he rolled himself up in his sleeping bag and closed his eyes.

"It'll seem different in the morning.", he said sleepily, and it was.

Epilogue

There was no doubt about it, the Station clock had stopped. The slow steady "tick" of more than a hundred years had ceased and the man bending over it sighed regretfully.

"Well, it's a delicate thing," he murmured contemplatively. "I told Mr Oswald these are temperamental! Now I can't promise anything, but it's valuable in its own right, and a station without a clock isn't a station in my eyes!"

Sam grinned ruefully, "No more'n a station without trains!", he chipped back, adding cheerfully, "and how the bloody hell are you?", as his best man carefully folded his fine watchmaker's tools away. Gerry Richards laughed, saying, "All the better for seeing you, and how's your wife? That book of hers is advertised all over the place. I fell over a flyer in W.H.Smith's right out in Bournemouth the other day. Oddly enough I'd been over to value a clock for Miss Silversmith. You know that new school venture of hers fell flat on its face I suppose?", and Sam shook his head, dumbfounded.

"Yes.", Gerry nodded, "and I'm not surprised. She treated half the parents as if they had no right to question what daughters learned. We've got neighbours who can tell you a lot about her shortcomings.", he added grimly before asking awkwardly,

"Now do you want me to take this in for open heart surgery Sam? It won't come cheap I'm afraid. I wouldn't undertake it myself, but my father-in-law's been repairing clocks for more years than I can remember. It's because of him I finally turned my hobby into a job, a bit like you I suppose, though how you manage all this on your own I don't know."

He gave a shout of laughter as Sam invited him for a last brew-up in the ticket office, and went away carrying the clock carefully wrapped in cloth, as the Bentley purred into the old loading bay.

Seconds later a radiant Ellen, made up to the nines appeared, with Howard at her heels carrying a bag over his arm, which (Sam deduced), hid the dress she intended to wear at her book launch.

Howard came over, handed Sam a letter written in Rob's neat script, then assisted Ellen to hang her new clothes as Sam tore open the flap. He chuckled, then said to Howard, "The answer to Rob's question is yes indeed Howard.", then he laughed uproariously as Howard extended a beautifully printed pack of acceptance cards, saying primly,

"The correct form of reply Mr Smart is to fill in this card. I'll undertake its delivery immediately. You won't need evening dress by the way, Lord

Alexander doesn't dress for dinner unless otherwise stated."

Sam growled in disgust. "There's no need to turn into a proper butler with us!", as Howard grinned and left whistling "Love Me Do!"

"Now what's got into him?", Ellen watched as Howard sashayed out to the Bentley, then smiled and said "I wonder?", as she went back to their living-room to admire her dress. Sam came up behind her, drawing her back against him, and sighed with pleasure.

"That peacock blue will suit you very nicely.", he said in a satisfied voice. "I'm going to wear my dark grey suit, and I'll go into Christchurch and get a tie to match that dress."

She turned in his arms and said in surprise, "You're coming up to my book signing?", but he shook his head grinning.

"Nope, I'll leave you, your publisher's and the resultant melee to handle that, but I am accepting the loan of the Bentley and Howard for a day. I want you to arrive in style, have someone to whisk you away to the hotel when you need, and to get you safely home for Saturday. We have our own private launch party all set up, and that's where I'll be wearing my suit. Now darling, there's nobody else here, no more ghosts to lay. Can we just rest and enjoy the last two days of your holiday before it all gets crazy again?"

They went in a flash, then she was away, rosebuds of excitement burning in her cheeks, and Sam waved her off, Alex and Rob at his heels. Rob looked solemnly at the pale patch where the Station clock had been and raised his eyes questioningly.

"Beyond repair?", he queried, then as Sam explained what he'd done, Alex looked round and said quietly,

"You must let us stand the cost Sam, I insist. It's the least I can do, Ellen and you are very dear to me you know.", and Rob said quietly,

"Absolutely Sam, it would be a pleasure.", then all too soon they were gone, and Sam settled down with the book-keeping. After three hours of trying to reconcile figures, he was relieved to be interrupted by the phone, expecting it to be Ellen announcing her safe arrival at the hotel, but it was Tom Collier. He made a hesitant start, then said hurriedly,

"It's no good Sam, you'll probably hate me, but some time back a little bird told me that you and Ellen planned to get an old ambulance and convert it into a shop. I'd had a similar idea myself, so I waited for you to do it, but then you bought Silver Street, and you've never raised the subject since. As it happens I'm retiring earlier than I thought. Wellworthy are cutting the workforce and I've been offered a good settlement if I go now. So, if you don't mind, I'd like to pinch your idea.

I'll make it up to you by buying all my veg at Silver Street. I've got a sweet deal with my brother for his strawberries, and Jack Sherrington is bottling cream.", his enthusiasm waned under Sam's stunned silence, and he spluttered to a stop.

Sam had no doubts at all. He couldn't see Ellen driving an ambulance now, and he had more than enough on his plate, so he allowed his voice to warm as he said firmly, "Tom! That's brilliant. We'll look forward to seeing you and the orders will be reciprocated if you're thinking of general goods. Talk to Emma Fleet, I'm sure she'll tell you what she doesn't stock, there's no need to set backs up before you start."

He walked the down-line platform that evening, remembering how he had talked to the squirrel, and when he turned into bed, it was easy to think of Ellen, busy at her official book launch without jealousy, hugging himself as he thought of his own surprise waiting for her when she came home.

On Saturday their modest dinner party hosted by Lord Fullingford was full of the joy of success and friendship. Only part of the Manor had been restored to anything like the style Rob plainly wanted to set, but it was enough, and the small number of guests had chattered happily, enthused over Ellen's book, and now only Martin, Jane, and Melanie remained as Sam broke his own news.

"I had a phone call from "Lost Locations" the other day," he said diffidently. Alan Harper was talking to some bod in the BBC, and it seems that they have an archive of railway film footage that I can research for them. They've offered me the chance to work on a programme as a technical advisor, and they might put me in touch with a publisher myself.", and Ellen glowed at him, her eyes sparkling with unreserved joy. However, she had a mischievous look, and after they'd taken their leave, driving home in Lady Jane, she suddenly said,

"Stop the car Sam. I want to look at Silver Street in the moonlight.", he'd agreed, and they had pulled in, gazing down at their domain as it slept peacefully below their vantage point. Then she turned, lifting his hand to cup her face as she whispered mysteriously.

"I can beat your secret Sam, although I think adding a television expert to my retinue is pretty damn good. I can definitely cap that!", then as he stared at her bewildered, she dropped the final bombshell.

"You'd better get ready for an eventful summer sweetheart. We're going to have a baby!"

The End
(or just the beginning?)

If you have enjoyed the first novel in "The Last of the Line" series
you might like to continue reading;

The Last Charger – by Jez & Julia Caesar
(arima publishing 2015)

"The Tapestry of Tten", a gripping series of Fantasy Fiction novels by Julia Caesar is published by Arima Publishing.

'The Tapestry of Tten', what is it? Where is it? and why must they find it? The story begins at the

"Dawn of Darkness"

They were all doomed until the Sorceress remembered an ancient incantation, but as she chanted the forbidden words, what has Ikella unleashed on her unsuspecting world?

Hidden in the brilliantly hued deserts of Pelshar are the clues to its secret past. Strict obedience to the 'Way', has prevented their discovery until, engulfed in an apocalyptic storm, a party of Healers accidently fulfils ancient prophecy. Now launched on a perilous journey of self-discovery and emotional awakening, Ikella reaches far beyond her previously circumscribed existence, as she adopts a foundling of the Storm. Facing a choice between the child she loves, and the security of a world teetering on the brink of ecological disaster, she must discover why the word "Sandsinger" haunts her dreams, and how their very existence depends on finding a mysterious 'Tapestry of Tten'.

The reader will agonize with her over baby Daro's future, relax in the reassuring company of an aged Apothecary, and be on the edge of their seats, waiting for the sequel, "Curse of Night."

If you enjoy the first book, follow the unfolding mystery in …

"Curse of Night"

Following the Storm, Jentaroth (the annual Rite of Passage), takes on new significance. Amidst mourning rituals, Ikella must protect the Union of the Sands from treachery within, whilst resisting her growing emotional attachment to the frail orphan she longs to adopt. Beset by premonitions as she gathers her Sisters in Sorcery at Selesh, Ikella is forced to defend the Gathering as one of three new Candidates reveals herself as a practising heretic, with command of Dark Magic. As she confines Adruna and her followers to her own Sands, Ikella cannot prevent her cursing baby Daro, but did her curse have any effect?

As Daro grows up, how many Rotations must Ikella endure his relentless obsession with the ancient mages of the past? Is this something to do with 'The Curse of Night'? As his obsession leads him into perilous places, can he survive to find 'Another Shade of Mystery'?

For more details read on…

The Tapestry of Tten - Book 3 by Julia Cæsar

"Another Shade of Mystery"

Having exiled Daro for his obsession with the ancient mages of their secret past, life is still far from peaceful in Selesh. The aging Sorceress has found no relief from troublesome children, for she has given refuge to Jalni. The girl, hotly pursued into the heart of the community, has an intriguing (though erratic) command of power. Admitted as a novice, Jalni commits a catalogue of crimes, and is on probation when Daro returns empowered, to challenge his foster-mother's long held beliefs.

Determined to ignore the personal price he has paid for his power, the Opal Sandsinger takes Jalni as his guide, and sets out to save the children of Scartel. Encountering Myst-cats, Wanderers, Storm horses and a mysterious mentor, Daro must also find his feet in a strange new world, looking for 'Another Shade of Mystery', to help him understand, 'The Song of Sorcery'.

The story continues in…

"Song of Sorcery"

Returning from Scartel to safety, Daro and Jalni are shaken by the death of a child. As Daro questions his faith in magic, Jalni decides that if he can face the past of a world, she can face her own, and slips away unseen.

En route to Jerritol, followed by an old friend, she encounters Orto and decides to help him find the Tapestry of Tten. At the Temple of the Winds there's no trace of the relic, but the Oracle predicts, Jalni will become, 'Mother to the Tenth Wind'.

Jalni goes into retreat, but when the Sorceress Tirjella is poisoned, she usurps Sandsinger powers and saves her. Returning to Selesh, Jalni can predict Ikella's reaction, but Daro's she couldn't have foreseen in a thousand Rotations!

Empathise with Jalni's struggle to control her own destiny. Watch Daro confront the limitations of his power, and smile as Jalni finds love. Does it last? Read the sequel, 'Sword of Sanctuary' to find out.

Now the latest twist of this saga …

"Sword of Sanctuary"

Marran Dorenard never thought he would find it difficult to follow the Ranger Code. Honouring the memory of the Grandfather who gave his life to save him, he must deal with a web of divided loyalties. Can he support the Lord of the Opal in his desire to break free from the constraints of Selesh and his obligations, or should he protect the vulnerable girl who has been the mainstay and support for his Tawn of Rangers? As for Jalni…

Deeply distressed by constant bickering, worried about Ikella's increasing frailty, and concerned about her own erratic powers, she discovers she's pregnant. The Oracle's prediction was true! Frightened into running back to Scartel, she decides not to tell Daro, who seems intent on rejecting her. With the firm intention of surrendering the Sandsingers child to the Temple of the Winds, she returns to the Ashgenar with only Marran's sword for protection as she comes to terms with her destiny. Can she take the child where his father can't find it? Or has the Shadow of the Singer cast itself ahead of her?

To order any of the books in this series, please visit our website, http://www.arimapublishing.co.uk, or write to us at:

Arima publishing
ASK House
Northgate Avenue
Bury St Edmunds
Suffolk
IP32 6BB
UK